CITY OF THE DEAD

Illustrated by Richard Pace

JOHN C. HOCKING

TITAN BOOKS

CONAN: CITY OF THE DEAD
Print edition ISBN: 9781803366562
E-book edition ISBN: 9781803366326

Published by Titan Books
A division of Titan Publishing Group Ltd
144 Southwark St, London SE1 0UP

First edition: June 2024
10 9 8 7 6 5 4 3 2 1

Interior illustrations by Richard Pace.

John C. Hocking asserts the moral right to be identified as the authors of this work.

A CIP catalogue record for this title is available from the British Library.

Printed and bound by CPI Group (UK) Ltd, Croydon CR0 4YY.

This omnibus is dedicated to all who love Sword & Sorcery and especially to those who have anticipated the second novel for so long.

CONTENTS

THE
HYBORIAN
AGE
WHEN CONAN
·WALKED THE EARTH·

CONAN
AND THE
EMERALD
LOTUS

PROLOGUE

Ethram-Fal stood in the ancient chamber and looked upon bones. Dark and pitted, they lay strewn in the thick dust of the stone floor. Ruddy torchlight flared, filling the circular room with leaping shadows. A tall soldier in full armor stood motionless beside the single doorway, torch held high in one steady hand.

Ethram-Fal knelt, his gray robes rustling, and pulled an ornate dagger of irregular shape from a concealed sheath. Though he was a young man, the sorcerer's hunched and shrunken form gave the impression of great age. Thin hair of mouse-brown was beginning to grow from a scalp recently shaved clean. He frowned in contemplation, furrowing his bulbous and malformed brow. He probed among the bones and dust with the dagger's tip and felt the slow welling of despair.

It's dead now, he thought. Of course it's dead now, but I had hoped that there would be something remaining, if only husks. The dagger tip disturbed the dust of centuries, revealing nothing. Ethram-Fal stood suddenly, and the soldier with the torch flinched.

"Fangs of Set," he cursed. "Have I come so far for nothing?" His voice was a hollow echo. The sorcerer looked up. The ceiling of the circular room was so high that it was lost in the flickering darkness beyond the torchlight's reach. An even band of engraved hieroglyphics ran around the walls at twice the height of a man. The markings seemed to writhe tortuously in the dim light.

"There is no doubt," said Ethram-Fal dully, "this is the room." He turned, and in doing so set his sandal upon something that gave a muffled *crack*. Stepping to one side, he looked down and went rigid.

"Ath, lower the torch." The soldier dutifully lowered the torch to illuminate the floor while Ethram-Fal knelt again. He had tread upon what appeared to be a human rib and had snapped it in two. A fine black powder seeped out of the broken bone. Ethram-Fal gave a choked cry of triumph.

"Of course! It's gone dormant. It must have absorbed all nourishment down to the marrow and then spored. Set grant that there is still life!" He gestured with a gray-clad arm. "Ath, bring my apprentice."

The soldier left the room, the light of his torch receding down the empty corridor, leaving Ethram-Fal in darkness. But it was not darkness to Ethram-Fal, who saw his future looming bright and glorious before him. His breathing quickened, the only sound in the stony silence.

In a few moments Ath returned, his hawklike Stygian features stern and impassive. Behind him trailed a slender adolescent boy clad in yellow robes. Though taller than Ethram-Fal, the top of the boy's tousled head came to well below Ath's chin. The boy looked about the room with obvious impatience.

"I was helping the men set up camp in the large chamber," he said petulantly. "Have you finally found something useful for me to do?"

Ethram-Fal did not reply, but fixed his gaze upon the bones at his feet.

"Ath," he said, "kill him."

With a single fluid motion the soldier drew his broadsword, buried it in the youth's belly, twisted it, and withdrew. The apprentice uttered a high-pitched wail, clutched himself, and dropped to lie writhing weakly in the dust. When the boy stopped breathing, Ath wiped his blade upon the body and sheathed it. He looked at Ethram-Fal expectantly. The hand gripping the torch had not faltered.

The sorcerer produced a thick reddish leaf from a leather pouch on his belt. He handed it to Ath, who immediately put it into his mouth. The soldier's eyes closed and his cheeks drew hollow as he sucked upon the leaf.

Ethram-Fal paid this no heed. Bending at the waist, he gingerly picked up the broken rib between thumb and forefinger. Tilting the bone with exaggerated care, he spilled a thin stream of black powder over the sprawled body of his apprentice. He emptied the macabre vessel, concentrating its contents on the dark stain spreading upon the corpse's midriff. When the dust ceased to fall, he tossed the rib aside and stood staring at the body in silence.

An hour passed, during which Ath chewed and swallowed his leaf and Ethram-Fal moved not at all. Toward the close of the second hour, Ethram-Fal cocked his head, as though he sought to hear a soft sound from a great distance. The body on the floor shuddered and the sorcerer clasped his hands together in an ecstasy of anticipation.

A moist crackling filled the still air. The corpse jerked and trembled as though endowed with tormented life. Ethram-Fal caught his breath as fist-sized swellings erupted all but instantaneously from the dead flesh of his apprentice. The body was grotesquely distorted in a score of places, with such swift violence that the limbs convulsed and the yellow robes ripped open.

Green blossoms the size of a man's open hand burst from the corpse, leaping forth in such profusion that the body was almost hidden from view. Iridescent and six-petaled, the blooms pushed free of enclosing flesh, bobbing and shaking as if in a strong wind. In a moment they were still, and a sharp, musky odor, redolent of both nectar and corruption, rose slowly to fill the chamber.

The peals of Ethram-Fal's laughter reverberated from the stone walls like the tolling of a great bell.

The night air was warm and close, but it was of polar freshness compared to the dense atmosphere within the tavern. A stout, sturdily built man in the mail of a mercenary of Akkharia shoved open the door and surveyed the scene within. The main room was spacious, but crowded with a motley variety of locals, mercenaries, and travelers. The visitor ran a callused hand through his graying hair and scanned the gathering for the man he'd come to see. In the closest corner a number of men were throwing dice, alternately crowing in triumph and cursing in defeat. The center of the sawdust-strewn floor was dominated by a huge table bearing the nearly denuded carcass of an entire roasted pig.

Men clustered about it, drinking and stuffing themselves.

"Ho, Shamtare!" a voice thundered over the tavern's clamor. There, in the farthest corner, was the man he sought. Shamtare made his way across the floor, dodging gesticulating drunks and busy serving wenches with practiced ease.

The one who had called his name lounged against the tavern's rear wall with his long muscular legs propped up on a table. He was a hulking, powerful-looking man whose skin had been burnt to a dark bronze by ceaseless exposure to the elements. He was clad in a chain-mail shirt and faded breeches of black cotton. At his waist hung a massive broadsword in a worn leather scabbard. A white smile split a face that seemed better suited to scowl, and piercing blue eyes flashed as he hoisted his wine jug in a rakish salute, gesturing for Shamtare to join him. The scarred tabletop held a loaf of bread and a joint of beef, as well as heaping platters of fruits, cheese, and nuts. From the crusts and rinds scattered about, it would seem that a celebration of sorts had been going on for some time.

"Conan," said Shamtare, "I thought you said your money was running low."

"So it is," answered the other with a barbarous accent. "What of it? Tomorrow I shall surely be working for one of this cursed city's mercenary troops, and tonight I find that I have missed civilization more than I had realized." The barbarian washed the words down with a great swallow of wine.

Shamtare sat and helped himself to a handful of ripe fruit. "Traveled far, have you?" he asked, popping pomegranate seeds into his mouth.

"Aye, from the heart of Kush across the Stygian deserts. It seems that I'm no longer welcome in the southern kingdoms."

Shamtare raised his thick eyebrows in puzzlement. "But surely you are a Northman..."

"A Cimmerian," said Conan. "But I have done much traveling."

"Indeed," murmured Shamtare, to whom Cimmeria was a chill and distant place of myth. "But about your choice of mercenary employment..."

Conan took a bite out of the beef joint and chewed enthusiastically.

"Still trying to get me to join your troop?"

Shamtare lifted his hands. "You can't blame me for that. When I saw your performance on the practice field, I knew that you'd be an asset to any troop that signed you on. And you know I'm paid a bounty for each new recruit. I admit that when I asked where you'd be dining tonight, I had more in mind than tipping a jug with you. I say again that Mamluke's Legion could well use a man like yourself."

Conan shrugged, shaking his square-cut black mane. "I've been to see all four troops in this pestilent city, and they all offer the same wages. The king must keep close watch on his mercenary commanders that none of them can outbid the other for an experienced soldier. What in Ymir's name does King Sumuabi need with four troops of sellswords anyway?"

"The king watches over his mercenaries because he has plans for them."

Shamtare's voice dropped to hushed, conspiratorial tones. "Rumor has it that Sumuabi may need all four armies very soon."

"Crom, it seems that all you Shemites do is hole up in your little city-states and venture out once a year to try to conquer your neighbor. It is but a larger version of the clan feuds of my homeland. You fight a few battles and then slink back home with nothing gained. And this with Koth hungering at your border."

"True," said Shamtare tolerantly. "But this time it is whispered that we may go to aid a revolt in Anakia. Sumuabi may soon king it over two cities. If this comes to pass, then the plunder should be rich for even the lowliest foot soldier."

Conan thought on this while Shamtare borrowed the wine jug. "That is good news, yet it still matters little which troop I join."

"Come now, Conan." Shamtare set the empty jug down with a hollow thump. "What do you want of me? I tell you, I'm great friends with the troop's armorer, and I promise you a shirt of the best Akbitanan mail if you sign up with us. The shirt you're wearing looks as though it's been through hell."

Conan snorted with laughter, looking down at his tarnished mail. Long vertical tears in the mesh had been crudely repaired with inferior links that were beginning to show traces of rust.

"Perhaps not hell itself, but a pig-faced demon from thereabouts. You have a deal, Shamtare."

The Shemite grinned in his beard, opened his mouth to ask a question, and then shut it again. The tavern's door had swung wide, and now two figures entered the room. The foremost was almost as tall as Conan and clearly a warrior. He wore a black-lacquered breastplate over brightly polished steel mail. A black-crested helmet was held under one thick arm. Blue-black hair fell in a thick mass over his square shoulders. A wide white scar parted his carefully trimmed beard just to the right of his stern mouth. He looked around the room with an almost-tangible aura of scorn. The crowd in the tavern quieted somewhat at the two men's arrival, but those who stopped to gaze at the newcomers did not study the warrior but his companion.

The man who stood in the dark doorway was also tall, but he was somewhat stooped as though ill or injured. From head to foot he was wrapped in a cowl of lush green velvet. His hands, where they emerged from their sleeves, wore green velvet gloves. His face was hidden in the shadow beneath his hood.

The strange pair hesitated a moment, then walked quickly through the tavern's crowd, which parted easily before them. They passed through a door into a back room and were lost from view.

"Who the hell was that?" asked Conan, reaching for the jug.

"Someone best left unknown," said Shamtare softly.

"No matter. What's this? No wine? Ho, wench!" Conan brandished the empty jug above his head. "More wine! I'm parched!" Spurred by the barbarian's bellow, a serving girl leapt into action. Hefting a full jug onto one shoulder, she made her way toward Conan's table. Her thin cotton shift, damp with sweat and spilt wine, clung to her shapely torso as she moved. The barbarian grinned broadly, watching her approach with frank admiration. Blushing, she thumped the heavy jug down on the table, her eyes seeking the floorboards.

"Five coppers, milord," she murmured.

"A silver piece," said Conan. He tossed her the coin, which she snatched from the air with the effortless speed born of long practice.

"Keep the change," he added needlessly, for she had already turned away. He caught up the fresh jug as a heavy hand fell upon his shoulder. Conan looked up into the craggy face of the black-armored warrior who had entered with the man clad in emerald velvet.

"My master would speak with you," rasped the warrior. Conan shrugged off his hand and turned to face Shamtare. But the chair across the table was empty. Conan noticed that the tavern door was just swinging shut.

"Mitra preserve me from civilized comrades," muttered the barbarian.

"You would be wise to do exactly as my master requests." The warrior towered over the seated Cimmerian, the scar in his beard broadening as his lips tightened in a disapproving grimace. Reflected firelight gleamed upon his lacquered breastplate. Conan took several slow, noisy swallows of wine, pointedly ignoring his unwanted companion, then carefully set the jug down on the table.

"Am I a dog that I come when a stranger calls?"

The warrior started slightly, then drew a deep, audible breath in an obvious effort to control himself. His dark eyes glared into Conan's, blazing with pent fury, then flicked away.

"There is," he bit out through clenched teeth, "gold in it for you. Much gold."

Conan belched, then stood up casually, still grasping the neck of his wine jug. "You should have said so in the first place. Lead on to your master."

The warrior stood still, his expression betraying an indignant rage held in place by will alone; then he turned stiffly and walked toward the door at the tavern's rear. He looked back over one armored shoulder.

"You won't be needing that," he said, pointing to the jug Conan carried.

The Cimmerian took another drink, walking past the warrior. "I just bought it." He put a hand on the heavy door and pushed through.

T he room beyond the door was long and narrow, dominated by a lengthy rectangular table set with three brass candelabra. All four walls were hung with dark curtains thickly woven with brocade to deaden sound. At the table's far end the man in the green velvet cowl sat motionless in a high-backed chair. The candle flames danced briefly in the draft from the opened door. Conan strode into the room, stopped at the base of the table, and looked down its length at the man who had summoned him.

"You are Conan of Cimmeria." The voice was strong and masculine, yet possessed a peculiar underlying tremor, as if it took an effort to speak.

"I am," rumbled the barbarian. "And who are you?"

The dark-armored warrior pushed the door closed behind him and stepped up beside the Cimmerian.

"Dog," gritted the bearded warrior, "you are here to answer questions, not to ask them."

"Gulbanda!" The cowled man raised a green-gloved hand and Conan saw that it trembled. "Come stand beside me. I'll make a few indulgences for a simple barbarian." The warrior stalked to his master's side and stood there sullenly, mailed arms crossed over his deep chest.

"Who I am is of little importance to you. It is important only that you know that if you perform a service for me, I shall make you a rich man," said the man in green.

"Why me?"

Hoarse, wheezing laughter came from within the velvet hood. The green man gestured to Gulbanda beside him.

"My bodyguard spotted you coming into Akkharia and recognized you. I have since done some investigating of my own and found that you may well live up to your distinctive reputation."

"Recognized me?" Conan's blue eyes shifted hotly from one man to the other.

"Some years ago, I saw you taken by the City Guard of Shadizar. Men knew you as a great thief." Gulbanda spoke with reluctance, apparently finding even secondhand praise of the Cimmerian distasteful. The man in velvet leaned forward intently, placing both hands flat upon the table.

"It is said that you stole the Eye of Erlik and the Hesharkna Tiara. An old Zamoran thief even told me that you had taken the Heart of the Elephant from Yara's tower in Arenjun."

"That's a lie," said Conan flatly.

"No matter," purred the man in green. "No matter. Let us simply agree that you are a thief among thieves and that I need such a man. I will pay you a hundredfold more for one night's work than you would receive for a full month of selling your sword as a lowly mercenary for King Sumuabi."

Conan dragged a chair away from the table and sat down heavily. He drank from his wine jug and leaned back in the chair.

"What is it that you would have me do?"

The green man produced a rolled scroll of parchment from a sleeve and slid it down the length of the table to Conan, who caught and unrolled it.

"That is a precise map of the mansion of Lady Zelandra. Do you know of her?"

"She is a sorceress seeking position in King Sumuabi's court, is she not?" Conan's tone was skeptical.

"That is true. Since the death of King Sumuabi's court wizard, several pretenders to his position have come forward. Lady Zelandra is among them. Be assured that her skills are greatly overrated."

The barbarian frowned and shifted uncomfortably in his seat. Talk of magic set him ill at ease.

"Cimmerian," continued the man in green, "tonight you shall break into the house of the Lady Zelandra. There you will slay her and steal for me a silver box. The box is the twin of this one."

A delicately chased silver casket, the size of a man's fists held together, was placed upon the table. It gleamed in the yellow candlelight.

"I am told by a most reliable source that Zelandra's box is like my own in every detail. It is vital that you secure this small casket and bring it directly to me. You may take anything else in the mansion that catches your eye. The casket will be kept in her inner chambers, probably beside her bed. I must have it."

As he spoke, the man in green's voice grew louder, and his words tumbled urgently over one another. When he stopped, his breathing was raggedly distinct in the soundproofed room. His gloved hands twitched where he held them on the table.

Conan drew himself up straight in his chair. A corded forearm slid slowly along its armrest until the Cimmerian's right hand hung idly over the worn hilt of his broadsword.

"For all your studies, you seem to know me not at all," Conan said tersely. "I am not an assassin, nor do I make war upon women. Seek another for this task."

The green-cowled man flinched as if slapped.

Beside him, Gulbanda's features hardened into a mask of rage.

"I will pay," croaked the green man in a strangled voice, "a roomful of gold. You'll never need to work again. You could be a rich man, with the leisure to wench and carouse the rest of your life."

Gulbanda's arms dropped to his sides and Conan's hand fell upon his hilt. A deadly tension coiled in the closed room, poisonous as an adder.

"Seek another for this task," repeated the barbarian.

"You would deny me?" The cowled man's tone fell to a caustic hiss. "So be it. Think you that my investigations halted with your career as a thief? I know well your whereabouts these past few years, Amra! There is no city in Shem that would not gleefully hang the bloodiest pirate of the Western Ocean from a gibbet! You will do as I say, or I'll see that you spend your last days in the hands of King Sumuabi's Sabatean torturers!"

Conan's response was an explosive burst of action that sent his chair hurtling back against the door as he sprang forward, toward the two men, his blade whistling from its scabbard. The man in green cried out in wordless shock, falling sideways from his chair even as Gulbanda stepped in to shield him from the infuriated barbarian. The bodyguard's blade came out just as Conan's came down. Steel rang on steel as Gulbanda blocked the heavy broadsword's stroke, staggering under the terrific impact. The warrior had barely time to be astonished at his adversary's strength before he found himself frenziedly fending off a flurry of savage blows. Wielding his massive blade as lightly as if it were a slender rapier, the Cimmerian put the bodyguard on a desperate defensive, driving him back against the curtained wall and holding him there. Gulbanda, trapped in a relentless storm of steel, saw Conan's face go grim with intent and felt a chill lance his bowels. The bodyguard blocked each sledgehammer blow by inches, hoping that the barbarian's strength would falter or that the raging attack would flag, if only for a moment.

Abruptly, his wishes were granted as Conan seemed to overextend himself. A hard horizontal slash glanced from Gulbanda's guard and swung wide, leaving the barbarian's torso open to a thrust. As the bodyguard lunged forward to transfix the Cimmerian on his point, Conan's sword reversed itself with impossible speed. The barbarian's blade struck the hilt and the fist that gripped it, tearing the sword and two fingers from Gulbanda's hand on a flying ribbon of blood. The warrior fell back against the wall with a howl of animal agony, clutching his mangled hand and tangling himself in the drapery. With feline suppleness, Conan spun about to face his second foe.

The man in the green cowl stood weaponless beside his chair. His right hand made a sudden throwing motion and something tinkled against the mail over Conan's chest. The barbarian recoiled.

He looked down and saw that there was moisture shining on his breast and broken slivers of glass glittering upon the floor. A wave of dizziness swept through his frame and a sharp, sweet odor filled his nostrils. Conan took a staggering step forward, raising a sword grown almost too heavy to hold. His foe had become an emerald blur.

"Damn you," he whispered through lips gone numb. The earth tilted violently beneath his feet, and he never felt himself hit the floor.

3

Shamtare sat in the corner of a bar he didn't know and drank wine without tasting it. He stared into his chipped ceramic mug, taking no notice of those around him. The mercenary had walked into the first tavern he had found, sat down, and commenced drinking in earnest. Since then his fear had faded, replaced by a searing shame.

Shamtare the Shemite had been a mercenary for almost twenty-five years and feared no combatant who would confront him with muscle and steel. He had seen violence aplenty in more battles than he could remember. But ever since he had watched half his troop swallowed screaming by a black cloud conjured up by a Zuagir shaman, Shamtare had no love of sorcery. It was unnatural, unmanly, and it turned his bones to water.

The mercenary took another deep pull at his wine, feeling a little less than manly himself.

"Ho, white brother." A dark figure sat at his table, pulling up a chair and leaning forward confidentially. Shamtare blinked, setting his cup down. The newcomer was a slim Kushite in the brightly decorated armor of the mercenary company of Atlach the Mace. A thick cluster of fat braids was bound behind his head.

Crimson-dyed ostrich feathers were woven into the shoulders of his white cloak.

"Have you looked about yourself, friend?" The black's voice was deep and vaguely amused. "This tavern is frequented by those riding for Atlach the Mace. Do you see anyone from Mamluke's outfit except yourself?"

Shamtare took in his surroundings for the first time. His stomach clenched.

"Indeed," continued his new companion, "do you see anyone of your color at all?" He waited for the Shemite to shake his head in response. "Now, all's the same to me. We fight for the same king, and against the same enemies, yet there are those who see all freelance troops as rivals. In fact, some of the men here are of such a mind. Thus far only your graying hair has kept you from being accosted by these characters. Be wise, white brother, and take your thirst elsewhere."

Shamtare stood, touched his brow in a salute, and headed for the door.

The night breeze was cool along the dim street. He walked to the corner and found himself looking for a tall barbarian among the passersby. He could stand no more. Setting his teeth, Shamtare walked back to the tavern in which he had met Conan the Cimmerian. He thrust thoughts of the green-clad man from his mind as he strode in the door.

The tavern was quieter now, as the dinner hour was past and the greater revels of the evening were yet to commence. The roast pig was gone from its table, and many of the torches had been allowed to burn low. The gamblers in the corner were still busy, but now they wagered in softer, more earnest tones. Shamtare saw no sign of the barbarian. He hailed the barkeep.

"Good evening. Might I have a word with you?"

"If you don't dally about it. I've a tavern to run." The barkeep mopped at his balding pate with a greasy rag. A tattered yellow beard could not obscure his sagging jowls and sour expression.

"There was a tall, black-haired barbarian in here earlier. Did you see him leave?"

"I saw no barbarian. It's bad business to carry tales about customers."

The barkeep turned as if to walk away from Shamtare, but the mercenary's hand fell upon his shoulder and arrested his progress.

"A moment more," said Shamtare quietly. "What is that room in the back for?"

"Private parties for paying customers. Take your hand off me."

"Who paid for its use tonight?"

"Take your hand off me, mercenary, or I'll tell my sons to call the city guard." Shamtare's hand dropped away from the barkeep's shoulder and fell upon the hilt of his sword.

"I don't know the man's name," continued the barkeep hastily. "I just know that he has had his way in this part of the city for almost three moons. He is said to be a wizard, and his gold is good. These are reasons enough for me to rent him the room and leave him in peace."

Shamtare turned from the barkeep and made his way to the rear of the tavern. His sword whispered from its sheath as he hit the door to the back room. He almost tripped over a fallen chair that lay just within.

Three brightly lit candelabra were set upon the room's central table. Their warm glow revealed an empty chamber. Dark blood shone wetly on the carpet, and more spattered the woven curtains. The point of Shamtare's sword lowered to the floor.

He made his way quickly across the room, to where the drapes hung awry behind the high-backed chair. A door was concealed there, obscured by the curtains. It swung open at his touch, revealing a black alley, choked with stinking refuse. Shamtare thrust his head into the dark passage, looked about, and swore foully.

"Lose your barbarian friend?" The barkeep had followed him

into the chamber. His voice was not unsympathetic. "It wouldn't be the first time that someone had an audience with the Green Man and wasn't seen again. I won't even let the serving girls come back here anymore. It is said that the Green Man wishes to become King Sumuabi's new mage and will let nothing stand between himself and his goal. I'm sorry about your friend. A wise man doesn't trifle with sorcery."

"I know that," said Shamtare.

"Come, there is nothing to be done now. Perhaps the Green Man hasn't slain him. I'll buy you a mug of wine."

"Damn." Shamtare sheathed his sword.

"That's better," said the barkeep. "Was the barbarian an old friend of yours?"

"No, a new friend who'll never get to be an old one."

"Forget him, then. His turn today, our turn tomorrow. Come on."

The stout mercenary followed the barkeep from the back room to the bar.

He took a seat and accepted the man's offer of a mug of wine. Shamtare recognized the vintage as one of the best out of Ghaza, yet it seemed, at that moment, strangely bitter.

4

The first thing that Conan became aware of was a sultry breeze smelling of moist earth. He blinked and a vortex of nausea roiled in his guts.

He was seated in a heavily built steel chair. Metal bands held his ankles, calves, wrists, and belly tightly in place. Slouched forward, his head hanging, Conan focused his bleary eyes and saw that the chair was bolted to the chamber's glossy marble floor. He had vague memories, little more than disjointed impressions, of being dragged along a noisome alleyway before being tossed bodily into a wagon full of damp straw.

A gust of warm air stirred his hair, and he raised his head with ponderous effort in order to look about. Before him, bronze-bound double doors of glass opened out into the night, revealing a shadowed garden that sloped down and away. Beyond, through a screen of trees, the lights of Akkharia lay spread out like spilled gems on an ebony table. There was no moon, but the stars told him that it was almost midnight.

"Awake, dog?" There were footfalls behind him. It was Gulbanda, his right hand bound in a white bandage. He walked a leisurely circle around the helpless Cimmerian, who silently set all of his strength to testing his bonds. The bodyguard saw the powerful muscles of Conan's arms and legs leap out into ridged relief and laughed humorlessly. His dark eyes flashed in the dim room.

"You cannot break free. Your efforts would be better spent begging me to make your death swift and easy." Gulbanda drew to a halt in front of the barbarian and pulled a dagger from its sheath with great deliberation.

Conan relaxed, staring straight ahead in stoic silence. The bared blade made a silvery flourish before the Cimmerian's expressionless face.

"Speak." The dagger came forward until its point indented the skin beneath Conan's right eye. "You have nothing to say?"

Gulbanda moved the blade to the barbarian's forearm and lay the cold steel on bronzed skin. "Why don't you beg your heathen gods for rescue? They might answer if you cried out to them loudly enough."

The razor-sharp edge drew slowly across flesh and a thin scarlet stream broke free in its wake. Conan bared his teeth in a feral snarl, fixing his eyes upon Gulbanda with such elemental hatred that his tormentor withdrew the knife and took an involuntary step backward.

"Gulbanda, you are mistreating our guest."

The dagger made a hasty return to its sheath as the warrior retreated to a dark corner of the room.

"I did him no harm," he said in a voice thick with frustration.

"I should hope not," said the man in the green cowl. "He has important work to do tonight." The robed man stood over Conan, inspecting the shallow but painful gash inflicted by his servant. The hood lay in heavy folds about his shoulders, baring his head. He was a black man with sharp, aristocratic features. A high-domed forehead and a strong jaw might have made him handsome, but there was a weathered, weary aspect to his face that belied his obvious youth. The eyes were as rheumy and reddened as those of an old man. The skin of his face appeared to hang on his skull, slack and dull as a mask. Conan noticed a greenish smear beneath his captor's lower lip. Under the barbarian's gaze, he turned away as if ashamed, wiping his mouth on a velvet sleeve.

"You must learn to show restraint, Gulbanda. This man is a valuable tool. If you treat your tools well, they will serve you well." The black man turned back to Conan, pulled a lace handkerchief from his robe, and daubed it gently in the blood on the Cimmerian's forearm.

Folding the cloth with care, he replaced it in his pocket. He gazed down at Conan, his eyes dark wells of fathomless emotion.

"I am Shakar the Keshanian. Do you know me?"

"No, but you must be another who seeks to become King Sumuabi's toy mage. What did you do to me?"

"You have some wit for a barbarian. I broke a glass ball upon your breast. The ball was filled with a weak distillate of the Black Lotus. The fumes produce unconsciousness but do no lasting harm. You will feel dizzy and ill for a time, though. I hope that this will not inconvenience you on your mission tonight."

Conan spat at Shakar's feet. "Get your lapdog to run your errands." He jerked his head toward Gulbanda. "I'll not serve you."

Shakar nodded absently, pressing gloved hands together and turning away from his prisoner. He strode to a low chest of drawers set against one of the marble walls.

"The priests of Keshia had little liking for me," he said thoughtfully. "They made my life difficult. So, before I left that city, I stole much knowledge from them. Much knowledge and several precious items to make my life outside Keshan easier. The glass balls are one thing I acquired. These are another." Shakar arose from the chest and held his hands out to Conan.

Suspended from each fist was an amulet the size and shape of a hen's egg. They were the color of tarnished brass and inscribed in black with a single serpentine rune. Instead of a chain, each amulet dangled from a flexible loop of thin golden wire. With a quick motion, Shakar flipped one wire noose over the top of Conan's head and released it.

The strange pendant fell heavily upon the Cimmerian's breast. The black warlock leaned forward, pulling the barbarian's long hair out from beneath the encircling wire until the metal rested against his flesh.

"There," he murmured. "There." He stroked the amulet lovingly. Then his eyes narrowed, his lips tightened against his teeth, and he bent over to stare Conan full in the face.

"Hie Vakallar-Ftagn," he whispered in a voice like the stirring of dead leaves. Conan went rigid. The wire necklace contracted around his neck until the cold weight of the amulet nestled unpleasantly into the hollow of his throat. A thrill of horror coursed along the barbarian's spine. Shakar stood up straight and grinned in satisfaction. He held the other amulet away from his velvet-clad body.

"Now you shall do as I require, barbarian. You must do it because your life will be forfeit if you do not. This night you will go to the estate of Lady Zelandra, slay her, and steal for me her silver casket. And you shall have it back here by sunrise, thief, or I will speak to your amulet thus."

Held at arm's length, Shakar's remaining pendant swung slowly on its necklace of wire. The man in green stared at it and spoke.

"Hie Vakallar-Nectos." His voice died and there was an expectant silence. Then the dangling amulet flared with white incandescence and a sharp sizzling sound filled the room. A wave of heat hit Conan's face like the rush of air from an opened forge. The blaze of light stabbed fiercely at his eyes. For a moment the amulet hung from its wire as a fusing gobbet of nigh-intolerable brilliance; then it fell in a molten stream to spatter brightly on the polished floor. Acrid smoke arose in whorls as the liquid metal gnawed into the marble. It burned out after a long moment, leaving the floor deeply pitted and scarred. A shrill laugh broke from Shakar's lips.

"O Damballah! An ugly way to die, is it not? If you are not back by sunrise, I speak the words. If you attempt to remove the amulet, it will blaze up of its own accord. If you displease me in any way, I shall speak the words. Do you understand?" Mad triumph trembled in the warlock's voice. In the corner, Gulbanda moved uneasily. "Let him loose," Shakar ordered.

"Master?" Gulbanda hesitated and Shakar spun on him in sudden fury, cloak swirling.

"Now, fool!" The warrior hastened to Conan's side and bent to his task.

In a moment the barbarian was free of the steel chair, if not of all bonds. He stretched hugely, bending to chafe his legs where the metal cuffs had cut into his flesh.

"Do you know the Street of the Seven Roses?" asked the black sorcerer.

Conan nodded curtly. "It is where they store the shipments of wine in from Kyros."

"That is the warehouse district. Zelandra's mansion is in the residential district at the opposite end of the street. Across the city from the warehouses. It is a respectable area and often patrolled by the city guard."

"It has a very high wall," said Gulbanda coldly. "A smooth one." Conan met the bodyguard's eyes with a gaze as bleak and stark as the blade of a stiletto.

"I want my sword," he said.

Shakar nodded. "Of course. Fetch it, Gulbanda." For a moment the warrior seemed to pause, then he strode quickly from the room. The black mage looked upon Conan and lifted his gloved hands imploringly.

"Do you need to see the map again?"

"No. Do you give me your word that if I bring you the casket, you will remove this thing?" The barbarian touched the amulet about his neck as though it were a sleeping serpent coiled there.

"I swear it. And if it happens that you do not slay the woman, I shall still free you if you bring me the silver box. I must have it. Do you understand?"

The Cimmerian showed his teeth in a mirthless grin. "I understand that well enough."

"Another thing, barbarian, do you know of a Shemite named Eldred the Trader?" Shakar watched Conan intently for a reaction and was visibly disappointed by his reply.

"No. The name means nothing. Another of your rivals seeking position as the king's court wizard?"

"No. It need not concern you." At that moment Gulbanda returned, bearing Conan's sword and scabbard.

He tossed them roughly to the Cimmerian, who snatched them from the air and affixed them to his belt while moving toward the garden window.

"Remember the amulet. Do not fail me," called Shakar, but Conan had already stepped into the night and disappeared.

5

The great wagon lumbered along the Street of the Seven Roses beneath the overarching darkness of a moonless night. Massively spoked wheels ground on the cobblestones as the driver reined his team around a bend.

Two huge wooden casks sat ponderously in the wagon's bed, their weight causing the axles to sag alarmingly. The driver called encouragement to his straining horses and, thus distracted, did not notice the shadow that detached itself from the murk of an alley to furtively sprint across the cobbles and leap up onto the back of the rearmost cask, clinging to it like a cat. The man held himself to the curved surface of the massive barrel with powerful arms as the wagon continued its laborious progress. In the next block a high wall arose on the left side of the street.

Seeing it, the man drew himself lithely atop the cask and crouched with his legs drawn up tightly beneath him. He swiftly removed a light leather helmet tucked into his belt at the small of his back and clapped it onto his head.

The wagon swayed, drawing closer to the wall. Its wheels scraped the stone curb and the man jumped, hurling himself into the air with all the strength of his mighty frame. Like a quarrel from a crossbow, the man shot up and against the wall. His body met it with bruising impact, hands clapping against the cold stone with the fingertips alone finding purchase and digging in atop the wall. He dangled, breath hissing between clenched teeth. Then he chinned himself, threw over a muscular leg, and pulled himself up so that he was lying along the top of the wall. He lay motionless for a moment, waiting for the surging vertigo to pass. It seemed that Shakar's Keshanian drug had not entirely left him. He shook his head like a troubled lion, trying to rid himself of the persistent dizziness and see into the darkness below.

An elaborate garden lay spread out in the shadows beneath him. Dim, tangled outlines of trees and undergrowth led up a gentle, landscaped slope to an expansive villa that loomed as an unlit and angular silhouette against the stars. The perfume of night-blooming flowers floated on the slow breeze.

Conan stood on the narrow top of the wall. Heedless of the height, he ran swiftly along it to where a tall tree thrust leafy branches toward the wall. He squatted, peering intently into the tree, then leapt abruptly from his perch, dropping down and forward to capture a sturdy limb in iron fingers. Leaves shook and rustled as the branch bent and then rebounded, holding his weight. The Cimmerian glanced down, then released the limb. He dropped, hit the ground, and rolled in the dewy grass. Conan came to his feet in a fighting crouch, hand on hilt and eyes raking the darkness for sign of a foe.

He was alone on a well-trimmed greensward. In front of him two dense clumps of shrubbery framed a white gravel path that shone dully in the starlight. The path wound up the hill toward the dark mass of Lady Zelandra's mansion. The barbarian moved parallel with the trail, skulking in the shadows as silently as a prowling wolf. Skirting a tiled courtyard adjacent to the manse, Conan approached a darkened window and froze in midstride.

Footfalls rattled gravel along the path. Conan ducked into the shadow of a manicured hedge, hand once again gripping his hilt. Two uniformed men walked into view along the trail. They conversed softly, voices carrying on the night air. The Cimmerian crouched motionless as the pair came to a halt not ten paces away. The men wore light armor with shortswords belted at the waist, and the larger of the two bore a long, barbed pike on one shoulder. Conan's body tensed, preparing for instant violence. The pike bearer produced a wineskin from beneath his cloak, drank deeply, and passed it to his companion. The other took a swallow and returned the skin, clapping his comrade on the back with crude good humor. The pair continued down the path, blithely unaware of how close they had stood to death.

Conan relaxed, once again feeling a slight stirring of vertigo. He cursed vehemently under his breath until it passed, calling down a plague upon all dabblers in the dark arts. Then he stole silently across the grass to the waiting window. The stout shutters were thrown wide to allow the cool air of evening to ease the day's accumulated heat.

There were bars, but they were slender. Inevitably there was some noise, but Conan worked slowly and with great deliberation, bending the bars rather than tearing them from their settings. Soon he had a space wide enough to squeeze through. With a last look behind, he pulled himself through the window and into the mansion of Lady Zelandra.

He dropped into a long hall lit by a single taper. The floor was thickly carpeted, and rich Vendhyan tapestries graced the walls. The faint odor of sandalwood hung on the still air. Silence lay over the house in a heavy shroud.

Recalling the map that Shakar had shown him, Conan took his bearings and then paced soundlessly down the dim hall. He drew his sword, and the taper's soft light glimmered liquidly along its burnished length.

Ahead, the corridor turned right. At the corner a short pedestal held an elegantly fluted vase of Khitan porcelain. Conan rounded the corner and stared down a wood-paneled hall that stretched into the heart of the manse. Another lonely taper lit the corridor with a diffuse amber glow.

A woman stood stiffly in the hallway, looking at him.

"Hush!" Conan lowered his sword and lifted a finger to his lips. "I mean you no—"

The woman quickly reached a hand behind her dark nimbus of hair, then whipped the hand forward with all the strength of her arm and shoulders. A dagger shot toward Conan as swiftly and directly as a hurled dart.

"Crom!" The barbarian twisted his upper body so that the blade nicked his flapping sleeve in passing rather than burying itself between his ribs. The dagger sank almost half its length into the wooden wall five paces behind him.

Conan lunged forward, covering the distance between himself and the woman in two great bounds. An outstretched forearm struck her across the collarbone, knocking her from her feet and sending her sprawling gracelessly on her back. The Cimmerian's sword made a short, blurred arc that stopped a hairsbreadth from her exposed neck. Cold, sharpened steel lay upon her pulsing throat.

"Hush," said Conan grimly.

"Miserable thief!" hissed the woman. "Damned assassin! Kill me and be done with it!"

The barbarian raised his brows. Here was a beautiful woman. And unafraid. Her thick hair spilled upon the carpet, an ebony cloud surrounding a fine-boned face now sneering in defiance. Her pale eyes shone in the gloom like polished opals.

"I have no wish to harm you or anyone else in this house." Conan stepped back, keeping his sword leveled at the prone woman, but removing it from her throat. She sat up, twisting her full lips with disdain.

"You're mad, then."

"No. I am not here of my own choosing. My life is in the balance. If you will aid me, I will be swiftly gone." Conan's hand went to the eldritch amulet wired at his throat. The dark-haired woman drew long legs up beneath her and regarded him steadily.

"I should scream. I am not afraid to die."

"Then why are you whispering?"

She was silent a moment.

"What is it that you seek?" she asked suddenly, her voice slightly louder and more animated than before. "Are you alone? How can I help you?" Her gaze flickered from Conan's face to a point somewhere over his right shoulder. From behind him came the almost inaudible creaking of a floorboard.

Conan spun about and received a blow to the head so savage that it tore off his helmet and sent him reeling blindly across the hall. His shoulder hit the wall with a crash that seemed to shake the building.

Stinging blood sluiced hotly into his left eye. Snarling, the barbarian lashed his sword to the left and right, but the blade met no resistance. He blinked, shaking the blood from his face.

Across the hall stood a giant of a man, naked to the waist. The taper's light gleamed upon his skin, casting yellow highlights over heavy arms and a wide, hairless chest that descended into a broad, firm paunch.

The man's head was shaved and his features were those of a pure-blooded Khitan. In his hands was a short wooden club, its head adorned with iron studs. The man was silent, but he brandished the club with casual purpose, slanted eyes glittering coldly.

Conan struck with furious speed, taking the offensive with such suddenness that the giant Khitan was nearly impaled upon his sword.

With an agile twist of his brawny body, the Khitan battered the barbarian's blade aside so that it scraped its length along the wooden bludgeon, throwing splinters. Unable to halt his headlong thrust, Conan's body slammed into that of his foe. They grappled, and the Khitan sought to seize his sword arm. With an explosive grunt, Conan tore free of the powerful grip and drove his mallet-like left fist home against the side of his enemy's face. Despite the unexpectedness of the move, the Khitan managed to react, attempting to roll with the blow. If he had not, it might well have broken his neck. Even the reduced impact drove him to one knee and started blood streaming from his lips.

As the Cimmerian's sword shot up for the death stroke, a tremendous blow struck the back of his skull. Vision ablaze with flying yellow sparks, Conan went down, his blade thumping on the carpet. In an exhibition of almost superhuman vitality, the barbarian writhed painfully onto his back. Through a thickening haze he saw the dark-haired woman, gaping at him, clutching a sturdy chair. Two of its legs were splintered stumps. The stinging sweet taste of Shakar's potion crept into the back of his throat like bile. Conan tried to rise and felt a sick vertigo, a drugged dizziness that rose from within to smother him in cloying darkness. He reached for his sword, put his hand on the hilt, and passed out.

6

There was stale straw in his mouth. The floor where he lay was strewn with the mildewed stuff. With effort, Conan spat, pushed himself into a sitting position, spat again, and leaned back against a dank stone wall. Though his head throbbed like a blacksmith's anvil, he put his hands first to his throat.

Shakar's lethal amulet was still in place, still promising searing, lingering death. Conan probed his battered skull with tentative fingers. Drying blood matted his hair over two conspicuously swollen lumps. He pressed his fingertips around them and winced, but found no evidence of serious damage. Satisfied, he cast his eyes about his prison.

It was a narrow, windowless slot of a cell, a little longer than the prone body of a tall man and barely wide enough for two men to stand abreast. The door was a heavily barred iron grate, scaled with flakes of red rust.

Conan wondered how long he had until morning. A hollowness opened deep in his belly. To be incinerated by magic while locked in a cage like a helpless animal was no way for a warrior to die.

He saw that the iron bars of the grate were far too thick for bending and that the hinges were set too deeply in stone to be wrenched free.

The barbarian rose slowly to his feet, staring at the bars and clenching his fists until the tendons stood out across the backs of his hands. Conan's will for freedom was as elemental as that of a penned wolf. No matter if it would avail him nothing, he would tear at the bars of his prison until the amulet burnt through his throat.

The Cimmerian's nostrils flared as he stepped to the door of his prison, peering through the holes in the encrusted grate into the dimness beyond.

"Who's there?" he growled.

Scarcely visible in the darkened corridor outside his cell was the lissome figure of the woman he had encountered in the halls of the mansion above. She shrank away from the grate, one pale hand at her throat.

"How did you know I was here?" she stammered.

"You wear a scent in your hair. It is out of place in this pit."

The woman fumbled awkwardly at her belt for a moment, then there was a bright spark of flint on steel. A small, golden flame began guttering from an oil lamp that she thrust forward with one hand.

"What is your name?" she asked in a stronger voice.

"Conan," he replied.

The mellow light revealed the woman in full, her skin gleaming dusky ivory. Dark leggings clung to shapely legs.

A simple brown tunic was belted tightly around her trim waist and fell open at her throat.

"Let me out," rumbled the Cimmerian. In spite of the situation, his eyes were drawn to her beauty, captured by the loose fall of her lush black hair and the elegant oval of her face.

"A curious name." Her gaze seemed to pierce the cell's iron door, moving over the Cimmerian with a restless curiosity.

"If you do not set me free before dawn, it will be the name of a dead man," Conan said.

"Then you have a few hours of life remaining. Who are you, thief?"

The barbarian heaved an exasperated sigh and gripped the bars of his prison with both hands.

"I am Conan, a Cimmerian."

"What kind of a thief breaks into the home of an accomplished sorceress and yet scruples to kill one who discovers him therein?" The tiny flame of the oil lamp was mirrored in her eyes.

"Listen to me, woman. This amulet around my neck was placed there by Shakar the Keshanian. He charged me with breaking into this house and stealing a small silver chest. If I do not return with the chest by sunrise, his amulet will slay me with hellfire. Set me free and I swear by Crom to do nothing to harm anyone in this house. I will return to Shakar without your silver box and seek to persuade him to remove the amulet at sword's point."

The woman's brow furrowed with interest and skepticism. She held the oil lamp aloft to better study Shakar's amulet, while Conan, dappled by the grate's shadow, stared back intently and awaited a response.

"Silver box," she murmured. "And what does Shakar the Keshanian want with milady's silver box?"

"Hanuman devour all silver boxes!" exploded the Cimmerian. "I neither know nor care what mad designs the Keshanian has upon Zelandra's belongings. I only know that the bastard's sorcerous toy will spell my death unless I can make him take it off. Set me free! Did I not spare you when you lay at my feet with a blade at your throat?"

The woman was silent, staring at him expressionlessly through the iron door. Conan wondered how long she had been standing outside his cell before he noticed her.

The woman reached a hand behind her head and pulled a throwing dagger from its sheath at her nape. She hefted it, flipping the knife in a glittering pinwheel and catching it again by the hilt.

"I am Neesa, scribe and bodyguard to Lady Zelandra. I can throw this dagger with some skill."

"I am well aware of that," growled Conan, feeling the faint stirring of hope.

"Heng Shih wanted to keep you shut up until the morning so as not to disturb milady. But I am of a mind to take you to Lady Zelandra and have you tell her your story. Do you swear by your gods that you will neither attempt to harm me nor escape if I free you from the cell?"

"You have the word of a Cimmerian."

Replacing the throwing dagger in its sheath, Neesa turned and pulled a stout set of manacles from a peg on the wall behind her. She pushed them through a hole in the grate, and Conan received them without comment. The manacles were of oiled steel and separated by a mere three links of heavy chain. The Cimmerian closed the manacles about his thick wrists one at a time. Each fastened with a metallic snap that rang disproportionately loud in the narrow stone cell. When he looked up, his gaze locked with the woman's for a long moment.

What Neesa saw in the barbarian's eyes she could not name, but she produced a jingling ring of keys from another wall peg. The key turned in the lock with a rust-choked rasp and the door swung wide, keening in protest. The hulking Cimmerian paused briefly in the open stone portal, then stepped free into the corridor. Neesa felt a surge of fear that dissipated when she saw Conan's face. He was grinning broadly.

"Lead on," he said. "By Crom, it's good to see I still have some luck left this ill-favored night."

7

Shakar the Keshanian paced restlessly within the vaulted marble walls of his bedchamber, from the side of his canopied bed, laden with silks and exotic furs, across the exposed marble floor, to a circular table of carved and polished oak. The tabletop was bare except for a small, intricately chased silver cask that sat alone at its center. The black sorcerer halted before the table, staring fixedly at the box. This time he could not wrench himself away to continue his nervous pacing.

Instead, he extended a gloveless hand, webbed with veins as prominent as those of a man twice his age, and laid it reverently upon the lid of the silver casket. A trembling coursed through his body as he opened the box. The inner lining of the cask was seamless and polished to a mirror surface. In one corner was a small pile of powder as deeply green as the needles of a northern pine. Beside it lay a tiny silver spoon of the kind used to feed infants. Shakar gazed hungrily at the emerald powder, his lips drawing back from yellowed teeth set in receding gums.

"So little left," he breathed. He snapped the box's lid shut with a convulsive movement and turned forcibly away to resume his pacing. He reached the bed and turned, robes hissing on the smooth floor, and felt his resolve crumble. The silver box on the table drew him forward until he found himself standing over it, opening the lid, and seizing the spoon in a desperately eager hand.

At that moment, just beyond the circular table, a silent ripple of roseate light danced across the naked wall. Shakar stiffened, fearful that his craving for the emerald dust had addled his mind. Slow streams of multicolored light were running fluidly over the wall of his bedchamber. As he watched, they began lacing themselves together, weaving their glowing fabric into a luminous haze. Soon a rainbow-hued expanse of churning fog covered the full breadth of the wall. Shakar watched in mute astonishment as the colors dimmed, giving way to a brilliant white light. The dark silhouette of a man solidified there, suspended motionless in the pale blaze of phosphorescent mist. The head, as dark and featureless as a shadow, turned toward Shakar and regarded him.

"Sweet Set!" The black sorcerer took a faltering step backward, bringing a spoonful of the green powder to his open mouth and thrusting it beneath his tongue. His body jerked as though struck by a heavy blow, and the spoon dropped to jingle merrily on the marble floor. An incoherent cry of rage burst from his lips and resounded in the still room. Savage strength radiated through his wasted limbs, and his face lit with an unholy glee.

"Invade my chambers and die, fool!" howled Shakar, spittle flying from his lips. His hands described a swift sequence of complex signs in the air before him. At their conclusion, his left hand shot up and twisted into a crooked talon. He extended it toward the figure floating in its luminous cloud and barked a series of guttural syllables, words in a language that was ancient before the oceans drank Atlantis.

An ethereal ring of rolling darkness solidified around his left wrist.

Sharp pinpoints of white light winked in the black coil and a bone-numbing chill radiated from it, turning Shakar's panting breath into plumes of steam. The Keshanian's hand drew back and then lashed forward, casting the black ring as a man might throw a stone. It moved toward the suspended silhouette with easy speed.

The figure lazily raised a shadow-hand amid the bright vapor. The dark coil hit the outstretched hand and shredded into fading black streamers.

Shakar gasped aloud. The invader had just shrugged off the most lethal death-spell in his repertoire. A flat, metallic laugh emanated from the suspended silhouette and a sourceless light shone upon the featureless mask of darkness. A face was revealed, and it was a face that Shakar the Keshanian knew well.

"Eldred!" cried the man in green. "Why do you torment me?" He fell to his knees on the hard floor, hands held out in shaking supplication. "I must have more of the Lotus! Anything I have is yours! What do you want of me? What must I do? Eldred?"

The fog of light upon the wall began to draw in upon itself, fading at its edges, hiding the dark figure from view.

Shakar's voice rose in frantic despair. "Eldred! Don't leave me!" But the sorcerous projection shrank and thinned until it was merely a few stray wisps of dispersing vapor.

Then he was facing a blank marble wall. Hot tears rose in the black warlock's eyes, spilling down his haggard cheeks despite his best efforts to contain them.

There was someone at his door.

"Master! Master, what troubles you?" Gulbanda's voice came muffled through the door's heavy panels. "Are you unwell?"

Shakar stood unsteadily, drawing a velvet sleeve across his face.

"Enter, Gulbanda. All is well. I had... an ill dream." He faced away from the door as it opened, admitting the bearded bodyguard, who looked quizzically around the bedchamber. Gulbanda's eyes narrowed as they fell upon the open silver box. Shakar composed his features, but did not turn to look upon his servant. He cleared his throat.

"Has the Cimmerian returned?"

"No, master. I would notify you at once. There are but four hours until dawn."

"The barbarian may still succeed. He does not seem to be a man easily thwarted. Still, go to the house of Lady Zelandra and keep watch over the gates. He may need your assistance in escaping. Go now."

Gulbanda grimaced in disapproval, his scar making a pallid flash in his black beard, but nodded obediently. The dark-armored bodyguard stepped out of the room, then hesitated in drawing the door closed.

"Master, if he returns without the cask, or even with it, may I have him? It will be months before I can wield a sword with any skill. It seems a small favor to grant to one as loyal as I."

"If he does not return, I shall slay him with my amulet. If he does return to this house, then he is yours, faithful Gulbanda."

The bodyguard grinned with clear pleasure. "Thank you, master. I would have him in the chair again, repenting that he ever took my fingers."

"Good evening, Gulbanda."

The door closed, leaving Shakar alone in his bedchamber. He walked slowly to his bed and sat, his body weighted with a weariness that left his mind free and ablaze with urgent energy. He considered trying to sleep, or at least lying down to rest for a while, but he didn't move.

Shakar simply sat on the edge of the bed with trembling hands clutched tight in his lap. He tried to fix his black eyes on the floor between his feet, but again and again his gaze rose helplessly to fasten upon the open silver cask.

C onan followed Neesa out of the little dungeon, through a
cobwebbed wine cellar, and up a worn flight of stone stairs.
They made their way silently down taper-lit corridors until they
stood before a broad double door inlaid with plaques of carved
ivory. Neesa laid a slim hand upon the heavy door and turned to
the barbarian.

"Milady is likely awake, but if she still sleeps, you must be
silent and allow me to wake her. If startled from sleep, she might
smite us with some spell."

Conan's face went dour and he stroked lightly at Shakar's
amulet with one hand.

"By Manannan, it seems the more I strive to avoid sorcery, the
more it strives to seek me out," he grumbled. "Lead on."

The doors swung open soundlessly at Neesa's touch, revealing
an ornate, painted screen that shielded from view the unlit room
beyond. Neesa took a tentative step within and the darkness
was abruptly split by a flicker of weird crimson light. The two
halted on the threshold, as the room was suddenly aglow with a
rainbow of brilliant colors. A soft feminine cry, half dismay and
half astonishment, came out of the dark.

Hearing it, Conan and Neesa lunged together around the screen and into Lady Zelandra's chamber, where they stopped short in amazement.

Vaporous light coruscated along the wall, illuminating the room with a shifting radiance. A luxurious bed stood against the left wall, flanked by massive shelves crammed with books. Tables were set on either side of the bed, and they too were heaped with books. A woman was sitting bolt-upright in the bed, half wrapped in a white froth of silken sheets. She stared at the wall across from her, where foggy strands of many-hued light were interlocking in a grid of translucent fire. The colors died and the wall became a sheet of phosphorescent mist. An ominous shadow coalesced there.

Conan's instinctive fear of the supernatural seized him in a frigid fist, lifting the hair on the nape of his neck.

"Heng Shih!" screamed the woman in the bed. "Heng Shih!"

A door on the opposite side of the chamber burst open and a man charged through, sliding to a stop beside the bed. It was the huge Khitan whom Conan had fought in the corridor. In his left hand was the wooden mace; in his right was a heavy scimitar, its flaring blade reflecting the sinister light that bathed the room. Holding both weapons before him, the Khitan advanced expressionlessly upon the black shadow suspended in light.

"Hold!" cried the woman. "Don't touch him, Heng Shih." The Khitan stopped his advance but moved sideways to put himself between the sorcerous projection and the woman in the bed.

"Oh, Lady Zelandra. You prove that your wisdom is the equal of your beauty." The voice was deep and resonant. It was not loud, yet seemed to reach into every corner of the room. Conan recoiled, his wilderness-bred senses assuring him that what he seemed to hear was not sound at all. It came from no discernible direction. The black figure spoke directly into the mind.

"Who are you? Why do you trespass here?" The woman in the bed seemed more enraged than afraid. The invader, etched starkly against shifting veils of white light, laughed and spoke again.

"You know me as Eldred the Trader."

The woman bristled, coming to her knees on the bed.

"Assassin! Have you come here to gloat over my impending death?" she spat.

"On the contrary, sweet lady, I have come to offer you life. I am the master of the Emerald Lotus. You have tasted its glorious power and felt its mortal demands. I am fresh from a visit to the home of Shakar the Keshanian, and I fear that he will not last another two days. His appetite escalates as his supply dwindles. You seem to be in much better health, so I infer that you have shown greater control than the Keshanian. You may live another week or two, but be aware that without a steady supply of my lotus, you are doomed."

"You have a price?" asked Zelandra bitterly. The shadow figure continued as though she had not spoken.

"The Emerald Lotus is a wondrous gift to sorcerers. You have experienced but a meager fraction of its strength in your own wizardry. Its power is limitless. With enough of the lotus a mage might become all-powerful, while those seduced by it and then abandoned must die. In the guise of Eldred the Trader, I approached both you and Shakar the Keshanian. Two petty sorcerers locked in a trifling rivalry over which would be privileged to become King Sumuabi's lackey. The lure of the mythical Emerald Lotus proved as strong as I knew it would be. I sold it to you for a pittance, but I would have given it to you for nothing had you chosen not to buy."

"Why?" The rage had faded from Zelandra's voice, leaving only a profound weariness.

"Why?" The veils of stark light throbbed brighter. "Because I wondered how much power such a small amount would grant you. Because I wondered how long you could make it last. But most of all, because I wondered how long it would take you to die once it was gone. I have learned so much from you, sweet lady, and from Shakar the Keshanian. It is knowledge I shall use to good effect. I have found the seeds of the Emerald Lotus, lost since the time of black Acheron, and I am its master. It shall strengthen me and slay my enemies. All the mages of Stygia shall soon have the opportunity to sample my lotus, and those who accept it will either obey me as loyal followers or be left to die.

"Can you not see it, sweet lady? I will command a legion of lotus-enslaved wizards, while that which holds them in bondage grants me greater and greater power. Who can say what the limits of my dominion might be?" The ebon outline fell silent, pausing as though to savor the moment. "I am destined to become a great force in the world, Zelandra, but you need not fear me. I am not here to slay you; rather, I would ask you, lady, would you share this power with me?"

"Who are you?" The woman on the bed spoke without emotion.

The moving curtains of fiery mist drew apart, dimming into the background as the figure became visible: a tall man dressed in a regal gray robe trimmed with ermine. Great dark eyes set in a noble, sharp-featured face surveyed the room with calm intensity. A subtle, golden radiance played about him as he bowed deeply toward the Lady Zelandra.

"I am called Ethram-Fal."

"Ethram-Fal?" Zelandra's voice cracked. "I have heard of you, Stygian. A reject of the Black Ring. Why do you present yourself as a normal man rather than the twisted dwarf that you are?"

"Bitch!" The invader all but choked in astonishment. "I offer you life and a place by my side, and you would mock me?" The sorcerer's words burst inside their skulls with staggering force, scalding with shock and rage. The figure fell in upon itself, its outline collapsing into the image of a much smaller, hunched man in plain gray robes. Bulging eyes glared furiously from beneath a dark and beetle brow. The haze of light around him paled and then vanished entirely, revealing a rocky desert landscape touched by the first pallid rays of dawn. Sharp spires of ruddy stone rose to his immediate left, while on his right a small, unusually regular formation of jagged peaks lay upon the azure horizon.

Ethram-Fal's clenched fists shook by his sides while his thin mouth worked in an uncontrollable fury of outrage.

"I will return to you in three days. By then my lotus will have tightened its grip. I swear by the Crawling Chaos that I shall hear you beg for my acceptance. And then, by Set, *then* I shall decide if you are worthy!"

The image winked out like a snuffed candle, leaving the four of them staring at a blank wall in a room gone suddenly dark.

9

The Lady Zelandra fell back among her pillows as if in a faint, then sat up abruptly, twisting one hand in the air. Four torches set in wall mounts flared into brilliant orange flame, flooding the room with light. She was still staring at the wall.

"Damn him," she said softly, "and damn me for a fool."

"Milady," cried Neesa as she crossed the bedchamber, towing Conan by one muscular arm. Heng Shih, the Khitan, brandished both of his weapons, the flare-bladed scimitar whistling as it cut the air. He did not speak.

"What's this?" Lady Zelandra swung her fine long legs over the bedclothes and came to her feet. She advanced upon the Cimmerian, her eyes slitted and mouth tight with contempt.

"Milady," said Neesa, "this is Conan. He broke into the house, and Heng Shih and I just managed to overcome him. He has an interesting story to tell. He is—"

"A pawn of Shakar's," cut in Zelandra. "The Keshanian amulet about his neck reveals the truth. Is that third-rate trickster so desperate that he sends barbarian thieves to rob me? What did you come seeking, oaf?"

Zelandra's hair was black, straight, and shot through with silver. Though she was well into middle age, her body was still erect and firm, beautiful in her silken nightrobe. Her keen black eyes inspected her uninvited visitor with obvious repugnance.

"I am no friend of Shakar's, lady. If you know the amulet, then you must know its purpose. If I do not return to the Keshanian by dawn, its flame will burn my head from my shoulders. Shakar sent me here to steal from you a silver box. I had no choice in the matter."

"Of course," muttered Zelandra as if speaking to herself, "without more lotus the rascal dies."

"With this damned amulet around my neck, I die in any case." Conan's voice grew louder. "Release me so that I may at least try to force the dog to remove it. Swear to give me that chance, and I shall help you against the Stygian who calls himself Ethram-Fal."

"Derketo, but you have gall." Zelandra grinned briefly in reluctant admiration. "And how might an unwashed savage like yourself be of assistance in a war of wizards?"

Conan tossed his black mane with manifest impatience. "The sorcerer who made himself appear upon the wall, the one who claimed mastery over the thing he called the Emerald Lotus—I know where he is to be found."

Heng Shih slid the scimitar into his wide yellow sash, then fluttered the fingers of his right hand as though drawing quick pictures in the air. Conan recognized the movements as a form of sign language, but had no notion of what message was conveyed.

"Perhaps," said Zelandra soberly, "but who can say?"

She took two swift steps to the Cimmerian's side and laid a cool hand upon his amulet and throat. Conan clenched his teeth. Expecting the thing to blaze into murderous life, he fought an impulse to shrink away.

"Hie Nostratos-Valkallar," she whispered, as her fingers slid between the egg-shaped amulet and Conan's throat. The muscles of the barbarian's frame locked into taut knots, but he held himself in place.

The sorceress smiled lazily into Conan's tense face and spoke: "Hie Nostratos-Nectos."

White fire erupted before the Cimmerian's eyes as Zelandra jerked the amulet free. She stepped back, her hand full of livid molten brilliance. The barbarian clasped both hands around his naked throat as a thick wave of searing heat struck his body.

"Crom and Ishtar!" The curse ripped from Conan's lips.

The sorceress opened her hand and liquid metal streamed down her fingers in bright rivulets, spilling to the floor. It seemed to flee her fingers, every drop shedding itself to sizzle in the carpet. Her hand was unmarked.

"Just a toy," she said. "Now, where is Ethram-Fal, and how do you come by such convenient information? If you are lying, I shall devise a death for you that will make the amulet seem most merciful."

"To hell with you and your threats," snarled Conan. "I've been drugged, beaten, and blackmailed all night long. I said I knew where he was, and I meant it. I could use a drink."

Heng Shih advanced menacingly, hefting his wooden mace. Conan stood his ground, glaring, and Neesa spoke up.

"I'll get some wine, milady. With your permission?"

"Certainly," said Zelandra, the reluctant smile playing about her lips again. "Being drugged, blackmailed, and beaten does sound like thirsty work."

Neesa bolted from the room, leaving Conan and Heng Shih to glower at one another while Zelandra examined the barbarian as though seeing him clearly for the first time.

"The Khitan is mute, then?" asked Conan, relaxing a little.

"Yes, though his hands and his weapons speak most eloquently when he wishes."

Conan rubbed the back of his head ruefully. "His club spoke to my skull earlier this evening, though I'll wager that if I had not felt the lingering fumes of Shakar's drugs, I would have heard him stealing up behind me." Heng Shih's round face split in a wolfish grin, the fingers of his right hand working in the air before him.

"He says that you have the hardest head of any man he's ever met," said Zelandra wryly.

"Others have said the same," replied the Cimmerian. "Tell him that he's the fastest-moving fat man I've ever seen."

The Khitan frowned darkly, drawing himself up to his full height as Neesa re-entered the room bearing a silver tray set with a jug of wine and a large pewter tankard.

"He understands you perfectly," said Lady Zelandra.

"So I thought." Conan snatched the jug from the platter with manacled hands and tore the cork out with his teeth. Disdaining the tankard, he drank directly from the bottle, taking several deep swallows before pulling it from his lips with an explosive sigh of satisfaction. He strode to the nearest table and, carelessly pushing books aside, sat on its edge. Nursing the bottle, he stretched his long legs out before him and gave every sign of being well pleased with himself.

"As soon as you are adequately refreshed, perhaps you would see fit to tell us where you believe Ethram-Fal can be found," said Zelandra sarcastically. Heng Shih drew his scimitar casually from his sash and absently began to test its edge with a thumb. None of this served to hurry Conan, who took a last, leisurely swallow from the bottle and set it on the table beside him.

"After you taunted the Stygian and he took on his true aspect, the scenery behind him became as clear as if we looked through a window of glass into a desert," said the Cimmerian.

"I angered him and his concentration faltered," said Lady Zelandra.

"What of it?"

"When the desert was revealed," went on Conan patiently, "I saw a ridge behind him. It is a row of small peaks that men call the Dragon's Spine."

"You have seen this ridge before?" asked Neesa in amazement.

"I have seen it twice. The last time was two months ago, when I took a caravan across Stygia from the Black Kingdoms. Before that, I saw it on the way to the dead city of demons called Pteion."

"You have been to Pteion?" Zelandra's eyes were wide in the torchlight.

"I was there once," replied Conan. "It is a place best avoided. Ethram-Fal is in eastern Stygia, a few days' travel from the Shemitish border. From the position of the Dragon's Spine, he is both west and south of Pteion, though what he is doing in that godforsaken wasteland only Crom knows. I give you my word that all I have said is true. Now, if you will remove these manacles, and give me back my sword, I will return to the house of Shakar the Keshanian. After my visit, I promise that he shall trouble neither you nor anyone else unless it be in hell."

At a gesture from Zelandra, Neesa came forward, drawing from within her tunic a small key which she fitted into the Cimmerian's manacles. In a moment they fell from his wrists, clattering to the floor.

"Barbarian..." said Zelandra. She hesitated, a rosy tint suffusing her features, then began again: "Conan, that area of Stygia is little known. I have scant time to find a reliable guide. If you lead me into that territory, your reward will be rich."

"But milady!" burst out Neesa in dismay. Zelandra silenced her with an imperious wave of a hand.

"What else is there for me?" she snapped. "Do I sit here passively and wait for madness and death? Or perhaps you would have me submit myself to Ethram-Fal?"

"No, milady," murmured Neesa, lowering her gaze. Heng Shih folded his thick arms impassively; only his bleak eyes revealed his emotion.

"Besides, Conan," Zelandra continued, "Shakar will die shortly for want of the Emerald Lotus. Slaying him would be an act of mercy. I need your aid now and can pay well for it."

The Cimmerian scowled, his blue eyes burning with distrust.

"I have little use for wizards—" he began, but Zelandra cut him off.

"Conan, I swear by Ishtar and Ashtoreth to do you no harm by sorcery or otherwise. Can you not see that my life is in the balance now? Without your aid, Ethram-Fal will claim my life with his lotus just as surely as Shakar would have claimed yours with his amulet. On the journey you could be guide and guard in one; but when we find his sanctuary, I shall confront Ethram-Fal alone. You needn't deal with him at all..." A note of pleading desperation had crept into her voice. Conan shifted in discomfort and suddenly felt Neesa's body pressed warmly against his side. In front of him, Lady Zelandra extended a hand in supplication more eloquent than words.

"Please, barbarian."

"What the hell," said Conan gruffly. "I trust that the wages will outstrip those of a mercenary."

"Tenfold," said Zelandra. "By Pteor, Conan, you shall never have reason to regret this." The Cimmerian felt Neesa remove herself from his side.

At the same moment, he noticed Heng Shih's face had taken on the expression of a man attempting to swallow a mouthful of spoiled meat.

"I'm damned if I don't regret it already," he grumbled. "When do we leave?"

"After sunrise." Zelandra spun about in a swirl of her silken robe. "I have many preparations to make, and you could doubtless use a little sleep after a night like this. Heng Shih, show our guest to one of the bedchambers."

The big Khitan thrust his scimitar once more through his sash and brusquely beckoned the Cimmerian to follow him. Neesa slipped out the door just ahead of them, not glancing at Conan, but heading off down the hallway in the direction opposite to that taken by Heng Shih and the barbarian.

Conan looked back over a broad shoulder and muttered a curse as he watched the woman round a corner out of sight. When he turned back to Heng Shih, the Khitan's round, yellow face was split by a grin that the barbarian found vexing.

In the mansion's opposite wing, the burning tapers were fewer and the rooms seemed unoccupied and unused. The hallway finally ended in a door that Heng Shih shoved open roughly. Within was a small, windowless, but elegantly appointed bedchamber. Conan stepped inside, and turned to the Khitan.

"My sword," he said. "Bring me my sword. I shall sleep poorly without it at hand." Heng Shih performed an elaborate shrug that seemed to indicate that he found the quality of the Cimmerian's rest of less than paramount concern. With that ambiguous gesture he closed the door upon the barbarian, leaving Conan wondering when he might hold his sword again.

Alone, Conan stretched like a weary panther as fatigue came over him despite what he had said to the Khitan. He examined the door, checked that it could not be locked from the outside, then sat down heavily on the bed. Falling back to sprawl among the velvet blankets, he let himself drift, confident that his senses would awaken him to any danger. He was sleeping soundly when there came a gentle knock at the door.

The Cimmerian snapped from slumber to complete waking clarity with the speed of a wild animal. He sat up on the bed, planted both feet on the floor, and wished that he had a weapon.

"Come," he rasped and waited. The door swung open soundlessly. The first thing that he saw was the proffered hilt of his sword.

"So," Conan began, "you decided..." He fell silent.

It was Neesa who brought him the sword. She stepped tentatively into the room, bare white arms extending from filmy sleeves as she held the hilt of the heavy broadsword out to him. Her only garment was a diaphanous robe that floated about her like a soft cloud of translucent vapor. The room's single taper illumined the long curves of her slender body through the robe's revealing gossamer.

"I..." Neesa's voice faltered. "I was afraid that Heng Shih would not bring you your sword and that you would think that we mistrusted you. I thought..." She flushed and thrust the sword out to him. Conan took his blade and held it uncertainly, his gaze fixed upon her. He had come to his feet without thinking, and now he became painfully aware of the woman's obvious discomfort.

"Neesa," said Conan hoarsely. "I'll take Zelandra's payment in gold."

"What? They don't know I'm..." she stammered. Her face twisted in mingled confusion and anger. "Damn me for an idiot!" she exclaimed savagely.

With that she lunged forward, throwing her arms around the barbarian and crushing her mouth against his. The sword was pinned between their bodies. Conan released it, his arms moving automatically around her.

Neesa laid her hands upon his wide chest and thrust him away, breaking the embrace. The sword dropped to the carpet, where it lay unnoticed.

Wild-eyed and panting, Neesa glared at the Cimmerian, who looked on in mute amazement.

"I am not payment," she gritted. "I thought... oh, to hell with what I thought!" She whirled and ran from the bedchamber, slamming the door behind her.

Conan stared at the door for a full minute. He glanced down at his sword to be certain that it was really there. Then he sat on the bed again and rubbed his jaw. He reflected that it made little difference how long he lived or how many women he knew, the opposite sex continued to provide surprises. Apparently Neesa had come to him of her own accord, and he had managed to drive her off with a few ill-chosen words.

It certainly wouldn't be the first time that he had shown poor judgment where women were concerned.

But there was little point in worrying about it. All and all, this was a superior close to a difficult day. He was employed, free of Shakar's magic, and lying on a fine bed with a belly full of wine. Conan lolled back on the blankets once again and kicked off his boots. Things had, indeed, been much worse. In a few moments, the barbarian was asleep.

10

A lone in her bedchamber, Zelandra brooded.

The torches burned as ruddy as dying embers, filling the room with a ruby twilight that matched the sorceress's mood. Her long, silken robes whispered on the marble floor as she moved among her books, studying the unwieldy piles on the tables and then methodically examining her shelves. In a corner, she knelt and pulled an armload of long leather tubes from behind a row of books.

Shoving the tomes aside, she piled the leather tubes on a table, peering at each in turn. Zelandra selected one that was pale and slender, and drew from it a rolled scroll of parchment. It was a map, darkened by age and inscribed in a dead language. The sorceress muttered to herself, smoothing the crackling scroll flat on the dusty tabletop.

The map depicted the eastern regions of what was now Stygia, but the highland areas were sketched in with little detail. Zelandra sighed.

The map seemed all but useless; still, it would have to suffice. She thrust the scroll into the tube and set it beside her bed. Then she hesitated, wrapped in indecision.

Zelandra's occult communication with Mithrelle

Resolution came to Zelandra, sending her striding to the far corner of the chamber. She reached for a torch, twisting it in its sconce, and a section of the bookshelf-lined wall swung open like a door. Within was a tiny, circular room hung with curtains of black velvet. A single chair sat at a round, ebony table that all but filled the little chamber. The sorceress stepped into the secret room and the door swung shut, sealing her in darkness.

Zelandra whispered a soft incantation, and an unearthly silver glow dispelled the gloom. Ten spheres of hematite were set in a circle on the tabletop, and they radiated a chill illumination.

The sorceress sat in the chair, touching each of the stones in turn.

Silver light raked her features, turning them stark and sinister. Her hands danced over the ring of stones, describing intricate patterns, and a patch of light appeared in the air before her. It rolled and seethed, suspended above the circle of silvery stones like a ball of glowing smoke.

"Mithrelle," said Zelandra clearly. "Mithrelle."

The ball of smoky light vanished, and it was as though a distorted mirror suddenly hung before Zelandra. The flattened image of a woman's face peered at the sorceress, floating above the table.

"Mithrelle," said Zelandra. The conjured face blinked as if startled.

It was a face of extraordinary beauty.

"Who dares?" The voice was rich and throaty, sounding as if its owner shared the little room with the Lady Zelandra.

"Who dares, indeed." Zelandra smiled casually, but her hands were clenched into tight fists, and the pulse fluttered visibly in her throat.

"Zelandra!" The woman called Mithrelle smiled in recognition. Black hair hung in heavy coils around her pale face. Eyes like pools of oil gleamed with dark humor. Her lips were stained so deeply red as to appear black. "To what do I owe this unexpected pleasure?"

"Greetings, Mithrelle. I'm loath to disturb you at this hour, but I have need of information. And everyone knows that there is no one so well informed as yourself."

Mithrelle laughed, throwing back her head and baring her white throat.

On her breast, a swollen garnet hung from a necklace of black pearls.

"Flattery! This is not like you, Zelandra."

"I need your help, Mithrelle."

"Even so? You have had little use for me since we studied together."

"Your path is not my path, Mithrelle."

"Oh no." Mithrelle's tones grew heavy with sarcasm. "The lady prefers the quiet life of a scholar. She hides away in Akkharia with her slaves, only venturing out to go to market."

"How is Sabatea, Mithrelle?" Zelandra's voice turned hard.

"Very well. I have performed a few favors for the sorcerers of the Black Ring, and they have been appropriately grateful. My life is full of pleasures. And your own? Is that strapping Khitan slave still keeping you company?"

"I freed Heng Shih long ago," said Zelandra tersely. She fought to control herself. Anger would accomplish nothing.

"Of course you did. I'd expect nothing less. You are the same woman you were a score of years ago. Yet, I have heard rumors as of late that the reclusive Lady Zelandra is seeking a more public position. I couldn't credit it." Mithrelle paused theatrically, lifting a long-fingered hand to stroke her chin. Her nails were sharp and gleamed with black lacquer.

Zelandra shrugged in resignation. She should have known that Mithrelle would ask at least as many questions as she answered.

"I'm seeking the position of court wizard to the king."

"It's true, then," exclaimed Mithrelle in mock surprise. "And why would the Lady Zelandra demean herself by working for another? Could it be that her inheritance is dwindling and that she must needs earn a living for the first time in her life?"

"I fail to see why you ask so many questions," Zelandra replied stiffly, "since you obviously know all the answers already."

Mithrelle laughed in delight, her mirth as sweet and cloying as poisoned honey.

"Indeed. That is why you sought audience with me, is it not? Now, how can I assist my old friend?"

"Tell me of the Stygian sorcerer named Ethram-Fal."

"Phaugh!" Mithrelle grimaced delicately. "What do you want with that one?"

"He has insinuated himself into my affairs. He claims that he can sell me magical talismans of unprecedented power."

"Ah." The Sabatean's eyes lit up. "I see. You wish to know if his goods can assist you in claiming the position of court wizard."

The sorceress nodded ruefully, as if admitting an unwelcome truth.

Inwardly, Zelandra rejoiced that Mithrelle was not as perceptive as she believed herself to be.

"Ethram-Fal is a laughingstock. I presume that you have heard how he came to Sabatea seeking membership in the Black Ring? Even the feeblest student of the dark arts knows that the Black Ring recruits its own members, yet still the dolt came calling. Perhaps he imagined that his greatness had escaped the notice of the Black Ring. They were more merciful than might be expected, however, merely casting him out of the city in disgrace. If Thoth-Amon had been about when Ethram-Fal made his plea, the upstart would probably still be screaming under the Steel Wings."

"Do you know where he dwells?"

"Ethram-Fal was born in Kheshatta, though I believe that he left the City of Magicians in order to take up residence here in Sabatea. The Dark Gods alone know where he has fled since his exile. You have seen him in Akkharia?"

"Yes, but his home is elsewhere."

Mithrelle's eyes grew hooded and lazy. "Why should this be so important to you? Ethram-Fal has little to his credit save his considerable skill in the magic of plants, fungi, and such. Still, I hardly imagined that his rejection by the Black Ring would drive him to become a merchant. What manner of magical talismans did he offer, that you felt it necessary to call me?"

"Just a handful of potions and philters. Magic intensifiers, mostly." Zelandra fought to keep the tension out of her voice, smiling sheepishly. "I shall need all the aid I can muster to be chosen as King Sumuabi's court mage."

"Yet you don't seem curious about your rivals. What is it that truly concerns you about Ethram-Fal, Zelandra?"

"It is small wonder that I do not converse with you more often, Mithrelle. You are the most suspicious woman I have ever known."

Zelandra's hands crept across the table toward the shining spheres of hematite. The image of Mithrelle swelled and throbbed brighter.

"Oh no, milady. Don't think to end this audience just yet. I can't abide unanswered questions, and you have made me very curious."

"Goodbye, Mithrelle." Zelandra slipped her hands down on two stones.

The flat image of the Sabatean sorceress flickered and dimmed, then abruptly flared to brilliant life.

"You would desert your old friend?" Mithrelle's voice dropped to a guttural growl. "Come to me, little Zelandra. Come to me and answer my questions and be my slave." The oval image expanded rapidly and acquired depth. Zelandra felt as if she stared into an open portal carved from empty air.

Mithrelle's bare white arms shot out of the image. Her hands seized Zelandra about the throat. Black nails scored Zelandra's flesh as the Sabatean sorceress reached into the chamber as if leaning over a windowsill.

"You would toy with me, Zelandra? Did you forget that I was always your better? Come!" Mithrelle's long-fingered hands squeezed off her breath, lifting Zelandra from her seat.

The blood roared in the sorceress's ears. She pulled back against the Sabatean's embrace, lifting her hands from the silver-glowing stones and clapping them upon Mithrelle's temples. Crimson lightning crackled from her palms. Mithrelle's mouth fell open like a castle's drawbridge, but no sound emerged. Her hands sprang from Zelandra's throat and clawed spastically at the air.

"You were always overconfident, Mithrelle," said Zelandra hoarsely. She dropped her hands onto the stones. Mithrelle's arms were wrenched forcibly back into the image, which shrank and flattened until it once again resembled a floating mirror.

"You can't!" The Sabatean found her voice. She snarled like a beast, a lank lock of black hair falling across her pale face. "You can't!"

"I can," said the Lady Zelandra. Her hands moved upon the stones and the image winked out in a scarlet flash, like a bursting bubble of blood.

The sorceress stood, stretching wearily and rubbing her bruised neck as the secret room's door swung open behind her. She returned to her bedchamber, where the torches burned ruddy and low. Casting a glance at the forsaken bed, Zelandra shook her head and sighed. There would be no more sleep tonight. She moved silently about the room, gathering her belongings for the long journey ahead.

11

B road beams of golden sunlight stretched across the floor of Shakar's study. The black sorcerer stood quietly, staring out the open window into the verdant splendor of his garden. A cooling breeze bore both the songs of birds and the perfume of greenery into the room, but the tranquil pleasures of the garden went unnoticed by the Keshanian mage today. He walked slowly from the window seat across the study, leaned listlessly against his wide mahogany desk, and tried not to think of the silver box he had placed within it.

The sound of a slamming door came to him and he started violently, turning eager sleepless eyes to the study's curtained entrance.

Gulbanda burst in, panting, his crested helmet clutched under one dark-armored arm.

"Master," Gulbanda said between gasps. "The barbarian, Lady Zelandra, and two of her servants have left the city!"

For a moment Shakar looked as though he might fall; then a surge of rage seemed to buoy him up.

"You lie!" screamed the Keshanian. His hands twisted through a series of swift movements, ending with his left hand raised, its fingers crooked into talons. Gulbanda knew the gestures that preceded the death-spell and fell to his knees.

"Master, I swear that it is true. I saw them leave by the caravan gate, and even now they ride the Caravan Road toward Sabatea. The amulet was gone from the barbarian's neck. I swear it." The sweat of fear shone on the warrior's face.

Shakar spun away from the kneeling man, waving his fists in uncontrolled fury.

"By the Black Gods, am I to be thwarted at every turn? Where were they bound?"

"So help me, Master, I know not. I watched the lady's house as you instructed, and when they departed, I followed them to the caravan gate. Then I came directly to you."

Facing the window, Shakar's arms dropped limply to his sides. He turned back to his bodyguard, face haggard but calmed.

"Arise, Gulbanda," he said quietly. "Forgive me for threatening my finest servant and most loyal friend." As Gulbanda faltered to his feet, Shakar took him by the arm and led him to the window seat.

"Here, sit down. You must be tired after your long vigil."

"I slept not a moment last night, master." Heavy lids half veiling his eyes attested to his honesty.

"Nor did I," said the mage. "Come, let me take your breastplate and helmet. We shall relax, eat, drink, and plan what is to be done." The Keshanian helped Gulbanda out of his breastplate, mail shirt, and helmet, setting them on a table across the room. He brought a split loaf of bread and a crystal decanter of wine from a cupboard against the far wall, and set them before Gulbanda as though he were the master and Shakar the servant. The bodyguard hid a grin of bemusement until Shakar had turned away again. He reflected that, if his master was losing his mind, then he had certainly picked the right way to go about it.

"Is the wine to your liking?" asked the Keshanian, slipping into the chair behind his desk and silently pulling open a drawer.

Gulbanda sipped thirstily from the bottle, finding the wine's taste odd but quite agreeable.

"It is sweet," said the warrior, tearing off a bit of bread. "I've never had its like."

"It is brewed from Brythunian apples and is a bit stronger than it may seem." Shakar's hands were busy in the drawer of his desk. "Tell me, my friend, how shall we avenge ourselves upon the barbarian and claim the cask from Lady Zelandra?" Gulbanda took another swallow of the sweet wine and found that it snaked a path of heat down into his belly.

"Well, if we move swiftly we could follow them to whatever their destination might be, then ambush and kill them. I would say that we could do it alone if not for my wounded hand and your..." he faltered, "...your sickness."

"Ah," said the Keshanian, "you suggest that I hire more men?" His hand drew the silver-chased casket from the velvet-lined interior of a drawer, set it on the desktop, and flipped open the lid.

"Yes, two or three bravos with ready daggers would even the odds."

Gulbanda washed down a bite of bread with another swallow of wine and found that the sweet stuff was going to his head. Behind him, Shakar lifted a tiny spoon to his mouth twice in rapid succession.

"Of course," added the bodyguard, "I would duel the barbarian alone if it were not for my wound."

The sorcerer tensed his body against the shudders that wracked it. He blinked back tears and drew a deep breath, shaking off the pain.

"Do you know where such men can be hired?" Shakar's voice had gone hoarse, but his bodyguard paid no heed. Gulbanda was taking another pull on the jug and relishing the warmth blossoming through his body.

"Yes, yes," he said. "I have a few men in mind right now."

"Tell me about them," said Shakar, though he wasn't listening. He was removing a number of distinctive items from the drawer of his desk and setting them before him. First was an eight-inch length of hollow bamboo, cut diagonally so that its base was an enclosed cup and its top a long tapering blade as sharp as broken glass. He stood it on its base. Next was a small vial of black crystal, which he uncorked, pouring a honey-thick, translucent fluid into the base of the bamboo spike. Last was a lace handkerchief baring a darkly crusted stain of dried blood. With a thumbnail, Shakar scraped flakes of coagulated blood from the fabric, dropping them into the bamboo receptacle. He then clutched the spike with both hands and muttered a word in a dialect sacred to the priests of Keshia. A thin, almost invisible curl of smoke arose from the bamboo spike. He palmed it as though it were a dagger and rose from behind his desk.

"Worthy cutthroats all," finished Gulbanda. "A few gold coins will secure their loyalty unto death, Shakar." His voice had taken on a barely noticeable slur.

The Keshanian showed nothing but calm interest, but he bristled inwardly as he advanced upon his bodyguard. The dog had addressed him by name rather than as master. That would make his task easier. He laid a cold hand on Gulbanda's shoulder, studying the thin leather jerkin that was now the only barrier protecting the warrior's full-muscled torso. The bodyguard shifted in his seat to face his employer. His bleary eyes focused on Shakar's expressionless countenance.

"But you, Gulbanda," said Shakar almost tenderly, "you will be loyal to me far, far beyond death." And he slammed the bamboo spike into the center of Gulbanda's chest with all of his strength. The bodyguard cried out, lurching to his feet with Shakar clinging to him like a leech. The Keshanian jammed the length of bamboo into Gulbanda's body, pouring the weapon's contents into the wound. A wild scream tore from the bodyguard's throat and his body spasmed, falling to the floor with Shakar still holding tight.

"Ayah Damballah!" chanted the sorcerer. "Kill Zelandra, bring me the casket, kill the barbarian, bring me the casket! Zereth Yog Ayah Damballah!"

Gulbanda thrashed convulsively on the floor, screaming like a man being flayed alive. His cries and Shakar's chanting mingled in an unholy chorus, each fighting for prominence until the screams died away and Shakar's voice rang alone in triumph.

12

E thram-Fal sat alone in a room carved from living rock and toasted his good fortune. His goblet was fashioned of gleaming silver set with lozenges of polished black onyx. It was brimming with an unwholesome-looking greenish liquid: wine blended with a heavy portion of Emerald Lotus powder. The Stygian swirled the thick mixture in the goblet, then tossed it back. He clamped his eyes shut, his thin throat working as he swallowed, guzzling the goblet's full contents. Pulling the emptied vessel from his lips, he gave a soft, shuddering cry. His gaunt, hunched body shivered within its gray robes.

"Hah! Yes, by Set!" Ethram-Fal's lips writhed away from his green-stained teeth, and his eyes blazed with a terrible light. He released the goblet, which remained suspended in midair before him.

The Stygian's pupils rolled back and his emaciated frame stiffened with effort. The floating goblet crumpled in upon itself as though in the grip of an invisible vise. A chip of onyx popped free of its setting and fell to the floor, while the rest of the vessel was slowly crushed together into a shapeless lump of metal. Ethram-Fal laughed with delight and allowed the rough ball of crumpled silver to drop.

He had become stronger than he had ever allowed himself to dream. Let Zelandra try to resist him now. The sorcerer sprawled back in the room's only chair, bulbous head lolling on narrow shoulders. Drugged ecstasy pulsed through him, fueling his fantasies. He remembered standing before her in the sorcerous disguise of Eldred the Trader. He remembered the way that her silver-threaded hair fell upon her slim, white neck. How beautiful she was! And a sorceress as well, by Derketo!

Surely here was a woman who could appreciate the true scope of his ambitions. Here was a mature sorceress worthy to stand at his side.

Yet she had rejected him. The memory lashed Ethram-Fal and his eyes flew wide, rolling as he gazed unseeing about the chamber. How could she be such a fool? It was all too obvious that she still had much to learn about him and his Emerald Lotus. But she would doubtless learn her lessons quickly as her supply of the drug dwindled away and her newfound power faded, replaced by the all-consuming hunger that presaged madness and an agonizing death.

The Stygian deliberately slowed his breathing and calmed himself. He needed only to wait and she would be his, crawling and begging for that which she had scorned.

All things that he desired would soon be his. Was he not master of the Emerald Lotus?

The sorcerer rose abruptly and picked his way with exaggerated care through the cluster of tables that stood about the stone room. Each held its own distinctive collection of sorcerous paraphernalia. He shuffled past the large central table whereon sat a glass box enclosing a small bush thickly covered with fat, ruddy leaves. The table he sought bore a darkly stained mortar and pestle, a collection of fluid-filled vials in a metal rack, and a long box of glossy ebony sealed with a small, golden clasp. With shaking hands, Ethram-Fal twisted the clasp. He opened the box and stared within with reverent eyes.

The black box was a little longer than a man's forearm and as wide and tall as a man's hand. It was about half full of deep green powder.

"Half gone," whispered the Stygian, unaware that he spoke aloud. He pursed dry lips as a frown wrinkled his protruding brow. The exuberant confidence that had lifted his spirits a moment ago now seemed a long-dead memory, distant and useless. A chill anxiety tightened his guts. He had been spending too much time experimenting with his new power and not enough tending to that which enabled him to exercise the power in the first place. He must see to the Emerald Lotus, and perhaps harvest more for his personal stock.

He swept aside the blanket that hung over the doorway—there were no doors in the Palace of Cetriss. The dark hall was a smooth shaft cut through solid stone. Ethram-Fal hastened along its length, his sandaled feet raising the dust of centuries. He passed down a spiral stair that coiled through the ancient rock and entered a short, vaulted room that ended in another hanging blanket. Beyond the blanket stood the Great Chamber, doubtless used as an audience hall by Cetriss in the days of Old Stygia. Now it served as an impromptu barracks for Ethram-Fal's twenty men-at-arms.

The three warriors lounging in the Great Chamber leapt to their feet when Ethram-Fal entered, slapping their right palms over their hearts.

The sorcerer smiled thinly, nodding his approval of their attentive devotion. When he had left Kheshatta in search of the Palace of Cetriss and his dreams, he had taken pains to hire the finest and most expensive squad of freelances that he could find. His riches and the fat, red leaves of the Vendhyan kaokao plant had fostered a powerful loyalty in them.

Threading his way among the cots in the Great Chamber, Ethram-Fal smiled. The wizards of the Black Ring had belittled him for devoting himself to the magics of plants and growing things. Such arrogance!

They had likened him to a Pictish druid, as if he had anything at all in common with those meek and feeble tree-worshippers. Those ignorant savages feared to so much as disturb the delicate balance of nature, much less to seize it and bend it to their will. Surely the pompous fools of the Black Ring would think differently of him now. He, a wizard whom they had mocked and rejected for his youth and unlikely fields of study, had truly come into his own. The specialized researches that they had disdained had finally led him to the lost palace of the mage Cetriss, creator of the mythical Emerald Lotus. Soon enough the Black Ring would learn that the lotus was no mere myth, but an ancient reality that he, Ethram-Fal, had personally resurrected. How they would marvel at his power! How they would beg to sample it! From the dust of three thousand years, he would breed a vengeance such as the world had never known.

Lost in his drugged reverie, Ethram-Fal moved down another hallway into a vast, unlit chamber. The Stygian started when he realized where he was and hastened his stride. To his left towered a sable shadow, a deeper darkness amid the dark. It was a great crouching statue of black stone, a sphinxlike, hulking god-thing whose name and nature were unknown to Ethram-Fal. When he had first found the palace and wandered through its deserted halls—the only visitor in many lifetimes—he had found something in this room as disturbing as the black and nameless idol itself. On the stone altar that lay between the proffered talons of the god was a dusty pile of offal. The tiny desiccated corpses of dozens of rodents, lizards, scorpions, and other even smaller vermin lay in a neat mound before the silent and implacable avatar. Now he hurried through the darkened temple and did not look upon the featureless face of the god of Cetriss where it loomed in the murk, staring blindly into the darkness as it had ever since the distant days of purple-towered Acheron.

Down a final length of hall and around a corner, the sorcerer came upon his captain, Ath, standing guard beside a doorway. A luminous sphere of crystal filled a niche in the wall. It gave off a steady yellow-green glow that painted the soldier's polished armor with warm light.

"My Lord," said Ath, bowing low.

"Light," commanded Ethram-Fal, striding past his tall captain and into the circular chamber. The small room remained as it had ever been, save that light globes had been placed in niches set to either side of the doorway. Ath touched these with his own globe, and they brightened so that the cylindrical room blazed with light.

Above their heads the band of writhing hieroglyphics that encircled the walls was clearly visible. Above that, a circular balcony of black metal spanning the room's circumference could now be seen. Higher still arched the chamber's domed roof. But the two men's eyes rose no higher than the floor.

In the center of the room lay the leathery husk of a human body wrapped in a tangle of dry, thorny growths. The withered corpse of Ethram-Fal's luckless apprentice, still clad in yellow tatters, was embedded in the tight embrace of dozens of crooked and browning branches. There were no flowers to be seen.

"Blood of Mordiggian!" Ethram-Fal cursed as fear swelled in his voice. "It is dying!"

A sick horror swept through his body, weakening his limbs and closing his throat. Had he killed his dreams even as they were being born, and done so with stupid negligence? The thought was too much to bear. The little sorcerer swayed on his feet.

"Ath," he rasped, "fetch a pack pony." The soldier turned to the door.

"Hurry!" cried his master, as Ath ran from the room.

The captain was gone long enough for Ethram-Fal to scourge himself a thousand times over because of the foolish and unnecessary nature of his predicament. When he finally heard the scuff of boots and hooves in the outer hall, he felt the relief that comes with action.

Ath led the party's smallest pack pony into the circular room. The horse was dun colored and long maned. Saddleless, it stood blinking in the unnatural yellow-green illumination as the soldier bent and hobbled its legs with lengths of rawhide.

"Here," said Ethram-Fal, "bring it here."

Ath cooed softly to the beast, drawing it forward. Suddenly, the pony seemed to notice the overgrown corpse and shied away, eyes rolling whitely.

"Here, Ath!" insisted the sorcerer. The tall soldier pulled helplessly at the horse's reins.

"He's afraid, my lord."

Ethram-Fal snatched out his irregularly shaped dagger and moved toward the hobbled pony with the abrupt swiftness of a pouncing spider.

Ath drew back involuntarily at the sight of his master advancing with clenched teeth, wild eyes, and bared steel. The sorcerer seized the pony's forelock and slashed its throat with a single quick, brutal stroke. The beast gave a pathetic whinnying cry as its blood splashed on the stone floor. It reared, then fell forward onto its knees as Ethram-Fal staggered back, crimsoned knife in one rigid fist.

There was a sound like the dry crumpling of aged parchment, and the fungus-riddled corpse moved. Barbed growths beneath the body stirred, rasping on rock, and the Emerald Lotus scuttled across the floor like a gargantuan crab. It battened onto the pony, climbing the animal's breast to sink thorned branches into its gaping throat.

"Holy Mitra!" Ath stumbled backward out of the room, his face pale as ash; but Ethram-Fal stood his ground, held by an astonished fascination that was stronger than fear.

The horse collapsed heavily with the nightmarish growth clutching it in a loathsome embrace, whipping suddenly animate branches around its body as it fell. The barbed and hooked limbs extended impossibly, lashing the air like the tentacles of an octopus.

Realizing his danger, Ethram-Fal tried to dodge past the monstrosity and out the door. A spiked branch flailed against his right leg in passing, laying open the flesh of his calf and drawing a cry of pain.

The sorcerer reeled, but Ath lunged back into the room, seizing his master's shoulders and dragging him bodily out into the hall. The two fell against the wall opposite the doorway, and would have fled had not the Emerald Lotus suddenly ceased to move. The room went silent and the pony's body lay still, half blanketed by the grotesque bulk of the vampiric fungus.

Ethram-Fal bent to nurse the wound in his calf, but Ath could only stare into the circular room with wide eyes.

"That was well done, Ath. There will be an extra leaf for you tonight."

The sorcerer's voice held a satisfaction and pleasure that were lost on his captain, who said nothing.

"I imagined that it might react more swiftly to nourishment since it did not have to revive itself from spores," said Ethram-Fal absently as he tightened a torn strip of his robe around his wounded calf. "I did not expect it to seek nourishment on its own. I see now why the room was designed as it is. We must feed it from the balcony above or its blood madness, like that of a shark of the Vilayet Sea, may lead it to attack us. You must have the men build some sort of door for the room as well, Ath."

The tall captain wiped his brow and nodded mutely. Then Ethram-Fal caught his breath as the Emerald Lotus, and its prey, shuddered briefly and broke into bloom.

13

A horseman rode through Akkharia's market square. A voluminous caftan swathed his rangy body, as though he and his mount had already traversed the desert wastelands far to the east. The rider sat atop his horse stiffly, looking neither to the right nor left at the teeming activity of the open-air market around him.

Beneath gaudy canopies, merchants hawked their wares to the interested and the disinterested alike, crying out the merits of their products in lilting, sing-song cadence. Stalls packed with richly woven clothing, worked metals, and medicines crowded others heaped high with Shem's bountiful harvest of dates, figs, grapes, pomegranates, and almonds.

All drew customers willing to haggle for what they sought, filling the dusty afternoon air with the clamor of a thousand disputing voices.

A potter, clad in the spattered robes of his profession, lunged from his sparsely attended stall brandishing a slender ceramic flask.

"Ho, warrior!" he shouted to the rider. "I have just the wine vessel a traveler needs! Flat enough to strap to your saddlebag and as sturdy as stone, it will outlast a wineskin by years! With Bel as my witness, I fired it myself and it is yours for the meager sum of three silvers!"

The man on the horse rode past as though he heard nothing, not even turning his head to look upon the insistent merchant. The potter's continued declamation of the wonders of his work were soon lost in the tumult as the rider moved on.

The city wall loomed ahead, a massive fortification of sun-bleached brick that rose to four times the height of a tall man. The imposing caravan gate stood wide open, but it was clogged with travelers both entering and leaving Akkharia. The arched opening was decorated with inlaid tiles of vivid blue; two golden ceramic dragons struggled above the gate in a time-worn bas relief.

The rider nudged his skittish horse into the slow stream of humanity before the towering gate. He drew the eyes of the guards, for most men led their beasts into or out of the city, and the mounted man overtopped all heads in the seething throng. But the guards took note of the rider's size and said nothing. After all, there was no law against riding from the city; dismounting was merely a courtesy to the thickly packed crowd.

Another man also noticed the horseman and shouldered into the press toward him. He was a stout Shemite with a florid face, dressed in colorful silks that marked him as a wealthy merchant.

"Your pardon, sir," he cried, as he struggled toward the rider. Ducking around a wooden cart bearing stacked cages full of squawking chickens, the merchant drew up beside the mounted man, who did not slow his pace or otherwise acknowledge the merchant's presence.

"You're not traveling the Caravan Road alone, are you? It is most dangerous for a single traveler, even a slayer like yourself." The merchant panted as he dodged along beside the rider, his florid face growing even redder. "Take passage with my party and be a guard. I pay as well as any betwixt here and Aghrapur."

The horseman did not respond. The merchant made a wordless sound of exasperation and snatched the horse's reins, drawing the beast up short amid the moving crowd.

"I tell you that the Caravan Road is dangerous for a man alone. Zuagirs roam the plains as well as the hills these days. You should—"

The rider bent rigidly from the waist, leaning over and thrusting his face into the merchant's. Eyes like frosted balls of black glass stared out of a sunken, yellowed visage. Bearded lips twitched over clenched teeth, throwing a pale scar into bold relief.

"Death," said the rider in a voice like two stones grating together.

The merchant released the reins and the rider put spurs to his mount, plunging forward into the throng, out through the gate, and into the open air beyond.

The crowd dispersed along the wide dirt road as the rider urged his horse to a full gallop. Around him the golden sun fell upon the sprawling, verdant grasslands of Shem, but the horseman was blind to all but his mission. Caftan flapping about him, Gulbanda looked to the horizon, his glazed eyes full of pain and purpose.

"Death," he said again, and the wind tore the word from his yellow lips.

14

Caravan routes lay across the length and breadth of Shem like an intricate system of arteries, bearing the ceaseless trade that was the mighty nation's lifeblood. From the gleaming ziggurats of the lush western coast to the sprawling tent-cities of the arid east, Shem, in all her contrasts, was united by the continuous flow of commerce. The routes the trading caravans followed ranged from broad roadways of bare, hard-packed earth to vague trails but rarely traversed.

Two days' travel east out of Akkharia, the Caravan Road forked, sending a branch questing north toward prosperous Eruk and ancient Shumir, while the original route continued east toward the ill-regarded city of Sabatea. Countless sub-routes broke south out of the main road, seeking the smaller cities and villages built along the fertile coast of the world-girdling River Styx.

Along the central route to Sabatea came four riders leading two well-laden pack horses. The party moved at a steady pace upon a dusty road that cleft luxuriant meadows blanketing low, rolling hills. The sun shone down from a cloudless, brassy sky. Off to the north, where the hills rose in slow undulations, a scattered herd of cattle grazed in a sea of waving grass.

Conan of Cimmeria tugged at the throat of his new shirt of white silk, popping stitches in the collar to loosen it around his bull neck. Also new were the blue cotton breeches tucked into the tops of his battered old boots. Heng Shih had reluctantly furnished the barbarian with clothes from his own wardrobe. The size and weight of the two men were similar, but the shape of their frames was so different that Conan found the garments binding where they should have been loose, and baggy where they should have been tight. The collar of the shirt emitted another pop as he pulled at it, then ripped jaggedly down across his breast, revealing Conan's weathered and rust-spotted mail beneath.

Heng Shih winced at the tearing sound and let loose a sigh audible even above the clomping of the horses' hooves. Turning in the saddle, Conan gave the Khitan a wide grin of infuriating friendliness. Then the Cimmerian nudged his mount up toward Neesa.

The scribe had never ceased looking about herself in wide-eyed wonder since they had passed through Akkharia's gates. As Conan moved up beside her, she took her eyes from the distant hills, lowered the hand shading her face from the sun, and favored him with a shy smile. The barbarian nodded expressionlessly. For the last two days Neesa had taken pains to address him only when necessary, and then to speak only in the most bland and businesslike fashion. Now her smile was warm and friendly, if somewhat wary. He wondered once again how long he would have to live before he found the ways of women to be predictable.

He reined up alongside the Lady Zelandra, who led the small caravan on her roan. The sorceress took little note of him, her eyes focused on the hazy, far-off point where the road met the horizon.

Conan noticed a bulky leather pouch attached to her belt. It thumped heavily against her rounded hip with each step her horse took.

"Milady," said Conan roughly, "that looks to be uncomfortable. There is room in my saddlebags. If you wish, you can stow it there."

Zelandra shook her head. "No, Conan, this is my cask of Emerald Lotus. I must have it on my person at all times, in case the craving grows too great." As she spoke, her voice softened with shame and her gaze fell to the road passing beneath the horses' hooves.

"Crom," murmured the Cimmerian, "you are a canny woman, and a sorceress into the bargain. How is it that you are enslaved to a magical powder?"

The barbarian's natural bluntness did not seem to disturb the Lady Zelandra. She sat up straight in her saddle. The warm breeze drew her silver-threaded hair out for a moment in a fluttering pennant.

"I have lived on an inheritance for all of my life, Conan. It left me free to indulge in my studies in sorcery and the healing arts. The inheritance is now much depleted. Of almost a score of servants, now only Heng Shih, Neesa, and a pair of drunken guardsmen remain."

Conan, having witnessed the incompetence of her guardsmen firsthand, merely nodded. "With the inheritance gone, you sought employment with King Sumuabi as his Court Wizard."

"Yes, it seemed a worthy way to continue my lifestyle as scholar and sorceress. I should have been granted the position immediately if Shakar the Keshanian had not also offered his services to the king. To think that Sumuabi cannot choose between that jester and me!"

The Cimmerian frowned reflectively. "I have heard rumors that King Sumuabi may soon lead Akkharia to war. If this be so, he would likely seek a wizard with war-like skills. Perhaps he meant to set you and the Keshanian at each other's throats and select the stronger as his sorcerer."

Zelandra looked at the barbarian, her brows raised in surprise. "I hadn't thought of that. How barbaric!" She flushed. "I'm sorry, Conan. I didn't mean—"

"It is nothing, though that sort of guile sounds damned civilized to me."

"Well, we were at a stand-off in any case. When Ethram-Fal sought audience with me in the guise of Eldred the Trader, I was pleased to see that he offered a number of rare and exotic magical components for sale. I should have been more wary when he claimed to have acquired a quantity of the Emerald Lotus."

"You knew of this lotus?"

"It is legend, supposedly created by Cetriss, a mage of Old Stygia, who bargained with the Dark Gods for it. It is said that the sorcerous power of the lotus helped the seers of Old Stygia keep the world-hungering empire of Acheron at bay almost three thousand years ago. Legends disagree as to its uses and effect, but all agree that Cetriss saw little value in his lotus, or in any of the works of man, and that he devoted his life to the pursuit of immortality. Disdaining his fame and power, he disappeared into the wilderness, taking the secret of the Emerald Lotus with him. You see? The Emerald Lotus is like the perfect love philter or the fountain whose waters bestow youth: a fable born of men's wishful imagining."

Conan squinted skeptically in the sunlight. "Yet you accepted it from a stranger?"

"It was easy to ascertain that it was not a natural lotus, and easier still to determine that it was not a poison. When Eldred—I mean Ethram-Fal—told me that he had just sold a casket of it to Shakar the Keshanian, I felt bound to at least experiment with the stuff. How could I know?" She paused, mouth twisting into a wry smile. "He sold it to me at a very reasonable price," she added with measured irony, drawing a gusty laugh from the barbarian.

"I'll wager he did at that. And the next thing you know the powder has you by the throat?"

Zelandra's left hand shot out to seize his thick right forearm in a cold-fingered grasp. She stared at the Cimmerian with darkly imploring eyes.

"You don't know what it's like. When I first sampled it, I felt that there was nothing in the world that I might attempt that would not come to success. There was a mad confidence and exhilaration unlike anything I have ever known. My sorcery almost doubled in its potency. Complex spells seemed obvious. Spells I knew increased in power and effectiveness. It was like a wild and glorious dream, until it began to fade. Then came the craving, and I knew that I was lost."

Her hand fell from his arm. She blinked rapidly, as though holding back tears. Conan pretended not to notice her discomfiture, looking ahead wordlessly.

"It is like a leech upon the flesh of my soul." Zelandra's voice had dropped to a husky whisper, but she continued to speak as though driven by some grim compulsion. "At first I could think of nothing but the damnable powder and the power it brought, but I held myself in check. I vowed that each dose I took would be smaller than the last, if only by a few grains. And so it has been since the first time I tasted it. I had hoped to lower the quantity until I needed none. It is not so easy. My supply is running low, and there is simply not enough left to safely purge myself of it. If I could get more, then I might be able to taper off completely, but without a greater supply of Emerald Lotus I shall surely die."

For a moment there was a silence, broken only by the scuff of hooves, the creaking of saddle gear, and the soft surge of the summer wind.

"So," Conan said evenly, "we ride into Stygia, and maybe into hell itself, just to get you more of this cursed powder?"

"No!" Zelandra's head snapped up, her profile hawklike against the clear sky. "No, Ethram-Fal deceived and poisoned me as an experiment. And now the arrogant bastard would use his drug's power over me to make me his slave. I'll see him die for it."

The Cimmerian grinned fiercely and, digging his heels into his horse's flanks, urged the beast to greater speed.

15

Though Shakar the Keshanian was exhausted after slaying his bodyguard and performing necromancy upon the corpse, the sorcerer could not take his rest. Time seemed to slow in its course, evening moving into night with glacial deliberation. All through the following day he meditated in his chambers, striving to stabilize his drugged metabolism and fill himself with strength. At first, he was successful. Shakar was proud of the power that he had exhibited in the ensorcellment of Gulbanda.

Without the unnatural augmentation of the Emerald Lotus, he doubted that he would have been able to accomplish it. Pride in his achievement gave him faith and courage.

But into the second day his body weakened and his consciousness fell into a tighter and tighter orbit around the small silver box which lay upon the mahogany desk in his study. Now he sat at his window, staring out through his garden without seeing it and sipping nervously from the crystal decanter of Brythunian wine he had used to lull Gulbanda.

Ignoring a growing tightness in his breast, the Keshanian turned his mind once again to the skilled wizardry he had worked upon his bodyguard, trying to draw comfort from the abomination that he had created and set in motion to accomplish his ends.

"He'll get it," said Shakar to the empty room. "He won't fail. He'll bring it to me, or I'll leave his soul sealed within his animated corpse forever. He won't fail because only I can release him into true death."

He paused, then repeated: "He will not fail." His voice trailed off as he began to fear that which he had not even allowed himself to imagine until this moment.

What if Gulbanda did not return in time?

The most impressive feat of sorcery that he had ever performed had been brought about by a great sacrifice. The silver-chased box on his desk was empty. The two spoonfuls he had taken before slaying Gulbanda with the bamboo spike had been the last, save for a few speckles of green residue.

The tightness in his breast grew more insistent, more difficult to ignore. Shakar turned his eyes away from the west, where the sun set in a bloody welter of tattered clouds, and looked upon the silver box where it gleamed dully in the study's serene twilight. The Keshanian rose from his chair in a halting manner, as though his body were not set on doing that which his mind desired. He walked slowly to the desk and stared down upon the burnished silver casket.

Pain blossomed in Shakar's chest, sending strident bands of tense agony around his torso. The sorcerer cried out and stumbled against the desk, seizing the silver box with hands that shook uncontrollably, hands that pried open the casket to reveal that which he already knew to be true.

"Empty," wept Shakar. "I know that it's empty." Slumping against the desk, he held the cold metal box to his breast and tried to draw a deep breath. The belt of pain that wrapped his ribs loosened a notch.

Through the door, the Keshanian saw a flicker of yellow light play along the wall of the hallway outside his study. He blinked in the deepening dusk. A sudden surge of hope drove new vitality through the sorcerer's veins. He pushed himself away from the desk with one hand and stumbled toward the door, still clutching his box. The sinking sun's last rays stained the floor scarlet before him as he half walked, half staggered down the hall. Ahead, flares of multicolored light shone through the open door of his bedchamber.

"Eldred?" The name was a harsh croak. "Eldred, I must speak with you!"

Shakar came into his chamber just as the vaporous haze of colored light finished weaving itself together and faded to white. He stood unsteadily before the supernatural projection as the ebony figure coalesced within its wall of witchfire and regarded him in inscrutable silence. Shakar's teeth ground together in the stillness.

"Speak, Jullah rend your soul! You are Eldred the Trader, are you not?"

The veils of light masking the dark form drew back, exposing a short, bearded Shemite in a merchant's silken garb. The image blurred almost immediately, wavering like a desert mirage.

"Fool," said a voice that was not a voice, "do you imagine that a trader would visit you thus?"

The Shemite merchant faded from view, becoming a hunched Stygian with a bald, misshapen skull. Bulging eyes afire with contempt seemed to sear into Shakar's body.

"Who are you?" cried the Keshanian. "Why do you torment me?"

"I am called Ethram-Fal, and I do not torment you. I study you. From your aspect I would hazard that your supply of lotus is gone."

Shakar's mind reeled in a rush of dizzy nausea. A hysterical laugh came through lips drawn back from teeth clenched in a death-like rictus.

"Study?" shouted the Keshanian. "Are you mad? Where is the lotus? I'll give you all I have for more of it!"

"Yes," said Ethram-Fal, "of course you would. Tell me, when did you use the last of it?"

Shakar forcibly calmed himself, drawing in a long, shuddering breath. The hand that gripped the silver box clung to its burden so tightly that pain rippled through the knuckles.

"Yesterday morning I used it in a feat of great sorcery. I need more to—"

"Yesterday morning? You are stronger than I had thought. Has the pain begun yet?" The voice of Ethram-Fal was clinical and expressionless.

Shakar could scarcely contain his rage and need.

"Yes!" he cried. "My chest is gripped in a vise of fire. Now give me the lotus!"

"Silence!" Ethram-Fal's command rang in the Keshanian's brain like a struck gong, driving him to his knees with its force.

A roiling cloud of inky blackness poured over the Stygian's scornful features, transforming him once again into an anonymous black figure suspended in a curtain of misty light.

"Who are you to command me, dog? You are too weak and witless to even make a good slave. Take solace in the fact that you have provided a lesson to Ethram-Fal of Stygia and thus aided him in his grand design."

With an inarticulate howl of hate, Shakar opened the silver box and brought it to his face. Thrusting out his tongue, he licked the polished inner surface clean. He hurled the box aside and staggered drunkenly to his feet.

"I'll kill you!" he railed, moving both hands in a swift, arcane series of motions that ceased with both fists extended toward the dark form of Ethram-Fal. A crystalline sphere of azure light shimmered into being before them. It hovered a brief moment, then fell in upon itself, extinguished like a torch in a downpour as Shakar cried out in anguish.

"Your powers fade," said the voice that was not a voice. "You might want to cut your own throat. That would be both quicker and easier than the death which now awaits you. Goodbye, Shakar."

The Keshanian lunged at the apparition with flailing fists, passed into it without resistance, and rebounded from the marble wall. He sprawled on the floor, stunned, with Ethram-Fal's frigid, metallic laughter sounding in his skull. Prone and helpless, Shakar watched the eldritch projection flow into itself and fade until all that remained was an afterimage etched upon his retina.

The Keshanian tried to get up, but his legs felt paralyzed. The tortured nerves of his body jerked spasmodically as pain screwed tightly back around his chest. The effect was spreading, flickering up the sides of his neck to drive nails of agony into his temples. A desperate sanity surfaced in the black warlock's brimming eyes.

Crawling from the room, Shakar dragged himself down the hallway to his study. The labored rasp of his breathing was the only sound in the dim and silent house. His legs were useless, and the bands around his chest constricted until he grew dizzy and held to conscious action only through sheer force of will.

In the study, he used his arms to draw himself up the front of his desk and jerk open a drawer. It fell from the desk, spilling its contents upon the floor. The black-crystal vial broke with a liquid crunch, spattering the marble with translucent syrup. Shakar let himself fall down beside it, his hands seeking and finding the bamboo spike. He held the bloodstained weapon before rheumy eyes that strained to focus on its razor edge. Both hands gripped the spike firmly by the hilt as he placed its keen length against the flesh of his throat.

Then Shakar the Keshanian took Ethram-Fal's advice.

16

E vening slumbered over the darkened mansion of Lady Zelandra. The single iron gate set in the encircling wall was chained and locked against the oncoming night. The two guards lounged in the kitchen, eating little and drinking much, swearing that they would take at least one more turn around the grounds before abandoning themselves to their cups. In time they did this, shuffling off along the garden's paths, passing their wineskin back and forth and speaking in hushed voices.

The stillness of dusky twilight filled the emptied mansion. The halls were dark, the windows curtained and the tapers all unlit. The manse seemed to lie tranquilly in wait for the return of its mistress. Yet amid the darkness and silence came a visitor unsuspected by the besotted guards.

The wall of Lady Zelandra's bedchamber was alight with blazing color.

Wild shadows leapt and capered over the book-lined walls and the opulent, unmade bed. Then a white glare shone from the wall, driving the shadows from every corner of the room.

Ethram-Fal's ebon outline floated in its fog of illumination and regarded an empty chamber. The black, featureless head turned this way and that, as though reluctant to believe that no one was there.

Frustrated, the Stygian sent an emphatic, wordless call through the still mansion.

"Zelandra! I have come for you!"

The sorcerer sensed no response, no activity at all. The dark form hesitated, standing motionless for a time, then moved tenebrous fingers in quick, precise patterns and lifted both arms above its head. Rays of brilliant green light bloomed around Ethram-Fal's image in a dazzling corona. Then, with the slow, unnatural movements of a man walking underwater, the black figure stepped down from the wall and stood within the room. It walked across the floor to the doorway and into the hall beyond.

Ethram-Fal passed through the deserted chambers of Lady Zelandra's mansion like a restless ghost, leaving behind him footprints of palely flickering witchfire. After a time he returned to the lady's bedchamber, ascended into his haze of sorcerous light, and vanished.

Zelandra's house was empty; its mistress had departed.

Ethram-Fal wondered if he might soon have visitors of his own.

17

The travelers crested the summit of a red clay ridge and viewed the broad expanse of the Styx River valley spread out before them. The trail zigzagged down a rolling slope through a thickening welter of vegetation. The land had grown more arid as they moved south and drew closer to Stygia, but the shores of the mighty Styx were anything but desert. Green brush crowded the path as they wended their way through clusters of swaying palms and plush meadows rippling in the slow breeze. Ahead, the land lowered further into irrigated fields that reached to the edge of the river itself. Yellow-brown along its shore and a rich, opalescent blue at its rolling median, the mother of all rivers stretched from horizon to horizon like a jeweled and sorcerous girdle bestowing a luxuriant fertility upon the grateful earth.

Though cultivated along much of its vast length, the shores of the Styx were but sparsely populated this far to the east. Scattered clusters of huts, raised upon stilts, were visible in the distance off to the west.

Directly before them, the party beheld a small, unwalled city squatting upon a low artificial plateau that lifted gently from the canal-crossed fields. A similarly raised road ran amongst the glittering irrigation ditches and broad, cultivated expanses like a sand-colored snake writhing across a bed of lush emerald moss. The road connected the raised city with the drier uplands, where it merged with the Caravan Road that stretched uninterrupted along the length of the River Styx.

As the four descended the trail into the river valley, they began to encounter the natives of this long-inhabited land. They waited at a crossroads while a herd of lowing cattle was ushered past by herdsmen brandishing stout sticks that they applied vigorously to the flanks of their charges. Farmers toiled in the irrigated fields of emmer wheat and barley that sprang in abundance from the land's black and silty breast.

The trail became an elevated road that soon afforded them a closer view of the white mud buildings of the city. Neesa waved a slender hand in the humid air, fanning herself. At the moment they rode single file, with the Lady Zelandra leading the way. Neesa knit her dark brows in thought, then edged her mount forward until she rode beside the Cimmerian.

"What city is this?" she asked of Conan. The barbarian grinned at her in open admiration, clearly pleased that she had overcome her unwillingness to speak with him. She continued to study the city ahead of them intently, apparently unnoticing of his attention, though her complexion began to grow rosy.

"It is called Aswana. It has a sister city just across the Styx called Bel-Phar. Aswana is a quiet village and should give us a fine place to cross the river without drawing too much attention."

"The Stygians are said to be unfond of visitors."

"Aye, the snake worshippers would deny every foreigner the right to enter their cursed country if they could. Their border patrols are few, but authorized by King Ctesphon to collar any intruder they wish and judge on the spot if he is worthy to stand on Stygian soil."

"And if he is judged unworthy?"

"Well, any merchant whose trade would fatten the land, or a fawning scholar come to pay homage to Father Set, would be left to his own ends. The best that most anyone else could hope for would be robbery and a quick kick back across the border. At worst, they'd be crucified at the roadside."

Neesa shivered despite the bright sun, then spat into the ditch.

"And here we come as uninvited visitors," she said.

Conan laughed, shaking back his black mane.

"Don't fret, woman. The patrols are few and the land is large. And besides, I'm going with you!"

Laughing, Neesa leaned from her saddle and pressed a swift kiss upon the barbarian's cheek. Then she put her heels to her mount, sending the beast trotting forward and away to Lady Zelandra's side, leaving Conan rubbing his cheek and grinning in bemused fascination. Neither the Cimmerian nor Neesa took notice of Heng Shih, who rode a short distance behind them. His incredulous expression attested that he had missed nothing of their exchange. The Khitan passed a wide hand over his smooth pate and shook his head in wonder. Lady Zelandra led her band of travelers along the river's flank.

Sweating workers clad only in breechclouts hoisted water from the darkly flowing body of the Styx with the aid of simple mechanisms made of lashed lengths of rough wood. A crude tripod supported an irregular pole with a heavy counterweight on one end, and a large bucket dangled from a rope on the other. The bucket was lowered until it was submerged, then the workers would add their bodies to the counterweight, lifting the full bucket from the river. Finally, the pole would be turned atop the tripod, swinging the bucket over the shore and dumping it into a waiting irrigation canal. To Conan it seemed a tedious way of making one's living.

Once among the white buildings of Aswana, the travelers became objects of much interest. Although the cobbled streets of the city were bustling with activity, Conan's band was conspicuous and exotic enough to draw the attention of the townsfolk. Naked children ran in the dust beside their horses' hooves, crying out to one another in shrill voices. A woman clad only in a diaphanous veil leaned from a second-story window and winked a kohl-darkened eye at the Cimmerian, who raised a hand in salutation, smiling until he felt the sharp and indignant eyes of Neesa upon him. When he turned his smile upon her, she looked away, flushing.

Conan slowed in front of a low, windowless building with a crude sign proclaiming it to be a tavern. As he reined in his mount, a lean man in a faded, sweat-stained tunic emerged from the curtained doorway and stood blinking in the afternoon sun.

"Ho, friend," called the barbarian. "Where can I find an honest ferryman in this town?" The man he addressed took on a sour expression as he fingered the dirty headband that confined his tousled, graying hair.

"Well, you won't find one now because Pesouris, may Set gnaw his cod, just took a load of acolytes across this morning. If I know that lazy cur, he shan't be back before nightfall."

"Isn't there another ferryman?"

"No, by the gods. I was a ferryman until the damned Stygians decided that one ferry was enough for Aswana and gave a royal seal to that pig Pesouris. Now he waxes rich, and I am left to test my luck fishing from a ferryboat."

Conan leaned toward the man conspiratorially, fixing him with a knowing gaze.

"What's your name, my friend?"

The fellow peered back at him with faded eyes touched with the bleariness of drink.

"I am Temoten. If you wish to speak further with me, ye'd best buy me a drink."

"Temoten, if you still have your ferryboat, why not take us across the Styx? You'll be plucking enough money from the purse of Pesouris to buy yourself a week's worth of wine."

Temoten drew back at the suggestion, his weathered face creased further by a skeptical frown. He shook his shaggy head.

"Nay. Pesouris would report me to the authorities of Bel-Phar, or even to the border patrol if he could. And if any Stygian soldiers were about when we made landfall, they'd want to see my ferryman's seal. As I have none, they'd behead me there on the docks. No thank you, stranger."

Temoten turned to walk off and almost collided with the Lady Zelandra, who had dismounted and now stood before him dangling a leather pouch from one delicate hand.

"My people and I need to cross the Styx without delay, Temoten," she said, "and I'm willing to pay well for the trip. Would you want this pouch to pass into the hands of Pesouris?"

The ferryman reached for the proffered pouch and poured a glittering stream of golden coins into a grimy palm. At once his eyes grew wider and more sober.

"Sweet Ishtar!" Temoten licked lips that had gone suddenly dry and wished mightily for a drink.

"Besides," continued Zelandra, "what fool in his right mind would contest the passage of my friends Heng Shih and Conan?"

Temoten spared a brief glance at the lady's hulking escorts before returning his gaze to enough gold to keep him living in comfort for the better part of a year.

"Only a very great fool, indeed," he breathed. "To nine hells with it. Let's go. What right do the stinking Stygians have to command a free Shemite anyway?"

"None at all, I should think," smiled Zelandra. "Now, where can we find your ferryboat?"

The boat was moored to a rotting dock behind Temoten's one-room hut on the outskirts of Aswana. It was a once-elegant vessel of sturdy cedar about twenty-four feet from stem to stern. A single slim mast rose above the deck, bearing a furled sail of faded yellow. A tattered ox-hide canopy mounted just ahead of the long steering oar offered the craft's only shelter from the sun. When Heng Shih came around the corner of Temoten's hut and saw the boat for the first time, he touched Zelandra's shoulder and communicated with her in a swift passage of sign language.

"My friends," called Lady Zelandra, "Heng Shih points out that there is no room in the ferry for our mounts."

Conan, pulling the saddle and saddlebags from his horse, spoke up: "That's just as well, milady. Camels are a superior mount for desert travel, anyway. Perhaps you and Heng Shih would take the horses into the city and sell them."

Zelandra raised dark eyebrows. "Are you leading this company now, barbarian?"

"No offense intended, milady, but we could use the gold earned from their sale to purchase camels in Bel-Phar."

"That sounds suitable," said the sorceress reluctantly, "but I am scarcely a bargain-mongering trader."

"You bargained me into this expedition easily enough. Just have Heng Shih stare at them if they try to swindle you. I'll wager that you'll get an excellent price."

"Very well. Temoten, is there a worthy dealer in horseflesh in the city?"

The ferryman, standing on the dock, nodded vigorously.

"Yes, mistress, my late wife's cousin, Nephtah, deals in horses and mules. You will find him at the northeast corner of the market square. Tell him that I sent you and he will treat you as his family."

The remaining saddles and packs were removed from the horses. Zelandra and Heng Shih mounted up, leading the string of riderless animals behind them. The Khitan looked back over his heavy shoulder and fixed his narrowed eyes upon the Cimmerian, who was busily loading saddlebags and provisions onto the boat. Conan heaped the stuff on the worn, red-painted planks of the deck beneath the ox-hide canopy as Zelandra and her bodyguard rode slowly out of sight.

Temoten leaned on one of the dock's cracked pilings, studiously examining the dirty fingernails of his left hand and making no effort to assist the Cimmerian.

"So, Outlander, you seem to know your way around a boat."

Conan stacked a packed saddlebag atop the pile he had built beneath the canopy. "I have some acquaintance with such things," he said quietly.

"Then you can steer, raise a sail, and the like?"

"I see that this craft would be difficult to run single-handed, Temoten. Do not fear, I shall help you get us across the river."

The ferryman looked disgruntled, but kept his silence, staring off into the reedy shallows. Neesa struggled down the sagging dock under the weight of a double waterskin, which Conan took from her and heaved into the boat. She then leapt nimbly onto the rear deck, catching the haft of the steering oar. Clinging to it for support, she leaned out over the vessel's side, gazing across the Styx with the wind in her thick, black hair.

In a moment Conan joined her. The broad, sunstruck river stretched away, flecked with distant skiffs full of fishermen plying their trade.

The air blowing in off the water was fresh and invigorating.

"It's beautiful," said Neesa dreamily. "I've never seen the Styx before. I haven't even been out of Akkharia since I was a child."

"Crom," said Conan in a strangely gentle tone, "that's no way to live. You have but one life and one world to live it in. Surely you should experience both as well as you are able? Ymir's beard, I'd go mad if I were cooped up in a single city all my life."

Neesa looked up at him, her black eyes afire with honesty. "I know it's wrong to say it, Conan, but this journey seems the finest thing I have ever done. All of my life I have been grateful to Lady Zelandra for her shelter from the world, and now I find that I am enjoying myself on a voyage made in the shadow of her death."

Conan turned his grim face to the wind. "All journeys are made in the shadow of death," he said simply. "Live now, and know that you will struggle with death when it comes."

The woman stepped into Conan's arms, pressing her lush body against him with feverish intensity. The barbarian, taken aback by her fervency, cupped a hand beneath her chin and lifted her face to his. Tears glimmered in her dark eyes.

"Kiss me," she whispered, and Conan crushed her mouth beneath his own, drawing her into an even closer embrace. After a moment one iron arm encircled her waist as the other swept under her knees and lifted her free of the deck. The kiss broke as the Cimmerian carried her to the canopy that covered their belongings. Neesa saw that he had built a hollow in the center of the pile and spread a blanket therein.

"Oh," she said huskily, "you think of everything." Conan ducked beneath the canopy and gently placed her in the hidden nest of blankets.

"Why do you think I sent those two to town?" he asked, but he gave her no chance to answer.

Out on the dock, Temoten looked from the boat back to his dirty fingernails. With a wistful sigh he turned toward his hut and went inside, looking for a drink.

18

The boat surged through the water, foam purling along its prow. The Styx shone a rich blue beneath the clear sky of afternoon. Small fishing boats made from bundles of papyrus reeds traveled in pairs, trolling nets between them. The busy fishermen paid little heed to Temoten's ferry; yet the ferryman seemed to grow markedly less nervous once they left the fishing boats behind and sailed out beyond the river's midpoint. The patched sail bellied full as Temoten leaned into the steering oar. Beside him, on the rear deck, Conan and Heng Shih relaxed, the barbarian sprawling along the gunwale and the Khitan sitting cross-legged, his face to the sun. Beneath the flapping ox-hide canopy, Lady Zelandra and Neesa sat in the shade and conversed in low tones.

The trio on the rear deck traveled in silence for some time. Temoten's curious gaze returned repeatedly to Heng Shih, sitting shirtless beside him, his yellow skin gleaming with perspiration.

"Does your friend speak at all?" the ferryman finally asked Conan, who grinned and stretched like a cat in the sunshine. Heng Shih did not open his eyes.

"He is a mute, though he speaks to Lady Zelandra with hand-language."

"What…" Temoten paused, then screwed up his courage. "What manner of man is he?"

Conan thought that he saw Heng Shih's eyes glimmer beneath slitted lids. "A Khitan from the distant east."

"I have never seen his like. Are all men of that country so big and fat?"

Now Conan was certain that Heng Shih's eyes drew open a crack. "Not at all," said the Cimmerian dryly. "He is truly exceptional in that regard."

Temoten said nothing for a time, clinging to the steering oar and looking off to the hazy outline of the far shore. Conan could sense further questions troubling the ferryman and was not surprised when a few moments later Temoten spoke again.

"Why are you in such a hurry to cross the Styx, Conan? And why pay me so much to take you? Are you fugitives? Does the Lady Zelandra flee enemies, perhaps?" The words came quickly until Temoten bit them off. "Not that it is any of my concern," he added, shamefaced.

"Temoten," said Conan seriously, "Heng Shih is a Khitan and Khitans are cannibals. They eat the curious."

At this Heng Shih opened his eyes and squinted at the barbarian; then he turned to the ferryman. Looking up at him, the Khitan slowly and ominously licked his lips.

"My apologies, friends," stammered Temoten.

The remainder of the crossing was made in silence. Conan napped, a bronzed arm thrown over his eyes, until he was prodded awake by Temoten, who needed help to furl the sail.

The city of Bel-Phar was even smaller than Aswana. Its waterfront lay somnolently along a raised foundation of mammoth stone blocks. The Stygians were fond of cyclopean architecture, and it was a rare city of Stygia that did not show some evidence of this fondness. The stained and eroded stone docks of Bel-Phar thrust out into the eternally passing Styx. Papyrus boats of all sizes, and even a few luxurious wooden dhows, were moored in clusters about them. The center of the waterfront appeared to be an open bazaar full of milling people and animals. Temoten wrenched the tiller about, steering his ferry left and to the east.

"Fewer people around the eastern docks," he said, half to himself.

"Conan, can you…"

But the big Cimmerian was already moving toward the prow of the boat, bending to catch up a long, wooden pole that lay along the starboard gunwale. Heng Shih lifted the pole on the boat's port side and Temoten nodded his disheveled gray head in approval.

The sun had begun its slow fall to the west and shadows appeared in the white city before them. The rolling Styx had gradually dimmed from transparent blue to a murky violet. The docks hove closer as the ferryman steered his vessel to their eastern extremity.

Conan and Heng Shih drove their poles against the oncoming dock, slowing their progress and letting the ferry slide smoothly into place beside a worn stair carved into a solid block of stone. Temoten scrambled forward, snatching a looped line and casting it neatly over a bronze stay set in the dock. The man was suddenly very animated.

"All right, then. Let's move. I've fulfilled my part of the bargain. Let's see you off."

He dragged a bulky pack from beneath the canopy and heaved it over a bony shoulder. With his eager assistance, Conan and Heng Shih soon had all their provisions piled upon the dock.

"We'll have to leave this here and go into the market for camels and water," said Conan. "Temoten, will you stay and watch over our belongings?"

"Stay?" burst out the ferryman incredulously. "I'm leaving as swiftly as I can push off."

"I'll stay," volunteered Neesa. "I feel somewhat poorly after the crossing anyway."

Lady Zelandra, Conan, and Heng Shih headed down the dock, leaving Neesa perched atop the heap of baggage. Temoten hesitated at the top of the stone stair.

"Farewell, mistress," he called hesitantly. "Farewell, Conan and Heng Shih." Zelandra turned without breaking stride and waved.

"A good wind to you," shouted Conan, raising a hand. Heng Shih did not even look back.

Bel-Phar's entire waterfront was paved with wide plates of stone.

Though the buildings were almost identical to those of Aswana, the atmosphere of the city was much more subdued. The quiet warehouses at the base of the dock were soon replaced by open shops and then the central market itself. The market was busy, if not overly crowded, but its customers seemed warier and less outgoing than their counterparts across the Styx. A stable of camels was located shortly, and Lady Zelandra was immediately joined in friendly argument with its wizened, one-eyed proprietor. Conan, who had been prepared to do the bartering, found himself standing to one side while the sorceress examined the proffered beasts and made derisive comments about each one in turn in fluent Stygian. The little proprietor rose to the occasion, rubbing his hands together with unconcealed delight and chattering pained protests of her harsh judgments. It seemed to Conan that this was set to go on for some time, so he cast his eyes about for a likely tavern.

Out of the moving throng of the marketplace, Neesa came running. There was such urgency in her movements that Conan froze. She stumbled to a halt before him, her bosom rising and falling as she panted.

"Temoten," she gasped. "Stygian soldiers hailed him just as he was casting off. I walked right past them as they came down the dock. They didn't seem angry, but called out that they needed to see his ferryman's seal. Conan, their captain has a kind of bow..."

"How many?" said the barbarian in a low voice. His blue eyes kindled with a dangerous light.

"Five, I think. Six?" She lifted ivory hands helplessly.

The Cimmerian pushed past her, stepping swiftly into the crowd. A voice rose behind him.

"Conan, no!" It was Lady Zelandra. But he was already running heedlessly through the market toward the docks. People either dodged or were thrust from the path of the tall outlander, who leapt over a vegetable cart in his headlong haste. Protesting outcries rang out in his wake but slowed him not at all.

At the foot of the dock, six saddled camels waited restlessly. Out on the dock itself stood six Stygian soldiers of the border patrol, arrayed in gray silk and burnished mail. A pair were at the dock's far end, appraising Temoten's ferry. One of these rubbed a stubbled chin thoughtfully, as if gauging the craft's value. Two other soldiers were closer, bent over and arrogantly rummaging in the pile of provisions on the dock. The last two were closest, accosting Temoten. The taller of this pair wore the gilded gorget of an officer and was berating the ferryman scornfully. A small crossbow hung at the officer's belt. The other was a shirtless hulk of a man who brandished a heavy-bladed sword before Temoten's terrified eyes with sadistic relish.

Temoten made feeble protests, his lean frame trembling visibly. The tall officer seized the front of the ferryman's scruffy tunic in a mailed fist and jerked him forcibly to his knees. Temoten struggled to rise, and the captain abruptly drove a knee into his unprotected midsection, doubling the ferryman up in agony.

The officer stepped back and nodded perfunctorily to the shirtless soldier with the naked sword. The executioner flexed the thick muscles of his arms, raised the blade above his head, and heard the sound of rapid footfalls behind him.

A length of silver steel sprang from the center of his bare breast. It caught the sun, throwing it back into his goggling eyes, then disappeared in a gout of bright blood. As the executioner sank down dying, Conan vaulted the body, whirling his stained broadsword about his head.

The officer scrabbled desperately for his belted scimitar as the Cimmerian bore down upon him with terrible swiftness. He drove a booted foot into the captain's belly with lithe savagery, knocking the man from his feet and sending him skidding over the stones to the dock's edge.

The remaining soldiers scarcely had time to perceive the fate of their companions before the barbarian was among them like a wind hot from the mouth of hell. The first of the two men rifling through the heap of baggage managed to turn and get his sword half drawn before being cut down by a blow that split helmet and head. The other soldier among the packs got his blade free and lunged at Conan as the Cimmerian wheeled from his second kill. The Stygian's hasty, vicious thrust was hammered aside with such force that the sword was nearly torn from his grip. Conan's return stroke was a blur of speed, bursting his foe's mail at the shoulder, shearing through the collarbone and lodging in the spine. The barbarian yanked on the hilt, but found that his blade was stuck fast in the sagging body.

Seeing his weapon entrapped in the corpse of their comrade, the last two soldiers advanced toward Conan from their position at the dock's end. As they moved to attack him from two sides, the Cimmerian acted.

Gripping his hilt with both hands, the barbarian hoisted the dead man bodily over his head and hurled him off his sword with a convulsive heave of his mighty shoulders. The torn corpse flopped onto the stone at the soldiers' feet.

"Come join him in hell," snarled Conan in Stygian, his eyes aflame with unfettered bloodlust.

The soldiers were of two minds about this. The stout soldier on the left leapt over the bloody body of his fellow and engaged

Conan, while his more gangly companion hesitated a moment before dodging around the combatants and sprinting away down the dock. If the fighter was dismayed by his erstwhile comrade's desertion, he didn't show it. He carried the fight to the barbarian, sending a whistling series of expertly aimed blows at the Cimmerian's head and torso. The strident clangor of steel on steel rang out over the calm river. Their blades flickered and clashed in a dire but elegant dance of death. The Stygian rallied, driving Conan back among the scattered packs with a flurry of skillful cuts and slashes. The heel of the barbarian's boot trod upon the corner of a saddlebag, and he staggered, seeming to lose his balance. His arms shot out to steady himself, and his foe lunged in.

The stumble was a ruse. Conan abruptly dropped to one knee and brought his blade forward point-first. The Stygian's killing thrust drove him directly onto Conan's sword. The man was transfixed, his own blade passing harmlessly beside the barbarian's head.

For a suspended instant the tableau held; then the impaled soldier dropped his sword to clatter loudly on the stone, and Conan sensed movement behind him. Wrenching his weapon free of the falling body, Conan spun about to see the Stygian captain advancing upon him with a small crossbow held cocked in shaking hands.

"Are you a demon?" choked the ashen-faced officer. "A bolt from my crossbow will send you back to hell!"

As his fingers tightened on the crossbow's trigger, Conan dove headlong to the side, rolling over packs and saddlebags and sliding into a crouch.

But the captain had not fired. He pointed the crossbow steadily at the Cimmerian's breast. The barbarian's fingers sank into the cool leather of a waterskin. He gripped it, his mind in a split-second debate as to whether he should shield himself with the waterskin or hurl it at his foe.

"You're damned fast," said the officer, "but now—"

The Stygian's head shot from his shoulders on a jet of liquid scarlet. It sailed through the summer air like a child's thrown ball, falling into the Styx with a hollow splash. The headless body stood in place for a moment, then collapsed bonelessly. Heng Shih stood behind the corpse. Bending ponderously, he wiped his flare-bladed scimitar upon the captain's silken breeches.

Conan shoved himself to his feet and pointed down the length of the dock with his dripping sword.

"That one escapes," he said grimly.

The gangly soldier who had fled from Conan was now mounted upon one of the camels at the base of the dock. He turned a white face to the men standing among the sprawled bodies of his fallen companions.

"You are already dead!" he shouted in a shrill voice. "I will lead the king's men to you no matter where you hide! I'll see you dead!" His voice broke as Conan suddenly advanced down the dock. Wheeling his camel around, the soldier drove the beast forward and away. The ungainly creature broke into a gallop, passing both Lady Zelandra and Neesa upon the waterfront's stone boulevard.

As the camel and its rider hurtled toward the bazaar, Neesa turned smoothly, watching them go by. With supple grace, she pulled the knife from her nape sheath and drew her arm back as though cocking it.

Conan's lips grew tight as the rider moved swiftly away from the woman.

Precious seconds fled, and Neesa stood motionless. Then her body uncoiled, sending the knife flying after the Stygian. It struck square between the man's shoulder blades.

The soldier slouched lifeless over the neck of his mount. The camel slowed to a trot, then a walk, and then stopped altogether. The man's limp body fell to the pavement, where his mount sniffed at it indifferently.

Temoten was crouched cowering on the carven stone stair. His mouth opened and closed several times before words issued forth.

"Ishtar, Ashtoreth, Mitra, and Set! I have never seen such things in all my life!" He stared at Conan as though the barbarian had sprouted antlers. "Where did you learn to fight like that? Who is this woman who can hurl a dagger so? Who in nine hells are you people?"

Conan cleaned his blade and sheathed it.

"Be silent, Temoten, else I shall wish I had let the headsman finish his job."

"Yes, yes," sputtered the ferryman. "I thank you."

A small crowd was gathering at the base of the dock. From their midst came Lady Zelandra, her noble face dark with fury. Heng Shih ran a hand over his bald pate and became interested in the setting sun.

"You great idiots! Now we shall have to fight the entire Stygian army!"

"I doubt it," said Conan easily. "I'm surprised that there were this many soldiers in town. And I couldn't let them behead Temoten and steal our gear, could I?"

Zelandra's anger did not abate.

"And how shall we deal with these people?" She waved a hand toward the burgeoning crowd. "Shall we kill them, too?"

"We need not deal with them at all. The soldiers have kindly left us their camels. We shall be gone before the good people of Bel-Phar decide if they wish to fight us or not. Come, let us load our packs onto our new mounts. Temoten, you should get the hell out of here."

The ferryman hurriedly cast off his line and leapt from the dock without another word. Using one of the poles, he pushed his ferry into the river and then poled out beyond the shallows. As the four looked on, his sail unfurled and caught the wind with a resounding snap.

Neesa led back the camel whose rider she had slain, and the party busied themselves loading their gear onto the uncooperative beasts. The crowd grew larger, some men even venturing down the dock to examine the bodies, but no one hindered the imminent departure of the travelers.

The soldiers did not seem to have been popular men. When Conan and his comrades rode out of Bel-Phar, the crowd parted to let them pass. The Cimmerian saw curious faces and fearful faces, but none who threatened to bar his passage.

As they rode free of the town's stone foundation and out onto the arid soil of Stygia, Conan turned in his saddle and looked back across the Styx.

The sail of Temoten's ferry was a small, sable silhouette moving against the purple breast of the evening sky. For a long moment, Conan watched it surging away, then turned back to the road that lay ahead.

19

Ethram-Fal and his captain, Ath, rode down from highlands of stone into a measureless desert of sand and gravel. They led eight riderless camels through an oppressive haze of heat. The unrelenting sun blasted the landscape with an implacable glare, hammering the crumbling soil so that waves of dizzying heat were reflected up from the ground to meet those falling from the sky.

The jagged saw-teeth of the Dragon's Spine lay against the horizon behind them. From the rugged, rocky crests of the highland ridges, the land descended gradually in an irregular series of broken foothills and canyon-cracked plateaus until it opened out into level desert.

The pair rode in silence. Ath wore full armor beneath a flowing white cloak but seemed to take little notice of the heat. Ethram-Fal wore a baggy hooded caftan that was far too large for his stunted body. Every few moments, with mechanical regularity, he brought a goatskin full of watered wine and Emerald Lotus powder to his lips and drank.

As the white sun hove past its apogee in the colorless dome of the sky, the crusted gravel beneath their camels' hooves slowly gave way to rolling dunes of ochre sand. The flowing dunes reached to the shimmering horizon, seeming to stretch to the rim of the world. Only an occasional outcrop of ruddy stone, carved cruelly by erosion, broke the monotony of the vast sea of sand.

It was well into the afternoon when the sorcerer and his soldier crested a massive dune and looked down its long slope at a sight to give a traveler joy. An oasis lay upon the naked desert like a bright brooch of emerald and turquoise pinned to the breast of a withered mummy. A cluster of vegetation, impossibly vivid against the sand, surrounded a pool struck radiant by the sun.

"There," said Ath needlessly, lifting a long arm to point. Ethram-Fal merely nodded and urged his camel on.

Only hardy scrub clung to the outer boundaries of the oasis, but close to the pool the growth was lush and plentiful. A tall date palm stood beside the water. At the base of its trunk lay the tattered remnants of a simple lean-to, left behind by some traveler.

The two men rode to the pool's edge and dismounted, falling to their bellies to drink the warm, clear water. Ath finished his drink, splashed his face, and went to work. A set of four large ceramic water jugs was strapped across the back of each camel. Ath began filling them one at a time, wading out into the pool to submerge the jug, and then climbing out to refasten it to a camel's saddle. Ethram-Fal sat cross-legged in the shade of a date palm and watched.

"Ath," he said after a time, "I have been so absorbed in my researches that I have seen little of the men. Do they grow lax from inactivity?"

"No, milord," panted Ath, hoisting a heavy-laden jug from the pool. "I drill them three times each day in the courtyard, and they entertain themselves sparring with one another or hunting the rest of the day."

Rills of water ran along the captain's arms as he tied the full jug into place upon the disgruntled animal, who shifted unhappily beneath the added weight.

"They hunt? What is there to hunt?"

"Tiny antelope, milord. The men have only caught one and now place bets as to who shall catch the next."

Ethram-Fal scowled in resentment. "If they catch another, I want a portion of its flesh. Fresh meat would be much superior to our tedious provisions."

Ath waded back into the pool, relishing the flow of water over his skin. "Yes, milord." The next jug bubbled as it filled.

"So, their morale is good?" The sorcerer drank from his wineskin and gave a barely perceptible shudder. Ath hesitated a moment before replying.

"There were some complaints when you forbade torches within the palace, and the glass balls of light that you gave us to take their place made some of the men nervous."

Ethram-Fal frowned, then waved a hand in dismissal. "There will be no fire of any kind inside the palace. I touched a petal of the lotus to a candle and it burned faster than dry pine. Tell the men that any who break this rule will pay with their lives."

"Yes, milord."

"And why the concern about my light-globes? Are the superstitious fools afraid of them?"

"Some said that they were unnatural and feared to touch them. I proved that they were harmless by holding several at once. All seem to accept them now."

"By Set's shining coils," Ethram-Fal chuckled dryly, shaking his head. "These warriors are a weak-minded lot. The light-globes are merely a sea plant sealed in crystal. The magical enhancement is minimal. Well then, are they otherwise content? Do they quarrel amongst themselves?"

"No quarrels, milord. But I've added an additional guard to each shift after nightfall."

"Two men per shift? That's of little consequence. But why? Does the night watch grow lonely?"

"Not lonely enough, milord. The past two nights the sentries of the third shift reported that something was skulking among the rocks at the canyon mouth."

Ethram-Fal sat up straight.

"Something or someone?" he demanded. "What did they see?"

"By Derketo's ivory teats, milord, I had hoped not to tell you of this. I am shamed to say that the men simply grow fearful when left on guard alone after dark, so I added an extra man to each shift."

"What did the guards see or hear, Ath? Answer my question now or know great pain." The sorcerer's voice was taut with displeasure.

"Y-yes," stuttered the soldier, dropping his jug so that it sank into the pool. "I do not mean to displease you, milord. The first night, Teh-Harpa thought that he heard something moving in the rocks, and when he went to investigate, thought he saw two shining eyes."

"An animal," declared Ethram-Fal.

"Just so," said Ath, bending to pick up his jug once again. "The second night, Phandoros heard sounds of movement and thought that he heard a voice speaking."

"A voice?" The sorcerer came to his feet. "Who was there?"

Ath flinched, holding the water jug before his chest as if it were a talisman against his master's imperious gaze.

"No one, milord. Phandoros scoured the canyon mouth with a torch and found nothing. He was too ashamed to tell me of his fear. I only learned of the matter when I overheard the men discussing it among themselves. All agreed that Phandoros was mistaken and that it was an animal foraging in the dark. I added the second sentry so that these stories would not work upon the imagination of guards left all alone."

"Yes," said Ethram-Fal, sitting down once again. "That was wise, Ath."

The tall soldier breathed easier and went back to the safe business of filling water jugs. He labored without speaking for some time, but the silent scrutiny of his master grew onerous.

"Our supply of water was quite good, milord. Do you need all these extra jugs filled for some great magic?"

Ethram-Fal laughed condescendingly, smoothing his caftan over bony knees. "It is my intention not to return to this oasis for some time. I wish us to be well supplied with water."

Ath hoped that his master would elaborate, but the sorcerer said nothing more. At last the final jug was sealed and lashed into place upon the shaggy back of an unhappy camel. Ath squatted beside the pool, sipping water from a cupped palm and catching his breath.

Ethram-Fal stood and stretched himself in the shade of the date palm. Hitching the strap of his wineskin over a shoulder, he walked to the pool's edge and pointed into the shallows.

"Ath, use your dagger to dig a small hole in the sand there."

"Milord?" The soldier obediently drew his dagger, but looked into the water quizzically.

"There," snapped Ethram-Fal impatiently, "beneath the surface before you."

Ath stepped into the pool, splashing diamond droplets in the sun as he hastened forward. Knee deep, he bent and used the blade of his dagger to carve a pit in the sandy mud of the pool's bottom.

"Deeper," commanded the sorcerer, peering over Ath's bent shoulder. "Not wide, but deep."

Swirling particles clouded the water as the soldier worked, obscuring his progress, but in a moment Ethram-Fal seemed satisfied.

"Good enough. Now, out of the way." Ath stepped back and climbed out of the pool, thrusting his dagger into the sand to dry. He regarded his master with wary curiosity.

Ethram-Fal waded awkwardly out into the water, his oversized caftan floating out behind him. He stopped beside the hole Ath had dug and pulled something from a pocket. He held it out in an open palm, and Ath saw that it was a flattened, black ovoid with a thick seam running around its edge. It filled the sorcerer's hand and had the organic appearance of a monstrously overgrown seed. Ath had never seen anything like it before.

Ethram-Fal whispered words in a language dead thirty centuries, and the black seed twitched in his palm. Bending slowly and reverently, the sorcerer lowered his hand to the smooth surface of the pool and whispered once again. The words rasped together like dry bones. A tangled network of veins appeared on the glossy, sable surface of the seed. Ethram-Fal thrust it under the water, pushing it into the hole and using his hands to bury it. Then he drew back, lifted his dripping hands from the pool, and moved them in a slow, circular pattern over the planted seed. He whispered a final time, turning his hands over abruptly before him. Lurid crimson glyphs blazed brilliantly upon each palm for an instant and vanished.

The Stygian sorcerer slogged out of the pool with a twisted smile on his face. His captain stared with intent apprehension at the spot where Ethram-Fal had planted the seed, as if expecting something horrible beyond words to burst from the waters at any moment.

"Come then, Ath, let us be gone," said Ethram-Fal jovially. He pulled himself atop his squatting camel and clung to its saddle as it rose to its feet. Ath tore his eyes from the pool and mounted his own beast hurriedly, as his master looked on in apparent amusement.

The camels snorted in distaste as they were forced to file out of the only patch of greenery on the parched expanse of desert. They moved steadily, if reluctantly, up the sifting side of the huge dune that flanked the oasis. A hot wind tore sand from the dune's crest and hurled it into the faces of the two men leading the column of camels.

Ethram-Fal noticed that the sun had already dried his caftan, which had been dripping wet only a moment past. Once over the dune, Ath drew up short, cursing.

"Set's scales! I left my best dagger stuck in the sand back there." The soldier pulled on the reins of his mount and prepared to turn about to retrieve his weapon.

"No," said Ethram-Fal firmly. "You must do without it. The next visitor to that oasis is in for a terrible surprise."

20

Pesouris the ferryman lounged in a well-padded chair set out upon his dock. At the end of a long day's toil, he often found it pleasant to relax here for a time before repairing to his house and the diligent attentions of his concubines. At times like this, when the sun had just dipped below the earth's rim and the breeze came cool and bracing down the twilit Styx, he felt it only proper that he should reflect upon his good fortune and perhaps offer up a discreet prayer of thanks to Father Set. It was the servants of the serpent god, after all, who had made his present prosperity possible. If he had not been granted a ferryman's seal by the Stygian authorities of Bel-Phar, he would still be competing for his livelihood with all manner of motley would-be ferrymen. Now that he alone was authorized to transport travelers across the Styx to Bel-Phar, his wealth and status had exceeded his fondest wishes. A fortnight ago he would have been unable even to rent this dock, and today it belonged to him. Paying even a single full-time concubine would have been beyond his meager means.

He heaved a deep sigh of satisfaction, his burgeoning paunch straining at his silken girdle. He locked stubby fingers together behind his thick neck and leaned back in the chair. His dark eyes narrowed thoughtfully. He wondered which of the two he should select tonight. An idea burst upon him, causing his thickly thatched eyebrows to raise abruptly. Couldn't they be made to compete for his affections?

Of course they could. Why hadn't he thought of this before?

The sudden stream of fantasies unleashed by this new inspiration was cut short by the nearly inaudible scuff of a boot sole on the dock behind him. The interruption displeased Pesouris, who twisted about in his padded chair to face the intruder.

Night and the shadows of two tall palms conspired to make the base of the dock a thick mass of impenetrable shadow. There was someone there, though; Pesouris could just make him out.

"Ahptut? Is that you?" The ferryman called the name of his hired servant and was dismayed at the weak sound of his voice. Bristling a little, he sat up and stared into the darkness.

"You! Who's there!"

The figure of a tall man was barely visible, standing motionless on the dock. A chill fluid seemed to course down the ferryman's back. He fumbled at his waist for the curved dirk on his belt, his mind awhirl with panicked surmise. Was it that drunken fool Temoten come to claim vengeance? Or a thief out to rob him of his hard-won riches?

Pesouris was still groping for his dagger when the man on the dock took two steps forward, emerging from the shadow of the palms into the pale starlight. He was a big man, standing tall and stiffly straight in a loose caftan that rippled gently in the night breeze. He said nothing, but his presence less than ten feet from the ferryman was mutely threatening. Pesouris finally got his hand on his hilt but did not draw the weapon. He looked into the blackness within the caftan's hood.

"What do you want?" he asked through lips gone suddenly dry. The man on the dock thrust out a hand and pointed at the smaller of Pesouris's two ferries, moored along the dock. Then he pointed out across the star-flecked Styx. The hand disappeared into a pocket of the caftan and came out clutching a fistful of coins. The man tossed them onto the dock at the ferryman's feet. There were several coins, and they clashed musically together as they hit the weathered wood of the dock. The weight of their impact and their vague yellow gleam were not lost on Pesouris. Gold.

"Your pardon, my lord, but I cannot ferry you across at this hour. The Stygians, in their wisdom, forbid it. If you come back at daybreak…"

An uncomfortable moment of silence lengthened until the ferryman felt his pulse quicken with new apprehension. The man on the dock moved, thrusting his hand once again into his pocket and drawing forth another handful of coins. The pile of gold on the dock grew twice as large.

Pesouris looked down upon the spilled coins in sorrow. "I'm truly sorry, master, but it is forbidden for me to take travelers across the river after sundown. Your offer is generous, but if the Stygians caught us they would slay us both." The ferryman spread his hands in a gesture of helplessness. He did not have to feign regret. That was a lot of gold.

The man on the dock stood still for a long moment, his flowing white garb giving him the appearance of a silently risen ghost. Then he lunged forward and seized Pesouris by the throat and belt.

The ferryman choked as he was drawn effortlessly up out of the chair.

The hand at his throat seemed sculpted from cold granite. The portly ferryman was tossed bodily into the smaller of his ferries. There was a sharp stab of pain as his right knee cracked against the gunwale. If he had not been so full of fear, the pain might well have incapacitated him. As it was, he had the strength to roll over, grasp the slender mast, and pull himself to his feet in the little craft.

"Please," he choked, "I'll take you. Don't…"

The silent man was lowering himself stiffly into the boat. He sat in the prow and regarded Pesouris impassively. Only the vaguest outline of his features was visible in the darkness. There came the dry whisper of steel on leather as the man drew a heavy-bladed sword and laid it across his knees.

The ferryman busied himself poling first off the dock and then along the muddy bottom of the Styx. The ferry was little more than an outsized rowboat fitted with a miniature sail. Pesouris had Ahptut use it to carry the smaller, less wealthy groups of travelers. Now he scrambled to set the little sail as the craft surged out onto the black breast of the Styx.

Once the ferry was well under way, there was nothing Pesouris could do except squint into the darkness for the lights of Bel-Phar and regard his unlikely passenger. The air was chill upon the nighted river and a cooling draft blew back along the length of the boat. It bore a strange scent to the ferryman's nostrils.

Once, when he was very young, Pesouris had traveled by caravan with his father to Khemi at the mouth of the Styx. One morning he had awakened early and set out into the dunes to relieve himself. In a sandy hollow he had found the corpse of a camel. The beast had been mummified by the relentless arid heat of the desert, and resembled a sagging leather facsimile of itself. The warm morning breeze had carried the same scent that he smelled now on the cool evening breath of the Styx.

Of a sudden, Pesouris longed to look at anything other than his passenger. Turning his head to one side, he noticed a brief flash of froth out on the dark water. Amazed, the ferryman realized that he had spotted a crocodile. There were more flashes, more signs of movement all around the little boat. Here a black, armored muzzle broke the surface, and there a ridged, lashing tail struck foam from a glossy swell. The hair stood up on the ferryman's arms. Crocodiles did not venture so far from shore. And they did not follow ferryboats. The breeze blew stronger, bearing that scent back to Pesouris once again, and suddenly he understood. Crocodiles are eaters of carrion. They smelled it, too.

By the time that the sparse lights of Bel-Phar's waterfront came into view, Pesouris had completed a long and most sincere prayer to Mitra.

He had briefly considered praying to Set before deciding upon the more merciful god of the Hyborians. If he survived this evening, he promised both a vastly generous donation to a temple of Mitra and a serious change of lifestyle. Looking to either side of the ferry, he felt certain that his prayers were falling on deaf ears. The man sitting in the prow of his boat had not changed position, and if he noticed the swarm of crocodiles following them, he gave no sign.

"Master," said Pesouris, hating the shrill sound of his voice, "we are almost across." No response. He mustered his flagging courage. "Master, the water is full of crocodiles."

The man in the prow remained silent.

Pesouris concentrated on bringing his ferry in to a darkened, deserted dock, pointedly ignoring both his somber companion and their reptilian escort. When the little boat grated against the stained stone blocks of the dock, the ferryman felt a surge of relief, immediately followed by a rush of stark terror.

The man in the prow stood up, naked sword in his hand. Pesouris fell to his knees in the bottom of the boat, clenching his eyes shut against the blow he knew would come.

"Please, master," he pleaded. "I'll tell no one of your passage. Spare your poor servant."

A weight lifted from the prow of the ferry. Pesouris opened his eyes to see his passenger standing on the steps carved into the stone of the dock. The waterfront seemed unnaturally silent. On the neighboring pier a lone torch flickered yellowly from a sconce set in stone. The man sheathed his sword with a swift movement and tugged back the hood of his caftan, paying no heed to Pesouris whatsoever. He turned and started up the steps.

"Master," called the ferryman. The tall man stopped, turned, and looked down at Pesouris, who cringed but spoke.

"Master, who are you? What do you seek here?"

The flesh of the man's face seemed impossibly drawn and sunken in the faint torchlight. The mouth opened and closed stiffly, as though its owner had forgotten how to speak. A scar shone pale through the lusterless growth of beard.

"Death," said Gulbanda, and moved away up the stairs into the night.

21

T'Cura of Darfar scrambled down from the jagged rock spur that he had been using as a lookout for most of the morning. Below him, twelve men lolled quietly beside their hobbled horses, clustered in what shade they could find atop the boulder-strewn ridge. Neb-Khot, the small band's leader, squinted in the merciless noonday glare, watching T'Cura descend and wondering what he had seen. He took a swig of warm, brackish water from a goatskin and motioned for T'Cura to hurry.

Neb-Khot was a thin, wiry man. His dusky Stygian complexion was darkened even further by ceaseless exposure to the desert sun. His burnoose was gray with dust, secured at the waist with a leather girdle that held a scimitar and three cruelly hooked daggers. His sharp brown eyes peered questioningly at T'Cura, who scuffed over the rocky soil toward him. The Darfari approached his chieftain, touched his scarred forehead in a salute, and spoke.

"Hai, Neb-Khot, riders were approaching, but now they have turned off the Caravan Road and ride into the waste."

Neb-Khot stared at his man incredulously.

"Telmesh, awaken and tell me if what T'Cura says is truth."

The one addressed as Telmesh arose from the shadow of a mottled boulder and jogged toward the rock spur at the ridge's edge.

"I speak the truth." T'Cura's lips drew back from filed teeth.

"Are they mad?" The Stygian met T'Cura's bloodshot gaze. The Darfari was a fine tracker and an excellent man in a fight, but he had to be kept in line. Their eyes locked for a moment; then T'Cura looked away, bringing his dark hand up to scratch at his crudely shaven head.

"They ride into the open desert," persisted the Darfari, "and there are but four of them. Two are women."

"Even so?" Neb-Khot clapped a hand onto the man's shoulder to show him that he was still respected. "This grows more interesting by the moment."

The other brigands were stirring, some rising to wander over to hear of what T'Cura had seen. Telmesh dropped from the rock spur and came breathlessly up to Neb-Khot. He was a Shemite outlaw with few friends in the band. Neb-Khot often used him for simple tasks so that he felt appreciated. Now he held up his hand to shield his black eyes from the sun, revealing the faded tattoo of a golden peacock upon his forearm.

"It is as T'Cura says," declared Telmesh. "I say that we leave them be. Only sorcerers would willingly leave the Caravan Road and ride into the desert."

"Two are women," said T'Cura again, and a murmur of approval swept the lawless band of men gathered atop the rocky ridge.

"I did not notice," said Telmesh, but his words were lost in the growing tumult of eager voices. Neb-Khot lifted his hands for silence.

"My brothers, what manner of travelers leave the Caravan Road to wander in the wastelands? Are they necromancers seeking wisdom amongst the sand and scrub? Or are they witless fools who know nothing of the desert and have made the last mistake of their useless lives?"

Bloodthirsty cries rose from the men, some of whom drew their swords and shook them at the hot, blue sky. Telmesh the Shemite looked dismayed, but held his tongue.

"And eagle-eyed T'Cura says that two of the four are women!" continued Neb-Khot, his voice rising. "So I say, if the women are ugly, perhaps they are ladies worth ransoming. And if they are comely, then we have been lonely men for far too long!"

A savage cheer rang in the bright air and the group turned as one to their horses. Neb-Khot hoisted himself into his saddle and nudged his mount to Telmesh's side. An extended hand helped the Shemite mount his roan.

"Courage," smiled the Stygian. "If they are beauties, I shall see that you get first pick." Telmesh nodded, loyalty burgeoning in his breast.

Neb-Khot reined his horse around, watching his men move into action and reflecting upon how his luck had never deserted him. It had made him the undisputed leader of this strong band of bandits, always kept him a step ahead of the Stygian militia, and seen to it that it was never too long between hapless travelers on the Caravan Road. He spurred forward.

Hooves thundered in the dust as twelve men swept down from the high ridge to rob and rape and slay.

22

After the gear in the saddlebags of their camels was sorted through and divided, each member of the party acquired a measure of protection against the desert heat. Zelandra and Neesa immediately made use of a pair of cotton cowls, pulling them over their traveling clothes and tugging up the loose hoods against the sun. Predictably, Conan and Heng-Shih had more difficulty. The Khitan found nothing that he could wear as it was meant to be worn, finally wrapping a gray silk tunic around his shaven skull in a crude turban. For an outer garment he produced from his own provisions a golden kimono embroidered with writhing dragons of scarlet silk. Though adequately protected from the harsh sun, he cut an odd figure. The Cimmerian was luckier, finding a cotton burnoose large enough to be serviceable, if not entirely comfortable. In motley array, the party moved through an empty landscape, the dry and barren miles passing slowly beneath their camels' feet.

Zelandra seemed unwell. Again and again, she looked back over her shoulder toward the road they had left behind, her face pale within the folds of her hood. When she spoke to Conan, her voice had developed an unsettling tremor.

"Are you certain that we should have left the Caravan Road? Shall we not become lost in this godforsaken waste?"

Conan shrugged his broad shoulders beneath the undersized Stygian burnoose. "The Dragon's Spine is not so easily found. It is near Pteion, remember, and no human road leads to that cursed ruin."

Lady Zelandra's left hand fluttered to her brow and she swayed slightly in the saddle. "And how am I to trust you, barbarian? How is it that I trust you to lead me through this hot and empty hell?"

The Cimmerian turned to fasten his probing gaze on her face. Zelandra's eyes rolled as though she were in the grip of a tropical fever and her jaw worked spasmodically. He saw that she gripped the box at her girdle with such fierce intensity that the tendons stood out rigidly across the back of her hand. Then Heng Shih was riding at their side. The Khitan leaned from his mount and caught the reins of Zelandra's camel.

The party drew up short in the midst of the rocky plain. The sun was so bright that its rays seemed to thicken the air, suffocating the travelers with its heat.

"Heng Shih," sobbed Zelandra, teetering in her seat. "Heng Shih, where are you?" The Khitan moved his mount in close beside the sorceress and laid a thick arm across her shaking shoulders. The woman half fell against his body, leaning against him while a series of visible shudders coursed through her slender frame. Conan drew back, casting a glance at Neesa.

"Crom," he murmured, "is she stricken?"

Neesa shook her dark head. "Her body cries for the lotus."

The barbarian cursed under his breath, feeling a creeping chill despite the cruel sun. He turned away from the little group, scanning the land around them. The ruddy, irregular plain was broken only by a rough ridge to their rear and by a widely separated group of eroded volcanic buttes before them. The wind rose from a dull whisper to a hot howl, drowning Zelandra's sobs. Conan looked back to the ridge behind them, where it rose sharply against the featureless blue of the desert sky.

His brow furrowed.

Heng Shih's hands pulled the silver box from its leather bindings and lifted the lid with gentle care. Within the box's mirrored silver rim lay velvety green shadow. Zelandra tossed her head back against the Khitan's breast, tears bright on her pallid cheeks.

"No, Heng Shih," she said weakly. "No, my love."

The Khitan put a blunt forefinger in his mouth, then thrust it into the open box. It came back out encrusted with emerald dust. He put it to Zelandra's lips.

"Riders!" The barbarian's voice rang with deadly urgency. "Bandits or worse. Follow me!"

Heng Shih carefully re-wrapped the silver box and fastened it securely to Zelandra's belt before looking up. Neesa wheeled about, standing in her stirrups to look behind them. The Lady Zelandra was shaking her head as though shrugging off a spell of dizziness. She wiped away the moisture on her cheeks, blinking quickly and suddenly seeming to focus once more on those around her. When she looked up, her gray eyes were clear.

"Derketo's loins," she cursed hoarsely, "listen to the barbarian."

"Crom and Mitra! Follow me or we're all food for the jackals!" Without looking to see if they heeded his words, Conan urged his camel to a loping gallop. He started off at an angle to their original path, heading toward the stony prominence of the nearest butte. The rest of the party followed.

Neesa stared back at the ridge a moment longer. A thin thread of rising dust was just visible, tracing a line down the ridge's rugged slope. How the barbarian had noticed this faint sign was beyond her. Marveling, she lashed her camel and started off after her companions.

The party, moving at top speed, drew nearer to the closest of the buttes, and Zelandra found herself questioning the wisdom of the Cimmerian's path. The butte they approached was the core of an eons-dead volcano, a huge, crumbling shaft of stone that rose almost vertically from the desert floor. Its base was cluttered with shattered boulders torn from the main body of the escarpment by the slow claws of erosion. There seemed to be little advantage in taking refuge among the jagged heaps of broken rock. Would they leave their camels and try to lose their pursuers by hiding in the jumble of boulders? Better to try to fight them off. Zelandra's hand sought and gripped the box that bounced at her hip. She breathed deeply of the wind that lashed her flowing cowl and cleared her mind in preparation for strong and deadly sorcery.

But Conan did not lead the party directly into the butte's base. He kept his camel galloping around the tower of stone, moving west and north until a new feature of the rock unveiled itself. This side of the butte was cleft by a narrow gorge. It was as though an angry god had split the stone with a titanic ax, opening a steep passage up into the body of the butte. Conan rode into the gorge's mouth, dismounting almost immediately as the ground became covered with loose stone. The rest of the party came up behind him and followed suit.

"We can take the high ground here. Lead your mounts; the footing is uncertain." The barbarian's words echoed in the stony passage.

They hastily moved up the gorge, over gravel and broken, treacherous plates of reddish rock, between looming walls of striated stone. The sun shone directly down into the steep cleft in the butte, filling it with oppressive heat and blinding light. Halfway up the little canyon their passage was almost blocked by a huge boulder.

"Get the camels up behind the rock," directed Conan. "We can hold this position until they're willing to bargain."

As Heng Shih, Zelandra, and Neesa led their mounts to shelter behind the boulder, the hammer of hooves echoed up from the gorge's mouth. The brigands had overtaken them and now moved to seal off the canyon.

Neb-Khot was displeased with the current course of events. His band's fresh horses had caught up with their prey's weary camels easily enough, but the bandit chieftain had not anticipated that they would find such a dangerous place to go to ground. The brigands could only get at the travelers by charging up the open slope. Even though there were only two warriors in the defending party, he might well lose several men before taking them down. A bit of bargaining might lower their guard, perhaps even intimidate them into throwing down their arms and surrendering. He rubbed his stubbled chin uncertainly. The little party had proved surprisingly skillful in protecting themselves thus far. The Stygian sighed, wondering what other surprises they might have for him. This was not as easy as he had anticipated, but it did not mean that his luck had deserted him.

The brigands dismounted, forming a loose phalanx facing up the passage.

Neb-Khot motioned for the two archers to take up flanking positions on each wall of the gorge and called Telmesh to him. The Shemite, black eyes bright with excitement, clutched his naked scimitar and looked to his leader in anticipation.

"Telmesh, how would you like to bargain with these fools?"

"I?" The bandit seemed stunned. "By the Steel Wings, I've never done such a thing."

"Bah," said Neb-Khot with friendly derision. "You underestimate yourself. Have a word with the dogs. Show them that we can be reasonable men while I ready the others to charge." He turned away before the Shemite could respond.

Up the gorge, Conan appeared atop the boulder sheltering the camels, while Heng Shih stepped out beside it. The Khitan moved a few steps down the slope, finding a niche in the rock wall that would afford cover from arrows. Conan stood in full view, black mane whipping in the hot wind that blew along the canyon.

Forty paces away, Telmesh leapt up on a block of stone and hailed him.

"Ho, travelers! Throw down your weapons, give us your goods, and we shall spare you!" The Shemite's voice rang strongly in the corridor of stone, and he straightened with pride at the sound of it. Conan's response was a harsh bark of laughter.

"We have no riches, dogs. Our mistress seeks medicinal herbs in the desert. We have nothing for you but steel. Come forward if you wish a taste of it."

At this the archers to either side of the gorge surreptitiously set shafts to string and looked to Neb-Khot for the order to loose them. The Stygian chieftain moved among the eight men on the gorge's floor, speaking to them in low tones.

Neesa struggled up onto the boulder's top beside the barbarian. As she stood, a gust of wind lifted her cowl, exposing her slim legs to the crowd below. A raucous cry of approval swept the bandits.

Telmesh laughed coarsely. "By Ashtoreth, give us a taste of her and you can all go free!"

As Conan turned to admonish Neesa to take cover, the woman's hand darted to her nape in a motion that the barbarian knew all too well.

Her arm snapped forward, sending a throwing dagger streaking down the gorge like a diving hawk. The blade drove into Telmesh's throat just above the collar of his dusty burnoose.

"Taste that!" shouted Neesa as Neb-Khot gave his archers the order to release. Conan swept out an arm, shoving Neesa from the top of the boulder and sending her skidding, cursing, down the far side. An arrow shot through the space where she'd stood, whistling

Conan confronts bandits in the desert canyon

up the gorge. The Cimmerian's sword licked out, clipping a second arrow aside in mid-flight. The eight men on the canyon's floor howled out a wild, discordant war cry and drove forward with blades bared.

Telmesh stood still on his rock, eyes wide with disbelief.

His hands groped for the dagger's hilt and found it just as his legs gave way beneath him.

Neb-Khot watched the Shemite fall and felt his luck running strong within him. The whim that had led him to avoid bargaining with this party had likely saved his life. Surely the gods protected him this day.

Behind the boulder, the Lady Zelandra heard the cries of the attacking bandits as an indistinct and distant murmur. She knelt in the gravel, her entire being focused upon the open box of Emerald Lotus perched in her lap. Inside the mirror-lined casket was a small seashell. She used it to spoon a bit of the deep-green powder into her mouth, pouring it under her tongue. Revulsion at the sharp, bitter taste was swiftly eclipsed by the shudder of raw power through her body. She snapped the box closed, lashed it to her belt, and stood up.

The first bandit up the slope closed on Heng Shih, who lunged from his niche in the rock wall to meet him. The flare-bladed scimitar flashed in the desert sun, driving down to rebound from the bandit's hasty block with a resounding metallic *clang*. T'Cura reeled back from the strength of the blow, his dark face twisting with determination, He moved back in, but this time Heng Shih's swing had all the power of the Khitan's body behind it. Again, T'Cura succeeded in blocking the stroke, but the sheer impact lifted him from his feet and hurled him backward down the gorge. The Darfari crashed to the ground, tumbling down the rocky incline in a series of painful somersaults. Heng Shih ducked back into his sheltering niche as an arrow splintered against the canyon wall beside him.

Another arrow shot past Conan's head as he dropped to a crouch, waiting for the oncoming bandits to climb the boulder to reach him. A moment later a bearded brigand pulled himself up to where the rock adjoined the wall of the gorge. Conan drove forward and met an arrow fired by a canny archer below. The point impacted the barbarian's left shoulder, failing to pierce his mail but delivering a powerful buffet that staggered him and sent pain flaring hotly down his arm. The climbing bandit came sword-first onto the boulder's top, where Conan, struck off balance by the arrow, lashed out at him with a wordless cry of rage.

The Cimmerian's blade tore across the breast of his foe, splitting his ribs and slamming him back over the boulder's lip. The brigand fell from sight with a hoarse cry as Conan's uncontrolled swing drove his sword against the gorge wall, where it broke with a brittle *crack*.

Cursing sulphurously, he tore his dagger from his belt, crouching low again as yet another arrow whispered past.

In the cover of his niche, Heng Shih gripped his hilt with both hands and prepared to go back out onto the slope to deal with the next set of attackers to struggle up the slope. His slanted eyes flew wide as the Lady Zelandra came from behind the sheltering boulder and strode boldly out in front of it. He hurtled from the niche, golden kimono billowing out behind him, to protect his mistress. He cut down a howling brigand with a single brutal stroke, sending the man flying back among his comrades and momentarily arresting their progress. Then the Khitan looked to Zelandra and froze in place.

The Lady Zelandra's hair blew back from her straining face. Her eyes stretched wide, lit up from within by a weird crimson light. A tortured stream of strange words poured from her lips as she flung her arms out as though to embrace the oncoming bandits.

Every man in the gorge stopped moving. They stared in horror at the sorceress as a fiery illumination gathered and seethed about her outstretched hands. Halfway down the slope, T'Cura turned to run.

"Heeyah Vramgoth Dero!" screamed Zelandra, her voice rising to a wail of supernatural intensity. "Aie Vramgoth Cthugua!"

A towering sheet of red-orange flame rose before her, filling the gorge from wall to wall, obscuring Zelandra and her comrades from the bandits. For an instant it stood still, raging like the blaze at the heart of a volcano; then it rolled down the canyon toward Neb-Khot's terror-stricken band. Men turned to flee and were caught in the roaring inferno like insects in a brush fire. Screams of fearful agony were half heard above the flame-wall's thunder.

Neb-Khot was astride his horse the moment that Zelandra began her chant. He tried to spur away, but his horse shied, its hooves slipping on the loose stone of the gorge's floor. The beast fell, sending the Stygian chieftain flying from its back to slide gracelessly down the slope. He dragged himself to his feet, twisting an ankle in the gravel, and ran as if hell were at his heels.

Conan stood on the boulder's crest, watching the flame-wall move away.

It rolled swiftly toward the mouth of the gorge, expanding and contracting to fill the defile. When it reached the end of the little canyon, it faded swiftly from view. The fearsome, ear-filling roar dwindled away to silence. The barbarian saw that three bandits had escaped the gorge and now rode intently away from the butte. Two of the men shared a single mount. None turned to look behind them.

Six brigands lay dead on the floor of the canyon. Their bodies were twisted and contorted as though they had died in terrible pain. There was not a mark upon any of them.

Conan clenched his jaw, feeling the barbarian's instinctive fear of the supernatural welling up in him even as his battle-hardened sensibilities rebelled at the cruel power of Zelandra's sorcery. He glanced down to where the sorceress had stood at the base of the boulder and saw that she now sat cross-legged in the dust, her head in her hands. As he looked on, Heng Shih approached Zelandra and knelt at her side, bending his head to hers.

The Cimmerian lowered himself to the boulder's edge and dropped over it, landing lightly beside the sprawled corpse of the brigand he had broken his sword in slaying. The man still clutched a scimitar. Conan took the weapon from his stiffening fingers and the leather scabbard from his bloody belt. The scimitar was of mediocre workmanship, yet its design was agreeable enough. The blade was curved, but not so much as to make it impractical for thrusting. It was not a broadsword, but it would have to serve.

When he turned, Zelandra was standing again, embraced by Neesa. Heng Shih approached him with a wide grin, his silken kimono bright and incongruously festive in the sun. The Khitan's hands went through a quick sequence of motions, ending by seizing Conan by the upper arms and giving him a vigorous shake. The Cimmerian pulled free of the smiling Khitan.

"He gives you thanks for saving our lives," said Neesa. The Cimmerian grunted in embarrassment, looking off down the gorge. Heng Shih slapped him on the shoulder and turned back to Zelandra, who stood leaning weakly against the boulder. Her posture spoke of enormous weariness.

The Khitan took her hand, and together they walked around the boulder to where the camels waited.

Neesa came to the barbarian where he stood affixing the looted sword and scabbard to his belt.

"I shouldn't have killed that man, should I?" she said. Her dark eyes sought his. "If you had time to bargain, perhaps..."

"Hell," grinned Conan, suddenly glad to be alive. "They had no intention of letting us go. You heard those dogs howl when they caught a glimpse of you. You don't think that I'd have traded you for safe passage, do you?"

"No," she said, and lifted her lips to his.

23

The riders allowed their horses, weary and lathered with foam, to stop and rest at the Caravan Road. Neb-Khot lowered himself awkwardly from the mount he shared with T'Cura, lit upon his twisted ankle, and swore savagely.

"Yog and Erlik! That was a close thing, brothers."

T'Cura eased off his horse and stood holding the reins while the third survivor remained mounted. The third was one of the archers, his bow now in place over his right shoulder. He was a young Shemite, his shock of black hair in sharp contrast to the pale flesh of his face.

"Telmesh was right," he panted, wiping his brow with a dirty sleeve. "They weren't human. Did you see the black-haired one knock my shaft from the air?"

"Be still, Nath," groaned Neb-Khot. He gave in to the pain in his ankle and sat down heavily on the hot, hard-packed earth of the Caravan Road.

The sun, just past its median, blazed down. It was still early afternoon. The Stygian chieftain marveled that the ill-fated pursuit of the travelers and the destruction of his band had taken so little time.

"I need a horse," he declared to no one in particular.

T'Cura was drinking noisily from a waterskin, still gripping the reins of his mount with one hand. He lowered the skin and studied his chieftain in a bemused fashion. The archer, Nath, shifted nervously in his saddle, looking back out across the shimmering expanse of the desert.

"The horses scattered, Neb-Khot," said Nath. "We'll never find one for you now."

"It's a long way to Sibu's oasis. And farther still to Bel-Phar," growled T'Cura.

"Ishtar." Neb-Khot rubbed his wounded ankle gingerly. "Give some of that water to your horse, T'Cura. The beast will need it to carry us both back to Sibu's."

The Darfari said nothing. He put the waterskin to his lips and took a long, deliberate pull. Lowering it, he looked upon Neb-Khot and bared his filed teeth in a cold and mirthless smile. Then he shoved the waterskin into a saddlebag with a single contemptuous motion.

Nath's gaze moved from T'Cura to his chieftain and back again, growing ever more apprehensive. Neb-Khot noticed none of this. His fingers probed his wounded ankle while his mind dwelt on this sudden reversal of fortune. He looked up to see that the Darfari had remounted his horse and was now stroking the polished blade of his unsheathed scimitar. For the first time, it occurred to Neb-Khot that his luck might have deserted him completely.

"Look!" cried Nath, his voice breaking. "A rider!"

Neb-Khot twisted around, coming to his knees on the hard road. It was true. A single horseman had come into view on the road along the far flank of the ridge. His form rippled liquidly in the haze of heat, a small black mark on the ruddy, sun-blasted landscape; but it was clear that he rode the Caravan Road alone.

"Hah," grinned Neb-Khot, getting to his feet. "The gods haven't forgotten me after all. T'Cura, bring me that fool's horse and I'll give you fifty pieces of gold."

The Darfari eyed his leader with a look of amused disbelief writ upon his dark features. Then he shook his head and spat in the dust.

"Jullah must love you, Neb-Khot," he said, and spurred his horse forward, toward the approaching horseman.

The Stygian chieftain laid a hand on the lathered neck of Nath's mount as they watched T'Cura rapidly close on the lone rider.

"Should I—" began the archer.

"No," said Neb-Khot firmly. "Stay here with me and make ready an arrow." Nath did as he was told, setting a shaft to string.

As they watched, T'Cura confronted the horseman, flourishing his sword threateningly in the brilliant sunlight. The traveler's mount seemed very weary, its head hanging, but it kept plodding toward them even as T'Cura accosted its rider. The Darfari's voice rang commandingly, the words indistinct and distant but unmistakable in intent. The horseman, wrapped in a voluminous caftan, did nothing, and his mount continued unperturbed in its slow, steady gait.

Neb-Khot licked dry lips. Was the man mad?

With a furious cry, T'Cura thrust his blade at the traveler's breast.

What happened next occurred with such speed that neither Nath nor Neb-Khot could immediately grasp it. The rider's left hand lashed out, literally slapping aside T'Cura's killing thrust, and then shot out to seize the Darfari by the throat. T'Cura's blade fell to the road and his horse shied away, pulling from beneath its rider and leaving him dangling at the end of an arm as rigid as the bar of a gallows.

"Mitra save us," gasped Nath.

Impossibly, the rider held T'Cura out at arm's length, kicking, and then gave him a powerful shake. The Darfari's thrashing limbs went abruptly lax, and he was released. He fell in a limp heap on the road as the horseman continued toward Neb-Khot and Nath at the same deliberate pace.

"Oh, Mitra! Mitra!" cried Nath hysterically.

"Be still!" shouted Neb-Khot, slapping the mounted man's leg. "Shoot the dog! Loose, damn it!"

The archer shook with fear, but drew and released with ease born of years' practice. The arrow flew true, slapping into the center of the rider's breast. The man lurched in his saddle with the impact, but stayed mounted. His horse maintained its leisurely gait.

"Excellent," said Neb-Khot. "Now again!"

Nath mechanically drew and loosed another arrow, which found its mark beside the first. The rider was jolted once again, but remained in the saddle as the horse came to within a dozen paces and slowed to a halt.

"Gods," breathed Neb-Khot, "what manner of man have we slain?"

Putting his bow back over a shoulder, Nath drew his scimitar and spurred forward, cautiously approaching the horseman.

Seen up close, the horse was in terrible condition. White foam dripped from slack jaws while its sides heaved in the last extremity of exhaustion. Spurs had torn bloody marks in its flanks and its legs quivered unsteadily beneath the weight of its rider. The man's appearance was obscured by his dust-caked caftan, which was nailed to his broad chest by Nath's arrows. He sat on his mount with the breathless silence of the dead.

Nath's horse snorted suddenly, but the Shemite jerked at the reins, pulling it up beside the lifeless rider. The archer poked at the horseman with the point of his scimitar, thinking to shove him from the saddle.

The dead man's hand knocked aside Nath's blade and swung back around in an arc of incredible speed. A fist like the head of a mace cracked into the side of Nath's skull, bowling him off of his horse and sending him sprawling unconscious in the dust.

The horseman swung a leg over his saddle and dismounted. Neb-Khot drew his sword without thinking. Then he was struck motionless, his limbs seeming to lock up in helpless horror. The rider had caught the reins of Nath's horse with one hand and was drawing one of the arrows out of his chest with the other. The shaft came out slowly and with a thick, grating rasp, as though it were being pulled from a wooden beam afflicted with dry rot. Bloodlessly, the arrow was removed and discarded. When the rider grasped at the second arrow, Neb-Khot's reason broke.

"Die, demon!" The Stygian chieftain stumbled forward, bringing his sword down in an overhand cut that should have cleft the crown of the rider's head. But his twisted ankle gave way beneath his weight even as the horseman sidestepped the attack. Neb-Khot fell awkwardly on the road, gravel scoring his palms as he caught himself.

There was no time to recover, to strike upward at his nemesis, or even to roll away. A knee came down solidly in the middle of Neb-Khot's back. A cold hand locked onto each shoulder, iron fingers sinking into his flesh. Struggling, the Stygian was bent backward with monstrous, irresistible strength.

Gulbanda spoke a single word, then snapped Neb-Khot's spine.

24

Zelandra's band of travelers traversed the waste beneath a molten sun. Conan led them unerringly across the desert's level floor, over red earth baked by centuries of ceaseless heat until it was the consistency of brick. As the long miles passed, the stony solidity of the soil gave way to crumbling gravel, and then to shifting sand.

The party crested a low rise and drew to a halt at the Cimmerian's command. Ahead stretched an ocean of rolling dunes, a seemingly endless expanse of ochre sand that reached for the shimmering horizon, raked by the sunlight of late morning and dappled by black shadow. A single band of cloud, burnt transparent by the sun, moved upon the blank blue slate of the sky.

"Here the true desert begins," said the barbarian. "Any sane caravan would traverse the dune sea only at night, but we are in haste and have no time for comforts. Drink sparingly. I doubt I'll be able to find another source of water until we've crossed the dunes and reached the highlands."

Zelandra bent in her saddle, digging a hand into her baggage. The sorceress produced a worn tube of pale leather, from which she drew a roll of yellowed parchment. Thrusting the tube beneath an arm, Zelandra unrolled the scroll for Conan to see.

"This is an ancient map of this part of Stygia," she explained. "I found it before we left. It dates back to the days of Old Stygia, and shows the city of Pteion and its environs. I doubt the map will be of much use, but I noticed that it depicted an oasis near the eastern highlands. Do you think it might still be there, Conan?"

The barbarian squinted at the map, lifting a thick forearm to shade his eyes. "It may be. I have heard of an old oasis in the dune sea, though not from anyone who claimed to have seen it with his own eyes. This part of the world is wisely avoided by most. Only men who wish to travel in secrecy cross these sands." Conan nudged his camel forward, and the travelers started down the gentle slope into the dunes.

Neesa pulled her hood over her tousled locks and said, "Do the caravans fear becoming lost amid the trackless sand? Traveling by night, as you say, could they not steer by the stars?"

"They fear losing their way, as they fear the heat and the absence of water, but they also fear the slumbering sorcery of the dead city of Pteion. These sands are said to be accursed."

"We are not going near Pteion," put in Zelandra. "We shall skirt its evil ruins by many miles. Your barbaric superstitions do you little credit, Conan. These sands are no more accursed than the grassy hills of Shem."

The Cimmerian made no reply. His blue eyes smoldered against his bronzed face as he scanned the horizon uneasily.

As the party rode into the sea of sand, the sun lifted into the sky and seemed to halt there, suspended in the heavens like a torch in a sconce. The camels labored over the dunes steadily, if unenthusiastically, occasionally snorting and moaning their distaste for the task.

Neesa followed Conan's example and draped herself in her cloak so that not an inch of skin was exposed to the merciless sun.

Closing her eyes against the glare, she settled back in the swaying saddle and tried to doze. Between the movement of the camel and the steady creaking of her gear, she could almost imagine herself back on the deck of Temoten's ferry. A cry from Zelandra snapped the scribe back into full awareness.

"Look there! Is that not a palm?" The sorceress stood in her stirrups at the crest of a tall dune. "Conan, is that our oasis?"

The barbarian pulled at his mount's reins, urging the camel up the dune's face until he was at Zelandra's side. Heng Shih pointed to the southeast, where a fleck of emerald glimmered in the haze of heat.

"It looks like it," agreed Conan, "though it is nowhere near where it is shown on your map."

Zelandra's high brows knitted in impatience. "Well, one could hardly expect the oasis to be in exactly the same position after the passage of so many centuries. Let us go fill our waterskins and lounge in the shade for a time. It will do us all good."

The Cimmerian said nothing, and the travelers turned from their trail.

The distant palms beckoned, wavering like a green flame on the face of the desert. Conan watched the palms draw nearer, coming into view as his camel slogged up a dune, then dropping from sight as his mount descended into the valleys between each hill of sand. Unlike his civilized companions, the barbarian had never learned to distrust or disregard his instincts. He was troubled by a vague and creeping unease.

The terrain altered as the party proceeded. The dunes flattened, and the sand became a hardened skin that crunched beneath their camels' feet. Conan stared at the oasis, now close enough for him to discern lazily swaying palms and the thick cluster of ground vegetation that marked the location of the waterhole. His nostrils flared.

"Something is amiss," said the barbarian. "The oasis appears green, yet I smell no water."

"For the love of Ishtar, Conan, would you attempt to contain your barbarian superstitions?" Zelandra sounded exasperated. "Pteion is many miles away. This oasis is a blessing that we shall not overlook. We—"

A wave of heat rolled over the travelers. Though the sky was clear, the sun brightened as if it had emerged from behind a thick wall of clouds.

Ahead, the oasis blurred like a waking dream, its outlines softening in the harsh glare. The brightness made Conan squint and look down. He saw that he rode over a hardened surface of solidified sand. The sculpted dunes had flattened into an uneven plain of fused glass. The ground resembled the congealed bottom of a glass-blower's forge. Conan jerked his camel to a halt, looked up, and saw that the oasis had vanished.

Where the palms and brush had been was now a stout, flat-topped cone of dark stone, standing almost as tall as a man. Its deep gray hue contrasted sharply with the ochre tones of the desert. The sand around the cone was frozen in concentric whorls of fused glass. It sat at the center of a mile-wide spiral of seared sand, like a gray spider in a web of brittle stone. The earth around it was strewn with dark debris.

A sheet of white fire rippled across the sky, and a cry went up from the party. The camels bellowed and stumbled as the air itself seemed to turn to flame. Conan dismounted, seizing the reins of his reeling mount, and pulled away from the false oasis.

"Come away!" he roared. "Sorcery!"

The heat intensified incredibly, dazzling their eyes and searing their skin. Heng Shih and Neesa could not control their mounts. The camels reared and staggered, with their riders pulling at the reins in vain.

Conan saw Zelandra jump awkwardly from her saddle and

fall, rolling on the ground beside her camel's stamping feet.

"Dismount!" bellowed the barbarian. "Leave the camels and flee or we'll be cooked in our skins!" Neesa and Heng Shih tried to obey as Zelandra scrambled away from her frenzied mount. Conan moved to help her. Hell seemed to swallow them all.

Blinding white fire filled the air. Breathing scorched the lips and tongue. The Cimmerian reached for Zelandra, and saw the sleeve of his burnoose was smoldering along the full length of his arm. Blisters sprang up on the back of his exposed hand.

"No!" shouted the sorceress "Stand away from me!"

Conan stepped back, and Zelandra knelt, lifting her hands to the incandescent sky.

"Dar-Asthkoth la Ithaqua!" her voice wailed. "Brykal Ithaqua Ftagn!"

The sky immediately lost much of its brilliance, and the heat waned.

Conan threw back the hood of his burnoose and looked about wildly. The acrid stench of burnt cloth filled the hot, still air. Heng Shih had been hurled from his camel's back. He rose from all fours, and limped to the side of his mistress. The Khitan drew his scimitar, as if his blade might protect Zelandra from the unnatural heat. Neesa had stayed in her saddle and succeeded in calming her mount, while the remainder of the camels milled about in a state of near panic.

Above the beleaguered party arced a translucent dome of azure light. The Lady Zelandra raised her palms to it, as though holding it aloft. Her breath came in short, harsh gasps. Outside the dome's circumference, the air blazed with rippling fire. The ominous cone of gray stone wavered in and out of visibility.

"What in the name of the gods is happening?" cried Neesa. She swung her long legs over her saddle and dismounted, hastening to Conan's side. The barbarian brushed roughly at the smoking hem of her cloak, extinguishing the embers glowing there.

"Some sort of sorcerous sentinel," he rumbled, "trying to burn us to death like insects under a glass. It's a good thing that Zelandra made quick use of her power, else we might all be piles of smoking bone by now."

"Is it a weapon of Ethram-Fal's?" asked the scribe.

"No," rasped the kneeling sorceress, "it is very old. And very hungry."

Her hands trembled, and a hot wind blew over the huddled group. "I can't hold it much longer. Our only hope is that it tires before I do."

"What is it?" Neesa's voice quavered. "What does it want with us?"

Zelandra did not answer. She had clenched her eyes shut and was now a study in stark concentration. Heng Shih knelt beside her, putting a reassuring hand on her slim shoulder.

"I can't say what it is," said Conan, "but I can tell you that it means to slay us. Look."

Neesa's gaze followed the barbarian's outstretched arm and fell upon a gruesome sight. Some twenty feet ahead of the travelers was a cluster of blackened bone, lying half-sunken into the fused glass of the desert floor. The jagged ribs of a camel were plainly visible, but more disturbing still was a scattered collection of rounded mounds that appeared to be charred human skulls.

"The cursed thing lures travelers by shamming the appearance of an oasis, and then cooks them to death when they come to drink."

"Why?" burst out Neesa, horror edging her voice with hysteria. "Would it kill us without reason?"

"It is hungry." Zelandra spoke without opening her eyes. The face of the sorceress was tense and drawn, as though she suffered a ceaseless pain she could barely endure. "It wants to burn us to death and feast upon our released souls. My resistance has made it curious. Look to its stone well, I think that it has come out to look us over."

Conan looked, and shuddered as though a spider had scurried down his spine. The space between Zelandra's protective dome and the gray stone well had cleared somewhat. Something hung above the well's dark prominence, floating suspended in the air. It was a shimmering tower of reflective light. It looked as though the desert's common mirage of distant, glistening water had been twisted into a living coil. The demon swayed like a stationary cyclone. Conan felt the distinct and unpleasant sensation of being watched.

The air outside the dome blazed up anew. White fire pressed in upon Zelandra's magical barrier, drawing a low moan from the sorceress.

"Ah, Ishtar, but it's strong! It is some guardian demon of old, freed of its well, yet bound to its guard post. I feel its mind. It knows only hunger and hatred. Ah!" The demon's body swelled suddenly, and the blue dome above the party dimmed and lowered. A flash of infernal heat fell upon the travelers, then dissipated as Zelandra marshaled her strength. "Damn! It means to have us all. Heng Shih, get me some lotus."

The Khitan obediently unlaced the silver box from Zelandra's girdle.

Tilting the lid open, he found the seashell within and scooped up a bit of the deep-green powder. He held it to his mistress's face and, when she opened her mouth, poured it under her tongue.

"Derketo," Zelandra cursed, shuddering. Then a terrible smile slowly spread over her features. Her teeth were smeared with green. Above them, the azure dome rose and darkened.

"How's that, old devil?" Zelandra opened her eyes and gazed upon the swaying form of her demon nemesis. Her voice was softer, almost sensual. "You've never met anyone like me before, have you?"

The whirling coil suddenly stretched up to twice its height, shooting skyward in a flash of blue-white light. Zelandra screamed hoarsely as her protective barrier was struck with enough force to drive it down directly over their heads. Neesa cried out and dropped to her knees, involuntarily lifting her arms to shield her head. The azure dome flickered, admitting quick pulsations of fiery heat.

"I can't hold it! I can't hold it!"

"Can steel harm it?" Conan had drawn his scimitar, and crouched beside the kneeling sorceress. His eyes blazed with reckless desperation.

"Strong blows might dissipate it momentarily, but it can't be slain by physical weapons. Don't be a fool! Ah!" Zelandra grimaced with effort as the demon hammered at her shield with all of its eldritch might.

Conan lunged to his camel's side and pulled a waterskin from its place beside the saddle. He tore it open, then upended the skin over his head. The Cimmerian poured water over his burnoose, trying to soak himself completely.

"Have you gone mad?" cried Neesa, grasping at the barbarian's arm.

Conan shook her off.

"It's our only chance. If I can distract it, flee." Without another word, the Cimmerian leapt through Zelandra's barrier into the inferno beyond. Breaking out of the azure dome, Conan felt a flash of sharp chill, as if he had splashed through an icy waterfall, then the demon's heat hit him like a toppling wall. Conan sprinted across the brittle sands with steam bursting from his sodden burnoose. It was like running across a lava flow. White light drove tears from the barbarian's eyes, but he could see the undulating coil of the demon's body ahead. He steered toward it, bounding over the blackened remains of a luckless caravan, and sliding to a stop before the gray cone of rock. It was a well of sorts. The tip of the cone was missing, revealing a shaft dropping away into darkness. A circular plate of gray stone, the size of a wagon's wheel, lay against the side of the well. The demon towered twenty feet above Conan, rising in sparkling, unbroken coils from the well's open mouth. It swung from side to side, then drew itself down, as if to examine the diminutive form of the man who dared approach it.

Conan heard the moisture sizzling from his burnoose, and smelled hair burning. The hilt of his sword seared his palm. He lashed out at the demon with a savage cry. It was like cleaving cobwebs. His blade passed through its insubstantial form but pulled a trail of glittering shadow-substance after it. The temperature dropped abruptly, though Conan scarcely noticed. With another war cry, he slashed his scimitar across the top of the well again, and yet again. The demon fell in upon itself, telescoping, until it stood only half a man taller than the barbarian. It bent over him, as if in benediction, and Conan's burnoose burst into flames.

The Cimmerian dropped and rolled on the hard ground, trying to smother the fire. Scorching pain bloomed along his shoulders and arms, then ceased abruptly. The flames died. Rolling onto his back, Conan saw the azure dome suspended above him. He jumped to his feet, heard the cries of his comrades, and realized that Zelandra was protecting him at their expense. The barbarian's sword whipped across the mouth of the well again and again, shredding the demon-thing's substance, drawing its attention back to himself. It dropped lower in the well. Sorcerous heat pressed upon the azure barrier, but could not penetrate. The twisted coil of rippling light shuddered, then dropped from view into the well.

The air was suddenly much cooler, and the sun less bright. The normal, fierce heat of the desert seemed pleasantly temperate after the demon's onslaught. Conan leaned against the faceted stone wall and fought for breath, peering into the well's blackness. A surge of heat billowed up from within and dried his eyeballs.

"Seal it!" Zelandra's voice carried across the blasted sand. "It will gather its strength and come back more powerful than before!"

Conan staggered back from the well. His eyes were drawn to the heavy plate of gray stone that leaned against the well's side. He bent and gripped it. The barbarian's arms stretched to their limit, his hands fastening onto the plate's rim and clamping tight. The great disk of stone had been carved, worked, and fashioned to cap the well. Weird runes, half obliterated by time, rose beneath his straining fingers.

He heaved up, muscles cracking in his mighty frame. The breath exploded from between his teeth. Balancing the massive plate against his heaving breast, the Cimmerian took a single, unsteady step, and the demon thrust itself from the well again.

The shimmering body of the creature shed a hellish heat and rose, resembling a cyclone of broken mirrors. With a convulsive heave, Conan dropped the lid. It fell across the well's mouth with a hollow boom, like distant thunder. The demon's body was lopped off cleanly. Its upper half dissipated like smoke on the wind, its luster fading rapidly to shadow. The stone lid rattled once, as if thrust up from within; then it was still.

Conan slumped against the well, drawing breaths that seemed as sweet as the wine of Kyros. His comrades joined him, stumbling across the fused sand.

"Get away from the well," snapped Zelandra. "I'll seal its bonds with magic." The sorceress muttered a brief incantation, then slapped her palms down on the well's cap. The plate of stone glowed a dusky, auroral blue, and a faint keening sound pained Conan's ears. Zelandra turned from the well with a triumphant grin.

"Congratulations, my friends. We have defeated a guardian demon that has haunted this desert since Acheron warred with Old Stygia." The lady's face was pinched with strain, yet lit by an unnatural energy.

She clutched her silver box of Emerald Lotus, gesturing with it. "Our barbarian friend was right again. We must learn to cease underestimating him. That was a creature of Pteion, set to guard its borders more than thirty centuries ago. I could feel its age as I grappled with it. It has a mind of sorts, and intelligence. If only I could stay and study it. What wonders the demon must have known in its youth."

Conan doffed his blackened burnoose, baring flesh scorched scarlet.

Wordlessly, he began rummaging through the pack camel's provisions, looking for new clothing. The barbarian shot a glance at Heng Shih, and smiled. The Khitan had lost his turban when he fell from his camel, and now his pate was reddened and dotted with angry blisters. His golden kimono was worn, dirty, and bore spots of black char. He noticed the Cimmerian's attention and grimaced, touching his blistered scalp ruefully.

"Can it get out of the well now?" asked Neesa.

"No, child," said Zelandra grandly. "My power has sealed the demon away until I see fit to set it free. Originally, all one had to do was open the well to release it, but I have fused the stone with sorcery. Go ahead, Conan, just try to lift the lid now. Even you shan't be able to do it. Go on. Try it."

"I believe you, milady," said Conan dryly, continuing his search through the provisions.

"But it got out of the well before," murmured Neesa dubiously.

"Some fool must have lifted the lid," said Zelandra. "Probably many years ago, though there is no sure way to tell. Pteor knows why anyone would do such a thing."

"Probably looking for treasure. The poor devils must have thought they had found a Stygian tomb." The Cimmerian finally found another burnoose in a saddlebag and pulled it over his stinging shoulders. It was too small, but it would have to do.

"They found their deaths. As we might have, if not for my lotus." Zelandra examined her silver box with pride.

"And Conan's courage," said Neesa.

"Yes. Yes, of course," said the sorceress absently. She opened the silver box and stared within. Zelandra's eyes grew vague and distant.

She licked her lips slowly. Her right hand seemed to rise of its own accord, stroking gently around the box's silver-chased rim.

Neesa snatched the box from her mistress's hands, snapping it shut. The scribe backed away from the sorceress, holding the box behind her body.

Her posture revealed fear and determination in equal measure.

"That's mine!" Zelandra snarled, her hands clenching into fists. "Give it back to me, or I'll…" Her gaze abruptly focused upon the slender form of her scribe. Their eyes met, and Zelandra's face fell.

Bewildered, she looked down at her hands and deliberately unclenched her fists.

"Forgive me, Neesa. You are a fine servant and a better friend. Forgive me." The voice of the sorceress was husky and halting.

"It is nothing, milady," said Neesa softly. "Here." The scribe handed her mistress the silver box, and Zelandra fastened it securely at her girdle, knotting it into place.

"Come then," the sorceress spoke up. "Let us mount and be off. I shall busy myself, as we travel, making a salve to soothe our burns. Lead on, Conan."

The barbarian rejoined his mount and swung into the saddle. His dark face was grim. As the little caravan began its slow crawl across the burning sands, he trained all his senses upon a single object. The Cimmerian had poured much of the party's water supply over his body to protect himself from the supernatural heat of the guardian demon. There was little left. Conan sniffed the air and scanned the landscape, searching for any evidence of a water source. If he did not find the oasis depicted upon Zelandra's ancient map, he had no doubt that the party would perish for lack of water.

25

Except for a single chair and several empty buckets, the little
room was devoid of furnishings. These few things sat in a
rough circle around the room's central feature. In the middle of
the smooth stone floor was a deep depression now filled with
hot water. In this impromptu tub lounged the naked form of
Ethram-Fal. The steaming water was dark and thick as syrup
with powdered Emerald Lotus. The sorcerer wallowed on his
back in the sunken pool, his slight, wizened body half floating
as he breathed the perfumed air through flaring nostrils and
stared upward with dilated eyes. He leaned his shaven head
back upon the sharp rim of the tub and idly created visions to
amuse himself.

Suspended in the air above his prone form, a silver flower
bloomed, its shining petals gleaming like polished steel. It rotated
a moment and then burst into a compact ball of scarlet fire.
The flame blazed brightly, then flew outward into a thousand
separate pinpoints that immediately contracted, spinning into a
miniature galaxy. The revolving disk of brilliant motes coalesced,
gradually outlining the tiny, perfect form of a woman. Once
complete, the fiery homunculus began to whirl in a wild dance,

slowly shedding its flames until it was a diminutive but perfect image of the Lady Zelandra. Naked, the little figure writhed in erotic abandon before Ethram-Fal's greedy eyes.

The sorcerer settled himself more deeply in the hot, lotus-laden water, feeling its power seeping into his bones. Above him, the homunculus caressed itself and thrust tiny hands out to Ethram-Fal in shameless supplication. Then, as he looked on, the figure began to tear at itself, rending its flesh with its own hands until it burst abruptly into a misty cloud of crimson droplets.

Ethram-Fal laughed, his mirth sounding metallic and inhuman in the closed stone room. The sorcerer rolled over, letting the image wink out, and turned his mind to more serious things.

He slouched low, letting the thickened water creep up to his lower lip, allowing a bit to slip into his mouth and savoring the bitter bite of it.

His continuing study of Cetriss's legendary discovery had taught him much about it, but had left him curious on a number of key points. Most notably, he had no idea how it had been conceived. It had no place in nature. The Emerald Lotus was a unique hybrid of plant and predatory fungus. Ethram-Fal believed that he now understood each distinctive stage in its odd life cycle. Thinking to feed it again before it went dormant, he'd had his soldiers drive a horse over the balcony railing and into the pit. It had taken six men with spears to do the job, and one of them had received a kick that stove in his ribs. The horse had fallen beside the lotus, which had remained motionless until sensing the blood from the beast's wounds. The lotus could be approached at any time, and its blossoms harvested, provided that it did not smell blood.

Exactly how it sensed blood he had yet to determine, but a few moments after the horse, wounded by prodding spearpoints, had landed at its side, the lotus had become violently animate, leaping on the beast and feeding upon it. After nearly draining the animal, it bloomed once again, the newer, brighter flowers almost obscuring the ones left unharvested from the pony that he and Ath had given it. Disturbingly, the lotus had seemed less than satisfied with its second horse, and continued to move about the chamber after flowering. Ethram-Fal wondered if it was possible to give the Emerald Lotus too much sustenance. Its appetite seemed limitless, and the blood it consumed added to its size and strength no matter how much it had already absorbed. The sorcerer had stared down into the cylindrical chamber and realized it would be as foolhardy to overfeed the lotus as it would be to starve it. The Emerald Lotus had to be kept alive and thriving, yet if overfed it might prove difficult to manage. The sorcerer had watched it continue to move after its feeding for almost an hour. The lotus prowled around the walls in a restless circle, dragging the body of the horse with it.

It never gave up its victims. They became a part of it, woven into its grisly fabric. The lotus was bigger now, a tangled mass of hardened branches, razor thorns, and lush, emerald blossoms. The nightmare plant now stood at nearly the height of a man, and fairly blanketed the floor of its chamber. Ethram-Fal knew that, in time, the blooms would dry out and fall away, leaving the bristling bulk of the lotus in a dormant state as it waited patiently for nourishment. Left even longer without blood, it would use the bones of its prey to go to seed, driving black spores into the marrow and letting its outer body fall slowly to dust.

It was fascinating, but frustrating as well. Though he now believed that he knew the lotus and how to control it, he had not developed even a tentative theory as to how Cetriss had created it. Even a sorcerer as skilled and knowledgeable in the ways of growing things as himself could not begin to imagine how such an unnatural conglomeration of plant, animal, and fungus could have been formed. To have created such a thing and have it live for mere moments in the laboratory would have been a triumph; that it was nearly immortal and yielded a powerful drug was practically beyond belief.

Ethram-Fal sat up in the tub, the water making green traceries over his bare shoulders. He mopped his brow and blinked in the steamy heat.

Perhaps the legends were right. Perhaps Cetriss had bargained with the Dark Gods for the lotus. If this was so, then the sorcerer had been a man of great courage as well as great skill. If this was so, then all his own efforts to fit the Emerald Lotus into earthly categories were doomed from the start. It might have been conceived in a place where the laws of nature as men knew them did not exist. Under what strange skies had the Emerald Lotus first blossomed? And who had been the first to harvest it?

Thinking on the accomplishments of Cetriss, Ethram-Fal felt an unaccustomed surge of admiration. No wonder the mage had abandoned all to seek immortality. His greatness had been such that all the brilliant sorcerers of Old Stygia must have seemed little more than insects in comparison. A man like that would have wanted the ages, the godlike power to rise above the paltry world of men.

Ethram-Fal sighed deeply. He, too, wanted the ages, but he would settle for power over the here and now. The lotus had already enhanced his abilities far beyond his expectations, and promised to make him stronger still. To seven scarlet hells with its origins, as long as he could continue to harvest its blossoms.

The Stygian slouched back in the tub's warm embrace, eyes slitted and glittering. He could wait a while to feed it now. Next time it shouldn't be a horse. That had proved to be much too difficult.

Ethram-Fal thought of the soldier who had been kicked and had his ribs broken, of how he now lay so uselessly in the Great Chamber. The sorcerer smiled.

Heavy footfalls in the hall outside the room woke him from his pleasant reverie. The blanket hanging over the doorway was thrust roughly aside, and Ath came panting into the room.

"Milord, I beg—" the tall soldier began.

"What is this? Did I not leave explicit orders that I was not to be disturbed?" Ethram-Fal sat up in his bath, a small, shrunken, and naked form that filled the armored warrior with a fear that jellied his guts.

"Milord, please, I would not have come here without reason."

There was a moment's silence while Ethram-Fal thought on this. The yellow-green illumination of the light-globe played along Ath's rangy form, highlighting the nervous tic that leapt beneath his right eye.

"No," said Ethram-Fal finally, "I suppose that you wouldn't. Speak. What is it?"

A lungful of air escaped from Ath's lips and he realized that he had been holding his breath. A hand went involuntarily to his cheek to quell the tic there.

"There is something that you must see, milord. One of the men has been killed."

"What? How?"

"Please, you must see for yourself, milord. It was one of the guards. He was found in the room of the great statue."

At that Ethram-Fal was up and out of his bath, scrubbing at his scrawny body with a towel and quickly struggling into his gray robes. He was following Ath down the stone hallway in mere moments, his bare feet leaving damp prints in the dust. They did not speak again until they came into the huge, circular chamber.

A soldier stood at the base of the black statue, thrusting his light-globe feebly at the encroaching darkness. He stared silently at them as they approached. Ethram-Fal hardly noticed the living man at first—his eyes were fixed upon the smooth block of stone between the god-thing's extended paws.

A man lay spread-eagled there, his head close to the black sphinx's glossy breast. His arms and legs were thrown out to each corner of the smoothly worn block, where black rings of untarnished metal were set in the stone. He was not bound. There was a ragged hole in his chest, piercing the mail. Bright blood spattered the sable stone in loops and strings. It pooled, cooling, beneath the body. The featureless oval of the sphinx's face hung above them like a black moon in the darkness, admitting nothing.

"What in Set's name?" Ethram-Fal's voice was a dry croak.

"It is Dakent, milord." Ath's tones were steady and emotionless. "He was on guard with Phandoros when it happened."

Ethram-Fal's gaze fixed on the man with the light-globe, and the slender Stygian flinched as if stabbed. He did not, however, speak until spoken to.

"What happened? How did your partner come to this?"

Phandoros licked his lips and spoke in a reedy voice. "It grew chill in the courtyard, milord. It was nearly dawn and a wind came up the canyon. I left Dakent alone at the portal to go and fetch my cloak. I found it, took a sip of wine, and returned to find him gone." Phandoros hesitated, swallowing audibly.

"What then?" urged Ethram-Fal impatiently.

"I called for him in the courtyard, then came back in to seek him inside. When I didn't find him, I woke Captain Ath and we searched the palace together. When we came to this room..." The soldier's voice choked off and he seemed unable to go on.

Ethram-Fal turned to his captain, "Ath, continue."

"Outside this room, we heard a voice."

"A voice? Who spoke?" The sorcerer held his hands at his waist, knotting and unknotting his fingers distractedly.

"I don't know, milord. We came in at the far entrance and heard the voice whispering. He spoke no words that I understood. When we lifted our lights and called out, whoever it was fled. We could hear his feet on the stone. We gave chase, but hesitated when we saw Dakent. By the time that we started after the intruder again, he had escaped out the portal."

"It's gone? You're sure it left the palace?"

"Positive, milord. I followed outside and heard the sounds of him climbing the canyon wall."

"Climbing that sheer wall?"

"Yes, milord."

"Does anyone else know of this?" demanded Ethram-Fal.

"No, milord. Everyone else sleeps," said Ath.

"Good. No one else shall hear of it. All shall know that Dakent was bitten by an adder while on watch and that his body was given to the lotus. Is that understood?"

"Yes, milord," said Ath.

"Phandoros?"

"Y-yes, milord. It is understood."

The small group of men stood in grim silence for a brief time. The light-globe shed its gently wavering illumination over the sprawled body, lending it the ghastly illusion of movement, while the shadows seemed to press inward and hold the living in place.

"Why didn't he cry out?" asked Phandoros in a small voice.

"Look at his throat," said Ethram-Fal. "His windpipe has been crushed shut."

"You mean he was seized, silenced, and dragged in here to be slain?" Ath's voice rose in repugnance and horror.

"Yes," said Ethram-Fal in softer tones. "And where is his heart?"

The two soldiers started and looked about themselves as if they might find the organ that had given Dakent life lying at their feet.

But it was gone.

26

An ancient lean-to of dry sticks and faded camel-skin tatters waved in the hot desert breeze. It sat forlorn and fallen in upon itself at the base of one of several palms that stood about the oasis like sentries swaying with weariness in the heat. The trees threw inviting splotches of dark shadow upon the sun-bright sand, but the eyes of the weary travelers were fixed on the pool.

Sunken into a sandy depression and half surrounded by grateful shrubs, the water gleamed a vivid blue, reflecting the cloudless sky above.

"Now that, by Crom, is a most welcome sight." Conan slid easily from his camel's back and led the others toward the pool's nearest shore.

His three comrades followed, stretching legs aching from hours in the saddle.

"Is the oasis where the map showed it to be?" Neesa pulled back her hood and shook out her tangled cloud of black hair. The scribe wondered if she could be patient enough to wait until everyone drank their fill before throwing herself headlong into the waterhole.

"More or less," said Conan. "I steered us by the map until I could smell water, then followed the scent."

Zelandra jogged to Conan's side, her silver-threaded hair bouncing with her movements. As they neared the pool's rim, her hand closed on his thick shoulder.

"Hold," she said urgently. "Something here is not right..."

Conan's eyes caught a trace of movement in the pool's clear shallows. A thin stream of bubbles rippled from a spot in the sand beneath the water. The stream widened as he watched, sending tiny concentric swells rolling across the still surface of the pool. Heng Shih and Neesa shouldered up to where Zelandra and Conan stood staring. The barbarian's skin crawled with a dread so strong and insistent that it was almost a premonition.

"Get back!" he bellowed as an explosive concussion ripped the surface of the pool, hurling white spray far up into the empty sky. Where the stream of bubbles had emerged from the pool's floor, a thick shaft of shining green, like the trunk of a tree, now thrust itself into view.

It shook, jerked, and stretched itself taller than a man, lashing the water to froth. A cluster of pale, bloated, petal-like growths covered the thing's crown. Its body was a densely wrinkled green cylinder, crisscrossed with pulsing veins. A pair of ridged tentacles burst from each side of its midsection, lashing the air. A thick mass of roiling roots formed its base, heaving at the pool's floor, lifting the grotesque thing up out of the water, moving it toward the shore and the stunned human intruders.

A whiplike tentacle whistled toward Conan, snapping itself around his right calf. It pulled forward with incredible strength, jerking his leg up, upending the barbarian's body, so that for a moment he was suspended head down. The Cimmerian's sword leapt into his hands, making a flashing arc that slashed through the hard, ridged arm and dropped him to the sand.

Heng Shih's hands caught Zelandra's waist and tossed her forcefully back. She stumbled out of range even as a tentacle curled around her bodyguard's torso. The emerald arm constricted, sinking sharply into Heng Shih's abdomen, drawing him in toward the hideous thing.

Conan sprang catlike up off the ground, ducking beneath one flailing tentacle as another struck him across neck and chest like a slavemaster's whip. He twisted away, stumbling in the sand, a line of dripping crimson bright on his bronzed throat.

The unnatural plant proceeded to pull itself out of the pool on its tangled carpet of roots while bone-white thorns began sprouting from the net of wrinkles on its swaying trunk. Wicked, needle-sharp spikes pushed into view, jutting the length of a man's hand. The unladen tentacles lengthened, whipping wildly about as the one gripping Heng Shih pulled steadily, tirelessly at him.

The Cimmerian lunged to his friend's aid. A questing tentacle writhed about the barbarian's left arm, biting into muscle and spoiling a stroke meant to free Heng Shih. The tentacle he had severed snaked clumsily between Conan's legs, seeking an ankle.

The Khitan's boots plowed twin furrows in the sandy soil as he was drawn irresistibly toward the thing. The tentacle sawed through his kimono and into his midsection, sending trickles of brilliant scarlet across golden silk. Clinging to the imprisoning appendage with one hand, Heng Shih managed to draw out his scimitar with the other.

The plant-thing, now well up onto the shore, gave a sudden heave on the tentacle grasping the Khitan. Heng Shih lost his footing and stumbled helplessly forward, toward the thing's body, which now bristled with dagger-like thorns. He made a desperate thrust with his scimitar and the point of his blade pierced the trunk's thick skin with a moist *crunch*. The Khitan's body jolted to a stop as he braced the pommel of the sword against his belly. To draw him closer, the monstrosity would be forced to drive his blade deeper into its own body. The length of his scimitar was all that kept Heng Shih from being pulled onto the murderous thorns.

Conan stomped the wounded tentacle into the sand while pulling against the horror gripping his arm. It jerked to and fro in a frenzy, confounding his efforts to hack himself free.

The ghastly thing kept inching forward, thick petals bobbing in the sunlight. Then it leaned back and gave another tremendous heave, nearly unbalancing Conan and driving half the length of Heng Shih's scimitar into its fibrous body. In the instant that it righted itself, the tension on its tentacles went slack and Conan moved. He staggered up to the abomination and, with a swift whirl of steel, struck off at the base the tentacle that gripped his arm. The appendage released him and dropped, writhing in the sand like a maddened serpent. The wounded tentacle, freed from beneath Conan's boot, finally found the Cimmerian's ankle, just as the last free tentacle snapped around Heng Shih's chest and added its relentless pressure to that already drawing the Khitan onto the spiked trunk. The ridged arm around Conan's ankle constricted with savage force and wrenched the Cimmerian away from the creature he had wounded. Conan fell heavily on his side and was pulled away, cursing and struggling.

Heng Shih's face was fixed in a grimace of agony as he bore up under the monstrous pressure exerted by the remorseless tentacles. His hands were white on the hilt of his sword, clinging doggedly to the only thing that kept him from embracing the nightmare plant's spined trunk. The pommel of his scimitar thrust painfully against his belly even as his blade slid an inch deeper into the monster's dense, wooden flesh.

Then a knife hurtled from nowhere, thudding into the horror's emerald trunk a handbreadth from Heng Shih's face. Neesa's aim was as true as ever, but if the sorcerous abomination perceived her marksmanship, it gave no sign.

The tentacle dragging Conan away from the fray suddenly released him and flew back to whip with vicious force around Heng Shih's shoulders. The breath was driven from the Khitan's lungs. The plant-thing was willfully impaling itself upon his blade in order to draw him to it. Heng Shih's scimitar was slowly being driven hilt-deep into its trunk, and now he held himself mere inches above the hungry thorns.

The Cimmerian leapt up and sprang back into the fray. Skidding to a halt in the damp sand, he braced his feet and delivered a terrific roundhouse cut to the plant-thing's body, hewing almost a third of the way through the trunk like a woodsman chopping a tree.

Colorless fluid gushed from the yawning wound, spraying Conan's arms and face. Its blood was cool and, where it touched the barbarian's lips, tasteless. It was water. Realization translated into instantaneous action. Conan hurled himself away from the thing even as the wounded tentacle released its grip on Heng Shih and darted toward the Cimmerian's legs with terrible speed. It dodged over his low slash with unnatural agility and wrapped itself around his throat. The tentacle drew taut and clenched furiously, instantly cutting off Conan's breath, wrenching him from his feet and dragging him, struggling, across the ground. A choked cry of pain and fury tore from the Cimmerian's throat as his body slid across the sand toward the waiting, wicked thorns. His free hand clutched at the tentacle encircling his throat, prying the cruelly ridged thing from his windpipe, while his sword hand whipped up and down in a convulsive surge of raw strength. The blade hewed through the oppressive arm, freeing him. Rolling, tearing the severed length of tentacle from his neck, Conan scrambled over the ground with the desperate speed of a wounded panther. The barbarian slid to a stop behind the obscene thing as four new tentacles erupted from its body.

From among the writhing nest of roots that formed the abomination's base came a thick cable as black and shiny as oiled leather. It was as big around as a man's thigh and led back across the sunbaked sand into the pool.

As the four new tentacles shot toward him, Conan rose on his knees, lifted his scimitar above his head, and slashed downward with all the remaining power in his body. The blade tore through the black cable and buried itself in the dry earth. Water burst from the sundered taproot like blood from a riven heart.

The plant-thing shuddered, the veins webbing its spiked trunk ceased throbbing, and its tentacles fell limply to the sand. It settled down heavily upon its bed of roots and then toppled sideways with slow grace, like a hewn tree. Its green skin was suddenly thick with dew, water running from its fallen trunk. It shriveled, giving up to the thirsting sand the water that had lent it life.

Heng Shih stood glassy-eyed where it had released him, bands of blood running freely down his torso. He staggered two unsteady steps away from the dead thing and collapsed onto the sand. The breath came loudly from his gaping mouth, and his shaven skull glistened with sweat.

Conan clambered over the corpse of the plant-thing, avoiding the sagging thorns, and fetched it a kick in its flowered crown. The drooping petals burst under his boot's impact, spattering water and vegetable pulp. He looked to Zelandra, who knelt beside Heng Shih, ministering to his wounds.

"I trust that was one of Ethram-Fal's guards," he said, tugging at his torn and bloodied shirt.

"Of course," said Zelandra absently, her attention on her bodyguard, who stared ahead stoically as she daubed at the wound that encircled his midriff. "That was a piece of work befitting a sorcerer dedicated to the magic of plants." She nodded at the toppled abomination, where it lay slowly dissolving into the sand. "A hell of an achievement, actually.

The Emerald Lotus must have improved his abilities by no small amount."

"Crom," grunted the barbarian, peeling off his shirt and standing in his tarnished mail. "So we can expect to meet more of his creations?"

"Little doubt of it. I'm fairly certain that he can only send forth his projected self to places that he has already been in the flesh. Even so, I imagine he has paid at least one more visit to my house, found me gone, and drawn his own conclusions. It shouldn't take a great deal of wit to figure that I'm coming for him and his lotus."

The Cimmerian wondered if she felt equal to the task of battling such an accomplished sorcerer. He wondered how she felt about closing in on a powerful enemy who was probably aware of her approach. He wondered, but said nothing.

Neesa dabbed at the gash across his neck and collarbone with a cloth she had dampened in the pool. He let her swab at it and the deeper incision about his left biceps, then pulled away.

"Ymir, woman, I've been hurt worse by a hangover. Help Zelandra tend to Heng Shih before his hide is bled white. I'll gather tinder for a fire and pitch the tents."

By the time that the sun had fallen below the western horizon, a tidy camp of three tents had been set up and a frugal meal of dried beef, hard bread, and oasis water had been served.

The campfire crackled, radiating a pleasant warmth onto sands now chill with the coming of night. Beyond the flaring glow of the fire and the dark ring of undergrowth, the desert receded in waves of sand, black and silver by moonlight, like a frozen sea. The slender scimitar of a quarter moon rode high in the heavens, skirting the icy torrent of the Milky Way.

"I'll take the first watch," said Conan, squatting beside the dying fire. Heng Shih nodded in gratitude as he rose with care from his seat and moved slowly toward his tent. Zelandra pulled her kettle from the red-orange coals and poured herself some tea.

The gentle aroma of jasmine rose with the steam from her cup. Neesa's head lay comfortably upon the Cimmerian's shoulder, his arm about her trim waist.

A thin cry echoed through the desert night, diminished by distance and quickly fading. Neesa's body tensed against Conan's.

"What was that?" she whispered uneasily.

"A jackal," grunted the barbarian.

"Perhaps the Yizil," said Zelandra, blowing across the top of her teacup. Firelight turned her eyes to flame.

"Yizil?" asked Neesa, now sitting up stiffly.

"Desert ghouls," said Conan. "Haunters of ruins and gnawers of bones. They shun the open desert."

"Do they?" Neesa's eyes probed the darkness beyond the campfire's glow. Conan laughed gustily.

"They do. Go to bed. I promise that if any Yizil come by, I shall feed them to their brethren."

Neesa got to her feet and sidled reluctantly toward the Cimmerian's tent. "Now I shan't sleep until you join me."

Conan watched her disappear through the flap and frowned across the fire at Zelandra. "Did you have to tell her that? You know that the Yizil are no danger here."

Zelandra grinned at him. She lifted her hands in an innocent shrug and nodded toward his tent.

"You should thank me," she said, and Conan smiled back at her.

"Seriously, my friend." Her voice grew softer as she continued. "I am concerned that we encountered a creature of Ethram-Fal's at such a distance from his lair."

"It is not such a distance. When we were atop the great sand dune beside this oasis, I could see the Dragon's Spine."

"Ishtar," she breathed. "So swiftly? You are truly a fine guide, Conan."

"Well," said the Cimmerian gruffly, "we aren't there yet. We must travel southeast into the foothills surrounding the Dragon's

Spine in order to approach it from the angle we saw in Ethram-Fal's sorcerous projection. Tomorrow we should get close enough to tell whether I am a good guide or not."

Zelandra nodded and Conan rose, dusted himself off, and went to walk the perimeter.

In a short time, he alone was awake, moving restlessly about the camp as silent as a shadow, disappearing in one direction to reappear in a few moments from another, memorizing the contours of the waste around them.

Conan stood watch, while overhead the moon rose, the stars wheeled, and a flight of meteors slashed the sky with fire.

27

The desert floor rose gradually, lifting into the rough uplands of rugged rock that held, somewhere in their labyrinthine vastness, the sculpted ridge that was the Dragon's Spine. The seemingly endless ocean of ochre dunes gave way to low hillocks of crumbling soil that gave way in turn to a new wilderness of stone outcrops and towers. Here the surface of the earth had buckled up, as though from unthinkable pressures within, shedding its skin of soil and baring raw and naked bones of mineral.

The party moved with excruciating slowness through this tortuous landscape. High up on the ragged rim of a ridge, Conan pointed off to the east, where the distinct and regular shape of the Dragon's Spine lay shimmering in the distance. From the lofty ridge they descended into even worse terrain—a literal maze of canyons and ravines that split the earth like cracks in the sunbaked bottom of a dry riverbed.

The weary quartet advanced and then retreated down narrow defiles that wound promisingly in the right direction, only to end abruptly in a vertical wall. Canyons that began as broad and as easy to traverse as the Caravan Road shrank along their length until the body of an unmounted man could not squeeze through.

Any passage they took initially seemed to lead in the direction that they sought, only to bend or double back until the travelers were riding away from their goal. Time and again the Cimmerian dismounted and climbed to a high vantage point in order to get his bearings. Agile as an ape, he would clamber up a rock wall or scale a stony spire to get a fix on the Dragon's Spine. The party would wait in dogged silence for him to return and order that they turn around, return to a fork, retry a passage that led in the wrong direction, or simply continue along the path that they were on.

It was well into the afternoon when they emerged from the mouth of a narrow gorge into a wide clearing that lay open to the sky. Passing from the cool shadows cast by rock walls into the golden glare of the sun, the party squinted, shaded their eyes, and looked about. The clearing formed an irregular hub into which three small canyons opened.

Off to the left, a slender cleft ran away to the northeast, its walls rising swiftly and sharply from the floor of the clearing into a high series of jagged pinnacles. To the right a larger defile dropped rapidly away to the southwest, its flattened path strewn with gravel and bracketed by low walls of broken stone. Directly in front of them the ground rose up into a worn hill of eroded rock, obscuring the opposite side of the clearing from view.

To the surprise of all, Conan nudged his camel to a trot and rode straight up the low hill before them. They followed in silence, having long since accepted the barbarian's guidance through this desert maze.

Heng Shih was as expressionless as ever, seemingly unperturbed by the bandaged wound that girdled his broad belly. Neesa rose nervously erect in her saddle, her eyes rarely leaving her mistress. The Lady Zelandra stared forward sightlessly, speaking only when spoken to and clutching the leather-wrapped box in her lap with both hands. She had made herself a turban and tucked her long, silver-shot hair inside it. Her face, sunburned and haggard, looked years older than it had only a few days before.

Once atop the hill, the party drew to a halt, their camels snuffling in gratitude. The far side of the hill descended steeply in a broad swath of loose stones and gravel. It fell away for many yards before ending abruptly at the edge of a precipitous cliff, where it apparently dropped away into an even lower canyon.

"There," said Conan, lifting a bare, bronzed arm. "The Dragon's Spine."

The party stared off to the northeast and saw that he was right. The saw-toothed formation was just visible over the walls of the canyon that opened on their left, and, for the first time, its alignment seemed correct. Its appearance closely matched their first view of it in the background of Ethram-Fal's sorcerous projection.

"At last," whispered the Lady Zelandra in a small, dry voice.

"We make camp here," said the Cimmerian. "I believe that narrow ravine will lead us to Ethram-Fal's lair, but I cannot be certain how distant it is."

"So there is something that you cannot do, barbarian?" said Zelandra. Her right hand crept up her ribs and pressed there as if stanching a wound. "I am astonished to hear you admit it. This is my expedition and I insist that we proceed down that canyon immediately. We have no time to make camp. We will close with Ethram-Fal and destroy him before this day is done."

"Zelandra," said Conan evenly, "the day is already nearly done. Darkness falls much swifter at the bottom of a canyon than it does in the open air. There are clouds on the western horizon that may bring a storm, and we have no way of knowing how much farther there is to travel. Moreover, you are tired, milady."

"Tired? You insolent fool. Even weary, I have strength enough to do what I must do. I say we go forward!" She wheeled upon her servants. "Would you follow this insubordinate savage instead of your mistress? I-I…" Her voice trailed off as her gaze passed over the concerned faces of Neesa and Heng Shih. Both of her hands clutched her torso as if they could unwind the bands of pain that tightened there. Tears glimmered in her dark eyes.

"Ah, sweet Ishtar's mercy," she said, her voice low and choked with shame. "I'm sorry, my friends. Our comrade Conan is right, we must camp here, for I am tired. So very tired."

Heng Shih seemed to appear at her camel's side. No one saw him dismount. His great hands gripped Zelandra gently about the waist, and plucked her from the saddle as lightly as if she were a mannequin of silk. He set her on her feet, swept the dirt from the top of a flattened stone, and motioned for her to sit. She did, pressing her face into her hands as though she could not bear to look upon her fellow travelers. Conan spoke again.

"Zelandra, after we set up camp, Heng Shih and I will scout down the narrow canyon. We will go as far as we can before nightfall. We may well find Ethram-Fal's hiding place. If all goes well, we will be planning our method of attack tonight and carrying it out tomorrow morning. Rest, be strong, and you shall have your revenge."

Zelandra nodded, taking her hands from her face but keeping her eyes lowered. The remainder of the party went about setting up camp.

Shortly, the three small tents were up, situated back and away from the hill's leading edge so that they would not be visible from any point in the clearing below. Conan forbade a fire, saying that they could have a cold supper whenever they hungered and that he wouldn't eat until he and Heng Shih returned from their scouting expedition. He balanced this unhappy news by breaking out one of the party's few bottles of wine and passing it around. Looking drawn and shaken, Zelandra took a token sip before retiring to her tent. As soon as she was out of earshot, the Cimmerian turned to Neesa.

"Has she used the last of her lotus?"

"No. I know that she has more, though I'm not certain how much. She does not want to use it. Not even the tiny bit that would ease her pain. She fears that if she does, her resolve will weaken and she will take too much—or all of it. She grows desperate. I'm sorry, Conan. You know that she meant you no insult, do you not?"

"Her words do not concern me; her actions do. Will she be strong enough to face the Stygian sorcerer when we finally find him?"

Neesa raised her pale hands in a helpless shrug. "How can I say? I think that she plans to use the last of the lotus to strengthen herself just before engaging Ethram-Fal. It really does seem to empower her sorcery. She took some just before sending the flame-wall against those bandits."

"She goes to battle with a wizard who claims to have an unlimited supply of the cursed drug. I wonder what manner of sorcery he will send against us."

To this Neesa made no reply. At her side, Heng Shih leaned forward and his hands made a series of deliberate motions in the air before him.

Conan looked to Neesa questioningly.

"He asks if you wish to leave. He says that he will hold no grudge against you if you do."

"Hell." Conan grinned wolfishly, tossing back his black mane. "I promised Zelandra my services, and will not back out now just because it's getting interesting."

The slightest trace of a smile came to the Khitan's lips and he extended his hand, offering the Cimmerian the wine bottle. Conan accepted it, threw back his head, and took a long pull, his throat working as he swallowed.

"Ah," he sighed with satisfaction. "That is a passing good wine. Come now, let us dig out this scorpion's nest. Neesa, you must keep watch on the mouths of the canyons. I doubt very much that anyone will come out of the other two, but watch them anyway. If anyone but Heng Shih and I come out of the one that we're heading into, that means we're probably dead. Keep low and awaken Zelandra. If intruders are about to discover you, flee. If you can't win free, kill as many as you can, however you can. Scream like the devil, and if Heng Shih and I still live, we'll hear you, for sound carries very far in this waste. If we can, we'll come to your aid or at least avenge you. Stay alert."

With that the Cimmerian threw an arm around the woman's waist and drew her to him. While they kissed with undisguised passion, Heng Shih fell to studying the sky. He noted that there was indeed a dark mass of clouds swelling on the western horizon. He had time to observe it quite closely before Conan clapped him on the shoulder.

"Come on, man, the day grows old."

The two men scuffled down the rocky slope and strode purposefully toward the dark slash of the canyon's mouth. Neesa dropped to a crouch at the crest of the hill's rise, nestling into the shadow of a boulder and wiping tingling lips with the back of a hand. As Conan and Heng Shih stepped into the narrow gap and disappeared from sight, she became conscious of a painful lump in her throat and cursed herself softly for a weakling. She reached back into the loose froth of her black hair and pulled the throwing dagger from her nape sheath. She thrust it into the hard ground before her and settled down to wait.

28

The red sun, bloated and sullen, lay impaled upon the sharp and broken ridges to the west when the thing that had been Gulbanda of Shem came to a halt.

He was a ragged figure now, his garments tattered and stained. His hands, face, and beard were caked with ochre grime that he had made no effort to wipe away. Eyes as glassy and expressionless as chips of black quartz peered into the dim canyon mouth that opened before him.

Gulbanda had been walking for a night and a day without cease. The nearly fresh horse that he had taken from Nath, the archer, had been ridden relentlessly until it collapsed beneath him. Then he had walked, heedless of the killing sun, moving onward because it was all that he was capable of doing.

Now Gulbanda stopped and stared into the impenetrable darkness. A breeze, cool as a spring, blew from within the canyon and stirred his torn cloak.

He felt the pull deep inside his breast. Deep, where Shakar the Keshanian had stabbed to his core. It was as though a strong fist had closed about his pierced and withered heart and pulled steadily upon it in the direction that he must go. The necromantic sorcery that kept Gulbanda moving among the living also gave him his unerring sense of direction.

Standing as silent and motionless as his stone surroundings, Gulbanda searched what remained of his memories. They were vague tatters now, like wisps of dank fog fading on the chill wind of approaching night.

He remembered a dark room and a man bound to a steel chair.

He remembered a dagger sliding over the corded muscles of that man's forearm.

He remembered his sword flying from his fist.

Gulbanda lifted his sword hand and studied the dry stumps of two fingers. The black-haired Cimmerian. It was he who was responsible for all of this. It was he whose blood burned and pulled so deeply within Gulbanda's breast, drawing him onward with an irresistible compulsion that could end only with the barbarian's death. Zelandra's death. The acquisition of the silver box that Shakar craved so terribly.

Shakar the Keshanian… Gulbanda remembered his master, though only as an imperious face making difficult demands of him. He must do the things that Shakar had asked of him so long ago. He would please Shakar and the sorcerer would help him.

How could he help him? Gulbanda groped among the shattered shards of his memory. He lowered his head, the only sign of the torment that surged within as he strove to grasp some small part of his vanished humanity and felt the ceaseless, tidal pull of Conan's blood drawing him forward and away.

Gulbanda remembered, and raised his head. If he did as Shakar wished, then the sorcerer would make the pulling in his breast cease and let him die. That was all that had to be done. If he killed the black-haired barbarian and the sorceress and got the silver box, then he would be allowed to die. There was nothing in all the world to desire except death.

The thing that had been a man and a warrior closed its dead eyes for the first time in days. Gulbanda saw his strong hands falling upon the Cimmerian, rending his flesh and breaking his limbs. He heard the barbarian's bones crack and his agonized cry of defeat.

Death was a most glorious reward for such a slight and agreeable service.

Gulbanda stalked into the canyon and was swallowed by darkness.

29

The canyon walls rose to either side of the two men, hemming them into a defile not ten paces across. Heng Shih fought a moment's claustrophobia as they passed from the open clearing into the shadowy, enclosed space of the narrow cleft.

The first thing he became aware of was the silence. When riding with the party, the desolate and deserted landscape seemed invested with their life and movement. Their speech and the steady sounds of their passage obscured the awesome silence of the wasteland. Walking with quiet caution behind the barbarian, whose catlike tread seemed not to disturb so much as a pebble, the full weight of the desert's silent emptiness seemed to bear down upon him. The only sound was the occasional rising of the wind, moaning like a ghost through the maze of canyons.

Heng Shih shook his bald head in a deliberate effort to rid himself of such useless thoughts. They were approaching the stronghold of an enemy.

They walked for almost an hour. The ridged walls of the narrow canyon rose slowly until they loomed at five times the height of a man. The path continued straight and the floor fairly even, cluttered only by the occasional pile of stone and sand that marked the site of a rock fall. As they stepped carefully about the base of one of these irregular heaps of debris, the sun broke free of the clouds on the western horizon and spilled its long rays across the empty desert. The stone passageway was immediately filled with a strange roseate illumination. Heng Shih looked about in wonder. The Cimmerian paid no heed, realizing that the sun's last light was rebounding from the red rock walls, tinting the cooling air with a lurid glow.

Conan raised his hand to signal a halt, and the Khitan shouldered up next to him. Ahead, the walls drew together as the canyon bent, turning sharply to the east. The Cimmerian lowered himself into a crouch and drew his scimitar, which in the ruddy light seemed dipped in blood.

Heng Shih left his weapon in its sheath, but bent down beside his leader.

"That," whispered Conan, gesturing with his bared sword, "is a fine place for a sentry. Or an ambush."

Heng Shih nodded to show that he understood, but the Cimmerian was already moving forward. He clung to the shadows at the base of the canyon wall, as silent as smoke on the desert wind. The Khitan followed, slowed by his desire to match Conan's stealth. The red glow of sunset faded abruptly, plunging the canyon into a murky gray twilight.

At the corner the barbarian drew up short, listening. Placing a palm on the cool stone of the canyon wall, he dropped to one knee and peered carefully around the bend. He stared ahead for a moment, then looked back at Heng Shih, who was still advancing with careful steps. When the big Khitan was finally at his side, he sheathed his sword and spoke softly.

"We have found it. Take a look." With that, Conan stood and leapt nimbly across the open bend in the passage. He lit soundlessly in the shadow of an ancient rock fall, crouched, and continued his judicious examination of whatever lay around the canyon's corner.

Heng Shih swallowed heavily, went to his knees, and slowly leaned forward until he could see around the bend. His eyes widened in amazement.

Ahead, the narrow canyon continued for another six or eight paces before lowering slightly and opening out into a broad, extended cul-de-sac. Hemmed by sheer walls, the canyon ended in a wide clearing with a floor as smooth and level as the courtyard of a castle. In the clearing's center, not twenty paces away, two men lingered about a circular pit. One squatted beside it, holding his hands toward it as if to warm himself. The other leaned upon a spear, regarding his companion and speaking in low tones. Each wore the gleaming mail and fine silk of a Stygian mercenary. Shortswords hung at their belts and their heads were protected by caps of steel.

But it was what lay beyond the sentries that captured the attention of the intruders and had them agape in the concealing shadows. Another twenty paces beyond the smoldering firepit rose the rear wall of the box canyon, and it was carved into the likeness of a great I facade. Twilight had begun to purple the sky above the clearing and the brilliant pinpoints of the first stars were just flickering into life, but there was still enough daylight to see the wonder that was the Palace of Cetriss.

A row of four massive pillars, each as great in girth as the mightiest tree, reached up from their roots in wide bases set into the clearing's floor to support the overhanging lip of the canyon rim high above.

Though obviously cut directly out of the cliff face, each pillar stood independently. An open black doorway was set between the two central pillars, and a broad flight of stairs descended from the ominous portal to the floor of the natural courtyard. Even at a distance and in the dying light, the carvings that surrounded the frame of the doorway appeared elaborate and passing strange. Spread out above the dark opening was a row of three equally dark windows, each bracketed with worn carvings similar to those that adorned the portal. A second row of open windows was arrayed above that, close to the tops of the towering pillars and the carved crest of the canyon rim.

Conan shivered in the cooling breeze. The palace had at least three stories and had been sculpted from living rock, a feat that would have astounded even the pyramid-building Stygians. Crom alone knew how deeply its halls and chambers bored into the desert's stony breast. Facing them in the deepening twilight, it projected an overpowering aura of unthinkable age and implacable purpose.

The Cimmerian's blue eyes burned upon the open doorway, narrowing in thought. There was no door or gate that he could discern, though he couldn't rule out some sort of sorcerous barrier. Even without any kind of closure, the passage could be held by very few men against a much more formidable force than the Lady Zelandra's little party. His gaze lifted to the open windows arrayed above the door, and then up to the second row of windows. He frowned as the voices of the sentries around the firepit rose in argument.

"So now we freeze?" demanded the fellow squatting beside the pit. "Why should we be forbidden fires without as well as within the palace? A late watch without hot mulled wine will be a pain in the arse. Come on, the last embers are almost out. Let me add a stick of firewood. No one will be the wiser."

"Hush," said the soldier who stood leaning upon his spear. "Don't be an idiot. Ath said there are to be no fires. The master obviously wishes to avoid showing our location to intruders."

"Intruders? Bah! Who would venture into this hellish land? And how would they find us if they did? I tell you, the master's gone soft in the head."

The spear carrier recoiled at this, shooting a glance at the darkened door of the palace. "Quiet, you fool! If the master hears you talking like that, you'll feed the lotus."

The other went silent, staring glumly into the fire pit. He drew a small, dried branch from beneath his silken cloak and thrust it down into the pit, working it into the ashes there.

"That will keep the coals alive," he said in sullen tones. "You'll thank me after I've made the mulled wine."

"If it starts to smoke, I'll put it out with your blood," replied the other curtly.

Conan leapt silently back across the canyon floor, landing on all fours beside Heng Shih, who twitched in surprise. He had a tense moment, wondering if the guards had spotted the barbarian, but there was no outcry. Even if they had glanced his way, the Cimmerian had been merely a shadow moving among shadows. He laid a hard hand upon the Khitan's shoulder.

"Come, let us return to camp."

The return journey along the darkening canyon seemed swifter and easier to Heng Shih. Conan was able to recall every irregularity in the path and led his companion as surely as though he had traversed its length a dozen times. As they drew close to camp, Heng Shih began to relax and stepped up his pace to walk beside the Cimmerian. He had been doing this for only a moment when Conan drew to a sudden stop. The Khitan stumbled to a halt, staring at the barbarian without comprehension. Lifting his face and flaring his nostrils, Conan leaned into the gentle breeze, while Heng Shih looked on in amazement. He reached out a hand to tap the Cimmerian's shoulder, but drew back when the barbarian shot a glance at him and spoke.

"They've built a fire."

Heng Shih's head snapped up, searching the slender slash of cobalt sky that was visible between the canyon's walls. No smoke trail could be seen there. When he lowered his gaze, he saw that Conan had started toward the camp at a dead run. Heng Shih took off in pursuit, wincing as the slap of his sandals on the rocky path was magnified and hurled back at him by the stone walls.

30

Ethram-Fal lay asleep and dreaming, and in his dream he knew fear.

In his dream he strode across a floor of black marble through pale and densely swirling mists. In his dream, it seemed to him that he had been walking for an eternity without encountering anything save the silent mist that moved and roiled without the benefit of a wind to stir it.

Then there arose in Ethram-Fal the absolute certainty that he was not alone in the limitless fog and that something was lurking ahead of him, just out of sight. Along with this certainty came an overpowering dread. Whatever it was that concealed itself in the mists, the Stygian did not wish to encounter it. Ethram-Fal abruptly changed the direction of his steps, swinging to the right and hastening forward.

Almost immediately he felt the foreboding presence once again, and this time a huge and shapeless shadow darkened the fog before him. He came to a fearful stop, his breath going ragged in his throat, then spun around and ran in the opposite direction.

In his dream Ethram-Fal had not taken a dozen steps in wild flight before the dark presence came out of the mist, in front of him yet again, as though his desperate drive to escape had only brought him nearer to that which he wished above all to avoid.

It was the idol of Cetriss's temple. The nameless, faceless sphinx of black stone lounged before him so that he ran full between its outstretched paws before sliding to a frantic halt. It was motionless, a thing of carved stone that appeared rooted to the mist-blanketed floor, yet it menaced the Stygian in a way that nothing in his life had ever done. He fell to his knees, his heart swelling painfully in his breast until crying out was impossible. Above him, the smoothly featureless face of the god blurred, losing its glossy sheen and becoming an even darker space: a black portal opening out upon a measureless void.

Ethram-Fal writhed on the marble floor before the god of Cetriss and found his voice. He begged for mercy in raw, shrill tones.

"Tribute," came a sourceless whisper, chill as the gulfs between the stars. "Sacrifice."

"Yes!" screamed the cowering sorcerer. "Yes! All that you desire!"

"Tribute," came the voice again, passionless as the wind. "Sacrifice."

Pain lanced through the Stygian's consciousness and suddenly the black sphinx was gone. Somehow there was a knotted rope around his chest, and someone was pulling cruelly upon it, tightening it until it dug into his ribs. He clutched at the rope, drawing a cramped breath and wincing at the stabbing sensation it produced. He looked ahead through tear-blinded eyes and saw that the rope's end was held by the Lady Zelandra. As he watched, she jerked brutally upon it, causing the cord to bite even deeper into his flesh. Her face was an expressionless mask. Ethram-Fal tore at the binding rope with both hands and cursed her.

"Release me, damn you! You are my slave! Release me!"

The Stygian sorcerer snapped awake, prone upon the floor of his laboratory. He was unsure if he had cried out loud.

It took him more than a moment to orient himself. He lifted his face from the cool and dusty stone of the floor. One of his arms was outstretched, the gray sleeve of his robe drawn back almost to his shoulder. He sat up stiffly and looked about himself with rheumy eyes.

He was alone in the room. How long had he lain here? What had he been doing? The muscles of his torso seemed to have been strained somehow. A tight belt of pain throbbed intermittently about his chest. That explained the dream, he thought, or part of it anyway. He lifted a hand to rub his brow and noticed with a start that there was a wound on the inside of his left forearm. He studied it in alarmed amazement.

An open gash about two inches long parted the flesh bloodlessly, resembling nothing so much as a cut in a piece of cooked pork.

Ethram-Fal put his right hand over the wound and stood up with careful deliberation. He leaned heavily against the table closest to him, saw what lay upon it, and immediately remembered everything.

Lying open upon the table was his long, ebony box of Emerald Lotus powder. Beside it, shining dully in the yellow radiance of the light-globes, was his irregularly shaped dagger. He could recall it all now. He had slashed the flesh of his arm in order to pour raw lotus powder into his blood. There was no lotus in or around the wound, so he imagined that he had collapsed immediately after cutting himself.

He felt as though he had just recovered from a long and debilitating illness. What in Set's name had he been doing? Though groggy, Ethram-Fal realized that he was thinking clearly for the first time in many days. He could not remember when he had last eaten or slept. All he had consumed was wine leavened with larger and larger portions of Emerald Lotus. Somehow his measured intake of the drug had become a thoughtless binge that only ended when it had endangered his life.

Ethram-Fal bandaged his forearm and thought dark thoughts.

When had his control over the lotus flagged? How long had he gone without taking any steps toward the completion of his grand design? He had done little but immerse himself in his newfound power when he should have been using it productively. He needed systematic harvesting, so that he would have enough lotus to snare the wizards of Stygia into his service. He needed to prepare more traps, in case the Lady Zelandra had found some way of locating him and came seeking vengeance.

"Thoughtless," he hissed to himself, jerking the bandage tight around his arm.

That was all over now, he thought. He had known that the lotus was powerful, but he had been incautious and allowed himself to indulge in it without control. It must be used like a tool, he reasoned. He was its master and not the other way around.

Now he must check on the health of the lotus in its chamber and muster his mercenaries. He would discretely ask Ath how long it had been since he had last seen him, and warn the soldiers about possible intruders.

Snatching a blue velvet sack full of kaokao leaves from a nearby table, Ethram-Fal started for the door—then came to an uncertain stop. The ring of pain around his breast flickered into being once again, constricting his breathing. What was it? Had he contracted some disease while lying unconscious on the cold stone floor?

A memory came unbidden to the Stygian. It was the memory of Shakar the Keshanian standing wild-eyed in his chambers, making threats that he was too weak and foolish to back up, claiming that his chest was gripped in a vise of fire.

Ethram-Fal turned and looked back upon his ebony box of lotus powder.

He wondered how long he had remained unconscious, and if it was possible that his body was already suffering for want of the drug. He squinted at the box, rubbing at his ribs with a cold hand. Surely a little dose would do him no harm. He need not overindulge.

"Milord!" Ath's voice came echoing hollowly down the stone corridor. "Milord, we have cornered it!"

Footfalls thudded outside the room; then the tall mercenary pushed through the blanket that hung over the doorway and confronted his employer. He hesitated a moment, staring and obviously trying to find his voice. Ethram-Fal became aware of his wrinkled and dusty robes.

"Forgive me for disturbing you," said Ath finally, "but we have cornered the intruder in the room of the great statue. It attacked the guards, knocking one senseless and dragging the other into the temple. He won free, crying out so loudly that he woke us all. Come quickly, I fear that it will try to escape and the men will be forced to slay it."

"It?" said Ethram-Fal. His captain nodded vigorously, starting to back out the door.

"It is not a man. Come quickly and see for yourself." The soldier waited in the doorway, holding the blanket to one side, looking to his motionless lord.

"Go," murmured the sorcerer. "I'll follow presently."

"But—" began Ath.

"Go!" shouted Ethram-Fal, and his mercenary disappeared through the blanket and hurried away.

The Stygian turned and walked purposefully to the table with the ebony box. He used three fingers to scoop a mouthful of deep green power from the box to his lips. Shudders coursed through his thin body and the ring of pain around his chest evaporated. He threw back his head in pleasure, sucking the last of the lotus from his fingertips. A surge of bright energy radiated along every nerve. His mind raced, borne up on a crest of superhuman confidence. He passed through the door and down the corridors of the palace in a haze of ecstasy. He muttered a brief incantation and his feet lifted up and away from the floor, so that he floated effortlessly along the hallway as quickly as a man could run. A slack grin spread across his wizened features. The spell of levitation usually took hours of preparation. With sudden, shocking clarity, he realized what a fool he was to doubt himself or his lotus. He was in control and there was nothing that he could not do, no spell that he could not conjure, no foe that he could not overcome.

As he drew near to the temple of the great sphinx, he allowed himself to slow somewhat. Passing around a corner, the armored backs of four of his mercenaries came into view. The men were crowded into one of the doorways of the temple. They held naked swords and were intent upon whatever lay before them.

"Your pardon," he said with gentle sarcasm, and the little crowd parted in dumbstruck astonishment to let him pass.

Once inside the great chamber, he banished the spell of levitation, allowing himself to settle down to the floor. Each of the huge, circular room's three doors was filled with armed men, and each group held aloft a number of brightly glowing light-globes, so that the chamber was well illuminated despite its size. Only the high ceiling remained unlit, arching up into a darkness like that of a starless night.

Standing before the black bulk of the statue was a pale man-like form: it stood fidgeting in front of the flat altar set between the extended paws of the faceless sphinx. Ethram-Fal walked a little closer, stopped, and marveled.

It was naked and shrunken, shorter even than he, but it had the appearance of animal strength. Tendons were wound like wires around its stark limbs. Hunched like a baboon, its skin was the color of the desert, hanging on its emaciated frame in reptilian folds. It twisted long, tapering fingers together, and the dirty talons clicked one against the other. Its brow receded sharply in bony furrows above the lambent yellow glow of its eyes. The nose was little more than two small pits above the lipless mouth, which opened and closed in quick, bestial pants, revealing a pointed, serpentine tongue.

"Iä Nyarlathotep," it whined.

"Holy Set!" Ethram-Fal was amazed. "It speaks!"

The soldiers at the doors stirred, murmuring to one another. The creature flinched at this, drawing back toward the statue that loomed behind it, as if seeking protection. It spoke again, and though it sounded much as though a python or some other great reptile were attempting human speech, Ethram-Fal found that he understood the words.

It was speaking an archaic version of his own tongue. It was speaking in Old Stygian.

"You die for Nyarlathotep." Needle talons stroked the air and its eyes burned brighter.

Ethram-Fal spoke haltingly in Old Stygian. "You make sacrifice?"

It bobbed its head, birdlike.

"Yes. Yes. Antelope. Scorpion. Man. Man best. You die for Nyarlathotep."

"Die for that?" The sorcerer gestured at the silent statue. The creature looked back and bobbed its head again, pressing long hands reverently to its ridged and reptilian breast.

"Yes! Iä Nyarlathotep." It took a hesitant, shuffling step toward Ethram-Fal, who seemed to pay it no heed.

"Why?"

"Live!" Its thin voice rose. "So I live! So Cetriss lives! You die for Nyarlathotep!" Quivering, it lunged toward the sorcerer, claws reaching for his breast and the heart that beat within. A cry arose from the massed mercenaries and they started forward, but Ethram-Fal halted the creature by merely raising a hand. It lurched to a stop not two paces away from the wizard, who held one palm out toward the thing. He crooked his fingers as if gripping something transparent in the air before him. The creature writhed in invisible bonds, held in place by sorcery.

"This is your immortality?" cried Ethram-Fal. "O Cetriss, mighty necromancer, did you abandon all your powers to live forever as a beast enslaved to a statue?" The sorcerer's face twisted in transcendent rage and his fingers clenched in a loose fist. The desert ghoul that was the mage Cetriss snarled mindlessly as it was lifted, writhing, off the floor.

"I followed you! I thought you a hero! You are a disgrace! You die for Nyarlathotep!" Cetriss's body lifted farther into the air and moved slowly backward until it hovered above the altar that lay waiting between its god's paws.

"Tribute!" screamed Ethram-Fal. "Sacrifice!" He clenched his fist and crushed Cetriss. The bones of the last survivor of Old Stygia broke like dry kindling and his blood spilled down upon the altar in a dark rain. Ethram-Fal gave his fist a last convulsive shake and let the broken body fall. It lay, twisted in upon itself, a discarded bit of offal that had once been one of the world's mightiest sorcerers. For the briefest instant the Stygian thought that he saw a ghostly tendril, a stream of pallid vapor, rising from the body of Cetriss and funneling into the black face of his god. He blinked. It was nothing.

The Stygian turned away from the corpse in disgust and saw that his soldiers were standing uncertainly about the doorways and regarding him with a mixture of astonishment and fear. This pleased the sorcerer.

"Ath," he called, bringing the captain jogging forward out of the cluster of men in the east door.

"Most impressive, milord," said Ath when he stood before his master.

The sorcerer pulled the blue velvet sack of kaokao leaves from his belt and tossed it to Ath, who caught it neatly in one hand.

"Excellent work, Ath. Distribute these among the men. Every

man should get one. You may keep all that remain." The tall captain nodded in grateful enthusiasm as Ethram-Fal raised his hands above his head and addressed the rest of his mercenaries.

"I am most pleased with your efficiency. Captain Ath has a reward for each of you. However, I wish to encourage the sentries to even greater vigilance, as I suspect that we may soon encounter other, more human, foes. I have reason to suspect that a sorceress may essay an attack on our palace. Capture her alive for me and I shall be greatly pleased."

The soldiers clapped naked swords against their shields and cheered in loyalty and anticipation of their reward of kaokao leaves. When Ethram-Fal turned away, they came forward and gathered swiftly around Ath, hands extended for their bounty. Ath, grinning widely, passed out the leaves as quickly as he could.

As the sorcerer reached the north doorway, a spontaneous cheer rose behind him. When he turned to acknowledge it, the cheer swelled twice more. He lifted a hand in a languid wave, smiling beneficently upon his men as he basked in their approval. The men were his. The Emerald Lotus was his. And now the mantle of Cetriss was his. How could anything stop him now?

A shout cut through the dwindling applause. A single soldier had run into the temple and now stood waving his arms and yelling for attention. Ethram-Fal frowned.

"Silence! Hear me!" The soldier's hands dropped to his sides as the gathering went silent and all eyes fell upon him.

"And where have you been, Phandoros?" came a voice from among the milling mercenaries.

"Captain Ath sent me to sentry duty when the beast was cornered," began the man defensively. "I come to tell the master that I saw a column of smoke to the southwest. There are intruders in the canyons."

31

When Heng Shih emerged into the clearing, he saw that Conan was already atop the hill. The Khitan broke into a sprint, his heavyset form shooting over the ground with surprising speed. Chest heaving, he reached the little grouping of tents just in time to see the Cimmerian kicking dirt over a small fire. Zelandra stood to one side, clutching her teapot and scowling at Conan with exaggerated disgust. Neesa squatted in front of one of the tents, rubbing at her brow in a gesture at once weary and frustrated.

Conan finished burying the fire and commenced packing the soil down upon it with the heel of his boot.

"I trust that you're satisfied now?" Zelandra's voice was so strange that both Heng Shih and Neesa looked at her in surprise. It was thin and rasped in her throat like a file.

"You may have given away our position for a cup of tea," said Conan without expression.

"I need my strength," said Zelandra loudly. "I need the tea to help me rest." She brandished the teapot to emphasize her point. Her left arm was held rigidly across her stomach, gripping her ribs.

Conan looked up into the freshly dark evening sky. The air was strangely still, the sky pellucid and speckled with stars except where the swelling clouds massed to the west.

"We should move the camp." He turned to Heng Shih. "Those guards seemed inattentive, but the smoke would have been easily seen had they but looked around."

"Guards?" Zelandra looked from the Cimmerian to the Khitan and back again. "You found Ethram-Fal's hiding place?"

"Yes, my lady. It is less than two leagues distant. If your smoke was spotted, they could have an armed party here any time now."

"Heng Shih! Was it a palace?" The voice of the sorceress quavered with desperate energy. Her bodyguard's hands passed through a number of signs. The movements were concise and measured, his face betraying no emotion.

"Yes!" cried Zelandra exultantly. "Just as the legends would have it! We attack first thing tomorrow morning. I'll teach that withered fool to trifle with me. I'll walk into his parlor and tear his bloody heart out!"

"This is madness," said Conan flatly. "We must move the camp. We could be set upon at any time."

"Be silent, barbarian. The fire lasted only a moment. I must rest now. Keep watch yourself if you are worried." Zelandra stepped forward and set her teapot down neatly in the center of the smothered fire, as though it might still be warmed thereon. "Awaken me if we are attacked, and I shall smite the fools with sorcery." With that, she turned about and ducked into her tent. The flap swung shut behind her.

Conan looked to Neesa, who nodded, came to her feet, and strode quickly across the camp. She followed Zelandra into her tent and immediately muted voices rose from it.

The Cimmerian strode to the hill's leading edge, looking down to the canyon that led to the Palace of Cetriss and Ethram-Fal.

Heng Shih followed, watching the barbarian as he scanned the clearing below.

"Nothing yet," grumbled Conan. "We must find the swiftest route of escape." He turned and loped back through the camp and on to the hill's far side, where it fell away in a long, gravel slope that ended sharply, far below, in a cliff's edge. The barbarian made his way easily down the loose incline. Heng Shih followed more carefully. Night had fallen and the slope was even more treacherous than it appeared.

Sand and gravel seemed to grease the hillside as it grew ever steeper. Heng Shih staggered, his boots losing purchase as his footing gave way. He caught himself, but not before kicking up a cloud of acrid dust.

The slope finally petered out into a short expanse of level, gravel-strewn stone that was sheared off a few paces away by the sharp edge of the cliff. Conan reached the rim and peered over. There was an almost vertical drop of thirty feet ending in a dry, sandy runoff cluttered with rounded boulders, gleaming as pale as scattered bones in the light of the rising moon.

"Morrigan and Macha," cursed the Cimmerian. "This is no good. We'll be best off if we head back along the canyon that brought us here. Listen." He turned abruptly and put a hand on Heng Shih's shoulder. "I know little about wizardry, and wish that I knew even less, but your mistress seems in poor condition to engage Ethram-Fal in any kind of combat, sorcerous or otherwise. You must convince her to attack by stealth. A frontal attack would be suicide. Tomorrow I can scout along the top of the canyon walls and try to find a way to approach the Stygian's palace from above. If I can find a path, we might be able to lower ourselves down through the open windows of the upper floor and take our enemies by surprise. What do you think?"

Heng Shih lifted his hands as if to sign, then dropped them to his sides with a sigh. He nodded.

"And can you get Zelandra to agree to move the camp?" asked the barbarian. "Her madness could bring death to us all."

The Khitan bristled, his hands becoming fists. He shook his head violently from side to side, scowling darkly.

"Don't be a fool. If you care for your mistress, then save her from herself. Enough jabbering, let's…"

The Cimmerian fell suddenly silent. A frigid finger traced a line along Heng Shih's spine.

"Did you hear something?" breathed Conan. Heng Shih shook his head and listened. The desert's ponderous silence filled his ears like thick cotton. The Khitan stepped carefully, turned his back to the cliff edge and stared up the slope, alert for any sound or sign of movement.

Conan's body lowered into a fighting crouch, his eyes taking on a feral gleam in the darkness. Heng Shih's breath slowed and thickened, seeming to clog his lungs.

Then came the sharp scrape of a boot on stone.

Heng Shih spun around, heart in his throat, hand scrabbling for his hilt. A black figure shot up over the rim of the cliff, springing from the sheer face like a monstrous spider. The Khitan had his sword half drawn before a fist like a war-hammer slammed into the side of his head. The muscles of his neck screamed in protest as his bald skull was wrenched to one side. Heng Shih reeled, his senses swimming, and stumbled helplessly into Conan. The Cimmerian sidestepped his stricken friend, who crashed to the ground, sprawling and sliding in the gravel.

Conan's sword flashed into his fist, but the black figure moved even faster. He dove in through the Cimmerian's guard, his extended hands locking around Conan's throat. Fingers like blunt daggers sank deeply into flesh, choking off his breath.

"Death," rasped Gulbanda, thrusting his drawn and grimy face into Conan's. The Cimmerian reared back and drove the fist clutching his scimitar into the lich's forehead with all the strength of his arm. The metal pommel crunched on bone and ripped skin the consistency of desiccated leather. The impact tore Gulbanda's hands from Conan's throat and sent him staggering back and away. The barbarian gave his attacker no time to recover, lunging in with a blinding, two-handed cut to the ribs. It was like hewing an oak. The blade thudded into Gulbanda's torso, sank in an inch, and stuck fast.

"Crom!" swore Conan, jerking back on his sword. The blade remained lodged in the dead man's hardened flesh. Retreating a step, the Cimmerian tripped over the prone body of Heng Shih and staggered, ducking low. Gulbanda's bony hands clawed the air where he had stood.

Conan stumbled sideways, still gripping the hilt of the scimitar with both hands, and delivered a savage kick to his opponent's chest. His boot landed with terrific force, slamming Gulbanda back off his steel in a cloud of ochre dust. The dead man reeled backward, recovered his balance, and came forward again without an instant's hesitation. Both sword and dagger swung in their sheaths at Gulbanda's belt. He had forgotten their use.

"Death," wheezed Gulbanda, coming toward the Cimmerian with his claw-like hands held out to grasp and rend. Icy gray moonlight shone full in his face as cracked lips peeled back from broken teeth and a pale scar parted the filthy thatch of beard.

Recognition and horror drove a frigid spike through Conan's belly. His heel slipped on stone and the Cimmerian realized that he was standing on the rim of the precipice. He flourished the scimitar in a moon-glittering figure eight, trying to make Gulbanda keep his distance. But the dead man did not fear his steel. He drew up short a moment, then dove headlong for the barbarian's throat.

Conan braced his feet and lashed the scimitar from right to left in a brutal, horizontal cut that struck Gulbanda's outstretched left arm at the elbow. Fibrous flesh and dried bone split under the impact. The severed limb flew from its bloodless stump even as the dead man's body slammed into Conan's, knocking him backward and sending both combatants hurtling over the edge of the cliff.

There was a moment of sick vertigo as the pair dropped into darkness; then Conan twisted in midair, shoving Gulbanda out and away from him.

The barbarian's falling body scraped against the cliff face in a small explosion of dirt and gravel. He clawed frantically at the wall, striving to slow his fall, struck the floor of the dry wash on his side, and blacked out.

There was an indeterminate time of darkness and silence during which Conan's consciousness struggled to rise, like a swimmer trapped beneath the surface of a black lake. At some point came the distant and dreamlike sound of feminine screams, but they faded back into the heavy silence and it was as if they had never been.

The Cimmerian sat up carefully, sand spilling from his hair. He had landed in the sculpted sand of the dry wash, which had cushioned the impact somewhat. His ribs ached abominably and his head spun. The scimitar lay at the base of the cliff, a crescent of silver in the gray rubble. Conan lunged for it, grasped it, and stood up unsteadily.

Standing in the shadow of the cliff, he watched the world reel. He shook his head in a leonine fashion, trying to clear it. Though it felt as if every inch of his body had been bruised by hammers, he seemed to have suffered no serious injury.

Gulbanda had fallen only a few paces away. He lay on his back, bent and broken over a small boulder. He writhed weakly but ceaselessly, like an insect on a pin. Bent backward almost double over the boulder that had snapped his spine, his remaining hand clawed listlessly at the air.

Conan's senses cleared and he stepped forward, gazing in fearful awe at his deathless adversary. Something small crawled from the

Conan finds Gulbanda on his back, bent and broken over a small boulder

shadow of the boulder and into the silvery moonlight. Gulbanda's severed left hand groped spider-like across the ground, dragging the dead weight of its forearm behind it. A surge of fresh horror lifted the hairs on the back of the Cimmerian's neck. The hand moved blindly away from Gulbanda's helpless body. Conan bent forward and plucked the dagger from the dingy sheath on his foe's girdle. Then he took two quick steps forward, knelt, and drove the blade through the thing's wrist, pinning the grisly limb to the earth. The pallid fingers clenched and unclenched in the sand.

"Death," hissed a voice, little more than a feeble whisper, yet as cold and piercing as an arctic blast. "Death."

Conan straightened. The breeze picked up, strangely warm, blowing his dark mane back from his face. He looked down upon the prone and broken form of Gulbanda of Shem.

"Death," sighed the dead man.

"Certainly," said Conan and lifting the scimitar, hewed off Gulbanda's head. The body jerked and slowed, but never ceased its restless movement. Gulbanda's skull struck the packed sand and rolled behind the boulder. The barbarian turned away and sheathed his sword in one smooth motion. He strode to the base of the cliff and began, with swift and certain movements, to climb it.

Behind him, in the shadow of the boulder, Gulbanda's head lay blinking up at the cold stars, lips twisting soundlessly as he called for a death that would not come.

32

onan came over the rim of the cliff in a low crouch. He scanned the long slope rising before him. After assuring himself that there was no one about, he looked to the sky, wondering how long he had lain senseless at the base of the cliff. The night sky was already half obscured by the dense clouds unfurling from the west. The stars wavered and disappeared before their leading edge as they raced across the heavens. An unnaturally warm breeze rolled through the canyons, growing slowly in strength as it moaned among the crags.

The Cimmerian dropped to one knee beside the sprawled form of Heng Shih. The Khitan lay face down, his bulky body partially covered by dirt and gravel. Conan gave him a firm shake and Heng Shih stirred feebly, then sat up. He looked about himself wildly, eyes wide with panicked surprise.

"By Ymir," rumbled the barbarian. "And you said that I had a hard head."

The Khitan ran a wide hand over the side of his shaven skull, touching gingerly above his left ear, where the skin was already beginning to swell and discolor. He stood up slowly, shaking the dirt from his clothing. He fixed his gaze upon Conan.

"That was an old friend of Shakar the Keshanian, come back to settle a score," said Conan, answering the unspoken query.

Heng Shih frowned uncertainly, setting a hand upon his hilt.

"Don't worry about him. He's done. Let's check the camp, I fear the worst." The Cimmerian turned suddenly and started up the treacherous slope with long, quick strides. The Khitan kept pace, though he fought off waves of dizziness with every step. The wind had picked up, throwing dust into their eyes and striving with invisible hands to thrust them back down the incline.

The camp was deserted.

Heng Shih stumbled into the center of the encampment, staring about with grim desperation, dismay apparent in his every movement. All three of the tents were empty and one had collapsed. Its crumpled fabric rippled and flapped forlornly with each fresh gust. The eroded stone of the hilltop showed no sign of struggle, but Conan pointed wordlessly to where the hill dropped away into the clearing. Two pale forms lay still in the darkness there. Heng Shih ran haltingly toward them, then slowed, breathing a sigh of relief when he saw that they were not the bodies of Neesa and the Lady Zelandra.

The corpses of two Stygian mercenaries lay not ten paces apart. The nearest of the pair had a charred blot for a face. Curls of steam rose from empty, blackened eye sockets and were torn away by the wind. The second soldier gripped with both hands the hilt of the dagger that had pierced his throat.

Heng Shih stared down at the dead men, then noticed that Conan had knelt beside the fallen tent. The Cimmerian was examining a bit of cloth that bore dark stains. He stood and held it out to the Khitan.

The wind toyed with the discolored fabric, tossing it about, but Heng Shih could see that it was the bloodstained remnants of Zelandra's turban.

He walked stiffly to Conan and tore the scrap from the barbarian's grasp. His face hardened into a mask of stone. The blood on the fabric had not yet congealed, and it came away on his fingers. He let the remains of the turban fall from his hands. The wind whipped the tattered cloth away into the night and the growing storm.

Heng Shih unsheathed his scimitar and started down the hill toward the narrow canyon that led to the Palace of Cetriss.

"Hold!" Conan's voice rang out above the wind like the clangor of steel on steel. "Don't be a fool."

Heng Shih drew to a halt, his back to the Cimmerian, then turned slowly to face him. The Khitan's eyes held a bleakness that was terrible to behold. He placed his right hand on the center of his broad breast, and then held it out in the direction of Ethram-Fal's lair.

"Yes," said the barbarian, "I understand." He bent over, rummaging in the crumpled remains of the fallen tent, and came up with a jug of wine. He plucked out the cork with his teeth, spat it away, and offered the bottle to Heng Shih.

"Have a drink and heed me well. Your mistress is alive, else the Stygians would have left her here as they did the bodies of their comrades. If you walk into their stronghold, you'll be butchered like a sheep and leave Zelandra alive in the hands of the Stygian wizard. Is that what you want?"

The Khitan shook his head painfully, shoulders slumping as the cruel tension wracking his body loosened its grasp.

"I thought not. Now, look to the sky. This is no ordinary storm that comes upon us, but a sandstorm out of hell itself. I've seen a few in my time on the desert, but never one that filled the heavens like this one. The damn thing probably sprang up around Harakht and has been growing larger over every league it's traveled. It should give us fine cover."

Conan thrust the wine at Heng Shih, who finally accepted it. The Cimmerian ducked into one of the two standing tents, leaving the big Khitan standing alone with the bottle. He squinted at it, took a sip, and cast it aside. The crockery shattered on stone. He had no time for such things.

The barbarian emerged from the tent carrying his leather helmet, a coil of rope, and two of Neesa's silk shirts. As Heng Shih watched, Conan donned the helmet, looped the rope over a brawny shoulder, then tossed one of the shirts to him. The Khitan caught it before the wind snatched the garment away, and stared at it without comprehension.

"We'll do as I said earlier. I'll lead us across the canyon tops to the sorcerer's fortress. The storm will not make it any easier for us, but it is our only real chance. Tie the shirt around your head so that it covers your mouth and nose. Leave a thin space to see through. It will provide a little protection from the sand."

Heng Shih stood in place lifelessly, glancing from the shirt in his hands to the place where the ragged tops of the canyon walls met the lowering belly of the storm. The wind whipped through the camp and rushed away into darkness.

"Come on," said Conan, knotting the shirt at the base of his bull neck.

Heng Shih nodded, then began wrapping the silken shirt around his head.

33

The moon's last light was quenched before rolling clouds. The wind raged past the climbers, bearing a scourge of sand that tore at their clothing and abraded their exposed skin. Despite the absent moon, an ethereal yellow half-light, vaporous and sickly, illuminated the storm-wracked sky. Heng Shih could just make out the form of Conan silhouetted against it as the Cimmerian drew himself up the irregular stone wall.

Heng Shih stood upon a narrow ledge, embracing the cliff face beneath the climbing barbarian. He scarcely dared move in the ceaseless wind.

Twenty feet below lay a scattered carpet of sharp boulders. The Khitan pressed his forehead against the hard stone, still warm from the sun's rays, waiting for Conan to reach safety and lower the rope.

They had proceeded in this fashion for hours. Heng Shih had entertained hopes that the tops of the canyons would be fairly level, at least allowing for occasional expanses of easy travel. It was not so. The upper portions of the canyon walls broke into a wildly uneven collection of jagged rock formations. They hadn't traveled forward as far as they climbed up and down over the canyon walls.

Conan had chosen an initial approach that took them across the canyon rim at its lowest point, and then dropped them into a gorge packed with huge boulders. Finding a path out of that jumble seemed to have taken half the night. From there they had made their way over a series of steep ridges. Nowhere did the stone afford much in the way of hand or footholds. The two men had developed a pattern: Conan climbed ahead, often disappearing entirely into the swirling sand; then the rope would come trailing down out of the yellow-tinged darkness, and Heng Shih would clamber up its length.

The far side of each ridge was generally shorter and less steep than its leading edge, as the canyons they flanked grew deeper and drew farther back into the highlands. Inevitably, the men would find themselves at the base of another almost sheer wall and be forced to climb once again. Heng Shih's pride goaded him to keep pace with Conan, but he soon discovered that his skill in scaling stone was no match for a Cimmerian hillman's.

Now the Khitan stood panting on his little ledge and waited for the rope. He blinked through the slender gap in sand-crusted silk. His lungs fought for air and his legs throbbed from exertion. The muscles around each knee were defined in every fiber by pain. Steeling himself, he thought of Zelandra and looked up for the rope. Conan had long since vanished into the whirling sandstorm above.

Heng Shih was all but blinded, but when he shifted position against the rock face to ease his cramping knees, his hand brushed against something. It was the rope. Visibility had grown so poor that it had fallen beside him without even being noticed. The Khitan seized the rope, set his teeth, and began to climb.

As he approached the summit the huge form of the Cimmerian loomed above him, etched against the tawny darkness of the sky. Heng Shih dragged himself over the rim, grateful that the stone was moderately level. Conan bent over him and yelled above the storm.

"Are you all right?"

The Khitan nodded and stood, resisting an impulse to check the bandages wrapped around his midsection beneath his clothing. The wound throbbed dully from strain, but he did not think he had reopened it.

The pair stood between two natural pillars of crooked and weathered stone that thrust skyward like the broken, skeletal fingers of some buried giant. Heng Shih leaned his weight against the nearest and stared doggedly ahead, trying to get some idea of the nature of the next section of terrain. He felt confident the canyon they had followed to the Palace of Cetriss was located somewhere to their right, and that the palace itself lay more or less in front of them. He couldn't hazard a guess as to how much farther they had to travel.

"Look!" shouted Conan, his voice half smothered by the roar of the wind. "The palace!" The barbarian extended a hand, pointing above and ahead of them. Heng Shih tried to stare through the blowing dust.

A dark mass, huge and angular, faded in and out of view in the weird yellow half-light. It seemed less than a league away, yet the space between the looming phantom and the two men was a sand-lashed void that made estimations of distance impossible.

"We'll go down here, along that ledge, and then up atop the palace. We're almost there."

Conan wrapped the rope in coils around his brawny arm while Heng Shih peered skeptically ahead, trying to identify the features that the Cimmerian had described. He abandoned his efforts when Conan moved forward, off the level top of the ridge, and down its uneven rear slope. The Khitan followed, keeping his comrade's broad back in view while stepping carefully on the treacherous stone.

The slope bottomed out into a narrow crevasse packed with broken slabs of fallen rock. Conan descended, leaping nimbly from one boulder to the next, avoiding the gaps and irregularities that could trap and break an ankle or even a leg. He made his way along the crevasse floor to their right, with Heng Shih keeping close through sheer force of will.

The narrow passage was abruptly sheared off. The crevasse opened out from a smoothly vertical stone wall into a vast open expanse seething with windblown sand. Conan crouched on a boulder at the opening's rim, looking down. Heng Shih caught up and stood gasping at his side.

"Below is the courtyard we saw when scouting the canyon!" bellowed Conan. "With luck, that thin ledge running along the courtyard wall will take us to a point where we can scale the palace roof."

The open space of the courtyard was a raging maelstrom of shrieking wind. Airborne sand and dust made it impossible to see more than a few paces ahead. One look down inspired a strange vertigo. The courtyard's floor might have been thirty feet down or three hundred. Heng Shih could just make out the slender ledge that Conan had indicated. It began six feet from, and six feet below, the opening in which they stood. The natural pathway stretched along the courtyard wall, leading up into the storm. Its width varied, but seemed to afford space enough to walk upon. The Khitan's stomach lurched as he realized that he and his companion would have to jump from the crevasse mouth along the courtyard wall to reach the stone path. The ledge abruptly appeared much narrower to his eyes.

The barbarian set his feet, bent his knees, and then leapt out into open air. He landed catlike upon the ledge. The Cimmerian put his back to the rock face and walked along the shelf with seeming ease, quickly disappearing from sight.

Heng Shih followed with intense deliberation, perching carefully on the boulder at the edge. He did not look down. It wasn't really much of a leap, he reasoned. A one-legged man could do it if the ground were level. Heng Shih took a deep breath and jumped. He lit on a ledge, but overestimated his leap and struck the canyon wall with force enough to rebound slightly. His hands scrabbled desperately on the stone, miraculously finding a handhold; and seizing it, pulling himself back in tight against the wall.

His heartbeat thundered in his ears, for a moment drowning out the sound of the wind. He allowed himself no time to recover, or to think on how he stood unsteadily upon a crumbling bit of stone suspended above a howling abyss. He proceeded along the precarious shelf, following Conan.

The ledge proved easy enough to negotiate for the first twenty or thirty paces, then it narrowed and became a rising series of sharp and irregular steps. Heng Shih half stumbled on the first, stopped to slap the dust from his improvised mask, and then began to climb. At the fifth step the path narrowed to nothing, disappearing into the cliff face. Heng Shih clung to the rock and looked in all directions. The courtyard's natural wall continued ahead, but without the benefit of the slightest foothold. The stone shone smooth as polished crystal.

Where was Conan? The thought battered the Khitan with the force of a blow. He peered frantically into the roiling storm below. Had the Cimmerian fallen? What could he do now?

Something struck him atop the head. He recoiled involuntarily, jerking backward so that he almost fell from the ledge. His right hand clawed at the air and caught the rope.

Conan was above him. Heng Shih gripped the line and stared up along the cliff face to where it vanished into lashing clouds of grit. The rock was almost featurelessly smooth, devoid of all but the tiniest irregularities. These had apparently sufficed. Conan had scaled the wall to its summit.

Heng Shih gave the rope a yank. It held fast. With repeated grunting and effort, the Khitan went hand-over-hand up the rope. He braced his feet and knees upon the slippery rock face when he could, but depended on the strength of his upper body to draw him to safety. The muscles of his shoulders quivered with effort, and he found himself slowing. Dust and sweat stung his eyes. His boots slid over stone, striving for purchase and finding none. Then the rope began to rise of its own accord, reeling him in like an ungainly fish until he was drawn over the edge of the cliff. Heng Shih scrambled onto level ground, released the rope, and stood with his hands on his knees, breathing deeply.

Conan of Cimmeria unwound the rope from his fists, clapped the Khitan on the back, and unleashed a guffaw audible even above the wind.

"Thought you'd lost me, eh? It takes more than a bit of climbing to stop a Cimmerian. Come, we're almost there."

The canyon wall continued only another dozen paces before it reached the courtyard's corner and angled sharply inward to form the back wall of the natural cul-de-sac. They had climbed to the far corner of the courtyard, and now stood a mere spear's cast from the Palace of Cetriss.

The Khitan found that he could discern the massive pillars of the palace's facade, flickering in and out of visibility between veils of windblown sand. Its outlines shifted, giving it the appearance of a sinister mirage created by the ferocious storm.

The footing was blessedly even. Conan and Heng Shih climbed a low ridge of weathered stone and passed beyond the courtyard. The dark and shadowy mass that they had seen through the storm now rose directly before them. Their harrowing climb had brought them up beside the palace roof. The uppermost portion of the Palace of Cetriss was fashioned from a section of canyon that rose in a promontory, towering above all around it. The palace's flank lifted from the stone at their feet as sharply as a man-made wall sprang from a city's cobbled sidewalk. Gazing up its face almost twenty feet to the tortured sky, Heng Shih found himself wishing that he could see so much as a single star. Conan

JOHN C. HOCKING

walked beside the wall, trailing the fingers of one hand along it. He turned to the Khitan, slapping his palm on the wall and shouting above the gusts.

"It's been worked. Leveled and sanded. Long ago."

Heng Shih nodded that he understood, wondering if this meant the Cimmerian would be unable to scale it. They walked for a few more moments, passing over almost-level stone, with Conan staring ceaselessly up at the wall. At length he stopped, pointing high to a single fissure marring the smooth surface. As Heng Shih looked on, the Cimmerian took several steps back, then ran forward and leapt up at the slender split in the stone wall. His body seemed to fly into place and stick, like a dagger hurled into soft wood. Steely fingers dug into the narrow gap, supporting the full weight of his powerful frame. He writhed, clawing his way up the wall with his fingertips alone. After an instant of breathless struggle, his hands found purchase atop the wall. Then his legs swung up and he was over the top, out of sight.

Heng Shih stood with his hands on his hips and shook his head. He reflected upon how reluctant he had been to allow the barbarian to accompany Lady Zelandra's expedition. He grimaced, tugged the wrapped silk away from his lips, and spat downwind. The rope came tumbling down the wall to him. He flexed his shoulders, cracked his knuckles, and climbed.

The roof of the Palace of Cetriss was as large as the courtyard, rectangular, and bounded by a low wall that reached to a man's hip. It was as level as a floor beneath their feet and patterned with whirling eddies of sand. In its center lay a wooden board as thick and heavy as a tavern's tabletop. Conan knelt beside this anomaly and, as Heng Shih watched nervously, pressed an ear to the rough wood. He rose quickly and padded to the Khitan's side.

"An entrance," he explained. "Probably guarded. Look here." The barbarian went to one knee again, pointing out a collection of odd items in the blowing sand of the rooftop. Five black candles

220

were set in congealed pools of their own melted wax. Each was
positioned at one of the five points of a large star inscribed upon
the roof's surface.

Strange symbols and traceries stained the stone on all sides of
the great pentagram.

"I'll wager this is where the Stygian cast forth his image to
pester your mistress," said Conan.

The mention of Zelandra drove a surge of fresh energy through
Heng Shih's tired body. He jogged to the front of the palace,
motioning for Conan to follow. Gripping the carved rim of the low
wall, the Khitan leaned over the courtyard and peered below. The
flattened facade above the great pillars stretched down about ten
feet. Below that he could make out the protruding cornice of one of
the pillars. Conan moved toward the facade's center, where another
slim fissure split the low wall, and began unspooling the rope.

"We'll go down here. We want to swing in between the
pillars."

Heng Shih watched as the Cimmerian tied a heavy knot in
the rope's tail. Conan stood on the cord and wrenched upon it to
tighten the knot.

Then he fit the rope into the fissure, wedging the knot flat
against the inside of the wall and carelessly tossing the remainder
over into the courtyard to dangle in space.

"It should hold, unless our weight tears the knot loose or the
stone cuts the rope." Conan stretched like a lazy tiger, seemingly
confident and unconcerned. Heng Shih swallowed heavily.

"I'll go first," said the barbarian as he straddled the wall and
grasped the line. With a lithe twist, Conan rolled over the edge
and began to lower himself down the rope. Sandy gusts tore at
him, trying to pluck him loose from the wall and swing his body
like a pendulum.

The Cimmerian fought the wind, staying in close to the carved
stone face. When Conan reached the base of the facade, he planted

the soles of his boots against the wall, kicked back, and slid down the rope.

Then he swung out of sight beneath the facade and between the pillars.

The skin between the Khitan's shoulder blades tingled as the rope stayed taut and Conan failed to reappear. After a long moment the rope went slack and trailed back into view, flailing loosely in the relentless wind. Heng Shih briefly considered that Conan might have fallen, or worse, swung right into a room full of waiting soldiers.

Then he seized the rope and drew himself over the wall.

He slid too quickly down over the facade; its ancient, faded inscriptions rasped his knees and elbows. The rope felt thin and inadequate in his fists. Heng Shih slipped, dropping below the facade and dangling between two of the pillars, which loomed to either side like huge and shadowy sentries. The wind spun him on the rope, swinging him to and fro helplessly. The black square of an open window beckoned to Heng Shih, recessed beneath the overhanging facade less than ten feet away. Hurling his legs forcibly out and away from the palace wall, the Khitan swung himself under the overhang and up to the window.

Deftly hooking a boot over the sill, he pulled himself toward safety.

When one fist released the rope and reached for the window's edge, a strong hand thrust out to catch him and drag him in. Heng Shih tumbled into a darkened room, landing on his much-abused knees. Conan stood beside him, his silken mask discarded, a fierce white grin creasing his hard countenance. His scimitar shone naked in his fist. Heng Shih stood and drew his own sword. He and the Cimmerian were inside the Palace of Cetriss.

34

The armored soldier thrust Neesa through the portal and into the huge stone room. She turned, snarling in hot-eyed defiance and straining at the chains that clasped her hands behind her back. Zelandra, similarly bound, stumbled against the scribe and staggered for balance. A lance of poignant pain thrust through Neesa, undercutting her rage with sorrow. Zelandra was moving like an aged and infirm crone.

"Are you all right, milady?" she asked, trying to sound strong and unafraid. The soldiers pushed into the room behind the women, surrounding them.

"You were told to stay silent. Obey or I'll slice out your tongue," said the Stygian who had shoved her. He thumbed the edge of his shortsword with crude suggestion.

The tallest of the soldiers spoke in a voice of calm authority. "Easy, Daphrah. The master wants them in one piece."

"Erlik's fangs," cursed the one called Daphrah. "This one threw a dagger into Teh-Harpa's throat as neat as you please. I hope the master feeds them to the lotus."

Wrenching her gaze from the raw hatred in the eyes of Daphrah, Neesa looked around the room. It was massively vaulted and circular, lighted by a collection of strange globes set around the walls. These crystalline spheres appeared to hold only water and some sort of leafy plant, yet they shone with strong yellow light. The center of the room was dominated by a statue the size of a small house. It was a carven sphinx of the sort occasionally seen in Stygia, but it was exceptionally large, fashioned of glossy black stone, and had no facial features. Between its paws lay a flat slab of similar black stone.

Gazing at the altar and its faceless idol, Neesa felt her blood slow and grow cold. What manner of men worshipped such a god?

The women were herded into the room's center until they stood beneath the overhanging oval of the statue's blank visage. Neesa retreated before the advancing mercenaries, halting when she backed into the altar slab. She sat upon it defiantly, curling her lips in a sneer of disdain. Zelandra shuffled to her side, head bent. The lady's silver-threaded hair was bloodied at the crown by the blow of a sword hilt. A cruel leather gag had been fastened about her head to prevent her from casting any spells. Neesa doubted that Zelandra would have been able to work any sorcery even without the gag. Her mistress seemed taxed by merely standing upright.

Neesa clenched her eyes shut. She should have physically fought Zelandra to keep her from building the fire.

The camp should have been moved immediately, just as Conan had said.

They had been taken so swiftly. It seemed only a moment ago that she was arguing with Zelandra inside the tent. Her mistress had been so adamant about being safe and only needing some rest, all the while clinging with hands like gnarled talons to that damned silver box. Then there were voices outside the tent, and even Zelandra, for all her illness, could tell that they were not the voices of Conan and Heng Shih. The women burst out of the tent together, and there were Stygian soldiers coming over the rim of the hill. Neesa had taken the foremost with her nape-dagger and Zelandra had just enough time to bark out a single spell. She sent an incandescent bolt of fiery green light from the palm of her hand into the horrified face of the second Stygian.

Then the soldiers were upon them. Zelandra had clawed at her silver box, trying to unwrap it, until the pommel of a sword dashed her turban from her head and sent her sprawling. Neesa drew another dagger, screaming out for Conan and Heng Shih, not quite able to believe that they weren't there. The warriors had encircled her, obviously unwilling to do harm unless it was necessary, and wary of the knife she held ready to throw. The blade of a shortsword held to the throat of the stunned Zelandra was sufficient threat to get her to toss her dagger aside.

Then she had been struck down by the mailed fist of the one called Daphrah. The mercenaries had milled about for a short time, looking for her companions, whom they shortly determined had fled. Satisfied that they had captured the sorceress that Ethram-Fal desired, and fearful of the coming storm, the soldiers escorted their captives back along the canyon. En route, the sandstorm fell upon them, railing and screaming in the narrow passage. Neesa had faced it numbly. Her thoughts seemed somehow paralyzed by the fact that Conan and Heng Shih had failed to come to her aid.

Even the marvelous facade of the Palace of Cetriss, wreathed in swirling, windblown dust, had made little impression upon her. The labyrinthine corridors within led them through empty rooms as silent as sepulchers, through a great hall full of neatly arranged cots, and finally to this fearful temple.

Now they waited for the one who ruled here.

Zelandra gave a low moan, grasping at her belt. Dangling leather thongs showed where the silver casket had been cut away. The tall, hawk-faced captain held the box in one hand. He observed Zelandra's distress dispassionately, glancing from her mindlessly grasping hands to the box in his grasp. Rage and helplessness warred in Neesa's breast until it felt as though her heart would be torn asunder.

Footfalls came from the far door. The clustered crowd of mercenaries parted, allowing a small, gray-robed figure to approach. The man was shorter than Neesa and hunched slightly, his head concealed beneath the hood of his robe. His sandaled feet slapped smartly on the smooth stone floor. Drawing to a stop before the women, he considered them for a moment, then crossed his arms over his narrow chest.

"Ah, Zelandra," came a soft voice from within the hood. It held pity and amusement in equal measures. "Your powers of endurance are nothing less than remarkable. I was a fool to underestimate you. But you were the greater fool to underestimate my Emerald Lotus."

Zelandra did not respond, but stared sightlessly forward, one arm crooked about her ribs and the other clutching uselessly at the place on her belt where the box of Emerald Lotus had once hung.

"Ath," called the wizard imperiously. "Loose the lady's companion from her bonds and affix her to the altar."

The tall soldier advanced as commanded, passing Zelandra's silver box to a comrade, and producing a key from within his polished breastplate.

Terror seized Neesa by the throat, sending a shuddering palsy down through her belly. She crouched and showed her teeth, clenching her fists to fight. The captain drew to a stop, his stern face betraying no emotion.

"Now, now," said the robed man gently. "Don't be a fool. You may still survive unscathed. All depends upon your mistress. It will be much the worse for you if you struggle. Think of what might befall you here if you displease me. Imagine."

Neesa went limp, half swooning as Ath unfastened her bonds. The captain put a hand beneath each of her arms and hoisted her easily up onto the altar. She went unresisting, clenching her eyes closed as he used lengths of rawhide to tie wrists and ankles to the black metal rings set in each of the altar's four corners.

"Very good," said the robed man, then louder: "Now, men, leave me. Be vigilant. These two may have friends. Hep-Kahl, give her box to me. Ath, you may stay."

Subdued grumbles of disappointment came to Neesa's ears. All of her senses seemed heightened to an unendurable pitch. The altar felt much colder against her spine than it should have. She lifted her head and saw the soldiers filtering out the doors. The last stragglers looked behind themselves wistfully.

"Ath, remove the lady's gag. Do not worry, I fear that she is beyond any wizardry at this point."

Neesa kept her head raised to watch even as the muscles of her neck began to ache dully. The gag fell away from Zelandra's mouth, though she seemed to take no notice. Her eyes were dull, staring at nothing.

The tall warrior stepped back uneasily, one hand on the hilt of his heavy, northern broadsword.

The sorcerer lifted his hands and lowered the hood. His countenance wrung an involuntary gasp from Neesa. The bulging brow and shrunken jaw marked Ethram-Fal as a man who would never be called handsome, but the ravages of the Emerald Lotus had transformed him into something that could scarcely be called human. Tufts of mouse-brown hair stood out from his mottled scalp. His complexion had faded from the dusky tone of a healthy Stygian to a grayish pallor better suited to a corpse. The wasted flesh of his face bore an infinitude of tiny wrinkles, giving him the appearance of an animated mummy. The whites of his eyes shone pale green.

"Now, lady, we have so much to discuss."

Zelandra might have been deaf. She stood like a sleepwalker, unaware of the grim tableau that surrounded her.

"Ah, I know what you need," said Ethram-Fal happily. "Look here, milady." With a flourish, he thrust the silver box aloft. Zelandra's eyes focused suddenly, locking onto the gleaming casket.

"Come, a few grains should make you more communicative." He opened the box and held it so that she could see the contents. Zelandra took a hesitant, dragging step forward. Her arms hung lax at her sides.

"Yes, that's very good. You want to feel better, don't you?"

Zelandra took three pained steps toward the Stygian and stretched out her hands blindly.

"So little left," mused Ethram-Fal. "Even so, you shall get only a taste." He used two fingers to scoop a bit of the deep green powder out of the box, and then extended his hand to the Lady Zelandra.

"There will be more if we can reach an agreement. All that you like, in fact."

The sorcerer caught his breath as Zelandra took two more steps toward him, grasped his wrist with both hands, and began to lick the Emerald Lotus from his proffered fingers.

Ethram-Fal threw back his head and laughed like a fiend out of hell.

35

The chamber was square, hewn directly from the canyon wall, and without any furnishings. It was obvious that it had not been occupied, or perhaps even visited, for a very long time. A small, hardened drift of sand stretched across the floor, the accumulation of ages. On the far wall a single portal opened on darkness. The storm raged unabated outside, scouring the window frame with whips of sand.

The two warriors leaned against the wall to either side of the window, resting a moment and taking stock of their situation. The only sound was that of the wind. Conan fumbled beneath his cloak, pulling into view a small, leather backpack that Heng Shih hadn't seen. The Cimmerian opened it and produced a wineskin.

"Here. It is not the finest vintage, and watered besides, but I'll wager that you won't cast it aside now," said the barbarian. Wearing a faintly sheepish expression, Heng Shin took the wineskin. The first swallow seemed to slice through the layer of dust coating his throat.

The second filled his mouth with rich flavor. The wine may have been second-rate and watered, but he could not remember ever appreciating a drink so thoroughly. After they both drank their fill, the skin was returned to the backpack, and the men advanced as one to the doorway.

Outside the room was an empty, lightless corridor leading away to both left and right. Conan's eyes adjusted to the darkness at once, and he perceived that vacant doorways flanked the one from which they emerged.

A moment's exploration revealed that both of these rooms had windows opening out onto the pillared facade, and were identical to the one that had admitted them to the palace. To either side, beyond the rooms, the corridor turned inward and tunneled deeper into the rock.

Conan chose the hallway to the right. Once they rounded the corner, the sound of the storm dwindled to a distant whispering and the air grew thick and stale. The stagnant smell of ancient dust filled their nostrils.

The corridor continued in gloom, uninterrupted for a space, then split in a three-way intersection. Ahead, and to the left, the hall went on as before, with no sign of light or another doorway. To their right a spiral stairway coiled downward. A vague yellow glow, faint as a vapor, shone along the stairwell's curving wall.

Conan thrust down with the sickle blade of his scimitar. The Khitan nodded, and the two stole down the stair. Conan led the way, keeping his back to the wall and his sword extended before him. The stairs opened out onto the second floor, where the two men hesitated. The Cimmerian crouched, leaning into the hallway, but all was darkness and silence. The phantom glow of light came from farther below. He withdrew and they continued.

The stairwell ended by opening out upon a broad hall that led away to the left and right. A single light, set in a niche carved into the wall, filled the long chamber with a soft illumination. It was not a torch. The light looked like nothing that Conan had ever seen before.

It appeared to be a hollow ball of glass containing water and a sprig of some leafy plant. The whole gave off a steady, not unpleasant, glow.

The barbarian noted its oddity, then gave it no further thought. Death stalked these corridors and would claim the unwary.

To Conan's right, the hall extended fifteen paces before ending in another open doorway. To his left, the corridor reached a similar length to a similar portal, but this one was covered by a hanging blanket of coarse brown cloth. Faint sounds, echoing and indistinguishable, came from beyond the fabric barrier, which twitched gently, as if touched by a gentle breeze.

Conan came out of the stairwell and padded stealthily toward the covered doorway. His boots made no sound on the stone floor. Heng Shih began to follow about four paces behind, but was struck into immobility when the Cimmerian suddenly thrust an open palm toward him.

A voice spoke in Stygian, startlingly loud in the pervasive silence.

For a terrible instant Conan and Heng Shih both stood stock-still; then the hanging over the doorway rippled and was thrust aside. Two men in bright mail pushed into view. Lights bobbed and flared behind them.

Conan had a split second of indecision. It was shattered by the rising voices of an unknown number of men, coming up behind the two that now stood, goggling, in the doorway. The Cimmerian lunged across the hallway, snatched the light-globe from its niche, spun, and ran straight at Heng Shih. The Khitan took an involuntary step backward.

"Run, damn it!" The barbarian shoved his comrade back into the stairwell as cries of alarm rang out behind them.

The sound of boots on stone filled the stairwell with rebounding echoes. Conan took the steps three at a time, easily driving past the laboring Khitan. At the second level he slid to a halt, bent, and rolled the light-globe down the darkened hallway to the north.

Yellow-white light blazed up eerily, splashing the walls with unnatural radiance as the sorcerous torch rolled swiftly away, scarcely bouncing on the smooth stone floor. Conan didn't stop to watch, but ran past the darkened second level and continued up to the third, bursting into the dim hallway at the three-way intersection with the shouts of his pursuers loud in his ears. Heng Shih followed the Cimmerian as he turned right, sprinting into the inner reaches of the palace's third floor.

They ran through another intersection and passed an open doorway on the right, but Conan did not even slow his pace. Then there was a curtained opening on the left and the barbarian was shoving the fabric aside, charging into the darkness beyond. Heng Shih was at his heels, sliding to a stop in complete blackness as Conan let the blanket fall across the doorway. They pressed their backs to the wall on either side of the door, ready to cut down any who might follow them. Heng Shih strove to muffle his gasps for breath and slow the rapid hammering of his heart.

Voices and footsteps came to them from an uncertain distance, fading and blurring together. Heng Shih wiped sweat from his pate with the dirty sleeve of his golden kimono. Across from him, Conan stood with his scimitar at the ready, as charged with potential energy as a leopard poised to spring.

The sounds of pursuit dwindled and disappeared. Conan grinned savagely, invisible in the gloom, and lowered his blade. His steel clinked softly against something on the wall. Turning, the barbarian reached out. His hand encountered something smooth and spherical sitting in a niche in the wall. When his fingers closed upon and lifted it, a dull pulse of light came from the thing. It was a light-globe like the one he had seized in the hall below. When he picked the thing up, the water within it rolled about and the light came more steadily. Conan gave the glass ball a good shake, and the room was revealed in the resulting yellow glow.

The first thing he saw was Heng Shih, pressed against the wall across from him, sword in hand and an incredulous frown wrinkling his smooth features. The Khitan extended a hand as if to knock the light-globe from Conan's grasp.

"Easy." The Cimmerian stepped away from the door. "They're chasing the light I rolled into the second floor. With any luck, they'll think we dropped it and are hiding down there. Probably wouldn't believe a man of your size could run fast enough to get this far anyway."

Heng Shih lowered his scimitar, but kept his frown, apparently seeing little humor in the situation.

The globe in Conan's fist showed the room to be an eldritch combination of sorcerous laboratory and unnatural greenhouse. The barbarian wrinkled his nose in puzzlement. The chamber smelled more like a humid jungle glade than a stone room in a desert ruin.

A single small chair stood in the center of one wall, overlooking the many tables that all but filled the chamber.

The tables were of varying sizes, each holding a bewildering array of odd paraphernalia, ranging from racks of liquid-filled vials to a set of flat, metal trays that apparently held only moist earth. One of the central tables held a box fashioned of transparent glass panels bound with bronze. Within the box was a round bush, thickly covered with fat, reddish leaves.

Along the wall across from the chair was a long table covered with a tent-like drape of thick black velvet. Heng Shih approached the shroud of dark fabric. The sharp tip of his scimitar lifted the fabric from the table and a brilliant ray of golden light shone out, stinging his eyes. It was as though he revealed the desert sun itself. The table beneath was set with a number of unrecognizable plants growing from ceramic pots full of soil. The velvet cowl was draped over a framework of thin metal struts that also held, at measured intervals, several extraordinarily bright light-globes.

Heng Shih let the cowl fall back into place and the golden light faded abruptly, like the sun falling behind a storm cloud. He turned to see Conan standing beside a small table. The Cimmerian had laid the light-globe on the tabletop. He was fastening his backpack and adjusting it beneath his dusty cloak. The barbarian gestured to the black and empty doorway across the room.

"We've tarried long enough."

The portal opened upon yet another dark and deserted hall. Conan held the light-globe muffled beneath his cloak, so that only a dim glow lit their way. They turned to the right, moving deeper into the palace's stone heart. The silence was as heavy as lead, weighting them down.

Ahead, the hallway ended in a high arch unlike anything they had seen thus far. Conan stopped, and drew from his belt the silken shirt he had used as a mask against the storm. He wrapped the light-globe in the shirt and set it against a wall. A gentle, yellow radiance shone faintly through the bundle of cloth. Heng Shih watched with a concealed impatience that the barbarian seemed to sense.

"Come," said the Cimmerian. "This room is different."

Conan passed beneath the open arch, stepping into an even deeper darkness. The stone floor of the hall ended at the arch. Within the circular room beyond there was no true floor, but rather a ring-like balcony made of a lusterless black metal. The balcony ran around the room's perimeter, encircling an open shaft of uncertain depth.

Heng Shih followed Conan into the strange chamber, pacing soundlessly a step behind and to the right. The pair drew to a halt on the metal balcony, straining their eyes into the dark, trying to see across the room's empty center. Conan laid a hand on the low railing and spoke in a harsh whisper.

"We can reach the other door from either side. But what is that scent?"

Heng Shih frowned in frustration. His dilated eyes could scarcely discern a darker smudge against a featureless background that had to be the far wall. It made sense that both branches of the balcony would meet at a doorway across from the one they had entered, but he could see nothing of it. The Cimmerian's vision was uncanny. Then Heng Shih noticed the scent.

The balcony, only wide enough for two men to walk abreast, bracketed a well of absolute darkness. And from the unfathomed depths below rose a faint odor, reminiscent of stale perfume. After a few breaths, Heng Shih found that its apparent sweetness masked a cloying undercurrent of decay. His hands ached to spell out questions in sign language, but he knew that Conan would not understand.

The barbarian stood rigidly at the balcony's lip, all of his senses focused into the darkness before him. The hair on his forearms prickled. There was something wrong about this room. Heng Shih stared at Conan in dismay, noting the Cimmerian's animal wariness and unable to account for it. The Khitan put his hand on the worn hilt of his scimitar.

Conan's sword lashed from its scabbard, hissing sharply as it cut the air.

"Soldiers. More than four of them, coming to the other door."

Heng Shih started in surprise, drew his sword from his sash, and stared in vain across the lightless room. He waited a suspended moment, every sense awakening. A faint and wavering yellow glow illuminated the opposite arch, revealing the room to be about twenty paces across. The scuff of boots on stone came to his ears. He tugged the wooden mace from his belt and looked to Conan. The Cimmerian cocked his head and grinned wolfishly at his comrade.

"No better time to shift the odds in our favor. Here we can take them one at a time. Are you game?"

The Khitan nodded his shaven head, stepping to the right branch of the balcony even as Conan moved onto the left. The pair advanced slowly, weapons at the ready. And then the opposite arch was abruptly full of light and armed men.

"They're here!"

Hands gripping luminous spheres of crystal were thrust into the room's darkness as twelve armored Stygians pushed out onto the balcony. They reacted smoothly, drawing blades and splitting into two groups without orders, moving like professional warriors who had trained long together.

Conan cursed under his breath. There were too many of them, and they were too good. The balcony forced the Stygians to advance in single file. The last man in each line held a light-globe high, so that his comrades could see.

"Intruders," cried the light-bearer on Heng Shih's side, "cast down your blades and be spared!"

Conan's reply was to charge his first challenger. A barbaric war cry resounded in the vaulted chamber as the Cimmerian sprinted forward, closing the distance between himself and his foe with terrible speed.

The Stygian mercenary was astonished by this unexpected tactic, recoiling into the soldier to his rear. Conan brought his scimitar down with all the power of his shoulders behind it. His blow dashed aside the attempted parry, cleaving through the steel helmet to split the Stygian's skull. The man fell back among his fellows, dead on his feet.

The second mercenary stumbled over the sprawling body, an outthrust hand catching at the balcony's rail. Stepping forward, Conan reversed his blade. His return cut brought the sword back up in a murderous swath that passed inside the staggering man's failing guard and up through the breastplate to split his sternum. The shattering impact of the blow lifted the man from his feet and sent him hurtling over the balcony in a shower of blood and a mad flurry of flailing limbs.

"Come ahead, dogs!" roared the barbarian. The battle-madness of the berserker raged through Conan's veins, driving him forward with such raw fury that his more numerous opponents found themselves drawing backward in an involuntary retreat.

Across the pit, Heng Shih feinted with his wooden mace. When the mercenary facing him parried the blow, the Khitan's scimitar lashed out with such strength that the man's head sprang from his shoulders and rebounded from the ceiling. The body collapsed like a dropped wineskin, sending a wash of crimson vintage spilling over the balcony's rim. The next Stygian lunged in, only to find his thrust blocked by a precise movement of the mace, and his belly laid open by a sudden slash of the scimitar.

Conan saw none of this, for his third opponent was a man of some ability. Cursing steadily in the name of Set and Bubastis, the warrior traded cuts with the Cimmerian, closing with him over the sprawled body of Conan's first kill. The barbarian's boot skidded on blood-smeared metal, and the Stygian drove forward, his thrust tearing through the patched portion of Conan's mail and searing along his ribs. Conan grunted in pain and, hooking the point of his scimitar in above his foe's gorget, thrust the mercenary through the throat. The blade burst through the man's neck, splintering his spine and lodging in the bone.

The luckless Stygian reeled backward with a gurgling cry, tearing the blade from Conan's hand and tumbling headlong over the railing to disappear into the darkness below.

The Cimmerian drew his dagger even as he watched his sword go. The fourth mercenary gave a hoarse shout of triumph to see the fearsome barbarian disarmed. The shout's timbre shifted as Conan dove headfirst into his oncoming foes, slamming bodily into the leading Stygian and bearing both of those following to the balcony in a cursing, writhing heap. No sooner had they struck the metal flooring than Conan was struggling up, wrenching his dagger from the entrails of his fourth opponent. The fifth, fighting for position, came to his knees and awkwardly brought his shortsword down on the head of the rising Cimmerian. The leather helmet saved his skull, but couldn't keep his scalp from splitting under the impact. Fire-shot blackness rolled across Conan's vision. Stunned by the blow, the barbarian half lunged and half fell forward, driving a clenched fist into the swordsman's face. The blow landed with a meaty crunch and the man spilled over backward with a broken jaw.

Conan's sole remaining opponent scrambled up from the balcony and turned to flee. Hurling himself forward across the floor, the Cimmerian caught at the mercenary's flying ankle, snagging a strap of his sandal. With a cry of terror, the man twisted in midstride, desperate to escape the barbarian's grip. The Stygian tore free of Conan's fist, but in doing so spun wildly into the railing, which struck him just below the waist. He upended, all but flying over the rail, and fell into the shaft with a horrible scream. There was a muffled *crunch* from below, as though the man had fallen into a dry thicket.

Conan seized a fallen shortsword in a bloodied fist. Gripping the railing with his other hand, he pulled himself slowly to his feet. The breath whistled between his clenched teeth, and sweat ran freely along his limbs. He looked across the pit to see how Heng Shih fared.

The Khitan stood splay-legged, holding the hilt of his scimitar against his broad belly with both hands. The point of the scimitar was embedded in the chest of the last Stygian mercenary, whose body hung as limply on the blade as an impaled rag. As Conan looked on, Heng Shih hoisted the body up, and with a powerful heave, hurled it into the pit.

The last soldiers had laid their light-globes on the balcony before engaging the invaders. Now the two men looked at each other in the eerie yellow glow. The Cimmerian bared his teeth in a grotesque approximation of a smile. He drew a hand across his brow to wipe away the blood seeping from his scalp wound.

"Crom and Ymir, that was as touchy a set-to as I have ever—"

A terrible screaming rose from the shaft and silenced him. A single human voice strained in notes of an unknowable agony. The hair rose on Conan's head. He drew away from the balcony's rim, pressing his broad back to the cool stone wall, as the screaming intensified into an inhuman siren and was suddenly cut off.

A new sound floated up from the hidden depths of the shaft. A subtle rustle that grew steadily in volume until it was a ragged rasping, as if the walls below were scraped by thousands of steel blades.

Conan shot a glance at Heng Shin and saw that the Khitan was moving carefully toward the arch through which the soldiers had come. The Cimmerian stepped in that direction too, moving stealthily, and then hastening as the sounds in the pit grew louder and, horribly, nearer.

Something was rising out of the shaft. It moved faster and faster, tearing at the walls around it, until it shot up past the balcony. To Conan's horrified eyes it resembled nothing so much as a tree of surging darkness, hurling its black branches aloft until they crunched against the domed ceiling. It paused there, suspended in the shaft, a tangled tower of rustling darkness, and then it fell down toward them.

"Crom!" The curse was wrenched from the barbarian's throat. Conan ducked and ran for the door, almost slamming into Heng Shih as the Khitan came through on his heels. They ran for their lives down a darkened corridor, while behind them a soul-searing scream was ripped from the man whose jaw Conan had broken. The cry was mercifully short, but superseded by the even more chilling sound of the swift, rasping progress of the blood-sotted Emerald Lotus as it pursued its prey.

36

When Zelandra was a girl of twelve, she contracted a fever that came close to ending her life. When the disease reached its critical phase, and her young body was wracked with chills and delirium, her parents wrapped her in woolen blankets and laid her upon a couch on a balcony overlooking the grounds of their estate. There they left her to fight for her life.

The strength of her youth, and the powerful Vendhyan medicines they had given her, gradually won out over the sickness. When she came to herself it was as though she was emerging from a long, winding tunnel of woven dreams. The events of the previous few days blurred into a fantastical skein of unfocused impressions, and she had no real idea of where she was or how she had come to be there. There was only a strong sensation of wellbeing: the sense that she was well at last and sitting safely in her home.

Now Zelandra felt that old feeling anew, and her stirring consciousness believed that she was back on that balcony in the summer of her twelfth year. The sensation of emerging from a half-recalled maze of unreal events was the same. Zelandra licked her dry lips and opened her mouth to call for her mother, but found that her voice would not respond. As her vision began to clear, she noticed that someone was speaking to her in a familiar voice. It was a hateful voice. It planted a germ of unease that took root within her, growing and spreading until her emerging awareness focused upon a simple and disturbing certainty. She was not on that balcony now.

Zelandra found herself looking down at her feet. There was a bitter, oddly familiar taste in her mouth. A frown creased her high forehead as she noticed the dismal condition of her fine riding boots. How had they come to be so battered and dirty? The hateful voice droned on, sounding very pleased with itself. Zelandra looked up to see who would speak to her in such an annoying fashion.

"Are you coming back to us now? Yes, I believe that you are. It is a great honor and a greater pleasure to have you as my guest, Lady Zelandra. First of all, you must tell me: how did you manage to use my lotus so slowly? Shakar, the poor fool, was dead within two days of finishing his supply. How is it that you still have some left after all this time?"

Zelandra stood up straight and ran a hand through her tangled hair. She knew where she must be, though she remained uncertain as to how and when she had arrived. Saying nothing, the sorceress looked slowly and carefully around the huge room, taking in her captors, the black statue, and the bound form of Neesa. Her eyes met those of her scribe for a moment; then Zelandra made herself look away. She could not recall the last time that she had seen Heng Shih or the Cimmerian. She wondered if they were dead. Her lips parted again, and when her voice came, it was like the creak of a rust-choked hinge.

"Shakar must not have seen your lotus for the poison that it is. Either that or he took too much at once and found himself unable to lower the dosage. I felt the craving from the start and tried to stave it off immediately. I used whatever power the drug gave me to strengthen myself against it. Would that you had done the same."

"Ah." Ethram-Fal was smiling at the spirit and cogency of her response.

His thin lips drew back from green-stained teeth in a loathsome grin that gave his face the appearance of a withered skull.

"Well done, milady. A small triumph of skill and determination. And yet, here you are now, a mere handful of hours from a painful death despite your best efforts. It seems most unjust, does it not? Perhaps this is the time to bargain?"

"Bargain?" Zelandra's eyelids fluttered and she put her left hand to her brow. She had to buy time, both to remember what she could about how she came here, and to plan some sort of action, however suicidal. Pretending greater weakness than she felt, the sorceress closed her eyes and rubbed at her forehead.

"Yes, of course," said Ethram-Fal with ill-concealed impatience. "You must remember—"

"You were Eldred the Trader?"

"Yes, yes, I thought that you understood all of that. I came to both you and Shakar the Keshanian in that guise so as to test the effects of my lotus upon you."

"A spell of hypnotism?"

"Ha! Hardly!" The little sorcerer puffed up like a preening sparrow. "Nothing so simplistic and easy to expose. It was a full-fledged glamour: a flawless illusion to any who might look upon it. Behold!"

As the Lady Zelandra watched, Ethram-Fal's slight body began to shimmer like a desert mirage. His image blurred over swiftly, then cleared, revealing an astonishing transformation. Where the stunted Stygian in stained robes had been, now stood a plump and stately Shemite dressed in the elegant silks of a successful merchant. His black beard parted in a broad smile. The illusion winked out and there was Ethram-Fal, grinning just as broadly.

"You see? Such mummery is nothing to me now."

"But the time, the preparations…" Zelandra dissembled. Feeling within for sorcerous strength, she was shocked by her own weakness. The bit of Emerald Lotus given to her by Ethram-Fal had apparently vented most of its strength in merely returning her to rational consciousness. A powerful offensive spell was out of the question. She had to conceive of a simple defensive tactic that would both take her captors by surprise and allow her adequate time to free Neesa and flee. Her mind raced frantically as she felt the borrowed power of the lotus fading, moment by moment.

"You disappoint me, milady. Either you have used my lotus so sparingly as to be unaware of its true strength, or you are much less perceptive than I had hoped. Such spells are little more than child's play to me. The Emerald Lotus has so enhanced my abilities that I daresay I'm more than a match for any of those arrogant, shortsighted pigs of the Black Ring."

Zelandra made her eyes go wide and took on a look of amazement. "As powerful as that?" she murmured. Her aura of awed astonishment served its purpose. Ethram-Fal swelled visibly with pride and continued in more strident tones, while she settled upon a simple spell of blindness and strove to recall the precise and elaborate details of its casting.

"Certainly! You are familiar with the spell called the Hand of Yimsha? It is a simple manipulator that can be performed by any apprentice of moderate talent to pick up small objects and move them about. It is a fine index of a sorcerer's skill. I have read that the creators of that spell were mighty enough to use it as a weapon, and heard it rumored that Thoth-Amon employed it to build his palace at the Oasis of Khajar.

"Understand this well, Zelandra: I no longer even need to conjure it. It is with me always. And I have used it to kill. Thus far I have seen nothing to indicate that there is an upper limit to the power bestowed by the Emerald Lotus. The more I immerse myself in it, the mightier I become. If you join me, milady, all the power I describe and more shall be yours. Do you understand what it is that I am offering you?" The Stygian leaned forward and lifted his hands imploringly, his tainted eyes shining green as a cat's. "We could become as gods!"

Zelandra thrust out both hands as though pushing him away. Thin streams of gray smoke coiled along the pale flesh of her forearms.

"Tieranog Dar Andurra!" Her voice snapped like the crack of a whip, abruptly free of any weariness. The eldritch spirals of soft gray did not seem to extend themselves from her arms, yet the air was suddenly choked with writhing tendrils of mist. Ethram-Fal cried out in shock as the blunt tips of the smoke trails moved for his eyes like so many trained cobras. Ath stumbled away, shouting incoherently in alarm, both hands covering his face. Zelandra kept her hands extended, her fingers working as if communicating in Heng Shih's sign language. On the altar, Neesa began to writhe against her bonds.

Ethram-Fal backed quickly away, dodging the questing streamers of smoke while muttering sibilant syllables under his breath. Beneath the blank countenance of the black sphinx, with her back to the altar between its paws, Zelandra struggled with her invocation, trying to strike her nemesis blind before he gathered his wits or her strength failed.

Ethram-Fal was forced to retreat all the way to one of the temple's doors, and now he stood motionless before it. He no longer sought to avoid Zelandra's tentacles of smoke. They swarmed into his calm face.

From the halls behind him came the muted sounds of outcry and struggle, distant yet drawing nearer. The Stygian sorcerer had no time for that.

He seemed to relax, his arms hanging limply at his sides, and the chamber was filled with the sound of a raging wind. The strands of the blindness spell were whipped about and shredded in a storm that was felt by no one in the room. Zelandra watched as her desperate bid for freedom disintegrated in a gale that did not so much as stir her hair.

"Clever!" yelled Ethram-Fal. "You led me to underestimate your strength. I salute your power, but this last betrayal is too much to bear. Feel the Hand of Yimsha, milady!"

The last gray streamers thinned and faded, like blood diluting in water, and the Lady Zelandra felt a giant's fist close about her torso. The pressure was immediate and excruciating. Tears sprang to her eyes as the breath wheezed from her compacted lungs.

"Blame yourself, Zelandra! You might have shared the world with me. I-I..." The Stygian appeared almost overcome by a sudden excess of emotion. His wizened face darkened, contorted by hatred and something less easy to identify. "Damn you! Do you think I can't find another to take your place? You're nothing to me! Nothing!"

Zelandra frantically sucked for breath and felt her feet leaving the floor. She was borne upward and back until she hung suspended above the prone form of Neesa, and directly in front of the smooth oval of the idol's face. Even through the haze of pain her eyes were drawn to it, fearfully seeking something in its blank and implacable emptiness. Against the black gloss of its face, a deeper darkness bloomed and grew.

"Tribute!" screamed Ethram-Fal, his body vibrating in every limb. "Sacrifice!" His fist shook and, away across the chamber, Zelandra's body shook with it. The Stygian readied himself for the final moment, opening his eyes wide so as to miss nothing.

There was a clamor in the hallway behind him. He thought to turn and was dealt a blow that lifted him off his feet and dashed him against the wall. His brow struck stone. Pain and blood blurred his vision as he fell to the floor, stunned.

Neesa saw two figures burst into the chamber behind the Stygian sorcerer. The foremost hurled Ethram-Fal aside with a casual blow of his forearm, sending the little man flying like a discarded doll to rebound limply from the wall. A pulse of excitement slammed through her as she saw that the intruders were Conan and Heng Shih. Then Zelandra, freed from the Hand of Yimsha, fell full upon her.

Ath advanced purposefully from the shadows beside the dark idol, his broadsword whisking from its sheath. He moved directly for Conan, who brandished his recently acquired shortsword and spoke.

"Flee, you fool! We're running from a devil out of hell!"

Ath responded with a swift overhand cut aimed at splitting the barbarian's skull. Conan's shorter blade licked out to deflect it with an echoing *clang*.

"I'll take this dog," he bellowed to Heng Shih. "Cut the girl free!"

The Cimmerian presented a picture of starkly primordial savagery. His huge body was entirely spattered with drying blood. A sluggish stream of it split his face like a smear of some macabre war paint. His mail shirt was tarnished and torn, hanging upon his mighty torso in tatters. Glacial blue eyes blazed volcanically through the crimson streaking his snarling visage, fastening upon the mercenary captain with chilling intent.

As Ath stared at his opponent in growing trepidation, the barbarian lashed out. The silvery sword darted for the Stygian's eyes. With a speed that belied his rangy form, Ath brought his weapon up and caught Conan's sword between the blade and quillion. With a practiced twist, Ethram-Fal's captain snapped the barbarian's sword off three inches above the hilt. The blade of the broken weapon sailed above the heads of the combatants, falling to strike the stone floor and rebound with a jingle. Ath skipped back to slash at his nigh-weaponless opponent, but the Cimmerian lunged forward to embrace him. Their bodies slammed together with a clash of mail. Ath's breath, sickly sweet with kaokao, hissed into Conan's face. They grappled. The Stygian could not bring his weapon to bear at such close quarters. The barbarian twisted his sword arm free, dragged the stump of his broken weapon up inside Ath's guard, and buried it in his throat. Then Conan shoved the Stygian away from him with all his strength. The stricken captain reeled away, falling on his back with a crash. His broadsword rattled across the floor and was intercepted by Conan, who took two quick steps, bent, and caught it neatly by the hilt. He snatched the blade up and turned toward the statue, leaving Ath dying on the stone behind him.

Heng Shih's flare-bladed scimitar had cut the bonds pinning Neesa to the black altar and she now stood beside it. The scribe rubbed at her thigh where Zelandra's knee had struck her. Zelandra herself was locked in an embrace with the brawny Khitan, her slender form almost engulfed in his powerful arms.

A distant series of horrified screams came echoing down the hallway. They were choked off almost at once, replaced by an indescribable rasping sound.

"Crom! It follows us! Run if you value your lives!"

"You are going nowhere!"

All heads turned to the doorway that had admitted Conan and Heng Shih.

There, Ethram-Fal had struggled to his feet and stood unsteadily, bracing himself against the portal's arch with one hand. The other hand wiped at the unnaturally dark blood streaming from his forehead, then extended, dripping, to point accusingly at the little group.

"Your luck is remarkable, Zelandra. But it will require more than the selfless efforts of your slaves to save you from my wrath. Nothing has changed. I shall—"

With the instinctive reflexes of the true barbarian, Conan chose that moment to charge his foe. The savage, ululating war cry of a

Cimmerian tribesman smote the ears of those in the chamber. It froze the blood.

Ethram-Fal lifted his encrimsoned hand toward Conan and, with a gesture, halted him in his tracks. A guttural grunt was torn from the barbarian's lips as the Hand of Yimsha clenched its sorcerous fist.

"All of your paltry physical strength is as nothing," spat the Stygian. "I shall crush you like the useless insect that you are."

His hand curled into a tighter fist and the Cimmerian jerked like a man stretched rigid on the rack.

"Watch closely, Zelandra! This fate awaits you, too!" The fist began to close.

Conan felt himself in the coils of some vast and invisible python. Sheets of agony rippled over his straining torso and his skull throbbed, filling his vision with billowing clouds of black and scarlet. His lungs heaved, starving for air and unable to expand. Sweat rolled down his contorted face to drip from his chin. Very slowly, he lifted Ath's broadsword higher and took a faltering step forward.

"Set's mercies!" Ethram-Fal stared in amazed horror as the barbarian took another dragging step toward him.

"Die, dog! Die!" screamed the sorcerer, clenching his fist and squeezing tight. There was a strange sound somewhere in the hallway behind him, but he had confined his attention to the barbarian. This man was damned hard to kill.

Conan felt as if he were walking across the bottom of an ocean. Pressure from all sides threatened to crush his body like a grape in a wine press. Although his sword weighed more than a mountain and the veins in his neck stood out like writhing serpents, all his besieged senses remained set upon his enemy. He lamented the distance that still lay between them while never wavering from his grim purpose. As he shuffled forward another step, his vision began to dim.

"Now!" shouted the Stygian sorcerer. "Now I have you!"

At that moment the Emerald Lotus burst through the doorway like the flood from a broken dam. It bore Ethram-Fal aloft before it, a mere chip upon its tide. The bristling plant-thing drove its bulk through the narrow gap of the doorway and thrust its thorned and flowering branches into the chamber.

The sorcerer found himself helpless on the forefront of a surging juggernaut. His startled cry became a full-throated scream as thorns like black daggers pierced his struggling body.

Ethram-Fal's sorcerous grip fell away from Conan. The barbarian staggered, looked up at the oncoming colossus, and blindly turned to run.

Heng Shih, Neesa, and Zelandra shook free of the paralysis of horror that had held them motionless. The Khitan seized the dazed Zelandra and spun her toward the closest doorway. Neesa followed, turning her back on the monstrosity that poured into the temple as she ran to grasp her mistress's arm. Heng Shih rushed to Conan's aid as the battered barbarian stumbled past him. The great scimitar lashed out at the first questing branch of the blood-hungry Emerald Lotus, lopping off a section the length of a man and sending it spiraling away. The huge bulk of the vampiric fungus slowed not at all. It bore down on the Khitan with Ethram-Fal, howling like a dying dog, still fastened to its swelling bosom. Spiked limbs festooned with vivid green flowers clawed their way over the altar that stood between the black sphinx's stone paws.

Conan hesitated in the portal's arch and saw the women fleeing toward safety down the hallway ahead. Then, turning back, he beheld Heng Shih sprinting straight at him with a towering mass of lotus looming up behind.

"Hurry!" roared the Cimmerian, hefting Ath's broadsword with an arm that still ached from the cruel grip of Ethram-Fal's spell. The Khitan shot past him through the arch and Conan followed. The Emerald Lotus hit the wall around the opening with the sound of a forest splintered by a lightning bolt. Tentacle-like branches whipped through the portal, seeking warm flesh and blood.

Conan and Heng Shih ran down the darkened hallway, chasing the shadows of Zelandra and Neesa, who were headed toward a vague and distant light. Behind them the lotus screwed itself through the doorway and pushed into the hall beyond. Its blood-gorged body almost filled the passage. A thousand thorns and branch-tips sought purchase on the stone walls, floor, and ceiling, pulling the abomination along with frightening speed. Ethram-Fal, driven back into the body of the lotus by its impact against the wall, writhed in his thorny prison and screamed prayers to Set.

The four invaders rounded a corner and fled down the length of a long, straight hall. Ahead loomed a pale arch. Neesa had time to sense a freshening of the air before she ran right out of the Palace of Cetriss. Suddenly there was a dark sky above her and a set of steps beneath her madly running feet. She leapt forward to keep her balance, landing with a clap of heels in the natural courtyard, where two huddled guardsmen rushed to get to their feet.

The blood thundered in Conan's temples and he felt his much-abused body falter. The climb into the palace followed by the pursuit and battle with the guards would have exhausted any ordinary man. Following those trials with Ethram-Fal's agonizing Hand of Yimsha had tested even his iron endurance to its utmost limits. His heavily muscled legs trembled with weariness and breathing filled his breast with flame. Ahead, he saw the running form of Heng Shih drawing away down a hallway that had gone vague and blurred. The floor seemed to pitch and roll beneath him like the deck of a ship in a storm. His balance failed, and his shoulder rebounded painfully from a wall, sending him staggering wildly forward. Behind the barbarian, both the raging rasp of the lotus and the now-feeble cries of its master drew nearer.

Conan shot through the portal and out of the Palace of Cetriss in a horizontal fall. When he hit the steps, he kicked forward with both feet, sending himself across the courtyard in a headlong dive. As his body struck the polished stone of the clearing's floor with punishing impact, he skidded forward and lay still.

The Emerald Lotus exploded through the portal into the outside world. Conan heard muffled shouts and cries. There was a momentary clash of steel against steel; then a woman's voice rose above all.

"Cease, you idiots! The demon has devoured your master!"

Whipping back his sweat-soaked hair, Conan shot a glance over a shoulder and saw the writhing mass of the Emerald Lotus come slithering down the palace steps. The exhausted Cimmerian dragged himself forward, his knees sliding over the smooth stone.

Through the flowering tendrils that imprisoned him, Ethram-Fal watched the crawling form of the barbarian. As the Stygian tried to call a last curse down upon his enemy, a great, green blossom bloomed from the sorcerer's open mouth, cutting off sound and breath forever. Flowers burst from his corpse.

Conan lunged forward and fell heavily on his chest, driving both hands into the fluffy gray ashes of the firepit. He groped desperately as the lotus rose above him in a tidal wave of deadly thorns, verdant blossoms, and lashing branches. The first limbs fell across his outstretched legs. The Cimmerian seized something from the firepit that seared into his palm. He rolled over, and with a savage howl of rage, thrust the red-hot ember into the body of the Emerald Lotus.

The effect was immediate and overwhelming. Scarlet curls of flame erupted around the outthrust ember. It was as though he had torched a dead and dried evergreen. The Emerald Lotus recoiled in a convulsive heave, drawing away from the barbarian and pulling back onto the palace stairs. But a scarlet badge of fire clung to its branches and grew there, coursing over and through its misshapen form. It burned with a sharp, ear-piercing hiss. In a moment its interior was alive with flame and the silhouettes of its victims' bodies were etched in deepest black against the flaring red-orange light. Then the lotus withdrew into the palace like a snake fleeing down its hole. The glow of its burning dwindled down the dark hallway.

Conan the Cimmerian lay on his back, supporting himself on one elbow, and watched the death throes of the Emerald Lotus. From within the Palace of Cetriss came a relentless crashing and rasping as the demonic thing thrashed out its unnatural life within the confines of its creator's lair. Each of the windows shone briefly with fiery light as the lotus rampaged through the palace seeking succor.

In time it was still.

The sandstorm had passed, leaving behind a cloud-swept night sky full of clean, rushing wind. Neesa knelt at Conan's side. The barbarian struggled to rise, and Neesa laid a gentle hand on his shoulder. Heng Shih limped close, using his scimitar like a cane. His breathing was audible as his heavy hand joined Neesa's on Conan's brawny shoulder.

"Lie still," she whispered. "You must rest."

"No," growled the Cimmerian. "I want to stand." Conan stood up, his feet spread wide apart. The night wind cooled his burnt hand and pulled his black mane away from his bloodstained face. He looked across the courtyard at the two Stygian guardsmen, who stood in tense silence, swords clutched in rigid hands. He scowled and, wordlessly, they came forward and laid their weapons at his feet.

EXEUNT

Tossing back half the remaining flagon of watered wine, Conan wrapped his cloak around himself, leaned against the gorge's wall, and immediately dozed off. After a brief conversation in sign language with Zelandra, Heng Shih followed the barbarian's example. Neesa and her mistress spoke in hushed tones for some time. They cast suspicious glances at the two surviving mercenary soldiers of Ethram-Fal, who sat in dispirited silence. With their employer and comrades dead, the pair apparently saw scant reason to quarrel with the invaders. Sleepless, they sat against the canyon's far wall, awaiting the morning and their fate.

In time Neesa fell into an exhausted slumber, leaning against the shoulder of Lady Zelandra, who showed no apparent signs of weariness.

The lady stared straight ahead, and though her gaze made the Stygian captives cringe and look away, it was not directed at them. She looked ahead to her future and bided her time until the morning. Thus, when the sun drove the stars from the sky, she was the first into the Palace of Cetriss.

The gentle sounds of her rousing woke Conan, who stretched hugely, shook Heng Shih awake, and followed her. He slowed just long enough to cast a baleful glance at the Stygian captives. Behind him, the sun rose with slow inevitability until its fierce golden rays fell into the canyon cul-de-sac.

The interior of the Palace of Cetriss had been scourged by the death throes of the flaming Emerald Lotus. Most of the light-globes had been torn from their niches in the walls and smashed by its passing. Conan picked up one of the few surviving globes and used it to light their way. The cots in the Great Chamber were smashed into scorched kindling.

Ethram-Fal's laboratories and private rooms looked as if a fiery wind out of hell had blown through them, crushing and charring everything into black wreckage. Nowhere did they see a human body. Silence lay thick on the smoke-tainted air.

They found the Emerald Lotus in its chamber, as if in death it had sought out the place of its birth. It had burnt down to its twisted core. The lotus was reduced to a clenched coil of blackened, thorny branches gripping a ghastly collection of contorted skeletons. The incinerated corpses of its victims were crushed together in its death embrace, wound and woven into its shrunken fabric so that Conan and Zelandra found it impossible to tell one body from another. All—human and animal, master and slave— were joined in death. The smoke and intense heat had seared and darkened the chamber, staining the walls as far as the pair could see. The high band of hieroglyphics that encircled the room was obscured by soot.

Conan took the sword that had been Ath's and struck at a curled limb of the lotus. Though it looked as solid as black stone, the burnt branch broke apart more easily than coal, crumbling into loose ash and releasing the skull it gripped to fall and rattle hollowly on the scarred stone floor.

Tearing free a shred of his tattered shirt, the barbarian distastefully wiped the dark ash from his blade. He noticed that Zelandra was staring emptily at the corpse of the Emerald Lotus.

She stood still and silent, one arm crooked across her midsection. The sorceress breathed shallowly and did not seem to blink. Conan took her arm and led her away.

The palace's lowest levels seemed to have escaped the insensate fury of the dying lotus. In a crude series of rooms carved out below the desert floor, they found both the stables where the mercenaries kept their camels and ponies, and a room full of supplies. There were sacks of provisions, grain for the beasts, and a large collection of tall ceramic jugs of water. They led the animals into the light, where Heng Shih and Neesa anxiously awaited their return.

The Stygian captives were astonished when Conan gave each water and a camel and told them to be gone. The taller of the two stared mutely at the Cimmerian, while the other bowed low, as though he stood before a king. They wasted no time in taking the barbarian's advice and departing down the narrow canyon.

While Conan, Heng Shih, and Neesa prepared to leave by bathing in the plentiful water and eating freely of the mercenaries' provisions, Zelandra quietly disappeared into the palace. When all was in readiness, the three looked about for her. They found Lady Zelandra in the pillar-flanked doorway, her face glimmering as pale as a mask of alabaster against the darkness of the portal. When Zelandra emerged into the morning light, they saw that her body was bent forward and that she used one arm to clutch her ribs.

"Conan, Neesa," she called, and then more tenderly, "Heng Shih."

"Come along, milady," said Neesa, a faint quaver in her voice. "We've far to go."

"No," answered Zelandra. "I have scoured every inch of this ruin and can find none of the Emerald Lotus. The entire plant has been burnt to useless ash. You must leave me here; I would not burden you with my madness and my death. I have failed and despite his doom, Ethram-Fal has triumphed."

"Nay," said Conan as he swung his long legs over his camel's back and dismounted. "I must be getting old if a little fighting makes me so forgetful." The Cimmerian bounded up the stone steps of the palace toward the Lady Zelandra, and drew his backpack from beneath a bronzed arm. "I snatched this from the wizard's room of magics when Heng Shih and I hid from his guards."

A long, slender box of polished ebony emerged from the scruffy backpack and gleamed dully in the morning light. Conan twisted the golden clasp, lifted the lid, and held out the open box for Zelandra to see.

The sorceress could not restrain a gasp as she gazed upon a glittering drift of emerald dust.

"The Stygian's private stock, I'll warrant," grunted Conan. "I hope, lady, that this is enough to serve your need."

Zelandra took the box, closed it, and held it to her breast.

"Yes, barbarian, I will make it so."

Together they walked from the shadow of the Palace of Cetriss into the bright sun of Stygia. The Cimmerian lifted the weary sorceress onto her camel's back, and the little group moved as one down the canyon that led to the west and away. Conan took the lead, the desert wind tossing his black mane. He did not look back.

Behind them, the Palace of Cetriss returned to the silence in which it had slept for thirty centuries. Its weathered pillars warmed in the rising sun and cooled with the coming of night. Deep within, alone in its high and vaulted temple, the faceless statue of black stone stared into the darkness that it knew so well.

CONAN
AND THE
LIVING
PLAGUE

PROLOGUE

Adrastus, once of Koth, readied himself for magic. He stood before a gilt-framed mirror and straightened the lace at the neck of his blue velvet doublet. He shook back his cloak, inscribed with small, arcane sigils in white silk that shone as bright upon the deep blue fabric as stars against a twilit sky. Thick fingers combed through the tight, auburn curls of his beard. His reflection peered back at him skeptically, then put on a false smile. Running a hand over his burgeoning paunch, the Kothian bent to a low table beside the mirror, where a star-shaped pendant of transparent crystal sat in a nest of piled silk. Adrastus fastened it around his neck and buried the bright pendant in the lace at his throat. With a final, appraising glance at his reflection, he walked to the door.

Lost in his thoughts, Adrastus strode through the baronial palace of Dulcine. For the thousandth time he reflected upon the vagaries of fortune that had brought him to this strange and wondrous place. There was no one to break his reverie; the magnificent marble hall was deserted. His soft footfalls echoed in the silence.

Sorcery did not come easily to Adrastus. He had begun his studies late in life and had shown but marginal aptitude. Only the Kothian's fierce desire to develop magical skills had enabled him to attain even a modest level of competence. He was past thirty summers and still apprenticed to an older sorcerer. His lips drew tight with the shame of it. At times his whole life seemed an exercise in slow failure. Still, it was best not to dwell on the inalterable, but rather to consider his good fortune. His master might be an impatient dotard, but the old man was the finest sorcerer out of Stygia to even consider taking on an apprentice. The best wizards tended to be the most self-absorbed, unwilling to tolerate fellow magicians, much less apprentices. Old Tolbeth-Khar could teach him much, but only as long as Adrastus continued to swallow his pride.

The Kothian passed beneath a fretted arch and entered a large, circular chamber that was unique in all the world. The Baron of Dulcine, rich as the lords of Ophir, had spent much of his fortune building this room to the exacting specifications of sorcerers drawn from across the length and breadth of the continent. Their cooperation was paid for in part by the opportunity to use the Chamber of Conjuring they had helped create. The room was probably the most potent man-made magical nexus extant. Adrastus drew a deep breath, inhaled its charged atmosphere as one might sip a draft of strong wine. The very air seemed to purr and seethe with invisible power; a power that waited patiently to be tapped and controlled by those who knew how.

Tolbeth-Khar turned from the podium to face his tardy apprentice, disapproval writ large upon his wrinkled features. The old Stygian set hands on hips and stared wordlessly at his student. In the awkward silence, Adrastus looked away from his stern master and concentrated instead upon the striking beauty of the chamber.

The circular room was about forty paces across and its famed domed ceiling rose to nearly that height as well.

Fashioned entirely of stained glass, the luminous patchwork of entwined colors, shapes, and symbols arched in a web of glittering beauty. The ceiling had taken ten years to complete and some of the glass had been brought from as far away as Khitai and Kambuja. Alternating slabs of glossy black marble and plates of mirror paneled the walls. As he looked away from Tolbeth-Khar, Adrastus saw his own abashed expression reflected in a dozen sheets of polished glass. The floor was a single mammoth mosaic, countless tiny tiles of ivory and ebony laid in the shape of a vastly intricate compass. Wheels and arrows, black on white, interlocked and crisscrossed in what the untrained eye would see as a senseless welter of complexity. But there was order here, sinister and purposeful.

The sun emerged from a bank of cloud and its light seemed to burst through the stained-glass dome. When Adrastus looked back to his master, the Stygian's podium was a dark island in a sea of riotous color. Livid crimson fell across the old sorcerer's shoulders like a bloody mantle. Tolbeth-Khar's heavy brown cloak hung open over his narrow chest and revealed a white silk shirt spattered with tea stains.

Adrastus advanced, passing through patches of light tinted dusky cobalt, deep emerald, and tawny gold. He bowed deeply before Tolbeth-Khar.

"Does it please you to be late for every engagement? No matter how important?" The Stygian's voice was cold, but strong and youthful, in odd contrast to his hunched body.

Adrastus bit back a bitter retort.

"A thousand apologies, my lord," said the Kothian. "I find no pleasure in displeasing you. Forgive me."

Tolbeth-Khar frowned, then nodded absently. "Take your position then, apprentice. And be quick about it."

Adrastus did as he was bidden, and stepped into a whorl in the floor's mosaic five paces to the right of his master's podium.

In front of the rostrum, directly in the center of the circular chamber, was a low dais of black onyx. Centered atop the dais, a small ebony table had a tiny cube of incense placed in each corner and, at the precise center of the tabletop, a tall, slender vial of crystal, sparkling in the sun.

Adrastus looked upon the vial and felt a surge of pride. It was his creation, his primary contribution to the ceremony. The magic associated with glass and crystal was the only form of sorcery in which he had shown any true potential. Tolbeth-Khar might well have been able to fashion the vial himself, but he had asked Adrastus to do it.

"Are you ready?" A tinge of acid sarcasm still tainted the old Stygian's tone.

Adrastus clenched his hands into fists, but spoke mildly. "Yes, master."

Immediately, the walls and ceiling began to resound with the sonorous sound of Tolbeth-Khar's chanting. His voice rose and fell in cadences strange to the ear, speaking words few men had ever heard. The Kothian stared ceaselessly at his vial, waiting for its moment of glory.

There came a pause in the Stygian's chant. Adrastus took his cue, and spoke the twenty-seven words that were his part of the verbal ceremony. The syllables hurt his throat, but he pronounced them correctly.

As Tolbeth-Khar continued, the incantation slowly acquired an alien timbre. There was an inexplicable companion voice, as if an invisible phantom echoed each word the Stygian uttered. At first it spoke in a thin whisper, but it grew louder as the ceremony continued until it was as audible as Tolbeth-Khar himself. The voice was inflectionless, metallic, and inhuman. Adrastus grew tense. His fists, still tightly clenched beneath the velvet wings of his cloak, began to ache dully.

The cubes of incense at the ebony table's corners ignited spontaneously with a muffled hiss. Blue-gray smoke rose in concentric whorls and a weird medley of smells stung the

Kothian's nostrils: damp rot and poppies; acrid bile and fresh sea air.

The space around the vial suddenly blurred, the outlines of the table and the dais itself softened. Adrastus blinked, but his vision had not failed him. A distorting haze grew up around the vial until it filled the center of the chamber like a miraculously contained fog. Squinting into the unnatural haze, Adrastus heard Tolbeth-Khar's chant falter and cease.

The crystal vial grew dark, as if magically filled with a black syrup. Then it exploded, bursting into shining shards with a sharp treble report like the striking of some eldritch chime. Adrastus gasped and involuntarily stepped back out of his assigned position on the mosaic floor. The vial was supposed to be filled. The delicate ceremony had gone awry.

In the sorcerous haze that surrounded the dais, a vague shape took form. The shape solidified as the astonished apprentice stared in disbelief. It looked like a man.

"What in the name of Set?" choked out Tolbeth-Khar.

The haze was suddenly gone. It didn't dissipate, but blinked out like a burst bubble, and there was a tall, lean man standing in the room's center. He was naked and hairless, his head and body long and angular. His flesh was a golden amber and his face a still mask of frozen beauty. The man regarded the Stygian sorcerer expressionlessly, his eyes like dull pools of pitch. Adrastus blinked and the man was wearing clothes. His dress matched Tolbeth-Khar's in every detail. The heavy folds of a brown cloak fell open over his breast, revealing a white silk shirt patterned with tea stains.

"What— Who are you?" stammered the Stygian mage. "What are you doing here?"

Adrastus turned and ran from the room. He fled down the curved hallway to his chambers, ducked through the doorway, and seized from his desk a roll of velvet. When he swung back to the door, a scream came to his ears. He froze, and the scream came again, a ragged, hellish cry of pain and disbelief. Tormented though it was, the apprentice recognized the voice of Tolbeth-Khar.

Adrastus sprinted from the room, his boots sliding on the polished floor in desperate haste. Black fear devoured his thoughts and reduced him to a fleeing animal. He almost lost his footing on the stairs, but grasped the banister and slid along the wall a few paces before he caught his balance and took the steps two at a time. The Chamber of Conjuring was on the highest level of the baronial palace, and the huge spiral stairs seemed to wind down forever. Adrastus was portly and ill-suited to any physical activity, much less headlong flight.

The breath rasped painfully in his throat and his heart thundered within the confines of his ribs, seeming about to tear free of its moorings. When the Kothian reached the ground floor at last, his knees gave way and he fell to the carpet with a choked curse. Scarlet-faced and gasping, Adrastus forced himself to his feet and stumbled forward.

The broad, iron-bound doors of the palace stood open. Outside, bright sunshine and the pleasant sound of the baron's famous sweet water fountain filled the courtyard. Several armored guards and a pair of tradeswomen turned to stare at the man who staggered from the palace. Adrastus paid them no heed.

Leaving the splashing fountain and the inquiring calls of the guards behind, the fleeing man disappeared around the corner of the sheer-walled palace. He ran into the baron's stables and almost collided with a livery boy bearing a pitchfork full of straw. The freckled lad gaped at Adrastus. He saw a man garbed like a noble, yet running with sweat and gasping like a caught fish.

"A horse," wheezed the Kothian, "get me a horse. Now, damn your eyes!"

"Whose horse, sir? Yours? Are you well, sir?"

"Get me a fast horse; any horse, or I'll kill you where you stand!" Adrastus half-collapsed against the stable wall. He looked less than threatening as he leaned there, pale and atremble, yet his eyes blazed with such fearful intensity that the stable boy quailed with terror.

"Don't kill me, sir! Take the horse in the stable behind you. It's the baron's own, and as fleet as any here."

Adrastus turned, wrenched open the door of the stall behind him, and revealed a strapping black stallion, already saddled. He stumbled into the stall, snatched the beast's reins, and jerked forward. The horse snorted angrily as the apprentice dragged himself into the saddle and drove his heels hard into the animal's flanks. With a fearful cry, the stable boy hurled himself from the horse's path and went rolling in the straw.

The stallion pounded through the streets of Dulcine, scattering pedestrians as it headed for the small walled city's only gate. Adrastus rode like a madman, beating the animal mercilessly and caring nothing for the angry cries that rose in his wake.

The gate was closed. The Kothian heaved back on the reins with force enough to nearly dislocate his mount's jaw. He looked up the sun-bleached wall to the crenelated guard post high above.

"Ho there!" he bellowed. "Open the gate! Baron's business!"

A helmeted head thrust over the rim of the wall. A crossbow was leveled at Adrastus's breast.

"Who are you to declare baron's business?"

"Damn you, man! I'm Adrastus, one of the baron's wizards, and if you don't open the gate he shall hear of it."

"Aye, then," called the guard. "No disrespect. A soldier must do his job."

"Of course." The apprentice forced false friendliness into his voice. As the great double doors of Dulcine's gate creaked slowly open, his eyes darted back into the city behind him, and his ears strained for sounds he feared to hear.

The guard was surprised to see one of the king's own wizards wedge his fine horse through the gate as soon as it opened wide enough to pass. It seemed remarkably undignified behavior for a sorcerer.

"Close the gate," shouted Adrastus over his shoulder. "Lock it, guardsman!"

The Kothian hesitated just long enough to see the doors begin to reverse direction; then he wheeled and drove his stallion down the road and away from the walls. As the branches of the forest came overhead, he heard the first cries. He rode on as if in a day-lit nightmare, the thundering hooves of his mount unable to blot out the sudden, terrible clamor. A ghastly chorus of screams rose into the clear summer sky.

Adrastus fled and, behind him, Dulcine died.

D ark clouds rolled slowly across the sullen dome of the sky, gray and swollen with the promise of rain. The distant mutter of summer thunder rose and fell on the moist breeze. In a field beneath the darkening sky stood orderly ranks of armored men. A chill mist of rain began to fall, but the soldiers of Mamluke's Legion stood stiffly straight and seemed to pay it no heed.

Before the massed ranks of men stood a regal pavilion of scarlet silk, its glossy sides billowing in the rising wind. The flap was sealed to bar any view of the tent's interior. An open expanse of ground, its grass scythed short and even, stretched between the pavilion and the soldiers. Circular archery targets were set against bales of hay at the far end of this space, while two sturdy wooden posts, wrapped in thick cables, were set in the earth directly in front of the tent's flap. The soldiers in the front ranks futilely strained their ears to overhear the muted sounds of conversation within the pavilion.

In the second rank stood a giant of a man wearing a brightly silvered mail shirt. He stood out not merely for his brawn, which was remarkable, but for the fact that he was the only warrior in the first ten ranks without a uniform. All those around him wore black mail, blue leather gauntlets, and helmets with low crests dyed blue to match. Tapered shortswords of identical design hung at their belts. The young giant's unruly black mane spilled from beneath a simple leather helm. His big hands were bare, and at his waist was a great broadsword of northern design. He wore plain leather breeches and a battered, but sturdy looking, pair of boots. The nearest soldiers in garb as motley as his stood far back from the pavilion.

The slow rain collected on the rim of his helmet, overflowed, spilled into his hair, and ran coldly behind an ear. The man's grim face betrayed no discomfort. His eyes, as blue as glacial ice, stared straight ahead. The giant had, in his time, been a leader of men. But neither his current status as a lowly mercenary nor the seeping, chilling rain seemed to affect him in the slightest.

"Hssst, Cimmerian." The whisper came from his left. "Ho, Conan, have you fallen asleep?"

"Shamtare," said the giant softly, his whisper more of a rumble. "We are on inspection. Be still." Beside him, Shamtare shifted uncomfortably, shuffling his booted feet in the wet grass.

"We have short notice inspection in the rain, on a day of festival. Is this not strange?" Shamtare was a stout, sturdily built Shemite and he wore the armor of Mamluke's Legion as if he were born in it. Rainwater beaded his graying beard and thick black eyebrows. He pursed his lips ruefully.

"You're still angry with me, aren't you? By Ishtar, Conan, what must—"

"Silence," hissed Conan.

The flap of the pavilion was thrust aside and two men stepped from its dim interior. The first was Mamluke himself, commander of the mercenary troop, a man well known for his exploits in the service of half the petty kingdoms of Shem. His armor matched that worn by his men, save that the crest of his helmet was taller and the hilt of his short sword glittered with gems. Though only of middle height, he gave the impression of imposing size as he imperiously surveyed his soldiers. Behind him came a tall, slim man in a long cape as scarlet as the pavilion. His pointed features were fixed in a frown as he plucked nervously at his waxed mustache. He wore a gaudy, golden breastplate fashioned to resemble a muscular male torso wound about by a raised design in the form of twining vines. A slim rapier in a gilded sheath hung from his jeweled girdle.

"Prince Eoreck, or I'm a Stygian!" Shamtare's whisper rose dangerously loud. "What the hell is the king's nephew doing inspecting us?"

"Silence," said Conan again. Nervous mutters of agreement rose from the soldiers around him. Conan watched as Mamluke set his hands on his hips and addressed his troops.

"Good morning, soldiers." Mamluke's deep, resonant voice belied his stature. "Our employer, the King of Akkharia, has sent his noble nephew to examine us. He shall inspect our ranks and then we shall demonstrate our skill in archery and sword combat." He stroked his close-cut beard and looked over his men meaningfully. "I have no doubt that he shall be suitably impressed."

Prince Eoreck walked slowly along the rows of mercenaries and scrutinized each man in turn. Now and again, he would hesitate, bending to stare at a scuffed boot or patched bit of mail. He said nothing.

When Prince Eoreck came to Conan, he stopped and raised his brows. The prince's dark eyes took in the barbarian's powerful build and mismatched armor. "A northern outlander?"

"A Cimmerian," responded Conan.

"I have heard tales of your countrymen. A grim people worshipping a grim god. They are said to love bloodshed and hate travel."

The barbarian shrugged hulking shoulders. "In some respects, I am much like my countrymen; in others, I differ."

The prince grinned at this, then proceeded along the line of mercenaries. When he was several ranks behind Conan, Shamtare whispered again: "This is a damned odd business. Eoreck is known more for his interest in gambling and wenching than inspecting mercenaries. I wonder what this means for us."

"We'll know in time. Now be still."

The rain continued to fall in a slow, clinging mist, beading on helmets, working its way through mail to trickle maddeningly along limbs. Questions writhed unanswered in Shamtare's mind, making each minute more unendurable than the last. Conan stared ahead in stoic impassivity.

Eventually, Prince Eoreck completed his inspection and Mamluke called out a trio of archers to demonstrate their prowess. Conan was surprised to see that one of the archers was little more than a beardless lad. Shamtare took note of the Cimmerian's interest.

"The young one is Pezur. I signed him on to the troop just as I did yourself. Watch his skill. The lad shoots like a dream." Fatherly pride glowed in the Shemite's voice.

Shamtare's words proved correct. While the other two archers would have been a credit to any band of mercenaries, the young man named Pezur shot with astonishing precision.

After crowding the bullseye of his target, his last two arrows actually split the shafts of his prior shots, drawing admiring applause from the mercenaries, despite standing orders to remain silent during inspection. Mamluke, obviously too pleased to mind, smiled broadly as the archers returned to their places.

Four men were then selected to display their skill with swords. Beneath Prince Eoreck's probing gaze they warmed up by practicing forms upon the cable-wrapped posts set in the earth before the tent, then sparred vigorously with wooden blades. Conan watched each passage with interest, noting clever moves as well as lapses in technique. Though the speed and skill of the

Pezur shoots arrows as Conan and Shemtare watch

four swordsmen were exemplary, he had little doubt that he could teach them all something about swordplay. Eoreck called a halt to the bout and the mercenaries dropped their wooden weapons and rejoined the troop. The prince spoke into Mamluke's ear, and the commander's face grew stern. He turned to his soldiers and raised his arms.

"The prince is pleased with us, but asks for one more demonstration. A demonstration of his own devising. A demonstration of strength." With this, Mamluke walked purposefully into the ranks of his men, pushing soldiers aside until he stood before Conan. He looked the barbarian up and down.

"You. Shamtare tells me you're the best he's ever seen," said the commander softly. "Don't dishonor us."

The Cimmerian strode to the front of the troop, and waited wordlessly beside the prince as Mamluke brought another soldier from the troop's hindmost ranks.

Prince Eoreck ducked into the pavilion and was lost to view. The second soldier selected by Mamluke came to Conan's side and eyed him arrogantly. The man was a big Brythunian, sandy of hair and wide of face. Though not quite as tall as the barbarian, his body was heavier. His thick-limbed and fleshy bulk made him seem an ox beside the tigerish Cimmerian. The uniform he wore was dingy and too small for his brawny body. He carried no sword, but rather a huge-headed war-hammer that dangled from a strap down his back.

"My name is Bosk," said the Brythunian. "I hope the prince asks us to fight, for I hate barbarians."

"You should hope he does not," said Conan flatly, "as it would spare you the fate of being slain by one."

Bosk opened and closed his mouth in search of a response, but no reply was forthcoming. He was spared any attempt at repartee by the reappearance of Prince Eoreck, who came out of the pavilion carrying a heavy burden. The prince half-stumbled under the weight of two wooden swords the size of small logs. Each was better than four feet long and as big around as a man's thigh. The end of each was shaped into a rude hilt, but the rest was merely a rough length of heavy wood. He dropped them at the feet of the mercenaries, took an awkward step back, and drew a relieved breath. His gloved hands wiped flecks of bark from his shining breastplate as his scarlet cloak flapped in the blowing rain.

"True strength is all too uncommon these days. I need—Akkharia needs men of might to serve her. Pick up a sword, men."

"Do we fight, then?" asked Bosk, as he seized a log-like sword.

"Nay," said the prince. "You are not slaves in some Stygian arena, but free mercenaries of Shem. Let me see you wield these weapons against yonder posts. Standard practice forms will do."

Despite the prince's facile words, Conan realized their task was not to be an easy one. Each weapon was heavy and unwieldy to lift, but to grasp it by one end and wave it about like a sword would tax the strength and control of the most powerful of men. The Cimmerian set his teeth, clenched iron fingers around the uneven hilt, and hoisted the "sword" into a defensive posture. He approached the practice post, the muscles of his arms knotting beneath his bronze skin. The weapon jutted into the air before him. It did not even tremble. Conan heard Bosk's labored breathing and knew that the Brythunian was not faring so well. The Cimmerian put the other man out of his mind, concentrating entirely upon the task at hand with the total absorption of a seasoned warrior.

The barbarian's motions would have been recognized on any field where men practiced at weapons. An overhand cut slammed down upon the top of the post. The ponderous weapon slid to the right as swiftly as if it were a slender blade, and cut back in to rebound from the post's side. Then Conan hoisted the sword above his head, spun around, and brought his weapon back in a roundhouse blow against the post's opposite side. The moves were simple, and as old as blade combat, but the strength and control needed to execute them with this precision, while wielding a weapon of such size and weight, was breathtaking. Excited mutters rose from the ranks of mercenaries. Conan did not hear them. His body moved in perfect accord with his mind.

Beside the barbarian, Bosk sweated and grunted with strain. His initial overhand blow had bounced from the top of the post and slid down along its side. It had taken all his strength to keep his sword from dropping to the ground. He recovered, hoisted the weapon, and struck the right side of the post smartly. Lifting the wooden sword easily above his head, he turned and swung it in a circular arc against the post's left side. The impact produced a loud *crack* and a cry of pain as the weapon sprang from Bosk's fingers. It spun away, sliding on the sodden grass.

"Mitra's eyes!" cursed the Brythunian, and started after his lost sword. Mamluke caught his shoulder and stopped him in mid-stride.

"You did a creditable job. Now be still and watch a master."

Bosk turned to watch the barbarian with eyes that soon grew round with disbelief. Conan moved smoothly from one practice form to the next, his square jaw set grimly. Veins stood out from his neck and his thick arms rippled with muscles swollen almost to bursting. His repeated and constantly varied blows upon the post filled the air with a metronomic series of impacts that rang loudly in the quiet field.

"By Ishtar, I've never seen such a thing," said Mamluke.

He grinned and shouted to the laboring Cimmerian: "Ho, barbarian! Hew with some strength there! Your foe still stands!"

Conan responded by speeding up his assault. Now the breath rasped from his lungs and the wetness that soaked his hair and body was as much sweat as rain. His knuckles were white as bone upon the hilt. The huge weapon trembled in the air, but never slowed or faltered in its relentless attack.

"Come!" yelled Mamluke, grinning like a lunatic. "Finish your foe!"

A hoarse bellow broke from the barbarian's lips and he spun in a full circle, bringing the weapon around at head level in a tremendous circular slash. The sword struck with a *crack* that stung the ears, burst the ropes that wrapped the post, and drove the post itself from the ground in a spray of dark earth. The post bounced on the grass beside the raw pit from which it had been torn.

Conan turned to face Mamluke, who gaped at the barbarian in wordless amazement. The Cimmerian drew the massive wooden weapon up in a formal salute, then dropped it to the ground.

There was a moment's silence, immediately shattered by a chorus of ragged cheers from the mercenaries. Mamluke seized the barbarian's fist in a warrior's handshake and the cheers swelled louder.

"May Set eat me if I don't believe that Shamtare was right," said Mamluke into Conan's ear. "Stay with my troop and there is a bonus in gold and advancement in rank for you. You have my word." The commander stepped away from the barbarian. He waved Conan and Bosk back to their places. As the crowd quieted and the two men resumed their positions, the Brythunian flung a resentful glance at Conan's broad back.

The prince stepped to the fore with a flourish of his crimson cape. His thin voice rose as he addressed the assembled troop, contrasting poorly with Mamluke's more stentorian tones.

"I am very pleased with the quality of Mamluke's Legion. Despite a few lapses in dress and decorum, I should say that this is perhaps the most impressive mercenary unit currently serving my uncle, King Sumuabi. I bid you good day, and convey my royal uncle's command that you keep your warrior skills in prime condition for the day he requires them." With that the prince bowed foppishly and returned to the pavilion.

"All right, soldiers," Mamluke shouted, his harsh tones offset by the grin that revealed his pleasure. "Not a bad showing. You have the rest of the day off." Voices murmured in approval at this.

"But," continued the commander, "I expect all of you back in the barracks by midnight tonight. Tomorrow we drill all day."

The approving voices broke into moans at the thought of a full day's practice on the morrow. The ranks of mercenaries broke up into clusters of men, not a few of whom stopped to offer the Cimmerian congratulations on his remarkable feat.

"Ho, Pezur," Shamtare hailed the youthful archer. "Come meet the barbarian I was telling you about. Is he not the great warrior I described?"

Conan grimaced wearily, doffing his helm to reveal sweat-plastered hair. The muscles of his arms and chest throbbed deeply and steadily. Despite his show of stoicism, the exhibition of strength had not been easy. He stretched hugely, like a jungle cat.

"I would be honored if you would allow me to buy you a drink," said Pezur formally.

Conan snorted with laughter.

"As my purse is as empty as that Brythunian's head, I'll honor any drink you set before me."

"And I'll buy the next round," said Shamtare. "I'll wager that, if we proceed directly to the Red Hand, we can fit in a full evening's revel between now and midnight."

The three men walked from the field among their fellows. The mercenaries filtered slowly back to the dirt road that led through open pastures to where the dark walls of Akkharia loomed against the rain-swept sky. Shortly, the grassy expanse was empty save for Prince Eoreck's crimson pavilion. Its silken sides snapped in the growing breeze. The flap opened and a man clad in blue robes emerged. He looked toward Akkharia, his brown eyes dreamy and thoughtful. His hands stroked at the star-shaped crystal that hung about his neck.

To the north, a blue-white flash of lightning split the sky, and a peal of thunder, like the roar of an approaching dragon, rolled across the land.

2

The bunk was too short and its mattress was little more than a threadbare sack stuffed with ancient straw. Still, the man lying diagonally across the narrow pallet seemed to be sleeping soundly. Neither the markedly unluxurious bed nor the ceaseless snores and sighs of the slumbering barracks around him seemed to impinge upon his easy rest. The man had slept on silken coverlets and dank stone; in the bed of a princess and propped against a tree in the snow. The bunk was a less than ideal resting place, but he had made do with much worse.

A booted foot was set upon a floorboard beside the bunk. The floorboard emitted a soft creak, and the sleeping man sat up abruptly. His right hand flew out to seize the throat of the intruder standing at his bedside.

Mamluke choked, both hands tearing at the fingers that closed his windpipe. Conan released the mercenary commander as swiftly as he had seized him. The exchange had been almost instantaneous, and virtually soundless.

"Sweet Ishtar," whispered Mamluke, as he rubbed his aching throat. "I thought you were asleep."

"I was," rumbled the barbarian. "I wake easily."

"So it would seem." Mamluke's air of command returned as if it had not been dispelled. "Get up and follow me. Be silent about it. Let us awaken no one."

"Too late for that." The amused whisper came from the upper bunk across the aisle from Conan's. Shamtare's white grin shone in the dimness. "What's the occasion, captain?"

Mamluke seemed to hesitate, looking from the Cimmerian to the Shemite in indecision. He shrugged mailed shoulders.

"Ah, come along, Shamtare. Be quiet about it, though." The stout mercenary dropped soundlessly from his bunk, slipped on his boots, and followed the two men as they passed through the darkened barracks. The soldiers slept on unknowing.

Outside the building the rain had ceased, and the moist chill of morning's earliest hours hung in the air. The cloud cover had receded and the stars glimmered like bright points of frost. The three men walked across an open courtyard to the small building of rough-hewn logs that served as Mamluke's office and quarters. The door stood open and, within, the welcoming, yellow-gold glow of a fire beckoned.

Inside, silent men crowded the central room. Beside the roaring fireplace stood Mamluke's desk, and at the desk stood a heavy, bearded man in robes of blue velvet.

"Is everyone here now?" asked the man. His tone was warm and jovial, but his eyes gleamed with a cool, detached appraisal. Mamluke pushed through his men and joined the stranger at the fireside.

"Yes. These are some of my best." As Mamluke was not given to great praise of anyone or anything, there were few men in the room that did not stand a little straighter upon hearing those words.

"Excellent." The bearded man nodded. "Excellent." Conan chose that moment to look about the room.

Aside from himself and Shamtare, he noticed the young archer, Pezur, and the big Brythunian, Bosk. There were several others whom he had seen on the practice field but did not know by name. His eyes were drawn to a half-obscured figure standing behind the desk, in the dark corner between the fireplace and wall. A massive man in the heavy armor of the asshuri of Shumir stepped between Conan and the shadowy figure. The asshuri had a jaw like a shovel, and he thrust it at the Cimmerian in silent challenge. A bodyguard, Conan thought, though too aggressive to be a good one.

"You have all been honored tonight. Honored and given a rare opportunity." The bearded man spoke expressively, and spread his hands to take in all the men in the room. "My name is Adrastus, but I am of little significance in this affair. Allow me to present the man responsible for both summoning you here and offering you the greatest opportunity of your lives. His Highness, Prince Eoreck."

The figure in the shadows beside the fireplace moved forward as his shovel-jawed asshuri bodyguard stepped aside. Firelight gleamed on the surface of the prince's gilded breastplate. Eoreck tugged at his waxed mustache and nervously surveyed the men gathered before him.

"All of you know me," he said, "and I trust many of you wondered why I called inspection on your troop today. I daresay some of you were surprised to see that I would take the time to examine you personally. Well, I am always interested in the armies of my beloved Akkharia, but I confess that I had another motive."

Conan shifted uneasily. The prince's words were predictably pompous, but the pervasive aura of secrecy spoke of danger and treachery. The broadsword at the barbarian's waist had a comforting weight.

"I have fallen upon financially difficult times. My uncle, the king, looks with disfavor upon me and hence upon my father, his own brother. King Sumuabi is a stern monarch, and though I wish to speak no evil of him, I shall say that he is unjust in judging me so harshly. He has no male heirs as yet, and he might legitimately look upon me as a possible successor. Instead, my uncle condemns me as a gambler and socialite. He has barred me from gaming and gatherings of nobility, even though his rule might benefit from greater attention to such things. And he has forbidden my father to give me money. Sumuabi thinks this will leave me without resources and ready to change my ways. The king both misunderstands and underestimates me."

Prince Eoreck looked about the room, his sharp features flushed with indignation. "How many of you men have heard of Dulcine?"

Murmurs rippled across the little group of men. The Brythunian, Bosk, scowled and spoke out: "They call it Plague City, and say that all who come near its walls die."

Eoreck nodded patiently, as if he had anticipated just such a reaction. "True. Last year Dulcine was wracked by a plague more virulent and deadly than any known before. This has been a source of great sorrow to the king, for although the baron of Dulcine claimed independence from any throne, his city lies within the territories ruled by Akkharia. The plague might well be seen as a divine judgment against the baron for daring to resist the rightful rule of King Sumuabi."

Adrastus looked to his feet, stroked his crystal star-pendant, and tried to hide a facetious smirk. Divine judgment, indeed.

"In the days before the plague, Dulcine was known as one of the richest cities of Shem," continued the prince. "The baron struck a vein of diamonds in the uplands between Koth and Shem, and built his little city up around the mine. Though less than a quarter the size of Akkharia, Dulcine is much richer. The baron's vaults hold gold, silver, and treasures from across the world. But his greatest possession is diamonds. His mines have yielded thousands of them. And we are going to take them for ourselves."

A confused rush of conversation filled the room as the men erupted with questions. Eoreck smiled, suddenly more comfortable before his audience. He lifted his hands for silence and nodded patiently as the outburst quieted.

"Reliable reports inform me that the plague still festers in Dulcine, and that none can venture within its walls. But I say that is all for the best…" The prince smiled at the puzzled faces regarding him. "None can enter Dulcine. None, that is, except ourselves."

The prince extended an open hand toward the heavyset man who had introduced him, and Adrastus the Kothian bowed.

"Adrastus is a sorcerer of some skill," Eoreck went on, "and he has devised for us a method of protection from the plague."

"This—" the prince dug a hand into a pouch at his girdle, "—this mask has been magically treated to filter out the vapors of the pestilence." He brandished a white veil above his head. "Wearing these, we will steal into Dulcine and together we shall seize all the diamonds we can carry. Together, we shall perform the greatest theft of the age. Together, we shall make ourselves rich beyond our wildest dreams!" His enthusiasm was a radiant force that surged electrically through the room.

Most of the men cheered, though a few stood quietly, staring into a future suddenly alive with wealth and its possibilities.

Conan stepped forward and the crowd fell silent. He shook back his square-cut black mane and spoke to Eoreck without deference. "The plan is brazen and the plunder ripe and worthy. The weak link is the use of sorcery. I trust it not at all."

"Ah." Adrastus spoke from the shadows. "I should have expected some reluctance from the barbarian. Be assured, soldier, that the veils do nothing but prevent the plague from afflicting the wearer. As I am no Stygian master-sorcerer, I found this difficult enough to perform in itself. And I'll stake my life upon their utility; I shall be the first to enter the city."

"And I shall be the second," put in Prince Eoreck hastily. "Join us in this effort, Northman. Grow rich with us. Be with us," he hesitated meaningfully, "not against us."

Conan nodded slowly as he weighed the options. The prince's pregnant pause had not been lost on him. "Aye," he said finally. "I'm in. When do we leave?"

"At daybreak. Gather your belongings and settle your affairs, men. I trust I need not remind you to tell no one of this mission. We meet beside the stables at first light." Prince Eoreck turned to the rear door and lifted the hood of his scarlet cloak. "I expect to see all of you then." He stepped into the night with his bodyguard at his side, and left the room behind him seething with questions.

"What are our shares?"

"Does the king know of this?"

"Why did he choose men of our legion?"

Conan shouldered toward Mamluke and caught the older man's attention. "Are you coming with us, captain?"

"No, I must tend to my troop." Mamluke spoke tersely and would not meet the Cimmerian's gaze. The other men fell silent to listen to their commander.

"Tell me, captain, do you trust the prince?" Conan's bluntness drew a few gasps.

Mamluke bristled and raked a hand through his close-cut beard.

"Damn your suspicions, barbarian! I admit that I am in the prince's debt and allowed him to select men from my troop for this mission, but he is of the royal family of Akkharia, and entitled to your respect."

"If you owe the prince a favor," said Bosk slowly, "that explains why he chose men from your troop. It doesn't explain why he selected the men that he did. Some of us are fit enough soldiers." The big Brythunian's eyes went grudgingly to Conan, then flicked away. "Others are little more than children," he added, gesturing at Pezur. The young archer looked abashed, but said nothing. Bosk's voice grew somewhat more strident and it became apparent that he relished the attention of his fellows. "And the worst are scarcely soldiers at all." A thick finger pointed to a lean, wiry mercenary who had been silent throughout the secret meeting. "This one's little more than a sneak thief, and skilled with nothing but his knives."

The lean man's face darkened, but before he could find his tongue, Mamluke spoke again, and his voice dripped disdain. "Are you not mercenaries? Who are you to question the will of your master? The prince offers you the riches of a lifetime and you quibble like girls. He commands, we obey. It was ever thus. Prepare yourselves for the journey. Anyone who wishes to whine further can find their way to the kennel and keep company with the rest of the curs."

"Well," continued the Brythunian loudly, clearly infatuated with the sound of his own voice. "You dogs can go pack your saddlebags. I'm for Dalvern's House of Pleasures. I like a woman before I travel."

The men ignored him and retreated from the stinging gaze of their commander, filing out the door into the last of the night.

Halfway back to the barracks, a hand fell upon Conan's broad shoulder. He turned to face Shamtare and the young archer, Pezur. The older man's leathery countenance bore an expression of concern.

"You are coming with us?"

"I told Mamluke that I would, and I meant it."

"But Shamtare has told me that you hate sorcery even more than he does," put in Pezur.

"True enough," said the Cimmerian, "yet I will go despite that, and despite the fact that the entire expedition reeks of falseness and treachery."

Pezur's beardless face contorted in an almost comical frown of puzzlement.

"What troubles you, Conan? And if it is so dire, why do you insist on going along?"

"First of all, I don't trust the prince to simply give a band of secretly hired mercenaries all the riches they can steal. I've yet to meet a blue-blood willing to give plunder like that away. Secondly, despite that windbag Brythunian's blather, there is a clear pattern in the men selected for this mission."

A moment's silence passed on the cool night breeze. Shamtare coughed into his fist, and Pezur scratched at his close-cropped head.

"All right," said Shamtare sourly. "What is this 'pattern'?"

"We are all of us new recruits. Mercenaries hired within the past two moons."

"By Anu, Conan, you've gone soft in the head," grumbled Shamtare. "I've been with Mamluke's Legion for almost ten years."

"And Mamluke woke you by accident, letting you join us only after you asked him what we were doing. All but yourself are new men, and unlikely to be much missed if we disappear for a few days or forever. I'm going because I'm curious and because the riches of Dulcine are no mere legend. I knew an old thief who told me that the baron of Dulcine wore around his neck the largest single diamond in the world. I should like to see that necklace." The Cimmerian started back toward the barracks.

"What are you going to do now?" asked Pezur. The youth watched the barbarian with wide eyes, as if expecting him to perform some wonder at any moment.

"I'm going back to my bunk for some honest rest. I'll be sleeping with an eye open and a hand on my hilt until Eoreck's mission is over."

3

"Wait a moment," whispered Adrastus. "I would have a word with you." The man he addressed stepped to one side, allowing the last of his fellow mercenaries to pass through the door of Mamluke's office and into the courtyard. When they were alone, he looked to the Kothian with sullen inquisitiveness.

The sorcerer examined the soldier by the ruddy light of the dying fire. It was the lean, dark man that Bosk had insulted before his comrades. He was of middle height, but his wiry frame made him seem smaller. His narrow face appeared pinched by prominent cheekbones, and his dark eyes gleamed rebelliously. Light mail encased his torso, and two black-hilted daggers hung from his belt, one on each hip. He said nothing; his small mouth was tight-lipped and unsmiling.

"Mamluke and the prince selected the men for this expedition. All except you. I selected you, Balthano." Adrastus spoke as warmly as if he addressed an old friend. "Do you know why?"

"No," said the man named Balthano. There was no warmth in his voice. His gaze moved restlessly about the room, as though seeking enemies.

"Because you are full of hate," said the sorcerer, "and I have need of such a one."

"What do you want with me?" rasped Balthano.

"I'm going to do you a great service, and in return you are going to become my bodyguard and manservant." The gentle words brooked no dissent. Balthano took a step toward the door, hesitated, then turned back to face Adrastus.

"A service?"

"I will give you the power to effortlessly destroy fools like that impertinent Brythunian pig. Take off your mail shirt and leather jerkin." Firelight gleamed in the Kothian's auburn curls and sparkled from his crystal pendant. He smiled slowly, his round face kind and strangely compelling. The face loomed large in the mercenary's vision. He could see nothing else.

Balthano blinked, then drew his mail up over his head. He dropped the shirt of steel links to the floor, then pulled his stained leather jerkin off as well. His pale-skinned torso was lean and knotted with muscle. A jagged scar twisted down the center of his chest. He shook back his queue of black hair and regarded Adrastus, both dazed and defiant, naked to the waist.

The Kothian reached within his velvet doublet and drew forth a length of cracked and aged leather with a strange green crystal affixed to one end. Balthano saw that it was a belt. The mercenary stood by, strangely passive, as Adrastus passed the belt around his waist and drew it tight to his bare flesh.

"There," said the wizard. "How do you feel?"

Balthano shook his head as if dispelling a bout of dizziness. He felt as though he observed his own actions from a lofty distance. When he spoke, his tongue was as thick and dull as a drunkard's. "What are you doing to me?" he managed.

"Nothing that you won't thank me for later. Now, put your mail and jerkin back on over the belt." A thin dew of sweat shone on the sorcerer's face. His brow creased with strain as Balthano obeyed and donned his garments.

"What are you doing to me, sorcerer?" The mercenary's voice grew stronger, and clearer, as if he were slowly waking from a drugged slumber. As Balthano fastened his weapons belt, his hands fell upon the hilts of the twin Karpashian daggers. He swayed a little on his feet, and blinked eyes that refused to focus. "Tell me, or I'll kill you!"

"Kill me?" Adrastus took a step away from Balthano and drew a blue velvet sleeve across his damp forehead. "You would kill the man who made you invincible? No one has ever done you such a service as I. The belt you wear was stolen from the black crypts beneath the haunted pyramids of southern Stygia. I took it from its place about the waist of a mummy that was half again as tall as any man I've ever seen. The tomb was guarded by a titan serpent that slew my bearers, so that I had to carry all my hard-won plunder out of the desert alone. I might have died many times over in acquiring them, but the things I took from that tomb have given me a chance to begin my life anew. The belt shall do the same for you. Touch the gem, Balthano."

The mercenary hesitated, then pushed a hand beneath his weapons belt and jerkin to touch the smooth, cool surface of the green gem. The instant he laid his fingers upon it, a slight shudder and a flush of tingling warmth passed through his body.

"How do you feel?"

Balthano shrugged, flexed his limbs, and smiled. "Good. Warm and... strong."

"Excellent. You are stronger than you have ever been, and faster. Much faster. Draw your daggers, Balthano."

In response, the Argossean's hands whipped across his body and his knives leapt from their sheaths. The movement was so swift that the eye saw it as ragged blur. It seemed that one moment Balthano's hands hung empty at his sides, and then, instantly, each fist was extended and clutched a black-bladed dagger. The mercenary looked down at his own hands in astonishment. He opened his mouth and gave a hoarse bray of disbelieving laughter. Balthano replaced the blades and positioned his hands as if to draw them forth once again.

"Touch the gem," commanded Adrastus. Balthano obeyed and felt his newfound power fade. He seemed to slouch, as though he had stood at rigid attention for too long and could not help but slump in weariness. The bright energy that had lifted his spirits and made his body seem weightless had vanished utterly, and he was left feeling emptied and exhausted. His hand fumbled at his waist again; his fingers sought the gem.

"Stop," said Adrastus, and Balthano obeyed. "Be careful. The gem draws from your own store of life-energy rather than adding any eldritch power of its own. It hastens your life. Use it only when you must. You are mine now."

Balthano bristled. His dark eyes flashed above ridged cheekbones. "I belong to no man, sorcerer. Why should I not cut your throat and take the belt as my own?" The Argossean's hands fell yet again upon the hilts of his daggers. "Why shouldn't I—"

Adrastus clenched his right fist and spoke a single syllable in Old Stygian.

Balthano dropped to the floor as if struck down by a battle-ax. His lean body writhed and arched like a snake with a broken back. Froth burst from Balthano's lips, and his eyes rolled back in their sockets as his hands clawed at the floorboards in insensate agony. Adrastus muttered another syllable in the dead language and opened his fist. The Argossean's tormented body immediately relaxed, collapsed limply to lie quivering and gasping at the wizard's feet.

"The belt belongs to me and functions only as long as I live. Its use is a payment to you for loyal service. Now you see that it can punish as well as reward. Be of good cheer, Balthano. If I am your master, at least I am a kindly one. As I do not wish this punishment for insubordination to be your final memory of our bargain tonight, I shall allow you a taste of the full extent of your power. You'd like vengeance upon the Brythunian, would you not?"

Balthano sat up on the floor and wiped the spittle from his lips with a narrow forearm. He showed his teeth, like a whipped but still defiant dog. Though he did not open his mouth to speak, his eyes blazed an eloquent answer.

"Good. Do not hate me, Balthano. My sorcery will make you an unconquerable warrior and the plunder of Dulcine will make you as rich as a king. All you need do is obey my every command. You gain might and riches, and I gain a man whom I can trust implicitly. Do you accept my terms?"

"Yes." Balthano's voice was a hoarse whisper, raw as winter wind. "I accept your bargain."

"Excellent. We shall both benefit by this immeasurably. Now you may go out and experience the true extent of your new abilities. The Brythunian said he was headed for Dalvern's pleasure house. I believe the rooms on the second floor are reserved for those who wish to dally with Dalvern's harlots. Find the Brythunian and see how easy it is to kill him. Be back and prepared for travel before we leave for Dulcine. Go now. Learn well the value of the gift I have given you."

Balthano got to his feet and touched the gem at his belt; then he turned and left Mamluke's office without a backward glance.

Adrastus walked stiffly to the desk and all but fell into the chair behind it. His portly body was sticky with sweat, and tides of queasy weakness swept over him. Darkness pressed in at the fringes of his vision and he feared he might lose consciousness. Drawing deep breaths to steady himself, the Kothian remained still until the darkness receded and his strength began to return. Panic fluttered in his breast like a trapped bird.

I almost lost control, thought Adrastus. Balthano's will provided so much more resistance than I anticipated. He almost wrested free of my grip. He might have buried those daggers in my heart. I might well be dead right now. Damn all mental control spells anyway.

The Kothian's hands fumbled for the star-shaped crystal that hung at his throat. His fingers caressed it as his mind reached out and felt its structure at levels far too small to be touched. The symmetrical lattice of its atoms was comfortingly regular, predictable and understandable. Not like the human mind.

The sorcerer continued to breathe deeply and slowly calmed himself. It had been a close call, true enough, but he had accomplished all he had set out to do. He had even successfully utilized a genuine mental control spell to lull Balthano while he placed the belt about his waist. Tolbeth-Khar would have been surprised at his skill. Surprised and proud.

Perhaps even envious.

Adrastus stood and the dying fire raked his body with bloody light. A small, cruel smile twisted his lips. He allowed himself to feel pleased with his progress. His task was difficult, but nothing had been easy since the plague had come to Dulcine. Each little success was a step toward his ultimate goal. If he could continue to proceed as steadily and successfully as he had thus far, then his plan would come to its inevitable fruition and all difficult tasks would be at an end. If his plan came to completion then all the world would leap to do his bidding, just as Balthano did even now.

Balthano waited patiently for the women working the door to leave their post. The scantily clad doxies called out to every male passerby, and finally drew the attention of a lanky Corinthian, who stopped to grin at them as they posed and preened. They ran to his side, giggling. Each grasped an arm and pulled him toward the waiting door of Dalvern's House of Plentiful Pleasures. While they answered the Corinthian's joking protests with cooed promises, Balthano came out of the alley's concealing shadow, moved along the building's wall, and stole through the curtained doorway. There was a guard within, but the man was distracted by the spectacular gyrations of the dancer performing on the tavern's small stage. Balthano slid past like a cold night breeze, moved swiftly behind the guard and up the stairs to the dimly lit second floor.

An oil lamp guttered weakly from a sagging wall sconce and painted the worn walls with faded gold. Balthano's black boots paced along the short hall. He halted briefly to listen at three doors before hesitating at the fourth. Its battered face was painted with the crude image of a hare in mid-leap.

A tremor ran through the Argossean's body as he bent his head to the door and listened. The belt around his waist seemed to throb warmly and send the blood surging through his veins with intoxicating force. He heard a muffled voice through the panel, identified it, drew back, and kicked the heavy door from its hinges. The oak panels split under his boot and exploded into the room, with Balthano following before they rebounded from the floor.

The two figures on the bed sprang apart. Bosk the Brythunian came to his knees on the silk-strewn pallet, cursing in shock and rage. His companion quailed back among the pillows, and jerked the sheets up to cover her exposed body.

The bed almost filled the tiny room. Balthano stepped arrogantly to its foot and put his hands on his hips. The single candle's light revealed his narrow features, his darkly shining eyes.

"You! What the hell do you think you're doing?" Bosk blinked in angry astonishment.

"Interrupting your games, Bosk," drawled Balthano, his voice bland and slow. He gestured languidly at the cowering woman as his eyes drew slowly down the length of her body. "Such as they are."

"You-you—" The big man seemed unable to form words, so great was his emotion. "You must be drunk, Balthano. If you were sober, you would know that I will kill you for this."

"Kill me?" Balthano's lips peeled back from his teeth in a twisted leer. His shining eyes brightened and burned like yellow cinders. "What keeps you from the task? Is that not your war-hammer beside you? Have you forgotten how to use it?"

For a frozen instant Bosk seemed to swell with rage. Muscles tensed across his broad chest and bunched in his thick arms as his hands knotted into fists. Then he uncoiled with stunning swiftness, coming off the bed, snatching the hammer in both hands and lunging for Balthano with a ringing bellow of fury.

The Argossean skipped forward to meet him, then dodged back too quickly for the eye to follow. Bosk's maddened headlong attack came to a jarring stop, as though he had collided with an invisible barrier. His hammer fell from nerveless fingers and thumped heavily on the threadbare carpet. He looked down at his torso. Beneath each arm a black dagger hilt stood out from his ribs. Bosk lifted his eyes to Balthano in confusion.

"And what is this?" Balthano whispered dryly. "Are you surprised that the sneak thief can use his knives?" Sweat gleamed in tiny beads across the Argossean's brow and cheekbones. His lambent eyes glowed from their shadowed sockets. He leapt toward Bosk again, his movements a dark blur of speed, then sprang back. The daggers gleamed wetly in his fists.

"Too slow, Bosk."

The stricken man lifted his hands and opened his mouth to speak. Blood ran over his lips in a scarlet stream and Bosk toppled like a tower shorn of its foundations. His head struck the low cabinet beside the bed, sending the candle tumbling to the floor. The chamber went black.

Silence shuddered in the small room. Then silk sheets rustled.

"I am not your enemy." The woman on the bed spoke softly. "You may flee in safety. I won't scream."

She was answered by a faint sigh in the darkness. "I won't scream," repeated the woman.

"No," said Balthano, beside her. "You won't have time."

4

The day came that the creature began to understand something of time, and it was no longer content to stand in the empty Chamber of Conjuring, or to walk the palace's vacant halls. The countless details of the small, contained world of the palace ceased to be absorbing, and it hungered for new experiences and knowledge. So it walked from the shadowed interior of the palace into the bright light of morning.

It wore the shape of a man, but it was nothing human. Soulless eyes, as black and dull as lumps of tar, gazed upon the high-arched door, the marble flagstones, and the splashing fountain that frothed white in the sun. Overhead the sky arched as blue and translucent as the sea. The thing in the form of a man observed all, and understood none, of these things.

It walked slowly around the great basin of the sweet water fountain that the baron of Dulcine had named the Freshet, seeking a closer look at the hissing jet that rose above it to crest and splash down ceaselessly in a thin curtain of mist. As it did, a ragged figure, bending to drink, leapt up in surprise. The thing looked upon a face distorted by ebon swellings, and eyes that brimmed with scarlet tears. With a choked cry of terror, the man turned and fled. It watched the man go, momentarily interested in his movement and fear. The fountain's bright cascade drew its dark eyes back, and it stared for a long while.

The light in the heavens moved, as it was wont to do, rising toward the sky's apex. In time the thing grew bored of the ceaseless changes to be seen in the water's flow. It moved out of the keep's walled courtyard and into the city. The broad double-avenue that met at the open gates of the palace courtyard was deserted, strewn with debris and still, silent bodies.

The thing that wore a man's shape walked the verdant, tree-lined boulevard that divided the avenue, and took note of the softness of the grass beneath its feet. All was new to it.

The plethora of new sights and sensations threatened to overwhelm it, and it fought an urge to return to the dim silence of the palace, to the comforting haven it knew beneath the great prismatic dome. An overturned wagon caught its eye and sparked its curiosity. The wagon had struck the curb with force enough to crush the left front wheel and flip the entire vehicle onto one side. The load of garments the wagon had carried was strewn across the avenue and boulevard. Brightly colored scraps of muslin, silk, and velvet lay upon the grass, blew along the gutter, and clung to tree branches, where they flapped like lost flags. There was no sign of the horse that had drawn the cart.

It stepped off the grass into the street, walked around the toppled wagon, and found the driver. His blackened, shriveled corpse lay where it had been hurled by the cart's crash, spread-eagled in the center of the avenue. A small, brown dog gnawed at the driver's outstretched hand.

The thing that looked to be a man stood silently beside the wagon, and a sudden wind washed brilliant silks about its feet. It marveled at the dog, for this was a new form of life it had not yet encountered. A cloak of black silk, edged with cloth-of-gold, was blown against its thigh and clung there. It grasped the cloak in a long-fingered hand, identified it as a garment, and released it. The wind yanked the cloth away.

Watching the multicolored silks move in the wind, a thought came to it. The humble garb of Tolbeth-Khar faded from its body, shifted liquidly to become a similar outfit made of black silk edged with cloth-of-gold. It looked down upon itself in approval. It allowed the new black cloak to be tossed by the wind, and smiled thinly as the mantle streamed out behind it.

The cloak's sudden movement alerted the dog to the thing's presence. It cringed and then, stiff-legged and growling, backed away from the wagoneer's body. When the black-clad thing took a step forward, the dog yelped and fled, claws clicking on the avenue's cobblestones.

The thing in the shape of a man watched the dog go, and wondered: *Why am I not like that? It studied its own hands, flexed the fingers. Why do I wear this form?*

It turned, examined the toppled wagon, and took note of the seat and how it was constructed to hold a man's body. It remembered the furniture of the palace and the design of the stairs.

Beings of this form rule here, and shape this world to fit their ends. The recollection of its first day in Dulcine washed over it, vivid enough in its new-born mind to feel almost as though it were recurring. Masses of these helpless beings had fled before him. They had fallen, blackened and dying, and in doing so they had made him strong. The thing began to feel as though it understood its role in this fresh and unknown environment.

Beings of this form rule this world. And I rule those beings.

It strode down the avenue and rejoiced in its rich new senses. It smelled damp grass on the wind, felt soft silk on its skin, and saw the sun shine gold upon the rooftops of Dulcine.

What was I before this? Did I exist?

The thing that wore the shape of a man looked across the city and lifted its arms as if to embrace it all. The black and soulless eyes went hooded and dreamy.

What does it matter? I am here now. This world is mine.

5

North of Akkharia, civilized pasture lands eventually gave way to hills that rose wild into the Kothian Uplands and, to the east, the impenetrable and ceaselessly volcanic Flaming Mountains. Where the uplands lifted high, the roads and trails grew fewer and more rarely traveled. Pine and cedar forest blanketed the rolling slopes, cut through with clear streams and rivers, and there were many glades that had never known the woodsman's ax.

A group of soldiers camped in one such vale, four days' hard travel from Akkharia. Yesterday they had left the caravan road to Dulcine and began traveling cross-country to approach their destination with stealth. Now they set up camp as the failing light of evening turned the thunderheads on the horizon into turrets of crimson flame. A lazy stream stretched beside the campsite, then wound off into the surrounding forest. The low sun poured between the trees that flanked the little river and struck sharp pinpoints of light from its moving surface.

A huge man, clad only in a breechcloth, stood thigh deep in the cold stream. His big hands held a length of rawhide and a straight branch with one end split. He watched the shore impatiently as two men left the bustle of the camp and walked toward him along the raised bank.

"Here, Conan, I've brought Shamtare as you asked," said the younger of the two men.

"What is this nonsense about a fish dinner?" grumbled Shamtare. "We have no net, Conan."

The breeze tousled the barbarian's black mane, drawing errant locks across his bronzed face. He shook them back and held out a hand to Shamtare. "Throw me your stiletto and you'll be cooking fish in a few moments."

The bearded Shemite looked skeptical and laid his hand on a slender sheath at his belt. He drew the little dagger, frowned, and tossed it to Conan. "Be careful, that stiletto was a gift."

The Cimmerian admired the weapon's clean lines as he used the strip of rawhide to bind it into the split end of the branch. The hilt was wound with silver wire and the pommel was a small, simple ball of black iron. "I know it was a gift. Once, after much drinking, you told me how you came by it."

"By Erlik, I'd best go a little easier on the wine," mumbled Shamtare.

Pezur looked from the Cimmerian to the stout Shemite, his face screwed up with poorly contained curiosity. He was about to speak when he was distracted by Conan's sudden movements.

Having completed his impromptu spear, the barbarian abruptly whipped his weapon back and cast it into the stream. It pierced the surface with scarcely a splash, and Conan slid easily through the shallows to catch it up again. A fish wiggled on the stiletto's point. With a flip of his wrist, Conan sent his catch sailing through the air to rebound from Shamtare's mailed breast. The Shemite scrabbled for the animal as it flipped about in the grass on the stream's bank. He caught and held it: a beautiful animal, as long as his forearm, darkly patterned across its back and bearing an iridescent stripe along each flank.

"Hah! I should have known better than to underestimate you, Conan."

"I doubt this creek has ever been fished. Give me a little time and I warrant I'll have enough to feed the whole camp."

Pezur and Shamtare leisurely followed the Cimmerian and received a steady stream of fish. The young archer was prevailed upon to use his blue cape as a makeshift sack to carry Conan's catch. He was soon lamenting the weight of his burden, as well as the sodden, stained, and pungent condition of his garment. In time they returned to camp, where several bonfires now held the night at bay. The bounty of fresh fish was received with cheers by men resigned to a meal of dry bread and salted beef.

Soon Conan, Pezur, and Shamtare were sitting on a moss-grown log as they drank watered wine and cooked gutted fish impaled lengthwise on long, green sticks. The fire flared and crackled warmly, occasionally sending a gout of orange sparks up into the darkness between the overhanging trees.

Pezur laid his fine blue mantle over his knees and regarded it ruefully.

"Mitra forgive me, I've ruined the cape my father gave me."

"Ah," Shamtare snorted, "a quick rinse in the stream will set it right. You worry too much about things of little consequence."

"Easy for you to say, Shamtare. You have fine mail, a silver belt buckle, and a pouch full of gold. I have no money, and if my cape is ruined, no finery. I shall look less like a roguish mercenary and more like a beggar."

This drew a deep laugh from the barbarian. He plucked the fish from the end of his stick and bounced it in his palm as it steamed. "Most mercenaries I've known were but little better off than beggars."

"Pezur's parents were once among the nobility," explained Shamtare. "He has an odd notion of the mercenary's life."

"Well, look about you," said Pezur. "There's not a man here

without some odd bit of finery to make him look professional and experienced."

"Of which you are neither," put in Shamtare with a smile.

"That's beside the point. Conan has his Akbitanan mail, Orbash has his emerald earrings, even Balthano has his Karpashian daggers. All I had was this cape."

Conan bit into his fish and, chewing, bent backward and rummaged in his gear with one hand. He leaned into the firelight again, holding a small backpack of shabby leather.

The Cimmerian set the backpack on the ground between his feet, unfastened the flap, and groped about inside while continuing to eat his fast-disappearing fish. When his hand emerged it held what appeared to be a large black bracelet. He flipped it to Pezur. Taken by surprise, the archer caught and fumbled the object, almost dropping it into the flames.

"What's this?" Pezur held the dark ring out in the firelight. It was an armlet carved of some dense, black wood. It was two fingers wide and inscribed with deep vertical cuts in a simple, even pattern. Worn smooth by time and use, it felt surprisingly heavy in the archer's hands.

"That's the armband of a Bamula chieftain," said Conan. He tossed the remains of his first fish into the darkness behind him, affixed another to the end of his stick, and thrust it into the fire.

The young archer stared at the black ring with dawning amazement. "Bamulas? Aren't they Kushites? This was worn by a black chieftain of Kush?"

"Yes, it belonged to many such. But I was the last man to wear it."

Pezur's mouth fell open in something close to awe. "You were a chief among the Bamulas?"

"For a time. I annoyed the wrong people and had to flee in such haste there was no time to return the armlet. You can have it if you wish. It's too small for me."

Pezur slid the wooden ring up his right arm until it encircled his bicep. When he released it, it slid back down to his elbow.

"It's loose," he explained, "but I shall bind it with cloth until it's snug. Many thanks, Conan. Imagine, an armlet fashioned by the brutal barbarians of Kush adorning the arm of a civilized Shemite."

Shamtare shifted uncomfortably on the log and shot a glance at Conan. The Cimmerian seemed unperturbed by the archer's thoughtless remark.

"The men of Kush are no more brutish than the men of any other land," said Conan evenly. "Since I first came to the southern cities as a lad, many civilized men have called me barbarian as though it were a curse. Yet, the black barbarian who gave me that armband might have given any of them lessons in honesty and courage." The barbarian's blue eyes stared into the fire as if he saw through the flames and looked upon something that none other could see. "Civilization esteems itself too highly."

Pezur fell silent. Shamtare drew in his fish and nudged the archer. "Ho, Pezur, do you want to eat fish or charcoal?" The younger man started, then snatched his fish from the reaching flames. He blew on the steaming flesh to cool it, then bit into flaky white meat as firm and full-flavored as a chicken breast.

"Good evening, warriors. We're all eating well, thanks to the big Cimmerian, Conax." Prince Eoreck had approached unnoticed and now stood in the circle of their firelight. His asshuri bodyguard loomed silently behind him.

"My name is Conan," said the barbarian dryly.

"Ah, yes. That's what I said." The prince stepped closer, his ornate, golden breastplate aflame with reflected light. His unsteady stride, lax diction, and bleary gaze bespoke a man far gone in his cups. He drew his scarlet cloak beneath himself and sat down heavily on the ground beside the fire. The asshuri warrior stood stolidly still; his arms hung straight at his sides and his shovel jaw thrust forward pugnaciously. He was still garbed in full battle gear and hadn't even removed his helmet.

"I couldn't ask to travel with more worthy comrades. Pass me that wine, would you, fellow?"

The prince extended a hand to Shamtare, who mutely offered the wineskin.

"You are all destined to become rich men. Barons and lords." The prince took a drink and grimaced. "Fie, it's watered." He looked around the ring of fire-illumed faces as if to see if anyone might offer him a goblet of undiluted wine. When none was forthcoming, he took another pull on the skin, then wiped his lips and belched softly. "Ah well. Better than nothing."

"A rare pleasure this, milord," said Pezur.

"Huh?" The prince blinked at the young archer. "What?"

"This is the first time I've seen you visit the fire of any of the men," began Pezur. Shamtare's elbow made a sharp, discrete dig into his ribs. "And it's an honor to have you," added the archer hastily.

"Yes, I suppose so," said Eoreck expansively, "but it's necessary for a true leader to acquaint himself with those he leads. As I look about myself, I see the faces of brave and hardy men. Men who are soon to be rich. But what do you truly know of Dulcine's riches?"

"Little," replied Conan. "Tell us, prince."

The massive bodyguard stiffened slightly at the Cimmerian's tone, but Prince Eoreck took another drink from the wineskin and continued.

"The baron of Dulcine was a madman. Obsessed with gathering riches and hoarding them at all costs. His diamond mine made him as rich as an Ophirean's dreams, yet aside from that which he spent to safeguard the rest, scarcely a gold coin ever left the walls of his little city. He moved the whole of Dulcine from the valley in which it had sat for hundreds of years. Moved it to the top of a stony mountain, built it up around his precious diamond mine, and raised an impregnable keep within as his palace. The walls of his tiny city are bigger than those of Akkharia, and the walls of his palace are unlike any in all the world! The stones are fitted together so closely that no seams can be seen between them. There are no windows, barred or otherwise, until the fifth floor! And I've heard whispers that the baron deemed even these extraordinary precautions inadequate, and also safeguarded his keep with strange and powerful wizardry. There can be no doubt but that the man was mad."

"It sounds as though Dulcine could withstand a long siege," said Conan.

"Truly," agreed the prince. "He built the inner keep right beside a bottomless sweet water fountain, so that his city would never be without fresh water. It was said that he packed warehouses full of enough preserved food to last the city ten years. And sorcerers! He had a magical chamber built atop his palace that wizards traveled halfway around the world to see. So there was never a time that he couldn't defend his little realm with sorcery."

Conan finished his second fish, tossed it away, and gnawed into a crust of hard bread. "This explains why the baron saw no reason to pay Akkharia's taxes," he said thoughtfully. "Pass me that wine."

The prince leaned forward, held the skin out for the barbarian, and watched him take it. As Conan tilted his head back to drink, Eoreck stared off into the night and scowled darkly.

"Such arrogance! I understand there is some ancient conflict as to whether Akkharia or Eruk has claim to Dulcine's lands. But Akkharia has bespoken its right of possession for fifty years without dispute from anyone save the baron himself. The arrogance! Give me back that wine."

Conan had passed the skin to Pezur, who took a hurried sip and returned it to the prince. Eoreck drank deeply, then dropped the wineskin to the ground beside his thigh. His brow was furrowed with indignant anger and his lips shone wetly in the firelight.

"Imagine, refusing to pay Sumuabi's taxes for a full score of years! Imagine! And the king stood for it! Open treason in his lands and he stands idly by, letting the baron fatten on riches that were rightfully his. What manner of king is that?"

"With Dulcine as impregnable as you have described, it sounds as though Sumuabi had little choice in the matter," said Conan.

"Little choice?" Eoreck clenched his fists in his lap. "If Sumuabi were any true regent, he would have stormed Dulcine and taken it no matter what the cost. He should have raped it and razed it to the ground! In sparing it, he condones treason and undercuts the power of the throne itself." He brought the wineskin to his flushed face again. "It would be different if his brother—my father—wore the crown. My father, Lord Eannus, would be a real leader, the kind the realm needs. You can damn well trust that he wouldn't brook treason in his own domain. The kingdom of Akkharia and its environs would be run with rigorous efficiency. Father is a canny man. And a careful one. Did you know that he receives visitors from atop a balcony, guarded by soldiers with crossbows?"

"Even the king isn't so cautious," muttered Shamtare.

"Oh no?" Eoreck tossed his head. "Perhaps he should be."

An uncomfortable silence fell over the little group. The fire cracked loudly as a glowing log settled into the gray coals. The prince looked at the men around the fire, and frowned as if he had suddenly realized who they were. Eoreck set the skin down beside his thigh once more and opened his mouth to speak.

Conan sprang from his seat and drove the edge of his foot into the fire. A cloud of smoke and sparks exploded under his boot. The barbarian kicked dirt and ash over the blaze, his sword suddenly naked in his fist. His voice thundered out over the camp.

"Douse the fires! Swords out! There are riders across the river!"

6

Conan ran through the camp and bellowed warnings in a voice that drove even those who slumbered to their feet. He vaulted a dying fire and in an instant was out of the camp, free of the trees and sprinting along the grassy bank of the stream. A blazing spray of brilliant stars stretched across the open night sky. The gibbous moon floated above the tree line like a ghostly lantern.

The creek was full of armored horsemen. They poured out of the forest across the water and splashed through the stream toward the Akkharian camp. The Cimmerian saw that the first of them was driving his mount out of the muddy shallows and onto the raised bank of the shore.

The man wore the scale corselet and cylindrical helm of an asshuri warrior of Eruk. He spotted the oncoming barbarian and put spurs to his mount with an eager shout. As the horse struggled up the embankment, its rider braced his lance against his shoulder and lowered it smoothly. The leaf-shaped steel head gleamed like a silver icicle in the moonlight. Hooves dug in and propelled the huge horse and armored horseman toward Conan in an avalanche of flesh and steel. The spearhead shot forward, aligned to transfix the barbarian.

It was not to be. Conan slid to a stop beside the limbless trunk of a dead tree. He sidestepped the point with feline grace, and slapped the lance's shaft aside with the flat of his sword. The deflected steel head imbedded itself in the soft wood of the dead tree and the savage impact of its abrupt halt tore the lancer from his saddle. The lance splintered with a sharp *crack*. The Cimmerian heard a ragged cry and caught a brief glimpse of the horseman as he sailed backward, limbs pinwheeling. But the horse came on and Conan had to dodge around the galloping animal. He spun swiftly out of its path.

The lancer was formidable; already he sat up in the weeds and groped for the scimitar he wore strapped to his armored back. As Conan bore down on him, the man scrambled to his feet and brought his weapon, a gleaming length of steel with a golden hawk's-head pommel, to bear. The Cimmerian did not close with his stunned foe, but ran right by him. The point of his broadsword drove through the narrow eye-slit in the visor of the lancer's helm with a rasp and a crunch. The barbarian wrenched his blade free as he passed and did not turn to look as the man toppled.

The next horseman struggled with his mount at the shore's embankment. Conan braced his booted feet in the grass and waited. The horse found solid footing and reared up the slope. Its rider cursed and struck at the barbarian with a moon-gleaming tulwar. The broad slash was deflected with a metallic *clang*. Conan's unstoppable return stroke sheared through the man's breastplate of boiled leather and dashed him out of the saddle to splash lifeless in the muddy water.

Other defenders joined the Cimmerian. They lined the shore so that the invading horsemen were confined to wallowing in the stream. A determined trio tried to charge the bank and were repelled by Akkharians with ready spears.

When arrows began to fall among the attackers, they suddenly turned about and retreated to the stream's far shore. They rode up the opposite bank in brisk unison and passed into the obscuring trees.

Pezur stood beside the barbarian, notched a final arrow to string, drew it back to his ear, and let fly. The shaft sailed into darkness.

"Ishtar save me, wasn't that a fine bit of fighting, Conan? You must have heard the hooves of the leader as he rode into the creek, eh? Ishtar be my witness, all Shamtare says about you is…"

The archer fell silent as Conan wheeled and stared back toward the camp, his eyes wide and intent in the starlight.

Blood stained his broadsword and shone along his bare arm in a blackly shining spray.

"Too easy," grated Conan. At that moment the clangor of steel and the cries of battling men rose from the camp.

"It's a trick, a diversion!" roared the barbarian. "Back to camp, we've been surrounded!"

Pezur opened his mouth and Conan was gone. The archer carefully shouldered his bow, then drew his shortsword and followed.

The camp was embroiled in a frenzied melee. Soldiers on foot had struck at the camp while most of its defenders had gone to repel the horsemen at the streamside. The space around the fires was packed with swearing, hewing men.

Conan noted that the invaders seemed to outnumber his force by half, and sternly resolved to even the odds.

Prince Eoreck fought back-to-back with his massive asshuri bodyguard. The pair were the eye of a hurricane of flashing steel. The prince's slender rapier darted into the mob of encircling foes with as much drunken bravado as skill, but thus far he had managed to escape any serious injury. The asshuri whirled a weighty bastard sword about his head. Trusting his heavy armor to forestall any blow, he sporadically picked out a foe, stepped full into the ranks of the enemy, and cut him down. He bled from a gash along his jutting, exposed chin, and from a deep dig in the calf beside his greaves.

"To your prince," bayed the asshuri in a deep voice. "Save your prince!"

Eoreck blocked a hard-swung scimitar and staggered under the impact. His left foot tangled in a fallen branch, and he went to one knee. He swatted aside the deviously probing tip of a spear. The warrior with the scimitar lunged in and took another strong cut at the prince, who clumsily interposed the hilt of his rapier at the last possible moment. The blow rang on the rapier's quillions with numbing force and the sword sprang from the prince's grip. Eoreck yelped in pain, clutched his injured hand, and looked up to see the scimitar-wielder bearing down upon him with an evil, gap-toothed grin. The prince tried to heave himself onto his feet, but a great hand fell on his shoulder and shoved him back down to sit in the dirt.

Conan leaned over Eoreck's prone body in a long thrust that drove his blade through the torso of the charging scimitar-wielder with such force that it burst out a foot beyond his spine.

The man collapsed and his dead weight almost wrenched the hilt from Conan's fist. The barbarian stumbled over Eoreck as the prince tried to stand. The shining head of a spear thrust for Conan's eyes. He snatched at it with one hand and tore his blade out of the scimitar-wielder's corpse with the other. His fingers caught the spear just below the point, then jerked it forward with all the strength of his massive shoulders. The spearman was yanked headlong to meet a whistling chop of the Cimmerian's freed broadsword.

Savage shouts mingled with the clash of steel as the Akkharians who defended the stream returned to camp in force. The men that encircled Conan and Eoreck pressed in with desperate intensity to finish them.

"The prince!" bellowed the bodyguard. "Save the prince!"

Eoreck stood, seemed to realize that he was unarmed, and bent to retrieve his fallen rapier. Conan's broadsword deflected a shortsword that stabbed for the prince's throat, then split the wielder's skull. The barbarian stepped between Eoreck and his foes with a roar of berserk fury. Reclaiming his rapier, the prince looked up to see the constricting ring of foes break and run before the Cimmerian's murderous onslaught. His blade harvested men as a scythe harvests wheat, and brave warriors fled before it.

The two-pronged attack, having failed on its first front, was now faltering on its second. The men of Mamluke's Legion rallied as their swift response to the attack surprised and dismayed their enemies. The invaders were driven back into the forest, away from the camp, and there they broke when the Cimmerian led an impulsive charge into their ranks. They ran pell-mell among the dark trees in a full rout. The mercenaries who started off to pursue them were called back by Conan.

Fresh logs were tossed onto campfires as the victors returned. The barbarian loped back through camp toward the stream, briefly disappeared into the darkness there, then rejoined his comrades at Prince Eoreck's side. Voices rose as the men examined wounds, counted the dead, and congratulated one another.

"There he is! There's the man who saved my life!" The prince extended both hands, open-palmed, toward the barbarian. "Let it never be said that I was an ungrateful lord. I hereby promote you to the rank of captain. Now, of all those on this expedition, you are second in rank only to myself. Bravo, Captain Conan! You, Shullar." Eoreck elbowed his hulking asshuri bodyguard. "You could learn much from this man."

Shullar wiped at the blood clotting along his shovel-jaw and glared at the barbarian. He said nothing.

The Cimmerian nodded curtly. "My thanks, prince, but I think you ought to see this." In the barbarian's hands was a sealed pouch of soft leather. "The warrior who led the attack across the river carried this in a pouch at his belt. It bears a royal seal." Conan handed the pouch to Prince Eoreck, who studied the waxen seal with a knitted brow.

"Why… why, this is the royal seal of the city-state of Eruk. And inside…" Eoreck broke the wax stamp and pulled a rolled sheet of parchment from within the pouch. He bent his head and read. "This is a letter of introduction from the King of Eruk himself, commending the mercenary soldiers of the Gray Legion of Palanthar to a General Gilhane." The prince's voice trailed off and his eyes stared blindly at the page.

There was a rustle of undergrowth, and Balthano emerged from the shadow-clotted brush. He clutched a dagger in each hand and his arms were black with blood all the way to the shoulder. His hard, thin countenance shone with sweat, and his lips were drawn tight over gritted teeth. All heads seemed to turn toward him as he entered the firelight. The Argossean looked over the party of mercenaries with eyes that glittered like black chips of obsidian.

"Why did no one pursue the dogs? I took down three as they fled. Do I keep company with cowards?" His raw voice ground in his throat.

"Enough, Balthano," said Adrastus softly. "That's enough." The sorcerer stepped from the shadow of a thick oak and regarded his bodyguard in a fashion both fatherly and commanding.

Balthano's bright eyes sought the forest floor, and his bloody hands met at his midriff, smeared the mail there as he seemed to press both fists against his belly. The rigid tension that gripped him abruptly dissipated, apparently taking much of his strength with it. The Argossean staggered sideways. His limbs had gone lifeless and rubbery. Adrastus stepped quickly to the man's side, caught and braced him up.

"Forgive my friend his hasty words. The madness of battle was still upon him." The wizard's apologetic tones were lost upon most of the men, who gazed at Balthano with an uncertainty that bordered on fear.

The entire incident had escaped the prince, who still stared incredulously at the royal letter. He rolled and replaced the scroll in its pouch. "I don't understand it. What would the soldiers of Eruk be doing in the lands of Akkharia?"

Conan sat on the moss-grown log beside the strewn ashes of his campfire, and began cleaning his bloodstained broadsword. "It seems certain they were headed for Dulcine," he said grimly.

The prince all but boggled at the suggestion. He waved the pouch about in one limp hand, and used the other to shake an upbraiding forefinger at the Cimmerian. "What nonsense! That's absurd! Akkharia and Eruk haven't squabbled in decades."

"You yourself said that the Baron of Dulcine paid fealty to no one," rumbled the barbarian. "And that Eruk once claimed these lands. Defenseless, Dulcine is surely a plump enough fruit to tempt a city-state to risk war."

"But why did they set upon us, then? What does all this mean?" The prince's small store of leadership seemed to run from him like wine from a cracked jug. Drunken and confused, he stared at Conan and waited for an answer. The barbarian laid his bare blade across his knees.

"They attacked us because they correctly saw us as rivals in competition for the plunder of Dulcine. Perhaps they recognized us as soldiers of Akkharia and sought to wipe us out before we learned that the forces of Eruk were abroad in Akkharian territory. That doesn't matter. What matters to us is that letter of introduction. It means the men we fought were going to join with an army already in, or on its way to, Dulcine."

"Impossible!" snapped Adrastus. "No one can enter that city and live!"

"Perhaps they have entered the city. Perhaps they have not." Conan stared down at the sword in his lap and saw his eyes reflected in the burnished steel. "We won't know that until we've come within sight of Dulcine. But from now on we'll have to move both swiftly and silently. There is an army arrayed against us."

With that a leaden silence fell over the group of warriors. The prince apparently could think of nothing to add, and bent unsteadily to spread out his bedroll. Most of the mercenaries followed suit, smothering the last of the fires and bedding down. Several men volunteered for sentry duty and took to their posts with marked vigilance.

Above, the moon rose as scattered silvery clouds scudded against a high background of brittle stars. The wind picked up briefly and made the trees of the forest speak in a muted chorus of whispering leaves.

Conan sat quietly on his log as Shamtare and Pezur turned in. He took a whetstone from his gear and, in time, the only sound in camp was the soft susurration of the sharpening stone along the unyielding length of his steel.

7

The morning sun sent shafts of gold down through trees that thrust emerald branches into a sky as radiantly blue as lapis lazuli. The road, still muddy from the recent rain, wound along the slowly rising flank of a wooded hill. Birds fluttered and sang above the group that rode from the dappled shadows of the forest into the open air of the hill's summit.

There, at this lofty vantage point, the men slowed to stare out across the upland forest.

Conan of Cimmeria drew on the reins of his mount, lifted a heavy arm, and pointed out across the swelling hills to where low bluffs of rugged rock thrust from the lush green mass of the forest like boulders from the froth of an ocean wave.

"There," he said. "Little more than a day's ride ahead. Dulcine."

The men atop the grassy hill slowed their horses and shaded their eyes. All looked off to the northeast, and saw, past the closest cliffs of stone, the distant shape of a walled city sitting athwart a low, rocky bluff. The boxlike regularity of its outline made the city stand out in sharp relief from the natural contours of the landscape. Beyond where dead Dulcine lay dreaming in the morning stillness, half obscured by the cerulean haze of distance, the first peaks of the Flaming Mountains lifted their dark and craggy crests.

Pezur fancied he could see slim, blue-green towers rising above the far-off walls. He stood in his stirrups, squinted at the party's destination, and wondered what awaited them there. After a long moment the men began to move on, and the young archer turned away.

Conan led the group, followed by a pale Prince Eoreck, who nursed a vile hangover, and his truculent bodyguard Shullar. Behind them came the remainder of the party: twelve men, including Shamtare, Pezur, Balthano, and the wizard Adrastus. They had lost five warriors in the battle beside the stream. The prince voiced his dismay over the reduction in their forces, if not the loss of good men's lives, but Conan was more sanguine. The barbarian pointed out they had inflicted better than thrice the damage on a superior force that had surrounded and ambushed them. To his mind, they had very much made the best of a potentially disastrous encounter.

As they descended the gentle slope of the hill's far side, the party re-entered the forest's enveloping shadow. They had come across this backwoods spur of the caravan road while traveling cross-country, and the men, weary of rough trekking, had prevailed upon Prince Eoreck to follow it for a time.

Though narrow and overgrown in spots, the old byway made for easier travel.

They passed over a broad stream on a sturdy wooden bridge that showed signs of recent repair. A bend in the road took them into a clearing beside a bow in the stream, and in view of a small mill. The squat wooden structure sat beside the slow-rolling stream, its great wheel turning with lazy persistence. The eyes of the party did not fix long upon the building, for there was a woman bathing in the mill pond.

The men slowed beside the quiet expanse of water without command or comment. The woman stood thigh-deep with her back turned toward them as she bent to soak her long blonde hair. She whipped back her head, sending a scintillant spray through the air, turned, saw the men, and froze. Her hands moved to cover her breasts and loins, then fell to her sides as she realized the futility of the gesture. She stood naked in the pond, her body shining like a white candle against the cobalt water. There was a moment of terrible silence.

"Your pardon, milady," said Prince Eoreck in silken tones.

"My pardon," repeated the woman wryly. She began slogging through the water toward the men. Pezur noted that her clothes lay upon the grassy bank on the pond's far side. He watched her approach, and felt his face grow hot.

"I thought I'd seen all the soldiers I was likely to see this year," said the woman. She stepped up out of the pond, droplets clinging to her white flesh like diamonds.

"Give her your cloak, Pezur," said Conan. The Cimmerian's gaze had passed approvingly over the woman's body, but now studied the faces of the men around him.

"My cloak? But it's torn, and stained..."

"Give it to her." The barbarian's tone brooked no denial.

The archer obediently tugged the blue cloak from his shoulders, bent from his saddle, and offered it to the woman with a hand that visibly trembled. Conan saw that the archer wore the Bamula armband about his right arm, bound in place with strips of blue cloth. The woman took Pezur's cloak and wrapped it around shoulders that shone like wet alabaster.

"My thanks," she said sincerely, looking at Conan.

"You said you saw soldiers." Balthano sat rigidly erect in his saddle. His eyes burned upon the woman; sought the folds in the cloak over her bosom, traced the dulcet line of her hip where blue fabric clung to the damp flesh beneath. "What do you know of soldiers in the lands of Dulcine?"

"A legion out of Eruk rode by a fortnight ago. My father and I shut up the mill, fearing it would be looted and we would be robbed and slain." She paused, cast a glance at the mill, and Pezur saw that her eyes were green. "They rode by without stopping, though. Apparently, the men of Eruk have more noble goals than harassing a pair of millers." This last was spoken with an edge of defiance that brought a hard grin to Conan's face. Here was a brave woman.

"No," said the barbarian. "They've bigger game in mind, and have no wish to alarm the locals."

Balthano abruptly swung his leg over the saddle and dismounted. Two quick strides brought him face to face with the woman. His thin mouth twitched as his gauntleted hands hovered above the hilts of his twin daggers.

"She's a liar," he said hoarsely. "She's in league with them. I want her."

The woman stepped backward into the muddy shallows, the first clumsy movement she had made since the warriors had interrupted her bath. Balthano watched her face, and felt a flood of hot exaltation sweep through him as her white teeth bit down on her full lower lip, and her green eyes flicked fearfully about for succor. The eyes settled upon a point just behind him.

Something heavy fell on Balthano's left shoulder. The Argossean tore his gaze from the woman and saw that Conan had moved his horse in behind him. The barbarian had laid the naked blade of his northern broadsword upon Balthano's shoulder.

"What's this?" burst out the Argossean. He looked from the Cimmerian to Adrastus and back again, his face contorted with disbelief and indignation.

"Touch the woman and die, Balthano," said Conan.

Balthano shoved the sword from his shoulder with a snort of impatience. Conan's wrist rotated smoothly, bringing the point of the blade back up until it was leveled at the Argossean's throat. Balthano was too blind with passion and incredulity to take note of what all the men in the party saw: the barbarian's face had become a grim bronze mask from which his eyes shone like pent blue flames.

"What is this?" repeated Balthano. "So the Cimmerian barbarian is actually a Zingaran courtier? Whence comes such chivalry? I'll take that oversized sword away from you and make you eat it. I'll—" The Argossean's hands crept toward his waist, a movement that Conan misinterpreted.

"Draw your daggers and greet your ancestors in hell!" snarled the barbarian savagely.

Adrastus spurred forward and pushed between the two men, holding up both hands in protest. "My friends, my comrades. Enough. We are in the lands of our enemies. We have no time to fight amongst ourselves, or—" he looked pointedly at Balthano, "—to dally with unwilling ladies."

"Set and Derketo," swore the Argossean. "Who leads this expedition? Does the barbarian order us about like slaves now?"

"You will cease at once," yelled Prince Eoreck belatedly. "The woman is a loyal subject of my uncle, King Sumuabi, and will be treated with the courtesy due to a citizen of the realm. Balthano, I promoted Conan to captain, and you will follow his orders or be subject to military discipline."

"The hell you say! You're nothing but a—"

"Easy, Balthano." The level voice of Adrastus cut through the tumult with uncanny ease, seemingly little more than a whisper, yet silencing all who spoke. "That's all."

The Argossean looked into the wide brown eyes of his master and his voice stilled. A distracted frown creased his narrow brow, and he looked off across the pond. "Yes," he said softly. "I'm sorry."

"Good enough for the time being," snapped Eoreck. "Now, let us be off."

There was the velvet hiss of razor steel on leather as Conan sheathed his sword. He favored Balthano with a coldly expressionless stare, then urged his mount forward.

As the party moved slowly back onto the packed earth of the

road, Eoreck lagged behind. He waited, at the woman's side, until his men were riding past the mill. Shullar took note of his absence and drew rein. He motioned for the prince to catch up.

"I trust you realize what would have happened if I hadn't intervened?" asked Eoreck.

"Yes," said the woman, bending to wring her hair. "The big barbarian would have killed that bastard of an Argossean and anyone else who offered me harm."

"Ah, perhaps that is so. But the men might have fallen upon you anyway. I saved you from a dire fate."

The woman smiled. "If this is true, then I thank you for it."

The prince wondered if he detected an element of sarcasm in her tone and words. The momentary uncertainty faded as he continued. "You are in my debt. And you can repay that debt by telling no one of our passing here. We are on the king's business." He dug into the embroidered pouch hanging from his jeweled girdle. "Here. A golden royal."

The tossed coin caught the light as it flipped through the sunny air. The woman thrust out a hand and it slapped into her palm.

"That's worth your silence, isn't it?"

"I'll tell no one of your passing here," said the woman, "but not because of anything you did, your lordship. And not because of this fine piece of gold."

"Ah," began Eoreck, confused by her qualified acquiescence. "Whatever. Be assured that I shall remember such a fine, loyal subject." In response she merely nodded, a gesture the prince took for meek subservience. With a foppish salute, Eoreck spurred after his mercenaries, and soon joined Shullar by the mill. She watched their progress along the road until it lowered around a sweeping curve and they were lost from view.

The woman shook back her damp locks, wrapped her new cloak a little tighter, and walked toward the mill to wake her late-sleeping father.

8

Conan of Cimmeria clung in the swaying treetop like a sailor atop a mast. The barbarian's booted feet were planted firmly on a pair of branches, and his big hands gripped the sap-smeared trunk. The mighty pine's needle-heavy boughs moved and sighed beneath him. The crisp, pleasant scent of the tree filled Conan's nostrils as he looked off to the east and the walled city of Dulcine.

"Hallooo!" came a voice from far below. It sounded to be Prince Eoreck. "Halloo! What do you see up there?"

Conan shook his head, took a last deep breath of the pine-scented wind, and started down the tree. The barbarian had learned to expect little of the nobility that civilized people allowed to run their affairs, but the prince's haplessness provoked both disdain and amazement. Such a leader would have been endured in his native Cimmeria for little longer than it took to draw a sword.

The barbarian swung down from his lofty perch with the speed and ease of a mountain ape. In but a moment he leapt from the pine's lower branches, dropped twice a man's height to land neatly on legs that cushioned the impact like great springs. Conan was immediately surrounded by a mob of his fellow travelers, all of whom clamored for information.

The party had moved with a full measure of stealth since the previous morning's encounter at the mill. They had followed the old road until evening, then, at the Cimmerian's urging, left it to move through the forest itself. As they led their horses and stumbled through the brush, the mercenaries of Prince Eoreck's squadron had found much to complain about. Sleeping in a wooded clearing without the benefit of a fire did little to improve their spirits. But now, after an early rise and further cross-country travel throughout the morning, the men felt the surging excitement of proximity to their goal. Small matter if the barbarian had led them on a difficult path; ahead loomed both the bracing chance of an armed clash with the forces of Eruk, and the more enticing possibility of plunder beyond imagination. A brash energy seemed to animate the men. It lifted their spirits and gave their eyes the roguish gleam of a gambler who senses the beginning of a lucky streak.

"So, what did you see? Speak up, man!" Eoreck had given Shullar his armor to polish the previous evening and now the prince might well have been wearing a golden metal mirror. The sunlight was blinding on the ostentatious sculpted musculature of his breastplate. "Have you lost your tongue, captain?"

"Bad news," Conan grunted. "An army surrounds Dulcine. There were many tents, most covered with brush for concealment, and a few small fires, tended so as to give off little smoke. I saw no pennants or other heraldry, but I trust it is an army of Eruk."

"This is an outrage!" exploded the prince. "An army, you say? And in the lands of my royal uncle!"

Adrastus stepped forward and his blue robe hissed over the grass. "Were the gates open?" he asked intently. "Were there men within Dulcine?"

"The gates were closed," said Conan, "though I saw a few rope ladders strung over them. If anyone got in, they haven't opened the gates for the rest. The encampment outside the city seemed set back at some distance from the walls. There was movement in the camp, but none I could see inside the city."

"Rope ladders?" Eoreck's voice was skeptical. "How could you see them at this distance?"

"If Conan says that he saw rope ladders, then he saw rope ladders," said Pezur. The young archer frowned at his prince reproachfully.

"Anything else?" rapped Adrastus. "Anything at all? The men you saw around the camp seemed natural and unafflicted?"

"I saw that the tales of the baron's palace-keep are more than just idle fancy. There truly are no windows until the fifth floor. The damn thing looks like a marble mesa capped with towers. But the soldiers moving in the camp seemed normal enough, and busy with the sorts of tasks one might expect them to be doing."

Prince Eoreck pressed knuckles to his brow in frustration. "By all the gods, what are we to do? We can't very well ask the Eruki army to let us pass. Perhaps a diversion might draw them away. Or we might pretend to be scouts for a larger party..."

"There is an alternative," said Adrastus. All eyes fell upon the sorcerer. "We must hobble the horses and proceed on foot."

"But what's to be gained from that?" blurted Eoreck. "Without horses we shan't even be able to flee the Eruki should they discover us."

"Now, now, my prince," smiled the wizard. "Have some faith in me. There is another entrance to Dulcine."

"Even so? Well then, do as he says, men." The prince's voice swelled. "Hobble the horses and ready yourselves for a hike. Jump to it, you sluggards!"

While the mercenaries busied themselves, Eoreck and Adrastus walked off a distance among the trees, where they stopped to confer. Conan dealt quickly with his horse while unobtrusively watching the pair. The Kothian spoke to the prince in a low voice

and punctuated his purposeful speech with sharp gestures. When
the wizard had spoken his piece, Eoreck rubbed his chin, stroked
his mustache, and seemed to fidget in indecision. The prince
abruptly nodded, turned away from the sorcerer, then strode back
toward the mercenaries with his scarlet cape belling out behind.
The barbarian thought his face had grown somewhat pale.

"Men, the wizard has conceived of an alternate route into the
besieged city. With him as guide, we should be able to avoid the
Eruki entirely." Murmurs swept the little band in response to
Eoreck's words. Shamtare rose from beside his mount, ruffled its
mane with one hand, and spoke.

"The city is surrounded. Will Adrastus cast a spell of invisibility
upon us? Or call up a demon to spirit us over the walls? I'm as
loyal a man as can be bought, but with all due respect to yourself
and the wizard, the less sorcery the better."

The Kothian mage smiled tolerantly and laid a hand upon
Eoreck's shoulder to still the prince's reply. Adrastus's gaze sought
and held Shamtare's, and though the wizard's eyes were wide and
guileless, the Shemite looked away from something he saw deep
within them. There was contempt and hatred there, tempered by
the necessity of circumstance. And there was something else even
more disturbing that Shamtare was unable to identify.

"The difficulty with being a dabbler in magic is that everyone
seems to believe I must be the equal of Eibon or Skelos. I shall get
us into Dulcine, and I won't need to cast a spell to do it. Long
before the baron struck his vein of diamonds and moved his city
to the top of yonder bluff, Dulcine lay upon the fields before you.
I have been given to understand that a subterranean passage exists
between the remains of the old city and the site of the new. If we
can find the portal, we shall slip beneath our enemies, enter the
city, and filch its riches while the army of Eruk stands by helplessly.
I trust you doughty warriors won't be too disappointed by the
absence of a clash of arms from this scenario." The last bit of

sarcasm was wasted on the crowd of soldiers, who broke out with a volley of questions and exclamations of approval.

"Spread out and cover as much ground as you can," continued Adrastus, his smile growing wider at the reaction of the men. "We are far enough from the Eruki flank that discovery is unlikely, but be wary of sentries or scouts. Look for a carved stone slab or doorway set into the earth. If you find it, do not enter or touch it. Call me and do nothing."

"To it, then!" Prince Eoreck clapped his gauntleted hands. "Let's move!"

Conan walked from the shade of the trees into a broad field full of waving weeds bleached gold by the summer sun. Shamtare and Pezur followed as the rest of the mercenaries stretched out into a broken line on either side. The men drew apart, advanced slowly, and scanned the ground.

Rough foundations lay scattered about the wide clearing, tufted with grass and worn smooth by the elements. The old stones were the same ruddy tone as the low bluff that lifted above the treetops to the east. Shamtare's short legs carried him over the irregular terrain with impatient speed. He tramped across a cracked foundation slab, took off his low-crested helm, and mopped his brow.

"By Ishtar's ivory baubles, it looks as though the entire city was picked up and taken away."

"And such was likely the case," said Conan. "The town was probably moved to the top of the bluff piecemeal. No point in wasting the building materials."

"True enough," agreed the Shemite. His voice lowered. "Conan, do you still distrust this wizard?"

The tall weeds clutched at the Cimmerian's hanging scabbard. He stopped, removed and adjusted his sword belt, running it diagonally around his brawny torso so that the hilt projected above his left shoulder. He was silent a moment. "I would rather trust a coiled cobra. I've known but few wizards that were worthy company, and this one smells of falseness and guile."

Shamtare grinned humorlessly and his teeth flashed in his gray-shot beard. "I find that I agree with you more and more, my friend. Let us hope the riches are as great as promised. And let us hope we all live to enjoy them."

Pezur overheard this last as he trotted up, his helmet clutched under one arm. "We'll all be rich by the time this adventure is done. By Adonis, we'll be rich as lords! We can retire from the mercenary business. What will you do with your fortune, Conan?" The trio began to move again, and the archer found himself straining to match the apparently unhurried pace of the two veterans.

"Live in style for a time, probably," said the Cimmerian. "Drink, gamble, and wench until I'm weary of it. Then, if any gold is left, I might start my own mercenary troop."

"Why, that is little better than squandering!" exclaimed the archer.

Shamtare burst out with a raucous laugh. "Our friend is a barbarian, Pezur, and they're a breed little given to worry about the future. Myself, I think I'd like to buy a good tavern and tend it as my beard grows white. Perhaps I could even convince old Fasn'lar to sell me the Red Hand."

"I," began Pezur, "I am going to take all of my riches and return to that mill to ask that woman for her hand."

Shamtare's laughter returned with redoubled strength. "Hah, Pezur, you are a wonder. You don't even know the woman's name."

"True," admitted Pezur. "But she is the most beautiful woman I have ever seen. She was fearless before a legion of armored strangers. And she was kind. I could tell. What do you say, Conan?"

"She was brave enough," said the Cimmerian. "And good to look upon."

"But this is preposterous!" cried Shamtare. "Conan, the lad is serious. Tell him how foolish he is."

The barbarian's dark brows raised slightly. He bent to look at an odd-shaped stone, then stood tall again. "I have done many foolish things in matters concerning women. Let him do as he will."

"You shall make a great ass of yourself, Pezur. Nothing good can come of such childish sentimentality."

"On the way back to Akkharia, I shall ask her to marry me," persisted the archer stoutly. "You may consider the matter closed, Shamtare." The older man's protesting reply died in his throat as he noticed Conan's actions.

The trio's progress had taken them across the open field and through the wind-tossed shadow of a small copse of saplings. The ground here was littered with low blocks of worked stone that appeared to have been laid down in orderly rows. As Shamtare looked on, Conan moved along the ranks of stone in a low crouch. His bright eyes raked over the earth. The sun was hot on his shoulder blades beneath the mail. The barbarian paused in a small open area bordered by a thick ring of coarse weeds. The weeds outlined a rough rectangle about six feet square; the area was clear but for loose soil and a growth of pale moss. Conan dropped to all fours and brushed at the dirt with a wide hand. He stood up suddenly.

"This is the portal," he said grimly.

"Wonderful," said Shamtare. "You've the eye of a hawk, my friend."

"This is it?" Pezur frowned at the blank square of earth, then at the Cimmerian. "You don't look to be very happy about it."

"This is the portal all right," said Conan. "But this," he held his hands out to indicate the area all around them, "this is a graveyard."

9

The mercenaries gathered about the spot Conan had found. Soon the soil was cleared away and a great slab of dark and somber stone was revealed. It was clearly a door set into a frame of bedrock that receded into the earth on all sides. The slab's surface was worked with stately designs that surrounded a much-faded depiction of the baronial crest of Dulcine.

"This is the entrance to a tomb," grumbled Conan.

"Correct," said Adrastus in matter-of-fact tones. "The nobility of Dulcine have long favored interring their dead in catacombs. They still do, and the tombs of the old city are connected with the tombs of the new. I, ah, paid a grave robber well for this information."

Conan looked to where Balthano crawled about the slab's circumference, using a dagger to dig black moss out of the space between the door and its frame. He shrugged sullenly. No grave robber had passed through this portal in generations.

Prince Eoreck stood in Shullar's shadow. He held out a hand to his bodyguard, and the asshuri pulled a heavy wineskin from beneath his arm and gave it to the prince. Eoreck flourished his bright cloak and cleared his throat for attention.

"I see there are a number of superstitious ninnies among us. Young Pezur looks ready to weep, and Orbash has made the sign of the horns so many times his hand must be growing sore. Are we old women that we cower from an empty tomb? Come, here is a skin of the best and strongest wine that the king's nephew can afford. I'll share it with you. Let us not shrink away from a few shadows and dry skeletons. Let us drink, journey through the catacombs, and help ourselves to the riches of Dulcine. Here, Captain Conan, take the skin and drink. You know the dead can never hurt you."

The barbarian could have told him differently; instead, he accepted the wineskin and took a huge swallow. As the vintage was fully as excellent as the prince had proclaimed, Conan took a second sizable gulp before he passed it to Shamtare.

"Now we must lift the slab," muttered Adrastus, half to himself. "How shall we accomplish that?"

Conan wiped his mouth by drawing a heavy forearm over his lips. He pointed to the upper left corner of the door's frame. "The stone is crumbling there. If we chip at it a bit, we should be able to get under the door and pry it up."

Orbash of the emerald earrings volunteered his stout Vanir dagger for use as a chisel, and Shullar used a small mace as a mallet. Soon, after much hammering and clearing away of debris, the corner of the door became visible.

The wineskin made a final round and was discarded as the men readied themselves for the task of hoisting the massive slab up out of its bed. Shullar's thick fingers couldn't wedge into the small gap he'd chiseled in the frame. Conan shouldered him aside and earned a resentful glare for his efforts. The barbarian dropped into a low squat, dug his hands in around the door's corner, threw back his powerful shoulders, and drew a deep breath. His legs tensed; the muscles of his thighs sprang into corded relief. He exhaled harshly through clenched teeth and began to stand. The slab shifted and a puff of fetid air erupted around its rim as the seal between the upper world and the lower was broken. The stone door rose slowly as the barbarian, shuddering with effort, heaved upward until its lower rim came free of the jealous earth.

The instant this handhold appeared, Shamtare, Orbash, and a dozen others hurled themselves against the door. The mercenaries jostled one another as they gripped the stone slab and hoisted with all the force they could muster. The air filled with grunts, gasps, and curses. The door lifted higher, and now all save Prince Eoreck and the wizard Adrastus plied their strength against its ponderous weight. One end ground against the bottom of its frame while the other rose painfully into a vertical position. The men skirted the black maw they had uncovered and heaved the door over.

"Get clear!" bellowed the barbarian as the giant slab teetered briefly on end. It toppled and struck the weed-grown ground with an impact that shook the earth. Dust rose in tawny billows around it.

A ragged cheer erupted from the sweating men—a cheer that faded weakly when they saw what had been revealed.

The inner surface of the door was carved with rows of blackly leering skulls. Clusters of pallid beetles scuttled in blind flight from the intrusive sunlight. The doorway itself was a black square cut from the heart of midnight, and the stench of death rose from it like an evil vapor.

"Sweet Ishtar," whispered Pezur.

Adrastus advanced to the portal's rim and peered within. The afternoon sun made small inroads into the stubborn world of night below. Conan could see that a hollow chamber of stone opened into the earth. The floor was smooth, damp, and stained where the light hit it. The mercenaries were so quiet one might imagine they held their breath.

The sorcerer looked them over and a sardonic smile pulled at his lips. He lowered himself awkwardly until he sat on the doorway's rim with his blue robes bunched up about his waist.

"Nothing to be afraid of," he said, and jumped in. The men stepped forward in unison, eyes wide as they stared into the open tomb. Adrastus stood in the patch of yellow sunlight ten feet below. He waved at them.

"Gather some brush to conceal the portal. We don't want any scouts of Eruk's army to happen upon our little secret, do we? Well, come on. Don't just stand about staring." The wizard's bantering tone shamed the mercenaries, some of whom went in search of brush, while the others leapt down into the crypt to join him. Conan was among the latter.

Shullar gripped Eoreck's arm, bent, and lowered him effortlessly through the portal while Conan examined the hidden tomb. The barbarian's instinctive fear of the supernatural caused his wilderness-bred senses to awaken to their fullest. His keen eyes cut through the gloom as his sword hand crept to his shoulder and touched at his hilt tensely.

The tomb was octagonal and ringed with funereal friezes cut directly into its bleak stone walls. Opening the portal had removed one of the panels of its domed ceiling. At the center of the room stood a low dais that held an empty stone coffin with a split lid; on the east wall was a black doorway protected by a grate of slender bars heavily encrusted with scarlet rust. Pezur, drawn to the metal gate, stared between its disintegrating bars into the murk beyond.

"There's a hall through here," he said in a small voice. "There's a hallway beneath the earth." His hand touched the bars, and flakes of soft rust stuck to his inquisitive fingers. He tugged at the gate, gently at first, then harder when it wouldn't come loose. It stuck, then broke free and lurched toward him with a screech like a crushed rat. The archer jerked away, snatching back his hand as if the cold bars had scalded him.

"Not yet, soldier," said Adrastus. "I've brought a few torches to light our way." Balthano struck flint and steel while the last remaining mercenaries above finished draping cut saplings and loose chunks of brush over the portal's mouth.

When all the men were in the room, Adrastus gave a torch to Conan, who was to lead the party. A second torch was given to the big Shemite Orbash, who apparently found the task of bringing up the rear quite agreeable. Many men seemed disappointed both with the perceived paucity of torches and the fact that they were not allowed to bear one.

"Follow me and this will be swiftly over," said Adrastus. "We are to proceed east with but few deviations, turns that I know well from the study of a fine map."

The gate was drawn open with a mournful squall of hinges, and the party filed into a dark passageway that snaked beneath the earth. Once away from the open portal, the air grew cool and thick with dank moisture. The men murmured softly to one another, as if reluctant to break the tomb's timeless silence. It was difficult to believe that the sun shone down on a warm field a few feet above their heads while they wandered through this forgotten corridor of eternal night.

Conan's torch illuminated a once elegant hallway, paneled with plates of discolored marble and decorated with morbid bas-reliefs. Sculpted death's heads grinned at the intruders from corners and cornices. The Cimmerian drew to a halt and held his torch out into a four-way intersection.

"Which way, sorcerer?"

"Straight on," said Adrastus without hesitation.

The passage seemed to lower more deeply into the earth. Open doorways gaped to either side, offering admittance to small chambers like the one they had used to gain entrance to this subterranean maze. The walls began to show greater signs of age and considerable water damage. At one point a thick marble slab lay fallen into the corridor, admitting a dark mass of moist soil that spilled over the floor. Conan thought the earth exposed by the fallen panel appeared hollowed, as if dug into the wall. He was struck by the horrible suspicion that if he were to dig at the loose earth there, he would uncover a tunnel that wound away in darkness to secret places beneath the hills, warrens forever hidden from the eyes of men. His scalp tingled.

Ahead, the knotted root of a tree thrust through a rent in the low-hanging ceiling. It seemed to probe blindly into the hall like the twisted tentacle of some misplaced squid. Conan ducked around it and came upon an arch that looked to be at the point of collapse.

The crumbling arch was blackened and gnawed by age. It opened on a dark chamber from which emanated a thin trickling sound, as of a small stream. Conan thrust the smoking torch into the room and wrinkled his nose at the stench within. As he advanced, Pezur and Adrastus followed close behind.

"A fountain!" exclaimed the archer. His thin face became childlike with wonder. "What is a fountain doing in a tomb?"

"Some faiths hold that a fountain freshens the air of a crypt. Others that it allows the departing spirits of loved ones a final drink," replied Adrastus absently. The sorcerer looked to each of the chamber's three additional doorways, one at each point of the compass, and rubbed his bearded chin in perplexity.

"I trust the spirits drank their fill, for the air in here is fouler than that of a kennel," growled Conan. The Cimmerian drew near the low fountain and muttered a curse. "Ymir and Bori! It's not ghosts that have been drinking here."

The fountain was a simple raised pool, the rim of which was a wide bench of pale and filthy marble. In the pool's center, dark water ran in a slender stream from the proffered hands of a small statue of the goddess Ashtoreth, scarcely identifiable beneath a disfiguring coat of black mold. The barbarian lowered his torch so that its light shimmered on the inky water. "Look."

The mold and dirt of the fountain's marble rim was smeared, marked by innumerable handprints. Where individual prints were discernible, the hands appeared strangely small, inordinately long-fingered, and sharply taloned.

"Ghouls, here?" Adrastus gasped, then thrust a hand to his mouth as if to silence himself. "It is nothing," he added hurriedly. "Ghouls are timid creatures and prefer the cold flesh of corpses. Let us move on. I believe the east passage is the correct one."

"You believe…" said Shamtare with bitter sarcasm. Adrastus turned as if to upbraid the Shemite, but when he parted his lips to speak there came a high, shrill chittering from the halls they had just traversed. The wizard spun and stared back through the crumbling arch. His eyes went hollow with fear and his mouth hung slackly open, still poised for a retort that was lost now and forever forgotten.

"Crom." Conan's sword came out, gleaming like a firebrand in the light of his torch. "Everyone to the east door. Follow the wizard."

The clustered men looked to Adrastus, who still stared as if hypnotized into the menacing darkness beyond the arch. He tore his gaze free and stumbled toward the exit he had chosen. His hands delved clumsily into the blue folds of his cloak and pulled forth a thick roll of black velvet. Balthano, knives bared, went after him, casting a single glance back over his shoulder.

Orbash and the others crowded close behind. Pezur began to follow, and hesitated when he saw that neither Conan nor Shamtare had moved.

"Aren't you coming?" The archer's voice had risen an octave, and might have made the Cimmerian smile under different circumstances.

"Go on, Shamtare," said the barbarian. "I'll bring up the rear."

"I won't let you face those things alone," said the older man. Shamtare's face shone pasty white in the dimness. The hand that gripped his sword trembled as if with a palsy.

"Go on, you dotard. I'm not going to stay here. I'll be right behind you."

"For Anu's mercy, come along, Shamtare," called Pezur. "Don't worry about Conan. You're holding us up."

As if in response, the sharp chittering came again, more loud and insistent than before. And this time it was answered from the south doorway by a low, whining snarl. A muted chorus of bestial mutters floated up out of the darkness like the whispering wings of a cloud of bats.

"Holy Ishtar!" Shamtare's bulging eyes darted from one black doorway to the other. Conan turned and shoved him toward Pezur. The archer seized Shamtare's arm and sought to draw him into the east hallway.

"Go!" bellowed the barbarian. He backed toward the corridor as low, black figures leapt from the south and west doorways.

Conan thrust out the torch with a savage roar of defiance. His skin crawled with superstitious dread. The flickering flame gave him a swift glimpse of three hurtling forms, manlike, yet traveling on all fours. Gleam-eyed shadows arose in an army behind them, following the leaders of their pack. The barbarian had a fragmented, nightmare vision of pallid canine faces with bristling muzzles that gaped to reveal jagged yellow fangs and lolling crimson tongues; of patchy, mold-clotted fur covering surging, wiry bodies.

Then they were upon the Cimmerian, slamming into him, swarming up his body and tearing at his limbs. The torch was ripped from his grasp and cast aside. It burst on the tomb's floor like a dying comet, scattering orange sparks.

Absolute darkness flooded the crypt. Cold, damp talons closed on Conan's throat. The sheer physical weight of the ghouls gave the barbarian a surge of berserker's confidence.

These were creatures of flesh, not bodiless specters of the night. And flesh is prey to steel.

With a mighty convulsion, Conan heaved the tomb-dwellers away from him. His sword sheared the ghoul at his throat nigh in half and sent its spouting body sailing into the far wall. The beast that tore at his torch-hand was hoisted high overhead and brought down upon the third, clinging at his waist, with a force that shattered bone.

He was free. The blackness that pressed in around him swarmed with shrill chitters and mewling. Hooves scuffed on the stone floor as the horde rushed forward. The war cry of a Cimmerian tribesman echoed through the catacombs as Conan whipped his heavy blade in an unstoppable circular swath from left to right and back again. The charging ghouls hit the barrier of steel and were cut down, crushed asunder, and hurled aside. Foul blood sprayed as the tomb-herd was thrown back upon itself. Thin, keening cries of rage and agony grated in the barbarian's ears. When his blade met no resistance, Conan ducked into the east doorway, lunged unerringly through the narrow opening in the impenetrable murk. The dim, welcome glow of a torch shone ahead.

The barbarian plunged down the passage. He snarled in repugnance at the memory of the crypt-dwellers' unclean touch. Raw wounds stung on his neck, thighs, and arms.

Behind came the patter and clatter of hoofed feet and the sick titter of the pursuing ghouls.

Ahead, the slender hall opened into a room-sized mausoleum. Two severely plain sarcophagi lay side by side upon a low platform of stone. In his desperate haste the Cimmerian saw only the haunting glow of the torch, faint as a will-o-the-wisp, as it receded through the opposite doorway.

He ran full into the side of the first sarcophagus and its hard rim struck him mid-thigh. The headlong impact drove the weighty coffin off its base with a rasp and clatter that obscured the barbarian's guttural cry of pain. Conan's body flew over the first sarcophagus and twisted in midair to slam lengthwise into the second. The Cimmerian hit the floor with all the breath shocked from his lungs. He lay, half stunned, while precious moments fled and his ghastly pursuers closed in.

Hooves clacked into the chamber, then clapped onto the lid of the dislodged coffin as the leading ghoul bounded atop it. A triumphant titter rose above the prone barbarian and a pair of eyes, as flaringly scarlet as stoked coals, gloated down upon him. Conan uncoiled, came to his feet, and lashed out with the sword in a tigerish explosion of violence. The ghoul on the sarcophagus was smashed back into his fellows. The horde snarled and gibbered in response, then surged forward in a tide of vile bodies.

Conan leapt up onto the second coffin and bent his knees to catch his balance as the lid shifted with a dull rattle. He faced his foes in darkness, and knew that if he turned his back on them now, they would drag him down like a pack of rabid hounds. The broadsword sang as it cut the stale air of the tomb, and again the night-creatures were hurled back by its relentless swath. A ghoul scuttled beneath his blade and battened onto the barbarian's left leg. Talons like chisels sank into his thigh and calf. Baboon-like fangs closed on his ankle in a grip like a steel vise. Only the thick leather of his boot saved his flesh from the jagged teeth, while the terrific pressure of the thing's jaws threatened to crush his ankle into splinters of bone. Conan whirled the blade about and drove its point down through the ghoul's spine, so that it struck and grated on the coffin lid beneath. The Cimmerian tore his weapon free, kicked the mortally wounded ghoul away, and yellow light abruptly filled the chamber.

"Conan!" came a familiar voice from behind him. "Here!"

The Cimmerian risked a glance back over his shoulder in time to see Shamtare standing in the chamber's opposite doorway, already in the act of tossing him a burning torch.

With a sulfurous oath, Conan twisted and snatched the brand from the air. He swung back to face the ghouls just as the ravening horde drove forward once again.

The torch's light revealed them to be even more hideous than his fearful imagination had painted them in the concealing darkness. They were short, hunched bipeds with hoofed feet and clawed, simian hands, yet the loathsome things appeared as comfortable on all fours as upright. The flesh of their arms, legs, and rat-like snouts was bare, corpse-pale and rubbery. Lank, hairless tails hung from their hindquarters, lending them further semblance to monstrously overgrown graveyard rats.

Fully a score of them bore down on the barbarian, chittering like maddened apes and squinting crimson eyes accustomed to midnight gloom. They met fire and steel. The sword swept three aside, spilled them over the stone floor in a tangled welter of limbs. The torch was thrust into the chest of a bold ghoul and ignited its moldy fur. It fell back, squalling and beating its burning breast. But the mass of them came on, apparently unmoved by the fate of their brethren. Conan's blade swung like a remorseless scythe, but he knew they would overwhelm him with sheer numbers if he were not soon relieved.

A star flew over Conan's right shoulder and lit among the clustered ghouls. The Cimmerian blinked as the fist-sized ball of white incandescence struck the tomb's floor, bounced, and blazed up to eye-searing brilliance. A horrid cry came from the crypt-dwellers. They pressed foul talons over blinded eyes and reeled away from the light.

The shining sphere emitted a hiss like an angry viper and burned still brighter. Conan lifted an arm to shield his dazzled eyes. The additional illumination proved too much for the ghouls, who broke and fled out the doorway, streaming away down the narrow passage amid much mewling lamentation. In a moment, the only ghouls that remained were those the barbarian had slain.

Conan faced the opposite doorway, where Shamtare stood beside Adrastus. Both looked pale and unwell in the stark, unnatural light. The Cimmerian laughed harshly. The thighs of his breeches were shredded and the top of his left boot was nearly torn away. There were talon marks on his bare arms and his own blood mingled with splashes of the ghouls' vile ichor. Yet his hard face was split by a wide, white grin, and his laughter rang through the bleak chambers of the dead.

"Hah! A neat enough trick, sorcerer. Why didn't you think of it sooner?"

Adrastus fumbled at his star pendant with one hand and clutched a fistful of blue cloak with the other. "I was frightened," he said finally. "I am a mage of small and specialized skills. Combat is new to me."

Conan nodded, still smiling. "An honest answer. More than I might have expected of you." The little fireball began to change color, fading slowly to russet gold. "Come along," continued the Cimmerian. "Let us be on our way before those corpse-gnawers decide we are a meal worth dying for."

They moved quickly into the east hall, met with Balthano and Pezur, and lit a precious additional torch. Adrastus led with one held high aloft; Shamtare and Conan brought up the rear with the other two.

Behind them, the sorcerous light dimmed to dusky crimson, as though it sprang from a lantern of garnet. Then it guttered out.

10

The room was long, narrow, and lined with broken coffins. The north and south walls were carved with niches to hold them, but the coffins were pulled out of their beds, smashed open and strewn about. Aside from the omnipresent charnel house stench, there was no evidence of any human remains. In the opposite doorway a bent and rusty iron gate dangled from a single hinge.

"That must be the room. The passage must lie through there." Adrastus hastened through the violated tomb and debris clattered about his feet. The party followed him through the decrepit gate, which fell from its decayed hinge when the wizard shoved it open. Beyond was a small, circular room containing a single coffin set in a niche in the opposite wall.

The chamber was unadorned, and more crudely cut than those they had seen thus far. There was no marble paneling, no somber decorations, and no exit.

"Set's shining coils! Have I been misled?" The sorcerer's calm demeanor fractured, and he looked about the chamber wildly.

"Where are we?" Prince Eoreck stood close to his asshuri bodyguard, his sharp features pale but intent. "Are you saying you've gotten us lost in this ghoul-haunted labyrinth?"

All pretense of reserve and control fled the sorcerer. He tore at his beard with both hands and spun around as though he might suddenly espy a new doorway in the blank walls. "This must be the room! I'm sure this is the place. First ghouls that attack the living, and now this! Why is there no door? I can't fail now!" The Kothian seemed almost about to weep.

The mercenaries observed Adrastus with expressions registering everything from pity to horror. Shamtare stood watch in the doorway and held a torch to illuminate the hall behind them. Conan came into the chamber, lifted his torch to examine the ceiling, and spoke.

"We've traveled far enough to have passed beneath the army of Eruk. Yet we have not risen a step since we first descended into this pit. If these catacombs truly connect to those atop the bluff in Dulcine, then the passage out of here should lead us upward as well."

"That makes sense," said Shullar in a voice like a kettle drum. "I've long been wondering how we were to reach the top of a high bluff by crawling about underground."

"Be silent," cried Adrastus. "Let me think!"

"Think fast," advised Shamtare. "There is movement in the hall behind us."

The Cimmerian had made a circuit of the room, and now stood in front of the single coffin in its niche. While his eyes had been focused on the ceiling, they now narrowed on the tapered flame of his torch. He moved the brand to and fro, watched it ripple, then abruptly turned and stared at the coffin. Loose strands of black hair floated back from his stern face. A gentle breeze was channeled up from behind the coffin.

"Here is your door," said the barbarian. His big hands seized the stone sarcophagus and dragged it from its recess. It grated forward with surprising ease. A circular hole had been bored into the inner wall of the niche; it appeared wide enough to admit

Conan's shoulders, but only just so. The barbarian jerked the coffin completely out of its bed and let it crash to the floor.

The hole was the mouth of a black tunnel. Its lip was chipped, ragged, and adorned with twists of coarse, grayish hair. A stunned silence fell over the party.

"I should have known," whispered the sorcerer. "Their pathways are not our pathways."

"They're coming," shouted Shamtare from the door. "The ghouls!"

Adrastus seemed to come to his senses. He bounded to the doorway and pulled from his doublet something that resembled a silver marble. He pushed Shamtare aside and stepped into the hall. The little crystal sphere shone in his proffered palm. The sounds that spat from the wizard's lips might have been the hissed curses of some sentient reptile. The sphere ignited with a snap and a sizzle, and Adrastus hurled it down the hallway. It sailed through the darkness like a lost meteor, burgeoning in size and shedding blinding brilliance.

Mewls of pain and the scuffle of hooves echoed from the corridor's end, then tapered off swiftly as the skulking ghouls withdrew before the unendurable light.

The wizard stormed back into the chamber and pointed at the tunnel's dark maw. "There is our path. Move quickly. The crystalline light won't last long."

While the rest of the men traded dubious glances, Conan climbed into the niche and thrust the torch, then his head and sword arm, into the opening.

"It goes back a bit, then angles almost straight up." The Cimmerian's voice had a sepulchral ring in the narrow tunnel. "We can climb it, but it won't be easy." Conan's muscular legs pulled back into the opening and it looked to the unhappy mercenaries as if he were being devoured by the wall.

Shamtare heard Pezur whisper a prayer.

"Go on then," snapped Prince Eoreck, gesturing at the niche with his drawn rapier. "You heard the wizard. This is our path."

Pezur pushed ahead of Shamtare, squirmed into the stone niche, and wiggled through the rough-edged hole.

Shamtare came on his heels, and the rest of the party followed doggedly. Strained curses rose as they wedged themselves into the uncomfortably close quarters of the narrow passage.

The tunnel stretched back a mere three feet before it bent in a sharp elbow and became a nearly vertical shaft. The walls were irregular, crudely chipped and torn from the ruddy rock of the bluff. The shaft's slight lean to the east and a multitude of rugged hand and footholds made the climb easier than Conan had feared, but the moistness of the stone and the flickering, torchlit darkness made the going slow.

A steady breeze, cool and dank, funneled down the shaft. It chilled the sweating limbs of the men as they clambered higher in the close stone passage. The climbers became keenly aware that anyone who slipped would fall upon those beneath him, bearing the lot down the shaft together. Soon they reached a height sufficient to make this possibility a deadly one. Progress was halting and the agile Cimmerian pulled ahead.

Conan braced a booted foot against the far wall of the shaft and held the torch in his teeth while his hands dug into a shallow channel chipped into the rock. He pulled himself up easily, drew his big body over a sharp lip, and found that the shaft leveled out and expanded into a rough, cavern-like chamber. He squatted, waited, and assisted those who followed, until the party began to gather in the small room.

Shullar's rough boost shoved Eoreck up over the rim so that the prince lost his footing and sprawled at the Cimmerian's feet.

"Damn you, man!" he choked, face damp with effort from the climb. Shullar slowly dragged his massive, fully armored body into the chamber and sat cross-legged on the stone. He panted harshly and responded to his master's curses with a dismissive shrug. Everyone caught their breath, wiped at perspiration, and seized the moment to sit or lie down. A water jug and a wine skin were passed around and swiftly dispatched. Shamtare leaned over the shaft's precipitous brink with his torch.

"None following that I can tell," he said.

"Good," said Eoreck as he dabbed at his brow with the hem of his scarlet cape. "Where to now, Adrastus?"

"Through there, I trust," answered the mage, still breathing hard from the climb. "That seems to be the only exit." He pointed to a small, circular tunnel mouth low on the wall opposite the shaft. It looked much like the hole in the coffin niche below, save that it was even smaller and level with the floor. Groans came from the mercenaries; the loudest from Orbash, whose face was still scarlet from strain.

Conan rose smoothly from his seat and strode to the dark opening. Something beside it made him hesitate and hold out his torch like a protective talisman of fire.

"Wizard. What is this?" There was such cold loathing in the Cimmerian's tone that the sorcerer climbed painfully to his feet and hastened to Conan's side. Adrastus found himself looking upon a crude altar.

Beside the black burrow, the wall was rudely carved with primitive designs. These clumsy marks surrounded, and made a frame for, a triangular niche clawed from stone in which sat a small, crudely fashioned statuette. The simple sculpture at first appeared all but formless, but upon closer examination it suggested the likeness of a bloated, beaked creature shaped somewhat like a squat toad. What looked to be a single bulging eye was incised upon its malformed brow.

"Gol-goroth!" gasped the mage, and drew a quick sign in the air.

Conan was not as disturbed by the crude idol as by the objects that lay stacked in a low pile before it. It was a heap of severed human hands. Some had rotted in the moist cavern air until there was little left but articulated bits of bone. Others looked almost fresh, save that they were spotted with what appeared to be black blisters. When Adrastus saw these, he blanched and tried to push Conan away from the little altar.

His effort met with little success. The Cimmerian took a step back and regarded the flustered Kothian in amazement.

"Don't stand too close to it," Adrastus panted. "Some of those hands were cut from men who suffered from the plague!"

"Ishtar's girdle," swore Shamtare. He peered around the barbarian's wide shoulder. "Do you mean we might catch this plague by simply standing beside the severed hand of one who died from it?"

"Unlikely," said Adrastus pensively. "Most unlikely. But now is as good a time as any to give you your protective masks." He beckoned to Balthano, who turned around so that the wizard could unfasten his backpack. From within the leathern pack, the wizard produced a number of filmy white veils and passed them out to the mercenaries. The warriors took the pieces of pale fabric and examined them without enthusiasm. When all had one, Adrastus held his own veil above his head so that everyone could see it.

"Watch, and I will show you how to place the veil over your mouth and nose. Know that it will protect you from the floating vapors of the scourge, but that physical contact with a plague victim may still infect you. Have no fears as to whether you have been unknowingly infected. This pestilence kills in minutes. Black eruptions appear on the skin. Swellings distend the flesh of the throat. The eyes weep blood. Death is inevitable and almost immediate. Watch," he added needlessly, for the mercenaries hung upon every word and stared at him unblinkingly.

Adrastus lifted his face to look at the ceiling and brought the veil slowly down to cover his features from below the eyes to his chin. The gossamer fabric seemed to blend with his flesh, smoothing invisibly into his cheeks and beard. When he lowered his head, the veil had all but disappeared; it showed only as a vague film over his lower face.

"The mask is removable at any time, but once we are within the walls of Dulcine, to remove it is to die. Eating is accomplished by sliding food up beneath the mask like so. You may drink directly through its fabric, though the taste of certain beverages will be slightly altered."

"Will it better the flavor of our wine?" asked Shamtare with false heartiness. No one laughed and Adrastus ignored him.

"Put them on then, comrades. A little more crawling about in the dark and we'll come out into the sun."

With a full measure of distasteful grumbles and colorful curses, the mercenaries complied. Conan and Shamtare exchanged uncertain glances. The Shemite looked at his bit of gauze as though it were a tarantula the sorcerer had asked him to place upon his face. When held at an angle to the torches, the gossamer threads of the fabric gleamed with reflected light, as if it were woven with slim filaments of glass. Seeing the others don the masks with no apparent ill effects, the barbarian spat and lifted his veil. Shamtare caught at his arm.

"No," said the older man. "I'll go first." With his lips pressed into a firm line of determination, Shamtare lifted his bearded face and dropped the veil over his mouth and chin. It fell into place and adhered effortlessly. The mercenary looked at Conan.

"How is it?" asked the barbarian.

"A little cold at first. Then nothing." He tapped at his cheeks with the fingertips of both hands. "Is it as hard to see as the wizard's?"

Conan nodded.

"I can tell it's there well enough," continued Shamtare. "Wearing a veil! By Pteor's manhood, I feel like a maiden."

"Be assured that you do not resemble one," said the Cimmerian. "Has the wizard won your trust at last?"

"He's given me no reason to alter my opinion of sorcery or sorcerers," whispered Shamtare. Then he raised an eyebrow and favored Conan with a wry grin. "But his masks seem to be all right."

Conan placed the veil over his face and recoiled a little at the cool tingle it produced, as if a tissue of ice had melted upon his skin. He looked at Shamtare and pulled the mask off. It came away easily enough, and he felt no different. He put the veil back on.

"Hanuman's stones. Would that good fortune dogged my tracks as oft as sorcery."

"Well, let's get going then," said Eoreck loudly. He stretched and glanced at the barbarian. "After you, captain."

Conan crawled into the claustrophobically tight opening, stoically ignoring the ghastly offering of human hands and the strange god they honored. His shoulders scraped along the tunnel walls as he wormed his way into the passage. It expanded somewhat, then described an elbow nearly identical to the one he had encountered in the coffin niche far below. The barbarian climbed another nearly vertical shaft, and found its end within a mere fifteen feet. The tunnel narrowed once more, its blunt terminus broken by another circular opening that punched through the rounded ceiling into open blackness. With a grunt of effort, Conan braced himself against one wall and shoved his torch up through the gap. It was as though he had thrust the torch into a closed box.

"Crom's devils," cursed the barbarian.

"What is it, Conan? Why do you halt?" came Shamtare's voice from below.

"Damned if I don't think we're all going to rise from the dead," said Conan. His boots found purchase on the walls and he rose through the ring of blackness. The top of his head thumped against something heavy that rattled. The smoke of his torch was suddenly suffocating in the enclosed space. The Cimmerian put the torch aside, pressed both hands against the flat surface above him, and heaved the stone lid up off a sarcophagus. It flew across the tomb, struck the floor with a crash, and broke into three equal pieces. Conan climbed up through the base of the niche, through the coffin that sat therein, and leapt from the sarcophagus into the silent crypt. He shook himself like a wet lion.

Ghostly voices floated up through the circular hole bored through the bottom of the coffin. Conan unsheathed his broadsword, moved lithely to the open doorway, and shot a glance down a vacant hall. He listened intently for a moment. Satisfied that no enemies were close by, the Cimmerian returned to the coffin and shouted down through its secret opening. "Ho, dog brothers. Come ahead if you'd like to know how it feels to climb out of your grave."

The party followed one at a time, and each in turn exclaimed in amazement and horror to find themselves literally emerging from a coffin. Conan's even teeth shone in an amused grin until the last of the men clambered out of the niche and stood in the dim tomb.

Adrastus leaned against the sarcophagus and breathed heavily. His corpulent face was florid and his cheeks flapped as he puffed and wheezed. It was apparent that the climb was the most vigorous exercise he'd had for some time. After a few moments he was able to speak again.

"We've made it. We are within the walls of Dulcine."

"Then let us leave these catacombs and find some fresh air. By Ymir, I've grown sick of graves," said Conan. The wizard pointed mutely to the chamber's only door, and the barbarian led the party onward.

The corridor was identical to those they had traversed at the base of the bluff, save that it was in somewhat better repair. The walls were mottled with mildew, and showed cracks and swellings from the ceaseless pressure of the earth, but nowhere did the hall threaten collapse.

The men came into an open four-way intersection.

Ahead and to the right lay unrelieved darkness. To the left shone a vague gray glow.

"Go left," said Adrastus unnecessarily. Conan had already rounded the corner and was pacing toward the phantom illumination. A scratching, scuffling sound came from the darkness of the right-hand corridor. The men hastened away as the noise was followed by an apelike chittering that echoed horribly through the empty labyrinth.

"More ghouls!" gasped Adrastus. His swift walk became a shuffling run. Boots trampled along the grimy stone floor as the men followed him in flight. The Cimmerian kicked open another rusted gate and the party piled into a mausoleum. Orbash shoved the gate shut, then threw a heavy shoulder against it, bending the gate in its frame to jam it in place. He peered through the bars for any sign of pursuers.

"We're safe," panted the Kothian wizard. "They won't dare face the light." He pointed to the ceiling. It was broken by four small iron grids which acted as skylights. Diffuse sunlight illuminated the glum chamber. Through the cross-hatching of the grids, bits of blue sky could be seen, like bright fragments of another world. Orbash shouldered his way to the chamber's other doorway and stared down an open gray-lit corridor.

"Ghouls! Why so many ghouls?" Adrastus caught his breath.

"There was a plague," growled Conan. "Their food supply is up and they're breeding."

"Of course," the magician nodded. "Of course."

"Not that there was ever any shortage of tomb-spawn hereabouts," continued the barbarian. "That passage we climbed wasn't made by men. It was made by ghouls hungry enough to claw through fathoms of stone and earth to reach another corpse." He spat explosively in disgust.

"True enough," admitted Adrastus. He stroked his crystal pendant. "But this is not so uncommon as you seem to believe.

The graveyards of many cities harbor ghouls."

"And how is it that you know their secret paths beneath the earth, wizard? No grave-robber ever dared the trails we've explored this day. And I don't believe that ghoulish warren was ever set down on any human map." Conan's terse words quieted the men and sent their eyes questing to Adrastus. There was a moment of uncomfortable silence.

The Kothian's brow darkened and his lips pulled down in an expression of contemptuous intolerance. His eyes grew wide and seemed to acquire an iridescent sheen in the dimness. They shone like orbs of quicksilver.

"I am a sorcerer," he hissed. "I have seen sights that would drive you to tear the eyes from your head. I have held concourse with beings that would blast your sanity. Ghouls are the least of my teachers. And I am not beholden to you or anyone else for explanations."

Conan's retort was obliterated by a sudden scream from the chamber's far door. Orbash staggered away from the opening in the grip of some new foe. While the big man's attention had been upon the sorcerer, someone had apparently crept down the hallway and attacked him. The mercenaries turned to meet this new threat, drawing blades and moving to their comrade's assistance.

To the eyes of the men in the dim mausoleum, Orbash appeared to struggle with a black man clad in filthy rags. The attacker had both his hands clenched about the mercenary's throat, and steely thumbs dug into the flesh of the Shemite's thick neck. Orbash made gargling sounds of distress and rage. Incoherent words streamed from the invader's black lips.

As his soldier's training took hold, Orbash drew his stout Vanir dagger, lifted it high, and then plunged it into his adversary's unprotected throat. A jet of dark blood burst over his hand, arm, and breast. His unknown assailant released him, staggered away, and fell against the wall. Orbash took a step back among his comrades, caught his balance, and coughed rackingly. Fifteen weapons were leveled at the attacker, who slid down the wall until he sat on the floor. His dark hands dropped from his torn throat and his head lolled loosely on his shoulders. The blackened face was covered with blisters.

"Another ghoul? What-what was that thing?" Orbash rubbed at his throat with a blood-wet hand. "I-I…" The words dissolved into a hideous choking cry. Orbash staggered forward, and suddenly bent at the waist as if stabbed in the belly. Then he jerked bolt upright and spun to face his astonished comrades. Another horribly strangled scream was ripped from his lungs.

Cries of horror rose from the assembled mercenaries, and they drew back from their stricken friend as though before a blaze of unendurable heat.

"Don't touch him! Don't touch him!" The wizard's words were all but lost in the tumult. Every man in the room stared helplessly at the swellings that distended the flesh of Orbash's throat, growing even as they watched. Countless black spots bloomed upon his pale skin like evil little flowers. Twin streams of liquid crimson overflowed his wide eyes and spilled down his cheeks. His cry was lopped off as abruptly as if he had been decapitated, and Orbash slumped bonelessly to the ground.

"Morrigan, Macha, and Nemain!" Conan's curse was as strident as the clash of steel. "What sorcery is this?"

"This," said Adrastus, "is the plague."

The sorcerer moved among the stunned mercenaries, pushed his way through the group of silent, staring men. He walked past Orbash's body and squatted down beside the corpse of the assailant, keeping a respectful distance.

"But the mask!" cried Pezur. "What of his mask?"

"The mask wards off the vapors of the pestilence. Direct contact with a plague victim may still cause the disease. Direct contact with infected blood will surely cause it. Our poor friend didn't stand a chance." The wizard sounded more interested than mournful.

"How could he attack Orbash if the plague kills so quickly?" asked Conan. He wrinkled his nose at the peculiar stench rising from the attacker's body.

"I don't know," said Adrastus slowly. "Look at this fellow. He's obviously in the plague's last stages and yet he was mobile and seemed aware. Wait, by Set! This is Botah-Aton, the cemetery groundskeeper. I recognize the robes. Hah! Fancy meeting you here, old skinflint! I've already made my passage, Stygian! You shan't be squeezing any gold pieces out of me today."

The mercenaries milled about uncertainly, taking care to keep well clear of the black spatters that stained the stone floor. Shamtare ran a callused hand through his gray-shot mane. "I still don't understand how the man attacked Orbash if he had the plague."

"Perhaps he was partially immune," said Adrastus. "Perhaps the plague isn't universally lethal, as I had thought."

"There are always those few who remain untouched by a pestilence," said Conan, "like the piper who survived the plague of Kova in Zingara. But this man seems to have been all but consumed by the scourge without having died of it. That is passing strange."

"Indeed," mused Adrastus. "Botah appears fairly riddled with the plague. He bears all the physical symptoms of the disease at its most advanced stage, yet he attacked our man with desperate strength. It's as if he lived on with the pestilence, and was maddened by it. Ishtar, his whole body is covered by the swellings. He must have been suspended in a kind of living death, like a zombie raised up by a shaman of Darfar. A plague-lich."

"Enough," said Prince Eoreck. Desperation quavered thinly in his voice. "Enough of this musing over the dead. I must see the sky again or I shall go mad. I demand that you lead us out of here. I command it."

Adrastus stood up and smiled mockingly. "Yes, my liege. Follow me." He turned down the empty corridor from which Botah-Aton had hurled himself upon the luckless Orbash. The mercenaries followed. Each gave the motionless bodies a wide berth. Pezur inclined his head and whispered a prayer for his fallen comrade.

"I trust this Botah fellow is unique," said the prince in an overloud voice. "Such an anomalous condition cannot be common." He paused. "Correct, Adrastus?"

"I shouldn't think so," replied the sorcerer. "I confess I don't truly know."

The party rounded a final corner and the corridor opened into another tomb. But their eyes passed over the coffin-lined walls, over the arching arabesque in black marble that formed the ceiling, and went to the barred door. It creaked faintly in a gust of fresh breeze that pushed between its bars and washed over the weary men. The wind was warm and smelled of greenery. Through the gate they could see the sun of late afternoon streaking through an untrimmed expanse of grass, reflecting from the polished marble faces of a row of simple tombstones.

Conan pulled the gate open and the men walked from the shadows of the underworld into the doomed city of Dulcine.

11

The thing that looked to be a man ventured out of its dark palace home, sat upon the marble rim of the fountain called the Freshet, and felt a strange weakness, a hollowness beneath its breast. It was harried by a hungry restlessness that it could not name nor understand. There was something it needed to do, yet its fresh-formed mind could not envision what that might be. This sensation had driven it into the sunlight from the comfortable shadows of its lair. Eyes like balls of tar squinted against the unfamiliar glare. Its garments hung heavily upon its man-shape. Despite the warm breeze they were as motionless as if carved of black onyx.

A raven sailed down from the cloudless sky and lit on the flagstones before it. The bird stalked to and fro in a lordly fashion, and the sun gleamed along its satin-black plumage. It cocked its sleek head at the thing, opened its stiletto beak, and cawed hoarsely. Once, many of those who came for water at the Freshet's broad pool brought with them crumbs of bread for the birds that gathered there. Not today.

The thing that was not a man admired the bird, seeing another creature that was new to it. It saw the sheen of the raven's wings, then looked upon its own garments and watched as they acquired the selfsame sheen. The creature felt a certain undefinable pleasure at this, and in its fledgling vanity it allowed its bountiful cloak to catch the wind and flap from its shoulders.

"Finish me, master." The voice was rasping and wretched, pleading from the last extreme of desperation. "Kill me, oh lord."

With a dire croak and a snap of black wings, the raven took to the air.

The thing turned its passionless face and saw that a man had come upon it unawares. It did not understand his words, for it had no true language, yet it felt a glimmer of comprehension and appreciation for the obeisance paid to it. It looked upon the man and knew curiosity.

This is one of those that have not stopped. It does not lie still. It lives.

The speaker was a stooped and heavyset man of middle years. He wore the silks of a successful merchant, cut in the latest style, but now his fashionable garb was wrinkled and smudged with grime. Beneath each of his ears protruded a lump like a swollen goiter. Everywhere his exposed skin was warped and mottled by black-bubbled blisters. They dotted his flesh, singly and in ghastly clusters, as if he had been spattered with molten tar. Worst of all, his pupils peered weakly from eyes awash with livid scarlet. Dark tears of blood lay congealed upon his blistered cheeks.

"Take me, master. As you took the others. I am sick with pain and can worship you no longer." The wretch reached into a pocket, drew out a handful of gold coins, and tossed them into the Freshet. He fell to his knees, then dropped to lay prostrate at the thing's feet.

Why does this one live? Can I make it stop?

The thing in black bent gracefully at the waist and laid a long hand upon the prone man's brow. The hand might have been a red-hot iron. The man flopped as if in the throes of a fit, cried out, and then went rigid. Rows of blisters ran across his features, coursing from beneath the thing's fingers. In seconds the man's face was unrecognizable. He went limp.

It watched the ebon carbuncles creep and swell.

My mark. The mark of my power over these little lives.

A hot billow of strength filled the creature, rose from within to fill the strange hollowness it had felt in its breast. With the renewed strength came an unmistakable sense of correctness. This was what it was meant to do.

I need this to live. They must end so that I may continue.

An eldritch epiphany came to it, and it felt as if it had opened a new eye on the world. It sensed the presence of human lives in the city around it. They moved like lost motes through the empty spaces, through the streets and structures of the city, like sparks tossed aloft by a fire set in darkness. There were many more survivors than it would have thought possible, but too few for what it now recognized as its appetite.

Its senses unfurled, languorously opened out into the world that it claimed as its own. The palace felt empty and hollow, and the uppermost room, the glass-domed chamber in which the demon had been born and knew as a haven, resisted its efforts to see within. It felt men clustered together in the stables beside the palace. There were more men outside the city, arrayed in a wide ring around its walls. And at a distance, far off to the south and west, was a great congregation of lives. It shut its lusterless eyes and felt the combined life force of the people of Akkharia shining like a living beacon from over the horizon. Here was a feast undreamed of.

It opened its eyes and stared longingly southwest. It gazed through the palace gate, beyond the walls and buildings of Dulcine.

Now I know what I am. Now I know what I shall do.

The raven floated down again on widespread wings, then seemed to think better of it and flapped away. It soared off into the open sky.

The man-thing watched the bird intently as it dwindled with distance. Huge, black-feathered wings unfolded from the thing's shoulders, massive duplicates of those of the fleeing raven. It stood still as they pulled slowly free of its back and opened, extended into great dark crescents that gleamed in the sun. It stretched its wings like a black angel risen fresh from hell. The beautiful, amber-skinned face showed no trace of expression. The dull eyes held no gleam of feeling.

I am the end of life given form. I am Death.

The giant wings resorbed, drew back into the thing's body without so much as disturbing the folds of its cloak. Then they were gone, and it seemed impossible that they had ever truly been. The thing that resembled a man stood as straight as before, apparently unmoved and untaxed by its momentary metamorphosis.

I hunger. I must seek those few who have escaped me, take them and gather strength.

It walked from the Freshet's side, through the courtyard gate, and into the waiting city. The rejuvenating strength that it felt melded with its new sense of purpose. Vistas of possibility it had been unable to envision now lay open before it.

Soon I shall leave this, the place of my birth, and go forth into the world outside. I shall take the men that encircle my walls. Then I shall find the great gathering of lives beyond the sunset and take them as well.

The thing that resembled a man strode leisurely through its kingdom and thought on the many things it would do now that it had come to an understanding of its destiny. There was much to be accomplished. And much to be enjoyed.

Soon it would leave these walls, perhaps forever, and explore to this land's farthest limits. Soon it would range over the length and breadth of this new world, and it would place its dark mark upon its subjects wherever it found them.

Soon.

12

The cemetery stretched beneath the clear summer sky, silent but for the buzzing of insects and the forlorn cries of birds. The untrimmed grass moved fitfully in the breeze. The mercenaries, soiled and weary from their long journey beneath the earth, were content to stand in the sun, sip from water skins, and congratulate one another on their safe passage into Dulcine.

While the men lounged about, Conan stole away among the tombstones. None noticed his absence until he returned, striding purposefully along the cobbled path that wound through a small copse of old oaks and led to the door of the mausoleum from which they had all emerged. The men, sitting on tombstones and lying on the grass, met the barbarian with shouted greetings, jests, and questions as to where he had been. Shamtare noted the Cimmerian's dour demeanor and rose to meet him.

"What is it, friend?" he asked softly.

"Do you never rest, captain?" said Eoreck. "Must you always be off scouting about? We're safe inside the city now and I give you leave to relax."

"We may be inside the city," said Conan, "but we're not safe. Follow me if you'd see why." Without another word the barbarian turned about and headed back the way he'd come, leaving the mercenaries to scramble up and follow.

Shouted questions went unanswered, and shortly the group of warriors formed a motley parade along the cobbled path. They passed through the cluster of old oaks, which perched atop a low hill like a leafy crown, then stared down across the graveyard and the city beyond. From their vantage point the men could see to the cemetery's limits and discern the colorful buildings of Dulcine, strangely still and peaceful. So motionless and silent was the city that it might have been sealed in crystal. Dulcine seemed frozen in a single suspended moment, and was strangely serene in its lifeless solitude.

Conan pointed wordlessly, drawing the eyes of the men to a spot at the base of the long sloping hill, just within the cemetery's iron gates. There was a paved clearing, like a city square, from which sprang a dozen cobbled paths that ran off into the graveyard's sprawling expanse. In the center of the clearing was a huge, irregular mound, perhaps twice the height of a man. It was dark in color, mostly black, and when the breeze shifted its stench made many of the hardened mercenaries gag and curse.

"What in Ishtar's name is that?" Eoreck asked the question in a tone that did not seem to invite response. At his side, Shullar glowered as sullenly as ever, and gave no answer.

The party came slowly down the hill, spreading out from the path to see the object on the pavement more clearly. As the men approached the dark mass they fell silent, and the only sound was the crunch of boots on dry grass and the clink and jingle of weapons and armor. In a moment, they all came to the rim of the paved clearing and stood in a half-ring around the abomination that lay heaped on the stone flags.

It was a gigantic funeral pyre. Blackened bodies, seared to the bone, formed a ghastly, tangled mountain of entwined limbs. At the base of the pyre the bodies were burnt to gray ash, but those piled above were twisted caricatures of humanity, skeletons of scorched ebony locked together in a deathly embrace.

"Who did this?" Pezur's voice was loud and hollow in the stillness. He looked from side to side, finally focused on Adrastus. "Who burnt these people?"

"The plague obviously spared a few. At least for a time," replied the Kothian thoughtfully. "Be at ease. When there are too many to bury, bodies must be burned. The people of any plague-struck city would do the same."

"And would they sever the heads of their dead neighbors?" snarled Conan. "Do you see a single skull in that great pile? Look to the fence and tell us again to be at ease."

The mercenaries looked away from the terrible pyre and gazed upon the cemetery's fence, a low wall of iron shafts topped with spearheads to deter intruders. Dark, globular objects capped many of the shafts. They were too far off to be seen with any clarity, but there was not a man in Prince Eoreck's party that did not feel a sudden chill and a sickened certainty as to what those objects were.

"Set's coils!" swore Adrastus. "The fools must have gone mad with the fear of death. Still, it is not so surprising when one considers it. Never before has a plague slain so many, so swiftly. The few with some immunity must have felt they witnessed the end of the world."

"Offerings," said Shamtare, still staring at the fence.

"What?" said Pezur.

"Come on then," shouted Prince Eoreck suddenly. He stepped in front of the half-ring of men that stood on the clearing's curb. He spun around in a self-conscious swirl of his brilliant cape and lifted a fist dramatically. "Let us not stand about gawking at death like green recruits. There is a city to be looted. Forward, men of Akkharia."

Though the prince's studied posing was apparent, and his words sounded empty to all but himself, the mercenaries responded to his call. They gratefully sloughed off the morbid malaise that held them staring at the pyre, and began to walk toward the cemetery's gate.

"Let us make for the palace immediately. I should like to take refuge there before dark," announced Adrastus.

"You'll get no argument from me, wizard," said Conan.

They filed through the gate, careful not to look too closely at the severed heads arrayed along its length. Conan set a brisk pace and all seemed content to hurry away from the cemetery, to follow the Cimmerian and get about their business.

Dulcine was a husk. The streets were like empty stone canyons, the buildings bright and in good repair, but lifeless and still save for the occasional gust of wind. The brilliant sun seemed incongruous as it spread warm light over a deserted marketplace. Stalls stood empty, wares still laid out upon tables with none to examine them or bicker over their price. Doors to shops and taverns gaped open, as though the people had fled or fallen abruptly, without warning. There were no bodies to be seen in the market, though Conan noted a pair of dark forms seated motionlessly in chairs on a second-story balcony. The plague would seem to have struck fast and hard here, to have left two victims sitting idly in their seats. The barbarian reasoned that the bodies of those who had fallen in the marketplace were likely among those in the funeral pyre.

Conan grimaced. The sooner they gathered what riches they could and got out of this charnel house, the better.

The dead city's oppressive silence fell over the mercenaries like an insidious spell, so that they spoke in whispers, if at all, and started sharply at any small sound that broke the unnatural stillness. Festive banners snapped in the breeze. A shutter swayed and creaked. In a craftsman's booth, jeweled wind chimes tinkled, the soft, musical sound at once ghostly and infused with a nameless melancholy.

"Those of you who distrusted my masks should know that by now we would all be dead without them," said Adrastus.

He seemed oblivious of the intrusive sound of his voice in the empty street. "Any who may still doubt me should feel free to remove their mask and thus provide an object lesson for the rest of us."

"Small comfort for poor Orbash," grumbled Shamtare.

"Orbash?" said Pezur. He pulled his over-bright eyes away from restlessly scanning blank windows. "Ishtar has taken Orbash. He's gone to a better place."

"Oh yes?" snapped Balthano. "I thought he was dead."

"That's enough talk," interrupted Prince Eoreck. "Be silent and pay close heed to the city around us."

"What for?" asked Balthano; his dark eyes glinted with yet darker amusement. "Everybody in the whole damn city is dead."

"Soldier, you will be silent!" shouted Eoreck. His pointed features went florid. He laid a hand on Shullar's massive shoulder, and the bodyguard stopped and stared at Balthano balefully.

"Balthano," said Adrastus quietly.

"Yes, milord," said the Argossean. "Your pardon." The party continued in silence.

Conan led the band out of the market, along a side street, and out onto a broad double avenue that reached through the city's lifeless heart to the gates of the baronial palace. The twin roads were laid with smooth cobblestones and divided by a lush greensward, planted at measured intervals with lofty trees. The grass was tall and untended. The wreckage of a toppled cart was visible some distance down the avenue. Looming over all was the palace of Dulcine.

It rose like a mountain above its own ponderous walls, and humbled the rooftops of the silent city. The base of the monolithic structure was a featurelessly smooth block of blue-green stone that stretched up five full stories like the rounded bole of some titanic tree. At the fifth story the body of the palace split into a collection of multiply-formed towers and minarets. At the center, and tallest of all, stood a thick, barrel-like tower capped with a dome from which the sun reflected in vivid glints of color. The mighty palace was as strange as it was regal, and not a few of the men in the party wondered at the sort of man who would build such a thing.

As they walked along the boulevard, they began to notice the bodies of the dead. A black and withered form leaned stiffly from a window as if to hail them as they passed. An ugly tangle of bodies jammed the doorway in which they had fallen, sacks and baggage still clutched tight in skeletal hands. Scavengers appeared to want little to do with the dead of Dulcine. Though there were the obvious and inevitable depredations of decay, very few of the corpses showed signs of being disturbed by vulture or jackal.

The square gates of the palace's courtyard stood open before the travelers. Solid steel they were, as bleakly functional as the doors of a prison, and mounted on hinges the size of a tall man. The walls were fully twenty feet thick, so that coming through the gate gave the impression of walking along an alley between tall and windowless buildings of somber stone.

The courtyard within was roughly circular and the size of a small town's square. The walls that loomed behind and the palace that towered before the party gave them the distinct and unpleasant sensation of standing at the bottom of a great pit. Between the gate and the arched double doors of the palace was the wide circular bowl of the bottomless Freshet, the baron's own sweet water fountain. It was thirty feet across from rim to white marble rim. Arranged around it were dozens of benches fashioned from the same white marble. Once this had been a gathering place for all of Dulcine. Now the benches were empty and the only visitors to the Freshet were trespassers from another city, armed invaders in search of plunder.

Just past the Freshet's center-point, closer to the palace, a plume of white water burst from the pool and sprayed skyward ceaselessly. The fountain hissed and splashed in the stillness. Conan noticed a single gold coin gleaming upon the fountain's niveous rim. As the party advanced, they could see beneath the surface of the pool. They saw that the shallows on their side of the Freshet dropped away precipitously into a dark opening that pierced the bowl's floor directly in front of the fountain's jet. The gap was the mouth of a shaft that drove down through murky blue depths and into the rock heart of the bluff upon which the city perched.

"Drink if you wish," said Adrastus, "but do so through your masks. I don't think the plague could have poisoned such a large source of moving water, but there is no profit in taking any chances."

Conan cupped his hand, dipped it into the startlingly cold water of the Freshet, and sipped tentatively through the nigh-transparent fibers of his mask. The water was sweet and refreshing. Its chill stung his palate. He scooped both hands into the pool and drank deeply.

The Cimmerian's blue-eyed gaze crept over the massive bulk of the palace. The wall rising before him was so seamlessly constructed that he doubted his ability to climb it.

His eyes dropped to the wall's base and narrowed in puzzlement. There was a dark space between the wall and the flagstones of the courtyard, a black slot, wide enough to admit a fist, that followed the length of the wall as far as he could see. It was as if the entire palace sat fitted into a base, like a torch set in a sconce. As he thought on this anomaly, he noted how the courtyard wrapped around the base of the palace.

The left side opened into a small garden planted with rows of fragrant fruit trees. The space to the right held a small collection of wooden outbuildings that appeared to be stables. When his eyes fell upon these innocuous structures a seemingly sourceless uneasiness came over the Cimmerian.

The stables were shut tight. The doors were closed and the windows were shuttered. Nothing seemed outwardly wrong, but Conan was a barbarian and trusted the instincts that sent a chill to tingle the flesh between his shoulder blades. He lifted his head, watching the stables suspiciously and sniffing at the air. His nostrils flared and he suddenly knew what it was that his wilderness-bred senses were trying to tell him. There was a faint scent on the breeze, and though it might be mistaken for the charnel stench of the dead, Conan knew it as the same scent he had first encountered on the body of Botah-Aton, the man who, though all but consumed by the plague, still had the mad strength to attack and slay Orbash.

The smell was distinctive; it was the unnatural tang of living corruption.

Adrastus leaned against the Freshet's rim. He looked across the courtyard and studied the high-arched palace doors.

Bound in bright brass, the smoothly finished panels still gleamed with wax. The sorcerer scratched at his beard. "If the doors are locked from within, we'll have the devil's own time getting them open. By Erlik's black throne! I should have thought of this. I can attempt to magically raise the bolt; otherwise, we'll have to bore our way through. The damn things are designed to resist a siege."

"Why don't you test them before abandoning all hope?" suggested Shamtare. "Why start complaining before you've a reason?"

"That mouth, old man," said Balthano lazily, "is going to talk you into a grave one day."

"Be silent," hissed Conan. His broadsword seemed to leap into his fist from the sheath on his shoulder. Balthano misconstrued the Cimmerian's intent and took a hasty step backward. He held both hands suspended over his belly while his eyes widened with defiance and anticipation. Only Pezur understood.

"What is it, Conan?" asked the archer.

His eyes followed the Cimmerian's gaze, and lit on the doors of the stable just as they burst open and those who had been lurking within lunged forth and gave tongue to an unholy medley of hideous cries. From out of the sheltering darkness of the sealed stable came a stream of warped and plague-marked men. Each brandished some manner of weapon and ran toward the mercenaries with murderous intent. Conan counted ten, then twenty, and then lost count as he beheld the aspect of the men who charged his party. There was no face that was not disfigured by black carbuncles, no eye that shone untainted with bloody crimson. A small army of plague-wracked human animals advanced upon them, and their blasphemous war cries were a nerve-shredding bedlam.

The mercenaries responded as any trained warriors would: they drew their weapons and readied themselves for the assault. Balthano slapped his belly and drew his knives in a motion so swift that his sleeves cracked like a whip.

"Crom! Your friend Botah-Aton wasn't alone, wizard. All those men are shot through with the scourge!" Conan's hot eyes flashed from the outstretched blade of his sword to the oncoming mob. "And we can't cut them down! Their touch... their blood is lethal! Flee, dogs!"

Adrastus and Balthano heeded the Cimmerian at once; they turned and ran unashamedly. Others seemed frozen, rooted to the flags. Eoreck was screaming at Shullar to get out of his way.

Then the plague-liches were upon them, and there were those who found themselves involuntarily engaged with opponents whose slightest touch might mean a grisly death.

Pezur, with no time to string his bow, wheeled around, caught sight of Conan's broad back, and followed it as the Cimmerian powered his way toward the gate.

Shamtare's shortsword deflected the running thrust of a pitchfork. The Shemite side-stepped his howling, hurtling foe, and struck him across the shoulder blades with the flat of his sword while simultaneously hooking a boot in front of an ankle. His attacker flew forward as if shot from a catapult, struck the flagstones with brutal impact, slid three feet, and lay still. Shamtare ducked around another bloody-eyed nightmare, spotted Pezur headed for the gate, and took off after him.

The courtyard was in pandemonium, a freakish scene drawn from hell's lowest level. Several of the mercenaries had fallen to the plague-liches who, driven by some inhuman frenzy, tore at them with weapons, hands, and teeth. Conan caught a glimpse of Adrastus and Balthano as they passed through the gateway, then he had to duck a butcher's cleaver flung at his head. Shullar loped past him, his face pale beneath his steel visor.

The barbarian ran for the gate, leapt a pair of wrestling combatants, reached his goal, and slid to a stop. A huge, armored figure blocked his path. At first Conan thought Shullar had turned around and now barred his exit from the courtyard, but it was another man of almost equal size. He wore full armor, complete with a faded plume atop his closed helmet. The tattered ribbons that adorned his tarnished breastplate proclaimed him a captain of the baron's personal guard. In his hands was a spike-headed mace the length of a tall man's arm. He hoisted it above his head with a wordless roar, and for a frozen instant Conan saw that while his right hand was gauntleted, his left was not. And it was plastered with inky bubbles that shone in the sun like black glass. All this the barbarian noticed before the mace came whistling down upon him. He twisted, and the blunt spikes grazed his shoulder, then his hip, then struck the courtyard floor with an ear-piercing *crack* and a shower of white sparks.

The Cimmerian reared back. He fought the ingrained swordsman's instinct that almost drove him to thrust his point into the narrow gap between his attacker's helm and breastplate. Such a throat wound might well shower him with the man's blood. So, the barbarian hesitated, and his foe brought the big mace back up with all the power of his broad shoulders. The steel-jacketed head hammered into Conan's mailed side, and the cruel spikes sank into his ribs. The sheer power of the blow lifted the barbarian from his feet and knocked him asprawl on the flagstones. All breath was struck from his lungs and pain flared fiercely through his torso. The armored warrior shambled forward, stood over him, and hoisted the mace aloft.

"You will die for him!" Guttural words choked from a blister-lined throat. "You will die!"

"Not today," rasped Conan. He moved; came to his knees on the flags with the fluid grace of a coiling cobra. Both hands gripped his hilt and whirled the broadsword in a short, brutal arc that slammed the flat of the blade against his opponent's shins. The plague-lich cried out as the powerful blow ripped his feet out from under him. His armored back crashed onto the stone paving. Curses and incoherent cries of rage burst through the shut visor.

Conan was on his feet, and he vaulted his opponent's thrashing body before the man could so much as sit up. The Cimmerian dashed through the gateway, past the towering doors of somber steel, and out into the open street. Shrill cries and the clash of arms sounded behind him, and he knew he was pursued.

Prince Eoreck was on his knees against the outer wall of the keep. He held his rapier up to catch an apparently unending stream of blows from a plague-blotched man wielding a blacksmith's hammer. The attacker wore a stained leather apron and his bald pate was thickly mottled with ebon bubbles. His hammer rose and fell with mechanical regularity, struck against Eoreck's desperately interposed sword again and again, as if working the blade on an anvil. The prince seemed unable to strike back or flee. Indeed, he seemed unable to do anything other than cower back against the base of the keep's massive rampart.

Conan used his headlong momentum to swing a savage kick into the back of Eoreck's attacker. His booted foot struck the hammer-wielder's spine with enough force to crush bone and slam the wretch into the keep. The black-blistered skull might have been a hen's egg hurled against the wall. Dark gore spattered the weathered stone.

Eoreck leapt up and staggered away from his foe as the man crumpled slowly down the wall. The prince held his hands out from his body as he looked frantically over himself for any trace of the plague-lich's blood.

"You dolt! Do you want to kill your prince? Do you see any blood? Did you get any on me? Am I infected?"

"You'll know soon enough," said Conan. "Let us be gone before we are overwhelmed."

Quick footfalls sounded on the cobbles behind, and Conan whirled to see both Pezur and Shamtare emerge from the keep's gate.

"Run!" bellowed the older man. "They follow us!"

Conan and Eoreck fled down the broad avenue with Pezur and Shamtare close at their heels. Behind them, the keep's gateway was flooded, choked with a wave of howling, plague-wracked men. Their blood-dimmed eyes scanned the vacant street and lit upon the swiftly receding forms of Conan and his comrades. A murderous cry rose from a score of throats as the mob lurched forward as one. Baying like a pack of wild dogs, the plague-liches loped after their prey.

13

"In here!" The barbarian's voice slashed through the near panic of the group and arrested their headlong flight. Conan lunged into the open mouth of a dark alleyway and his boots skidded in the rotting refuse that carpeted the dank cobblestones. Prince Eoreck, Pezur, and Shamtare followed, moved swiftly from the open air of the languishing afternoon into the damp twilight of the shaded alley. It ran between brick buildings that stood a full three stories high, a narrow passage strewn with trash and a collection of battered old crates, some still stuffed with moldering vegetables. Conan ran on ahead, sword in hand, only to halt before the alley's dead end. The barbarian faced a blank wall.

"Oh Anu!" The prince's voice broke like a stripling's. "We're trapped! I'm going to die here! Born in a palace only to die in a stinking alley! And all because of a stupid barbarian!" Eoreck's rapier dangled in its scabbard while his hands fretted aimlessly, making quick, nervous gestures in the air before him. His mustache was dark against the pale flesh of his face.

"Be still," said Shamtare in disgust. The prince fell silent and stared open-mouthed at him, apparently unable to grasp the enormity of the mercenary's insubordination.

Conan's eyes flashed like blue agates as his gaze raked the alleyway. He seized a half-rotted crate, dragged it across the alley, and shoved it against the south wall.

"Shamtare, help me. Pezur, ready your bow. Kill anything that comes around that corner."

"Yes, captain," said the archer. "I have but few arrows left," he added tersely.

"Best make each shaft count, then."

"Yes, captain." The bow came off Pezur's shoulder. He strung the weapon, with only a hissed exhalation of breath to reveal the strength necessary for the task. He pulled an arrow from his quiver, set it to string, and then drew the bowstring back to his ear and held it there. He stood like a martial statue, his brown eyes regarding the alley's mouth calmly.

Prince Eoreck watched as Conan and Shamtare gathered crates from about the alley and stacked them against the wall in a rough pyramid. The pile had grown as high as his shoulder before he realized it was being built beneath a boarded window.

"Oh," mumbled the prince. He put a hand to his lips. "But why would…"

"They're here," said Pezur, and the words mingled with the thrum of his released bowstring. A wordless howl of pain answered him, testament to his unerring marksmanship.

Conan sheathed his sword, leapt up the teetering pyramid of ramshackle crates, and seized upon the boards of the shut window. He grimaced and a board came away in his fists, accompanied by the protesting squall of nails being drawn from dense wood. His hands were on the second board when Eoreck began to climb the stack of crates. Shouts and babbling cries rose from the alley's mouth.

"Hurry! For the love of Ishtar, man, hurry!" wailed the prince. He awkwardly came to his knees on the second rank of crates, caused the entire structure to shake and sag.

"Stay back," roared the barbarian, tearing free another board with a surge of massive shoulders. "Shamtare!"

The old soldier reached up and grabbed a fistful of his prince's scarlet silk cape. Shamtare gave the gaudy mantle a forcible jerk, and Eoreck tumbled from his precarious perch to sprawl in the filth of the alley's floor.

Through all of this, Pezur's bowstring had sung its dire song. Now the cries of their pursuers rose into a ragged roar, and the archer shouted, "Draw steel! They are upon us!" The youth quickly re-slung his bow and drew his shortsword as the first of their foes closed with them in the narrow cul-de-sac.

They choked the alleyway, packed it full of reeking human flesh. Their twisted faces, darkened and disfigured with black boils, snarled and raged at the invaders. Clothed in tattered, grimy rags and waving weapons of all descriptions, they resembled an army of maddened beggars. Caution was unknown to them. They seemed to court death, and hurled themselves upon their foes with lunatic abandon and terrifying blood lust.

The final board was rotten and broke apart in Conan's hands. He wrenched the pieces free, cast them aside, caught up a crate from the top of the teetering pyramid, and thrust it through the pane of the exposed window. Glass shattered, and the sound was all but drowned out by the raging of the plague-liches. He stole a glance into the building and frowned.

Rather than climb to relative safety through the window, the Cimmerian turned to see how his friends fared.

The leader of the horde closed with Pezur and struck at him with a farmer's hoe. The archer sidestepped, clipped the rusty blade from his foeman's weapon and, without hesitation, drove his shortsword into the man's ribs. He released the hilt immediately and dodged back. Pezur helplessly checked his gauntleted hand for bloodstains as the man he had transfixed let out a gurgling cry and staggered forward with his arms extended as if to embrace the archer. Weaponless, Pezur backed away until Shamtare stepped up beside him and halted the impaled man by flourishing his blade before the lich's red-stained eyes.

The legion of plague-riddled berserkers pressed forward.

A clumsily thrown spear sailed over the mercenaries' heads and broke its point on the bricks of the alley's rear wall.

Eoreck began climbing the pile of crates again.

A bloodcurdling howl pierced the ears of all in the packed alleyway as Conan launched himself from the apex of the crate pyramid and dropped squarely between Shamtare, Pezur, and their oncoming foes. The crate the barbarian clutched was thrust forward. The wooden slats crunched against the pommel of Pezur's sword where it stood out from his victim's chest. The blade was driven in to the hilt and burst through the lich's spine. He coughed black blood and fell back among his fellows.

"Go!" bellowed the Cimmerian. "To the window!"

The mob of plague-liches seemed unmoved by the fate of their comrade. They shoved his sagging body aside, trampled it in their eagerness to fall upon Conan and rend him to bits.

Behind the Cimmerian, Eoreck was the first through the window. Pezur and Shamtare followed, scrambling up the crates in a frenzied dash for freedom. In his haste, the archer's elbow smashed shards of glass from the window frame.

Shamtare hesitated, one leg over the sill. "Conan!"

The embattled barbarian swung his crate like an unwieldy club. Trailing unrecognizable tatters of vegetable matter, the crate's corner raked across one lich's face and slammed into another's skull. Both reeled, and one fell, slowing the advance of their followers. Taking advantage of the hard-won space, Conan lifted the crate high above his helmeted head. Powerful muscles leapt into hard ridges beneath his gleaming mail.

"Back, dogs! Back, you plague-blasted bastards!" A thrown stone rebounded from the Cimmerian's chest with no visible effect.

Suddenly Conan's arms shot forward and sent the crate hurtling into the mob's front ranks, with devastating results. The wooden box slammed into his foes and disintegrated in an explosion of splinters, nails, vegetables, and blood. Spinning away from the carnage, Conan lunged up the ungainly pyramid of crates, reached the window before Shamtare could even pull in his leg, and shoved the older man over the sill. The pair spilled into a dark room and rolled on a wooden floor. The dim chamber's stagnant air was saturated with the pungent smell of aromatic oil.

"What are we to do?" Prince Eoreck's voice rose immediately in undiminished fear. "Quickly! Lean out the window and topple the crates lest they climb in after us!"

"No," said Conan. The barbarian regained his feet and looked about himself. The room appeared to be a warehouse of sorts. Barrels of every size lined the walls, both on the floor and on shelves that ran the length of the room. Dozens of metal lamps, in all stages of repair, hung from rows of pegs along the low rafters.

"We'll go through there." His outstretched hand pointed at a boarded window directly across the room from the one through which they had entered. Eoreck gaped at him.

"Have you gone mad? They'll simply follow us! We should use the building as a fortress. Seal ourselves in…"

"They'd starve us out even if the building were able to withstand a siege. We go out that way, now."

Pezur was already beside the indicated window and, as the prince looked on, the archer drove his boot through the glass. Voices rose from the alley behind them. They could hear the piled crates creak and grate against the building's wall. The mob was coming up after them.

"You'll get us all killed!" sputtered the prince.

"Shamtare," said Conan. The older mercenary grasped Eoreck by each shoulder and towed him toward the window that Pezur was rapidly kicking clear. Sunlight burst in yellow rays through the broken boards.

The Cimmerian bent over and set his feet, then dragged a stout barrel away from the wall and, with a grunt of effort, heaved it over on its side. It tipped and fell with a thump that rattled the lamps on their pegs. Conan drew his sword, and a snarling face rose into the shattered windowpane behind him. The barbarian took two quick steps toward the window, lithely drove his boot over the sill and into the splotched face. There was a fleshy impact, a choked yowl, and the face disappeared amid the clatter of dislodged crates. Enraged outcries rose outside. Conan grinned wolfishly, lifted his sword, and drove it, with a silvery flash, down upon the barrel. The blade sundered the wooden staves and sent a gush of pale fluid rolling across the floor.

"He's gone mad!" screeched Eoreck. Conan seized another, smaller barrel and hurled it against the wall so that it burst in a shower of viscous liquid. The pungent smell grew stifling.

Darkly blistered hands appeared on the windowsill behind the barbarian. If he noticed them, he paid no heed.

"There's a roof just outside the window," cried Pezur excitedly. "We can climb right out. Come on, Conan!" The youth ducked through the broken window and stepped onto a flat surface at the same level as the room's floor. Eoreck followed the archer into the sun, obviously as eager to leave behind the maddened barbarian as he was to escape the plague-liches.

"Shamtare," called the Cimmerian. "Flint and steel."

Shamtare's thick eyebrows shot upward. His leathery features looked pained above his gray-shot beard. "Ishtar's girdle, perhaps the prince is right. You have gone mad." Despite his words, the mercenary's hand plucked a leather pouch from his belt and tossed it neatly to the barbarian.

Conan caught the pouch and waved a hand at the window. "Go on, Shamtare. I'll be right behind you."

"As you say," said the older man, and stepped out onto the roof.

A broad-shouldered man in rusty scale mail dragged himself painfully over the sill behind the Cimmerian, a woodsman's ax clenched in one blister-mottled hand. He slipped in the oil coating the floorboards and caught himself on the window frame. Conan pulled a small barrel from its shelf, turned, and hurled the heavy vessel directly into the astonished face of the intruder. Barrel and skull broke against the wall beside the window, showering the floor with mingled oil and gore.

Another body squirmed over the sill and a pair of heads bobbed into view behind it. Conan turned his back on them and strode for the opposite window, where Shamtare squatted and peered in at him. The barbarian hesitated long enough to drive the point of his sword into another huge barrel, wrenching it free in a gout of liquid as thick and dark as blood.

"Get Pezur and Eoreck away from there, Shamtare," said Conan. Then he knelt beside the window, not looking to see if his friend obeyed, not looking to see the dark forms that poured from the alley through the opposite window. The figures shuffled forward, boots splashing.

Flint met steel in a burst of brilliant sparks.

The plague-stricken men hesitated for the briefest moment when they saw what the big barbarian was doing. Hesitated, then leapt forward with horrible cries to stop him.

Flint met steel again, and this time a spark struck the pool that spread beneath the barrel the Cimmerian had punctured. Blue flame leapt up, danced over the oil's surface in a shimmering wave. It skimmed brightly along the floor and shot a coil of fire up the stream of oil that ran from the massive barrel.

Conan whirled and dove headfirst out the window. He struck the tiles of the roof and rolled as a shattering concussion shook the building. A brilliant cloud of red-orange flame billowed out of the broken window, and lifted into the sky on a crest of thick, black smoke. If there were cries within the building, Conan couldn't hear them. A rapid series of muffled explosions blew tiles from the roof and sent a roaring torrent of flame spewing from the window as though it were the belching jaws of some mythical dragon.

Conan scrambled away from the geyser of fire, and joined Shamtare, Eoreck, and Pezur where they waited at the roof's edge.

They lowered one another from the rooftop, dropped into the street below, and fled through the silent streets of Dulcine as the sun sank into the west and evening swept in like a herald of the night.

14

"Hurry, Adrastus! Work your thrice-damned mummery quickly or we'll all be blistered corpses." Balthano leaned over his master's shoulder and watched the wizard's hands where they were pressed against the blond wood of the tavern's door.

"Set's eyes! Keep back! If you keep distracting me, I'll never be able to complete the spell."

Shullar's massive hand wrapped around Balthano's upper arm and jerked him effortlessly from the sorcerer's side. The Argossean found himself shoved against the tavern's wall and staring into the cold eyes of the asshuri bodyguard.

Shullar planted his ham-like right forearm across Balthano's throat and pushed.

"Act like a soldier," ground out the hulking asshuri. "You dishonor your uniform." He released the Argossean just as Adrastus began to mutter a series of slurred words in a soft monotone.

Balthano glared at Shullar through a rising scarlet haze.

Indignant rage boiled through him. His hands moved to his waist, hovered above the ensorcelled belt, and then dropped stiffly to his sides as he bit back the rising tide of passion.

There would be a time for vengeance later. Now, he and Adrastus might well have need of Shullar's formidable sword arm.

The empty street was lined with taverns and inns, and had doubtless once teemed with nightly revelers. Now it stretched empty and lifeless beneath the darkening sky, doors and windows sealed securely against a scourge no earthly barrier could hold at bay.

The three men had escaped their pursuers earlier, circled back to the baron's palace, and encountered them again. A wild, seemingly endless flight through the streets had finally put the bloodthirsty horde of plague-liches behind them. Though they had twice eluded their enemies, an occasional inhuman howl rose in the distance as if to remind the men that they were still the hunted, and the pack had not yet given up the hunt.

The three had selected this tavern solely because its door was neither gaping open nor boarded shut. The windows were covered with shutters that had been nailed in place, but the front door appeared merely bolted from within. If they got inside, they could bolt the door behind them and it would show no sign of their passage.

Now, Adrastus tried mightily to lift that bolt by means of a minor spell. His limited skill and the stress of the situation combined to produce a nightmare of uncertainty. The wizard's throat contracted and the strange, slurred stream of words came more strongly from his lips. He leaned, pressed all his weight down upon his hands where they lay flat on the door.

His lids were clenched tight, and sweat glimmered along his nose and in the orbits of his eyes. His mind probed through the wood, touched the bar, measured it, weighed it, and began, with agonizing slowness, to lift it from its bracket. He heard a soft scrape along the door's inner panel and his heart leapt. The white-knuckled hands inched up the door's surface, and brought the bar within up with them. The Kothian panted with exertion.

A drawn-out cry shuddered through the slow-descending night, unmistakably closer now. It was impossible to tell if it was voiced in pain, ecstasy, or some unhallowed blending of both. Shullar drew his bastard sword and stared off along the street in the direction of the scream. Balthano's head swiveled comically from the street's dim terminus to Adrastus and back again.

The wizard's hands shot upward along the door and a clatter came from within the tavern. "Hah! By Yog and Iod, I've done it." Adrastus shoved open the heavy portal. The trio quickly made their way inside and re-bolted the door behind them.

It took a moment for their eyes to adjust to the lightless interior. They stumbled urgently about in the gloom, piled chairs and tables against the door to reinforce it against attack. A few bottles of wine were selected at random from behind the bar and taken upstairs. After bolting the door to the second floor and cracking open a jug of wine, they began to feel some small measure of security.

The second story was a single room, apparently used as a combination office, flophouse, and storage room. There was no proper ceiling; the upper half of the room extended into the rafters, which were hung with blankets, towels, sacks, coils of rope, and fat lengths of sausage. Dusty boxes lined the walls. Adrastus pulled the single chair out from the lopsided table, sat down, and, after a brief struggle, managed to light a candle.

Sallow light ebbed and flared. Balthano stood beside the seated sorcerer and tugged at his fingers nervously. He was looking at Shullar.

The giant asshuri bodyguard stood just within the bolted door. A wine jug dangled lifelessly from one hand. He stared straight ahead as if somehow stunned. Adrastus smiled at him, but in his dark eyes lurked distrust and subtle calculation.

"Are you well, my friend?" he asked. A trembling cry came from outside, seemingly from the street directly in front of the tavern. All three men stiffened.

Shullar shrugged and raised a hand to rub at his shovel-jaw. He walked to the table, set his helmet upon it, and took a series of deep pulls on the wine jug. He put the bottle down beside his helm and gave Adrastus and Balthano a curt bow that was little more than a quick inclination of his black-haired head.

"I must leave you."

"What?" burst out Balthano. "Have you grown so tired of living, then?"

"You cannot," said Adrastus. "If you leave now, you may draw the attention of the plague-liches. You could give away our position."

"I've deserted my charge," said Shullar simply. "I am sworn to stand by the prince. If he dies and I am not at his side, I bring disgrace down upon all the asshuri."

"Spare me!" sneered Balthano. "Anyway, the prince is an ass."

"That's true enough. Nevertheless, I must reach his side or die trying. I am oath-bound."

Adrastus leaned back in his chair and steepled his fingers. His gentle smile never faltered. "How are you going to find the prince now? If he lives, doubtless by now he's hidden as well as we are. Will you wander the streets calling his name?" An icy edge of disdain cut through his false kindness.

Shullar frowned and drank again. "I must leave you," he repeated.

"No," said Adrastus with finality. "You'll not only get yourself killed, you'll bring the plague-liches down upon us. I forbid it."

Shullar's heavy jaw jutted belligerently and his lips twisted with contempt. "Forbid it? By Anu, who in nine hells are you to order about an asshuri warrior?"

Balthano stepped close beside the larger man and lowered his hands to his belt. "You'll do as Adrastus says, dog."

"Dog, am I?" Shullar's right fist snapped up in a backhand blow so sudden and unexpected that it took Balthano completely unaware. Knuckles like knots of oak struck squarely between his eyes with an impact that sounded much as if the asshuri had hit a block of hardwood with a hammer.

Balthano dropped to the floor in a loose bundle of limbs. "You should find a better manservant. That one is all but useless." Shullar's voice was as steady as the gaze he fixed upon Adrastus.

"Ah—he has his uses. I'm sorry he became impetuous."

"I trust I'll have no argument from you, wizard."

"Oh no. You're free to die pointlessly any time you wish. I won't stop you. I will, however, offer you an alternative."

"And what would that be?"

"I could use my magicks to show you an image of the prince, to reveal his whereabouts and his health. If he were well, would you be satisfied to wait until morning to go in search of him?"

Shullar shifted uneasily from one foot to the other. "Perhaps."

"Perhaps," said Adrastus acidly. "Perhaps you should go out and try your luck searching through every building in the city."

The asshuri heaved a sigh and nodded. "All right then. Use your sorcery. If he is safe, and you tell me where he is so that I can join him on the morrow, then I will sit out the night here with you."

"Excellent," said Adrastus. His eyes twinkled and he smiled as if at some secret joke. He reached into his doublet and drew forth a roll of black velvet. As Shullar watched, the velvet was unrolled on the tabletop into a thick strip about three hands long and one hand wide. Runes of glittering gilt shone upon the sable fabric, and a full-sized golden handprint was emblazoned at either end. The inner surface of the strip was composed of a row of long, narrow pockets. From each of the ten pockets the mage pulled a slender, blade-like crystal almost the length of a man's hand and about two fingers in width.

Each crystal was laid down atop its pocket. They gleamed in the candlelight like slivers of ice. Adrastus examined them with obvious pride, then looked up at Shullar with a coy grin.

"Oh. Do I have your word on that?"

"I have said what I will do. An asshuri's word is his bond. Will these bits of glass show us the prince?"

"Hm? Oh, yes. Certainly. Just bear with me a moment."

The mage laid his hands down on the golden handprints and shuddered visibly. From the floor, Balthano moaned like a drunkard awakening to a fearful hangover. Adrastus didn't smile. His lips were tight, and his eyes were screwed shut. He seemed to wince, almost to cringe, as if a sound loud enough to lance the ears with pain was audible to him alone.

The eyes snapped open. The wizard's hands lifted from the gilt handprints and leveled their forefingers at Shullar.

"Him," said Adrastus.

The crystals leapt from their places on the velvet strip and shot across the table at the asshuri. They avoided his armored breast. He had time for one hoarse bellow of horror before they sheathed themselves in the flesh of his face, neck, and throat. Each struck with the impact of a tiny crossbow quarrel. The swift series of staccato blows knocked Shullar away from the table, blood bursting in gouts from his riddled skull. The big man reeled, threw his armored arms wide, then fell flat on his back with such a crash that Adrastus half expected him to smash through the floor. The asshuri lay still. A black lake of blood formed rapidly beneath his ruined head.

"Well," said Adrastus happily. "They work even better than I hoped."

On the floor beside Shullar's corpse, Balthano shifted and moaned. Another shrill scream came from the street outside, farther away than the last.

The Kothian got up from his chair, stepped over Shullar's sprawled body, and went to the room's only window. There was no glass windowpane, merely a dingy shutter. Adrastus peered between the weathered slats into the night beyond. He groped beneath his cloak of blue velvet and pulled a pair of steel pliers from a pouch fastened at the small of his back. His hands toyed idly with the tool while he sought to espy some recognizable building in the city outside. It was difficult to make anything out in the darkness. Mild irritation caused a scowl to crease his broad brow. He had lived in Dulcine, under Tolbeth-Khar's tutelage, for better than a year, and he felt he should know the buildings here. They hadn't changed, even if everything else had.

It came to him that all the shadowed roofs he could see sheltered nothing but the silent bodies of the dead, and he found himself wondering what flaw had caused Tolbeth-Khar's ceremony to go so terribly awry. Perhaps the old man had done something as simple as transposing a few words of the chant. Any sorcerous ritual required exact performance in order to acquire exact results.

But perhaps the fault had lain in the crystal vial he himself had prepared. Adrastus clicked the pliers open and shut with one hand. The vial had been fashioned to Tolbeth-Khar's precise specifications. The Kothian was skilled in the use of crystals. He knew that, and so had Tolbeth-Khar. He was almost sure the error that had led to the depopulation of Dulcine had not been his. Yet he couldn't be certain.

Adrastus clenched his fist around the grips of the pliers and closed his eyes. Every man, woman, and child of Dulcine was either dead or reduced to the agonized, bestial life of a plague-lich.

What a price to pay. The Kothian rubbed his brow and turned from the window. A terrible price, perhaps, but the price of greatness is always high, he reminded himself. What had been a disaster to the people of Dulcine would, with some effort, prove to be a great boon to him. Of what account were their small sufferings when one thought of the power that might soon be his? Of what account were their ineffectual lives when one thought of the world-altering changes that might soon begin here? And in the end, of what account were their deaths since he, Adrastus, was alive? If luck was with him, if his plan continued on its steady progression toward inevitable success, then the death of Dulcine would seem but a small price to pay: merely a brief unpleasantness to be endured before the dawning of a new age. The age of Adrastus.

Outside, a bloodcurdling howl echoed out over the darkened city, like the cry of a jackal over a nighted veldt. The sorcerer shivered in his robes.

Balthano moaned like a dying man, rolled over, and flopped a limp hand into the pool of blood that formed a grisly halo around Shullar's shattered head. The Argossean sat up suddenly, uttered a choked gasp, and stared at his encrimsoned fingers. A livid lump was growing between his watery eyes. His gaze dropped to Shullar's still form. He cursed and pushed himself across the floor away from the corpse.

"Mitra and Bel! What have you done to him?" The Argossean gaped at the asshuri's macabre wounds. The transparent tips of the imbedded crystals stood out from either side of Shullar's throat and sparkled from the scarlet pools of his eyes.

"I stopped him from leaving us by using a new weapon of my own invention upon him." Adrastus walked from the window and bestrode the asshuri's body, pliers held in one casual hand. "The spell that sends the daggers flying to their target is encrypted into their crystalline fabric. I lay my hands on the avatar and indicate my foe. It's as simple as that. And it works even better than I hoped. Anyone could do it. Even you."

Balthano shrank away as his master bent over the dead man and began, with fastidious care, to wrench each crystal dagger free with the pliers.

15

Conan perched on the roof's corner and overlooked darkened Dulcine. The roof was rimmed by a low, tiled wall, and the barbarian sat upon this while his eyes roamed over the city below. Behind him, the flat roof held a collection of wrought-iron chairs, and a heavy, glass-topped table still set with the much-decayed remnants of a feast. Sunk into the roof beside the table, a trapdoor opened onto a flight of steps that led down into the expansive manor below.

Shamtare, Pezur, Eoreck, and the barbarian had found shelter in a walled villa that had obviously once belonged to one of Dulcine's wealthier residents. When he saw that the gate to the spacious grounds was sealed, Conan had scaled the wall and opened it from within. The party resealed the gate behind them, and found they had a luxurious mansion all to themselves. The plague-liches had apparently been unable or uninterested in scaling the outer wall, and as a result the villa had been protected from their depredations. Sealed inside its stone shell, the manor seemed to wait patiently for the outside world to return to its senses. Aside from the pathetic remains of the noble residents and their small coterie of servants, and the untended appearance of the grounds, there was little to indicate that a disaster had ever befallen the city outside the villa's quiet walls.

Once inside the great house, the men had found some edible food in the kitchen, and much drinkable wine in the cellar. Conan had instructed them to sup their fill, and then try to get some rest so they might attempt to enter the palace again on the morrow.

The barbarian now stood the first watch. Though he heard the occasional fearful howl from the streets outside, he had little concern that the plague-struck mob would attempt to breach the villa's wall, as they had no way of knowing that the intruders were concealed here.

The Cimmerian looked to the baron's palace, where it glowered darkly over the lesser buildings at its feet. From his vantage point he could see through the open steel gates all the way to the Freshet. The fountain was barely visible to his keen eyes, cloaked in thick shadow, yet limned by pale starlight. He heard feet on the steps and turned to see Pezur come up through the trapdoor, carrying a bottle of wine.

Conan looked back toward the palace and the cool night breeze stirred his black mane. Pezur approached him and held out the bottle.

"Have a drink. Shamtare says it's a very good vintage."

The barbarian accepted the wine wordlessly, took a loud gulp, and handed it back. "You should get some sleep."

"Indeed. Shamtare also says that a few drafts of wine should make me sleepy, yet it does not seem to be having that effect at all," said Pezur. He made a wry grimace. "It worked well enough for the prince, although I don't think I'd like to drink as much as he did."

"That worthless fop had best not be hungover tomorrow."

"If you'd seen the sheer quantity he consumed, you would know what a vain hope that is. I marvel at Shamtare. He drank a little water, lay down on a couch, and promptly fell asleep in his armor. I wish I had his nerve."

Conan grinned briefly. "Shamtare is an old soldier. I'll wager he's slept soundly in surroundings both more dangerous and less comfortable than this fine house."

"Tell me, Conan," said the archer tentatively. "Why does Shamtare so often behave as if he is in your debt? One would think he had wronged you."

"Ah, it is nothing. We ran afoul of a sorcerer in a tavern and Shamtare ducked out the door before I knew who or what I was trifling with. A good deal of complications followed, but nothing I couldn't sort out." The barbarian glanced back out toward the palace and tensed. "What's that?"

"What?" Pezur bent forward and squinted into the night.

"I thought I saw a light in the palace courtyard."

"Do you think so?" The archer saw nothing. His gaze swept over the darkened city. To the west a thick column of smoke, still flickeringly illuminated from below, rose toward the icy motes of the stars.

"The only light I see is the lamp-maker's shop you torched. And that." Pezur paused. "What in Ashtoreth's name is that?"

To the north and east a low overcast clung to the sky and obscured the stars. At off intervals crimson light rippled and flashed along the underbelly of the clouds. It came and went like distant heat lightning, soundless and ghostly, transforming the heavy blanket of cloud into a luminous blood-mist.

"A storm?" Pezur's voice betrayed his discomfort. "I've never seen..."

"Not a storm," said the barbarian. "That's light rising into the sky from the Flaming Mountains. They are bright tonight. Molten rock must be running from the earth in a river."

"Strange. Surely it is an omen."

Conan snorted with laughter. "Hereabouts the skin of the earth is thin and the molten stone that is its blood seeps through easily. Men often wish to find portents in the movements of the earth, but the Flaming Mountains are so often raging and smoking that one could read omens from them ceaselessly."

"Look! By Ishtar's mercies, you're right! There are lights in the courtyard." Pezur slapped the Cimmerian on his shoulder and pointed toward the looming bulk of the palace.

Bright sparks of flame now moved in the courtyard. A ring of torches encircled the Freshet, and illuminated the open area around it with a soft and ruddy radiance as ghostly as that which rose from the far-off Flaming Mountains. Spectral voices floated to them on the slow breeze, distant murmurs that might have been the restless voice of the night itself.

"Listen," whispered Pezur, eyes dark and wide in the starlight.

A ring of black figures had gathered around the Freshet, and now they held their torches aloft and raised their voices in a slow chant. The words filtered back to the two men on the roof, rising and falling in and out of audibility.

"Come death," sang the night. "Lord death. Come death."

"Crom," rumbled the barbarian.

There was movement in front of the Freshet. Some of the chanting figures lifted an object above their heads and then cast it into the fountain. There was the faint sound of a distant splash, and the chant continued as a low drone. Shortly, there was more movement, and another splash. The pattern was repeated again and again.

"Those are the survivors," muttered Pezur after a time. "The ones marked by the plague yet still alive. What are they doing?"

"That's worth knowing," said Conan. "But who is that?"

The Cimmerian pointed to a tiny balcony directly above the courtyard. From this distance it seemed but a small imperfection in the smooth, monolithic wall of the palace, a full five stories above the frothing crest of the Freshet. The torchlight from below scarcely served to pick out its outline, yet Pezur could discern it. And he could see that a single figure had stepped out onto the balcony.

The chanting grew louder and more frenzied. The strange splashing sounds came more quickly, and the torches tossed as if held in wildly gesticulating hands. The archer thought the figure laid its hands upon the rail and leaned forward, as if to better see the crowd gathered below it. The chanting became a raucous screaming.

"Who..." began Pezur. He swallowed. "Who is that?"

"I don't know." Conan's voice was dry.

The shadowed figure straightened, stood tall. The tiny, pallid oval of its face lifted, and a chill seared the archer's flesh. He felt a dreadful certainty that the figure gazed out of the courtyard, through the palace gate, across the unlit city, and directly into his eyes. Gooseflesh rippled up Pezur's arms and his stomach twisted with fear.

"Mitra save me! Who is that?" whispered the archer; his voice was that of a child locked in a nightmare.

The Cimmerian's sword had come into his hand unnoticed by either of the men. Pezur saw Conan bare his teeth in an unconscious snarl of defiance and felt a surge of kinship with the barbarian. He knew the Cimmerian felt the frigid touch of those distant eyes as keenly as he did.

Indeed, Conan sensed the unnatural scrutiny as well as if the dim figure had reached out across Dulcine and laid a cold hand upon his breast. The undulled instincts of the barbarian sent the same thrill along his nerves that he might have felt confronting a lion in a jungle grove. Though he could not give it a name, he knew there was danger here, a danger born of black sorcery.

"What are you, devil?" growled Conan.

The figure on the balcony stepped back into the palace's interior and was swallowed by darkness. The chanting of its worshippers swelled, their cries suddenly louder and more plaintive.

"What manner of man was that?" demanded Pezur. "I swear, I could feel his eyes upon me."

"I felt the same, yet I wonder if it was a man."

"Well, you saw him, just as I did," said Pezur in confusion.

"I saw well enough to wonder just what it was that I saw." Conan hefted his bared sword, examined the blade a moment, then sheathed it. A frown darkened his heavy brow and the transparent veil that sheathed his jaw gleamed like a faint rime of frost.

"Whatever it is, it waits for us in the palace."

Off on the horizon, the Flaming Mountains cast their bloody light upon the lowering clouds and rumbled deeply, as though the earth itself moaned in unquiet slumber.

16

The morning sun speared through the shutter's slats and fell upon Balthano's face. He felt a moment's disorientation, then sat up and wiped his eyes. The Argossean woke to discomfort, as he had spent the night sitting propped against the wall, and now his rump was numb and his spine ached.

His mouth tasted as if he had been chewing stale mustard seeds. Balthano also woke to mild astonishment, as he had not imagined that he would be able to fall asleep at all. The dark starburst stain of Shullar's blood had dried to an ugly crust on the floorboards. Balthano remembered dragging the big asshuri's body down the stairs to the first floor, and grimaced sourly. He became aware of a steady, recurrent rasp, and realized it was that sound that had awakened him.

He stood up slowly, trying to stretch out each kink as he did so. The gentle rasp was the sound of Adrastus snoring.

The portly mage sat sprawled in the chamber's only chair, his head tilted back and mouth open. The snores came steadily.

Balthano carefully made his way toward the shuttered window. He had no desire to disturb his master before the mage wished to be awakened. The Argossean gently took Shullar's jug of wine from the table, where it still sat beside the dead man's helmet. He uncorked it, then peered through the shutter and used the wine in a vain attempt to wash the miserable taste from his mouth.

The slats interfered with his view enough so that he reached out idly, gripped one, and tugged. The entire shutter came free with a sharp squeal and dropped from his surprised hand. Golden sunshine poured into the dusty attic as the shutter clattered loudly on the floor.

Adrastus sprang from his chair with a scream of terror. He crouched beside the table and squinted with wild eyes into the blaze of sunlight that burst through the open window. The mage saw his servant as a man-shaped shadow suspended in the glare.

"Mercy!" choked the Kothian. "In Set's name, mer..." His dazed eyes focused as Balthano stepped away from the window.

"By Bel's nimble fingers, what ails you, Adrastus?" cried the Argossean. The wizard sensed rather than heard the trace of contempt that mingled with the amazement in his servant's voice.

Adrastus stood tall, raised his right hand, and clenched it into a fist. His lips twisted as if about to speak the Old Stygian phrases that would turn Balthano's sorcerous belt into an instrument of infernal torment and leave him convulsing on the floor.

"No!" yelled the Argossean. "I have done no wrong! I did not mean to wake you, lord. It was an accident, I swear it!"

Adrastus's face was contorted with rage. Despite a slight quaver in his voice, he spoke with chill precision. "I was raised in Khorshemish, in the very shadow of the Scarlet Citadel. Tsotha-Lanti does not suffer other wizards to flourish in his domain. Yet I have prevailed. I have made myself into a mage of power. Too long have I endured the foolishness of my inferiors! I say I am a great sorcerer and I will not be toyed with! Do you toy with me?"

Balthano saw that his master grew ever more wroth, and dropped to his knees. "By all the gods, milord, the shutter broke free in my hand! I meant no harm!"

Adrastus was still for a moment. He blinked in the bright sunlight, slowly smiled down upon his servant where he knelt on the floor, and lowered his hand. "No. Of course you didn't. You're not a fool, are you?"

Balthano was afraid to stand. "No, master. I would not displease you."

"No. Of course not." Adrastus suddenly stepped around his servant and walked to the open window. The sorcerer thrust his head out and took a deep breath of the cool, quiet air of morning. The sky was cloudless, and the sun had just lifted clear of the mountains. He turned back within.

"We should proceed directly to the palace. I trust that the plague-liches, having spent the night roaming the streets, have sought their sleeping quarters by now."

"Probably back in those stables beside the palace," said Balthano as he rose slowly to his feet. He watched Adrastus with ill-concealed apprehension.

"Probably," said the mage blandly. "Here."

Balthano flinched as Adrastus abruptly tossed a small, metallic object at him. The Argossean caught it and held the thing out in the light. It was a slim vial of polished silver with a tiny wooden stopper. Balthano looked to the mage questioningly.

"It is an oil. Smear it upon your limbs. It will act as a protection against the plague."

"Your masks seem to work well enough."

"Yes, but the oil is repugnant to that which causes the plague."

Balthano opened his mouth to ask a question, but remained silent as Adrastus produced his own vial and began pouring the contents into a palm. The Kothian rubbed the dark oil into his exposed skin, and stroked handfuls of it over his garments. He even applied it to his boots. After a moment, Balthano followed his master's example. The oil was cold and slippery on his hands. It smelled unpleasantly of mustiness and decay. Balthano pursed his lips tightly as he applied it to his face. The odor was strange, oddly reminiscent of a moldered loaf of bread.

They cut a promising sausage down from the rafters and ate it with watered wine. Then the two men left their tavern sanctuary and walked into silent Dulcine. The low sun's light shone at an angle across the city and left the streets in the last shadows of night. The breeze was surprisingly chill, due both to the altitude and the slow wane of summer. Adrastus seemed relaxed and comfortable, but Balthano glanced about ceaselessly with furtive eyes, ready for an attack at any moment. Save for the calls of birds and the sigh of the wind, their footfalls seemed the only sound in the necropolis. The mass of the baron's palace came ever closer, and soon they passed into its huge shadow. Adrastus began to hum a soft tune under his breath.

"Your pardon, milord, but I cannot help but notice how calm you seem. Aren't you concerned that the plagued ones will ambush us again?"

"If they do, I shall use my magicks to defend us. But I think we shall have little difficulty this morning. The plague-liches were awake all night hunting us. Besides, I feel a true sense of destiny. My time of failures is past. Great things shall happen today, my friend. Great things, indeed."

Balthano shot a sideways glance at his master. "Of course," he said tentatively. "Today we both become rich men."

Adrastus laughed loudly enough to set Balthano to cringing and glancing about to see if the mage had drawn unwelcome attention. "Riches?" chuckled the Kothian. "To the nine hells with riches. Today we become men of might. Today I will learn the true meaning of power. Today I will learn how it feels to be a god!"

A sick uncertainty rose in Balthano's gut. Was his master going mad? He licked his lips. They drew near the gate, and saw the towering sheets of grim steel shine dully in the morning light.

"Well, I hope you don't mind if I gather a few gems," said the Argossean at last.

"Mind? Why should I mind? Please yourself," answered the wizard. Then the men fell silent as they passed through the portal and entered the courtyard. Their eyes sought the wooden stables, beside the vast stony bulk of the palace. The outbuilding was sealed and silent. Now Adrastus moved hesitantly. Despite his great assurance of a few moments past, the sorcerer clearly wished to make as little noise as possible in crossing the courtyard.

Balthano trusted the ceaseless splashing of the Freshet to cover the sound of their passage, fearing instead that a lookout in the stable would espy them and a full-fledged charge would follow in short order. He plucked at the sorcerer's sleeve in his haste.

"Come on," he hissed. "Come on."

Balthano's eyes were drawn to a quantity of gold coins that lay strewn and shining on the curved rim of the Freshet.

Others gleamed from the flagstones, and he saw a white flash that might have been a diamond. The double doors of the palace drew near, and he banished his curiosity. A terrible thought burst upon him.

"The door," said Balthano "Can you open it if it's barred?"

"It is almost certainly barred. Do not be concerned," replied Adrastus. "Did I not open the door of the tavern last night?"

"But that took so long, and it was much smaller, besides. Mitra, we can't stand around the courtyard just waiting for those disease-eaten dogs to come back and corner us against the palace!"

"Be silent, Balthano," said the sorcerer softly, and his servant obeyed. They approached the doors, a double arch of brass-bound, smoothly polished oak that rose to twice the height of a tall man.

Balthano wondered what Adrastus would do if the bolt proved too high to reach.

The mage seized the thick bronze ring on the door's left panel with both hands and pulled on it experimentally. His eyes flew wide as, with the merest whisper of oiled hinges, the door swung open.

17

"What is he doing in there?" demanded Prince Eoreck weakly. "How long are we supposed to wait?"

"Go on inside if you wish," said Shamtare. "I'll stand guard."

"No," replied the prince with a sigh. "I'll stay out in the fresh air." Eoreck was as hungover as any man Shamtare had seen in a life among hard-drinking soldiers. The prince had been so difficult to awaken that his comrades had considered simply leaving him in the villa. But when they had made ready to leave, Eoreck had lifted himself from his couch, discreetly vomited in a corner, and announced that he was ready to travel. Now, the prince's face was a waxy gray and his hands trembled so badly that he finally resorted to thrusting his thumbs into his jeweled girdle to hold them still. He leaned hunched against the wall of a blacksmith's shop, and let the chill morning breeze wash over him in the vain hope it might disperse the dismal vapors that fogged his thoughts.

Pezur stood in the middle of the open street and watched for any sign of their foes. When he heard Shamtare speak, he walked toward the looted blacksmith's shop.

"I'd like to go in. I'm curious as to what Conan is doing in there. And perhaps I can find a new sword."

"Go on in, then."

"But he said to stand watch outside."

"Ishtar's thighs, boy. Go in if you wish." Shamtare shot a sour glance at the prince. "The structure of command has eroded somewhat. I'll stay outside with the royalty." The old mercenary's sarcasm was wasted on Eoreck, who had closed his eyes and appeared to be taking a series of slow, meditative breaths.

Pezur went into the blacksmith's shop and looked about curiously for Conan. The soot-stained forge was unlit, and the sharpening wheel was still. The dim shop had been ransacked, probably raided for weapons by the plague-liches. Refuse was strewn about the dirty floor. In the corner, a shriveled, blackened corpse was pinned to the wall with a spear. A rack of old swords mounted on the wall beside the anvil caught the youth's eye.

The Cimmerian was behind the anvil, on one knee beside a barrel he had laid on its side. In the barbarian's hands was a long tube of brown leather, into which he appeared to be scooping handfuls of dark powder or dirt. He glanced at Pezur as the archer entered.

"What are you about, captain?"

The Cimmerian stood up abruptly and began tying off the end of the leather tube with strips of rawhide. Pezur saw that the hide sleeve was actually a hand-worked sheath, of the sort that a well-off warrior would use to protect a battle lance. Conan had nested one sheath within another and now tightly tied off both at about the five-foot mark. The Cimmerian hoisted the sheath, now a flexible tube of obvious and considerable weight, and draped it over one broad shoulder.

"Making a weapon," answered Conan finally. The leather sleeve drooped heavily over his back. "Grab yourself a new blade and come on. The baron's palace awaits." He stepped around the archer and walked back out into the sunshine.

Pezur hastily chose a shortsword, stained with age and unsightly, but sturdy-looking and still sharp. He checked that it fit into his scabbard, then followed the barbarian, stung by curiosity. The barbarian headed into the street. Shamtare fell in wordlessly beside him, and Prince Eoreck pushed off the shop's wall to shuffle along in their wake.

The streets were deserted, and it was easy to imagine that no one had walked abroad in Dulcine for long ages. The four men shortly emerged onto the broad double avenue that stretched to the palace gates. Overhead, dark birds circled silently, black glyphs against the china-blue sky.

"What shall we do?" asked the prince dully. "The plagued ones will just attack us again. Even now they probably await us in those stables beside the palace."

"That's possible," said Conan. "Though we slew a good many of them yesterday and I watched the survivors carouse most of the night. With luck they'll be asleep, and we can steal past them into the palace. If they're awake and feeling warlike, we'll be better prepared for them."

"How so?" mumbled Eoreck.

"Have you your torches, Shamtare?" asked the barbarian.

"Two left, Conan."

"And the oil?"

"One vial, only."

"Good enough. We can burn the stables if need be. And I can hold the diseased dogs at bay with this." Conan slapped the weighty tube of embossed leather that hung over his shoulder.

"What is it, Conan? What did you fill it with?" asked Pezur at last.

"It is a bludgeon, full of metal shavings and bits of scrap steel," said the Cimmerian.

Eoreck rolled bleary eyes in misgiving, but offered no comment. Shamtare grinned in admiration, his square teeth bright in his beard.

"An oversize blackjack you can wield like your broadsword," chuckled the Shemite. "And though it'll likely crush a few bones, it shouldn't draw much blood. You ought to work in an armory, Conan."

"My father was a blacksmith and knew well the crafting of weapons, though I don't think he ever made anything like this."

The boulevard's last tree fell behind them, and the stark steel doors of the palace gate stood open, waiting. It was cool in the shadowed passage between the thick walls. Conan held up a hand to slow the party's progress, and peered past the wall's worn corner into the courtyard. Aside from the ceaseless motion and splash of the Freshet, all was still and silent. The barbarian's gaze fell upon the glittering coins spread along the Freshet's rim and his brow furrowed. He did not point them out to his fellows. Of their comrades who had fallen here, there was no sign. The stables that had sheltered their foes were as closed and innocent in appearance as they had been just prior to yesterday's attack.

"Stay here," rasped the Cimmerian. Without waiting for an acknowledgment, he took off in a low run across the courtyard. He kept his head down, and his boots were all but soundless on the flags. His comrades peered around the wall's edge, watching the stables nervously, ready to send up an outcry should the doors be suddenly thrust open from within. In an instant, Conan stood before the high palace doors.

"Sweet Ishtar," breathed Pezur. "May Ishtar in her kindness grant that it's unbarred!"

The barbarian seized the left door's great ring and effortlessly pulled it wide. The morning sun momentarily etched him as a figure of sculpted bronze against the gaping, lightless portal. The door's panel seemed inordinately thick. He disappeared inside for a long moment, then reappeared and waved the others to join him.

"Damn me! As simple as that," laughed Shamtare. "Come on, brothers." The three stepped from the shade of the open gateway, took three steps, and a ragged cry rose from the outbuildings. The wooden doors of the stable flew open with a rattle and crash.

"No!" cried Eoreck, and fumbled for his hilt. Shamtare began to run for the palace's open door, but Pezur hesitated. Eoreck stood stock-still as he gaped in horror at the stream of red-eyed, plague-blasted men that streamed from the stable into the courtyard.

"Come on, milord!" Pezur gripped his prince by an elbow and pulled. Eoreck stumbled forward a step and faltered, his bloodshot eyes fixed on the oncoming mob. Their enraged howls rang brazenly from the stone enclosure's walls. "Damn it, Eoreck, come on!"

The prince blinked, as if awakening from a dream to a nightmare. "Yes," he mumbled, and fell into a loping run.

Pezur dashed along beside him, and saw that the plague-liches would intercept them before they reached the doors. He drew his new shortsword on the run. The Freshet was between them and their foes. Pezur could see the open palace door, see inside the darkened fortress, and knew that Conan had not shut them out.

Then the plague-liches were upon the two, and Pezur had just time enough to leap between their leader and his prince. Eoreck ran on blindly, dodged an outthrust spearpoint, and vanished through the darkened doorway.

The young archer faced a gigantic armored warrior wielding a long, spiked mace. A tattered plume bobbed above the giant's closed helm and the dirty rags of once brilliant ribbons adorned his discolored breastplate. The steel-headed mace swung around in a hissing arc aimed at the archer's skull. Pezur dropped to one knee and thrust at his enemy. The vicious spikes of the mace ruffled the low crest of the archer's helm, while his sword's point drove hard against the plague-lich's armored belly, and rebounded.

A titan's bellow rang out over the sudden din of combat, and Pezur knew that Conan had come to his aid. There was the raw clash of steel, the terrible cries of men, and a peculiar series of whistling thuds, but Pezur couldn't look away from his mighty foe. The armored giant had recovered from his missed two-handed blow with fearful speed. The warrior's mace shot up, then came straight down to crush the youth who knelt before him. Still on his knees, Pezur tried to leap to one side, but his boot slid on the polished flagstones. He fell forward and caught himself with both hands. The mace rocketed downward.

It never landed.

With a roar like an unleashed lion, Conan leapt between the fallen archer and his hulking foe. The Cimmerian's black mane flew like a war banner as his entire body strained to swing his ponderous leather weapon. The metal-stuffed sleeve tore through the air with a hollow swooping sound, brushed aside the descending mace as though it were a dry straw, and struck its owner in his armored ribs. The sound of the blow rang out like the toll of a broken bell, and the plague-lich was lifted from his feet and hurled aside like so much chaff. He crashed to the flags and clutched his ribs, rolled, and regained his feet.

"Up," snarled Conan to Pezur. "Up and into the palace." The archer obeyed, and as he did, he noted the sprawled bodies of a half dozen plague-liches. They lay in an irregular phalanx; some were still, others shifted and moaned, the battered harvest of the Cimmerian's strange new weapon. The remainder of the mob had drawn back, half out of fear of Conan, half out of curiosity as to who would prevail in the contest between the mighty barbarian and the armored giant. Pezur quickly withdrew into the palace, but slowed to watch the battle when he saw there was no pursuit.

The plague-lich who had once been a captain of the baron's personal guard faced Conan, and pulled a long dagger from a sheath at his belt. The giant slowly and deliberately drew the blade over the back of his bare left hand. Black blisters split under the

Conan fights the plague knight

dagger and spilled inky poison over its razor edge. He pointed at the Cimmerian with the stained weapon's needle-tip.

"You are a great warrior." The voice gurgled thickly, as if the man's throat were clogged with mud. "But you are his. We all belong to him. You blaspheme by not wearing his mark."

Conan began to back slowly toward the palace entrance. There, the mob would only be able to come at him in twos or threes. And perhaps he could close the doors against them.

"Who is this you speak of? Who is it that you are so proud to belong to?" The barbarian's big hands gripped the great leather bludgeon, held it ready to strike. His eyes burned volcanic blue, alive with the battle-lust of a born warrior.

"He is Death!" shouted the armored giant. "We belong to the dread Lord Death, who in his mercy lets us live when all others die! You, who walk unmarked in his domain, must pay him homage!"

"Come a step closer and I'll see you pay your lord the ultimate tribute," rumbled Conan. He took another step backward.

"Blasphemer! I'll give him your head!" The steel-helmed lich lunged forward and brought both mace and dagger into play. The Cimmerian surprised him, and those who watched, by leaping forward rather than dodging away. The two seemed to meet in midair. The mace blocked and stalled the bludgeon's impact, yet still the leather sheath struck an armored shoulder with enough power to throw the warrior off balance.

The envenomed dagger darted for Conan's exposed throat like a blue steel serpent, but the barbarian writhed away so that the point scraped across the bright links of his mailed chest. While his opponent still stumbled, Conan spun completely around, and as he turned, he held out the heavy sheath. It gathered fierce momentum, and he began to advance, whirling the weapon around his head as if it were an Aesir battle-ax. His foe regained his balance, but found himself withdrawing before the barbarian's onslaught. The lich backed into one of the marble benches scattered about the fountain and almost fell. With a roar, Conan drove forward, but his prey recovered quickly. The armored giant staggered around the bench, and retreated until he leaned against the white rim of the Freshet.

There, he took a fresh grip on his weapons, and waited.

The Cimmerian came on relentlessly, his heavy weapon flying in great circles. The plague-lich bided his time, paused until the leather bludgeon whipped past, then dove forward with his dagger outthrust and his spiked mace inscribing a short arc aimed at the barbarian's forehead. The move was well calculated, carefully drawn from the training of a lifetime. It should have worked.

But Conan, with a surge of thews that darkened his face, reversed the unwieldy weapon's path and swung it into his oncoming foe. The sheer force of the blow burst the leather sheath and arrested the warrior's body mid-lunge. The incredible impact blasted the dagger from the warrior's hand, dented his heavy breastplate, and lofted the man up over the Freshet's marble rim. Limbs aflail, the leader of the plague-liches sailed backward through a glittering cloud of flung metal dust, then plunged into the bowl of the Freshet in an explosion of creamy white foam. Conan hurled his ruined weapon after his foe and sprinted for the palace doors.

The few remaining plague-liches did not pursue him.

They stared in wide-eyed awe as their leader clawed wildly at the water, threw ropes of froth in a doomed effort to swim, then sank helplessly beneath the surface. His vainly struggling body slid along the steep slope of the Freshet's floor, then plummeted into the dim azure depths of the great shaft that drove down into the bluff. The metallic gleams of his armor were soon lost to sight.

As one, the plague-liches looked up to the small balcony that clung, like a barnacle on the flank of a whale, to the great sweep of the palace's wall five stories above the courtyard. A low moan ran through them like an icy wind through a winter forest. No one appeared on the high balcony. Almost regretfully, they turned their attention back to the fleeing Cimmerian.

Conan came into the palace at a dead run, and nearly trampled Shamtare underfoot in the process. The bronze ring affixed to the outside of the door had its twin on the inside.

The barbarian grabbed the ring with both hands and hauled the door shut.

They were in a foyer. Behind them an open arch adorned with a flamboyant coat-of-arms afforded entrance to the palace proper. The marble walls to either side were hung with tapestries embroidered with more elaborate versions of the same coat-of-arms. Though shadowed, the foyer was illuminated by a pallid white light emanating from somewhere deeper within the palace. A huge, iron-bound bolt, thicker than a man's thigh, lay in its channel beside the doors. Eoreck had to stand on tiptoe to grasp it. He did so, and tried in vain to slide the bolt home.

"Gods! It weighs a ton," he gasped.

Pezur added his strength to the prince's, and still the bolt wouldn't budge. Then Shamtare and Conan threw themselves upon it and, slowly, the sturdy length of hardwood ground reluctantly into place. The men fell away from the bolt with gasps of relief.

"Safe," crowed the prince, and clapped his hands together in satisfaction.

"What the hell?" panted Shamtare, gesturing at the door. His seamed face shone scarlet above his beard.

"The bolt hasn't been oiled for more than a year," said Conan. "We're lucky there were enough of us to throw it."

Despite the desperate action of mere moments past, Conan seemed unwearied and in good spirits. He showed little sign of exertion aside from a slight sheen of sweat over his forehead and temples. Indeed, a small smile pulled at his dour mouth and his blue eyes seemed to gleam with heightened vigor. "Save any of that wine, Shamtare?"

"A good soldier is prepared for any contingency," grinned the Shemite. He dug into his backpack with both hands and produced a bottle. The cork was drawn, and it was passed around to all. Eoreck took a notably smaller sip than his comrades, though whether from shame or the continued discomfort of his hangover, none could say.

"What now?" asked Shamtare as he licked his lips.

"Treasure," said Pezur. "Enough to pay off my parents' debts and make me rich!"

"Enough to make my father a king," said Eoreck hoarsely.

There was a sudden scraping sound from outside. It was followed by a heavy thud against the doors. The sounds came again, and they were repeated until they became an irregular, but steady, beating upon the doors.

"They're trying to get in," burst out Eoreck. He backed away from the entrance. "Don't the simpletons know they can't break these huge things down?"

Conan laid a hand on the polished oak of the door.

There was a thump and the thick panel quivered gently beneath his palm. "They're not trying to break in," he said tensely. "I think they're piling the marble benches up against the doors."

Abruptly a sharp series of staccato blows began to ring out. Shudders ran through the wood and tingled against Conan's fingers.

"That's hammering," said the barbarian. "They're nailing the doors together. They're not trying to break through." He looked squarely into Shamtare's eyes. "They're sealing us in."

18

The end of the foyer that opened into the palace had a second set of doors, stout and solid, but small in comparison to those that opened onto the courtyard. These inner doors were flung wide, flush against the walls of the room beyond. This was a large oval chamber hung with framed portraits of the baron and his family, along with a host of his apparently illustrious ancestors. The walls were of the same blue-green stone that composed most of the palace's exterior. The oval room opened on three expansive corridors, each of which allowed access to a different wing of the first floor. Rooted at the room's center was an imposingly wide flight of stairs, which stretched to a second-floor landing before splitting into three separate sets of steps.

The centermost coiled upward in a huge and stately spiral that rose into obscuring darkness. This central staircase was flanked by two more typical stairways that ascended to landings at the third and fourth floors.

Faceted crystals the size of a man's skull adhered to the walls at even intervals. These emitted a dull white glow that allowed the intruders to see adequately, yet still left much of the palace's interior masked in shadow. Only the great shaft of the central spiral stair was utterly devoid of light. A dusky twilight, silent and ominous, pervaded the dwelling place of the baron of Dulcine.

Conan stood in the oval room, hands on his hips. His shirt of Akbitanan mail shone dully in the half-light. The Cimmerian's face was grim. Voices floated on the musty air, and shortly Shamtare and Eoreck emerged from the left corridor.

"Ho, Conan!" Shamtare cried. "There's a great court back there, together with a half dozen other rooms that seem to have been built solely for fat nobles to gorge themselves in. The place has been well picked over, too," he added glumly. "Looters have pried golden sconces from the walls and even managed to cut down some hanging candelabras."

Pezur entered from the right hallway, glanced at the naked shortsword gripped in his right hand, and quickly sheathed it.

"Find any trouble?" asked Shamtare.

"No," answered the archer, shamefaced. "Just nervous. All I found were servant's quarters. And they, too, were looted. Someone even took the time to slash open the mattresses."

"How about you, captain," said Eoreck. "What have you found?"

"I found the stairs into the vaults beneath the palace, and the baron's fabled treasure rooms," said Conan. Eoreck's face lit up, but both Pezur and Shamtare heard the barbarian's flat tones and felt a sudden chill.

"Excellent!" bubbled the prince. "What are we waiting for? Let us gather all the riches we can carry!"

"The vaults are empty," said Conan.

Eoreck stared slack-jawed at the Cimmerian, apparently unable to credit his hearing. "What?"

"Aside from scattered coins and a few small chests, the baron's entire trove is gone."

"That's impossible!" exploded the prince. "You are mistaken."

"No mistake," said Conan. "The doors to the vault chambers have been broken down as if by a battering ram. There is plenty of open space where the treasure once lay heaped. But now it is gone."

"Set's fangs! How?" Eoreck looked stunned, almost ready to weep.

"Adrastus?" said Pezur. "Could he have survived and beaten us to the treasure?"

"Might someone else have had the ability to make the wizard's protective veils?" conjectured Shamtare. "Someone who came here well before us?"

"Pointless to wonder about it now," said Conan. "Our next concern is how we're going to get out of here alive."

"I—we can't leave here without the treasure!" cried the prince.

"There is no treasure," said the Cimmerian. He turned away and started up the stairs. "Let us explore the upper levels. We'll find a window and go down the wall."

"I can't climb that wall," said Pezur.

"I doubt that I could, either. Perhaps we can fashion a rope of some sort."

The wide stair was covered with deep green carpeting, thick with dust, but as soft and yielding beneath their feet as a loamy field. Their boots made no sound. The second-floor landing was almost wide enough to hold the villa where the men had spent the night. On the walls to either side was mounted a faceted white globe that glimmered faintly and painted pale streaks of light along the marble floor. A long table lay on its side, most of its semiprecious inlay broken out and removed. The base of the massive spiral staircase was shrouded in still shadow.

"Shall we split up again?" asked Eoreck.

"No," said Conan. "This corkscrew stair looks as though it must take us to the level with the balcony that overlooks the fountain. That balcony would be a good place to climb out of this damned prison, even though Pezur and I saw someone standing on it last night."

"Saw someone? Who?"

"I don't know," said the barbarian slowly. "But I think we should stay together from here on." The Cimmerian's deliberate tone lent weight to his simple words.

"Probably just another of the plagued ones," said the prince, but he drew his scarlet cloak about his shoulders as if he felt a draft.

The lightless stairwell opened before them like a darkly yawning mouth. The four ascended at an even pace, and their eyes sought ceaselessly in the gloom. They spotted several of the wall-mounted globes that lit much of the palace, but here they were broken, often little more than a few white spikes of glass protruding from the smooth stone wall. Conan led the way as the party made three circuits around the great stair.

They came to a small landing before an ebony door inlaid with engraved plaques of ivory. The barbarian hesitated before it.

The stairs continued, the curling banister stretching up into the dimness like a black python.

"See here," hissed the prince. "That door is intact! No one has pried out the ivory!" His fingertips flitted over the incised plaques.

"It should open onto the same floor as the balcony," said Conan. But he stood before the door in apparent indecision, and only Pezur truly understood his reluctance.

"Well, open it then. Perhaps the looters missed this entire tower! We may yet be rich men." Eoreck fretted impatiently, but he sensed enough of the Cimmerian's uncertainty to stand beside him and await his command.

Conan drew his broadsword with a motion as smooth as the flow of water. Then he laid a big palm against the inlaid door and shoved it open.

The room beyond was empty. A single white globe set in the ceiling lit up a chamber designed exclusively for pleasure. The center of the lushly carpeted floor was sunken, and this depression was almost filled by a single luxurious couch, spread with plush cushions, rare furs, and exotic silks. A long rack of glass shelves on the right wall held an impressive collection of eastern porcelains. A fine coating of dust lay over all. An empty arch beckoned from across the room, opening on a darkened hall.

"By Ashtoreth, these must be the baron's personal chambers," whispered Eoreck. "Those Khitan vessels were one of his passions. I know we'll find riches here. I know it!"

Conan stalked silently into the chamber, stepped around the sunken divan, and slipped through the opposite doorway. Shamtare and Pezur were quick to follow, but the prince slowed to examine the shelves. His gaze probed among the elegant pieces of porcelain for more valuable items.

Two arches opened into the hallway at its midpoint: doorways into dimly lit rooms. One was apparently a well-stocked library, the other a mirrored and marbled bath chamber. The barbarian glanced into each room long enough to determine that they were empty, then continued along the hall until it ended, opening out into an expansive chamber full of clean air and the pleasant, natural light of the sun.

It had once been some sort of reception room. Chairs and divans stood about the marble floor, all facing the arch through which Conan moved as silently as smoke. Beside the entrance was a small dais, and on the dais sat a throne.

Thickly upholstered in regal purple velvet, and bearing golden arms and legs fashioned to resemble the minutely scaled limbs of a dragon, the throne would have been somewhat ostentatious in the Grand Palace of Paikang. Sitting alone in this desolate place, presiding over a room full of empty seats, the throne seemed a hollow bit of vanity, the doomed hubris of a vainglorious man whose elaborate walls and high castle could not elevate him above the ranks of mortal men.

The throne faced the empty chairs, and the open, sunlit balcony. Curtains of purple velvet rippled in the bracing wind. Outside, the sky shone cloudless blue above the still and lifeless buildings of Dulcine. Black ravens rode the air currents, floated effortlessly high above the city. Conan could see past Dulcine's outer wall to the rolling emerald forest, and into the blue haze beyond to the ruddy ridges and bluffs that thrust like stone blades from the verdant flesh of the earth.

He also saw a body lying outstretched beside the right wall. The barbarian made his way across the chamber, satisfied there was no other exit and none here but the dead. Behind him, Pezur and Shamtare entered and exclaimed over the throne.

The body wore rich robes of purple velvet and red silk. The elegant fabrics were now a shroud wrapped about a wizened skeleton whose shriveled flesh was black as tar. Adorning the mummified skull was a simple silver circlet. The corpse's torso appeared somewhat hunched to Conan's eye, as if it lay upon something that propped it above the floor. Its bony hands seemed to reach in vain for the wall beside it, and the Cimmerian saw that a square segment of the marble wall had been drawn into the chamber, opening a thin black slot from floor to ceiling. The dead man had been attempting to flee through some sort of secret panel.

Conan knelt beside the body, slid the blade of his sword beneath it, and rolled it over. The corpse was as light as a bag of autumn leaves. Beneath the body was a small box of enameled wood. A deft move of the sword flipped the box's lid up and revealed its blue satin-lined interior. Nested within was a transparent, faceted stone the size of a small walnut. A simple mount affixed it to a chain of finely woven gold links.

Sunlight struck the gem and seemed to rebound with exaggerated brightness. It gleamed like a demon's eye, staring balefully at the barbarian.

Conan plucked the jewel from its box, snapped the golden chain over his dark-haired head, and dropped the gem inside the front of his mail shirt. His sword blade shut the wooden box, then shoved it beneath the corpse's voluminous robes. He stood and regarded the secret door as if nothing had transpired.

Pezur approached him, as the voices of Shamtare and the prince rose in some dispute. The archer looked down at the corpse and rubbed his beardless jaw.

"Is that the baron?"

"Yes. What are those two quarreling about?"

"The prince is upset about the lack of loot. Shamtare suggests they dismantle the throne, but Eoreck says that will devalue the thing and wants to remove it whole."

"He's welcome to carry it. What do you make of this?" asked Conan. The burnished tip of his broadsword thrust into the dark gap in the marble wall. Pezur frowned while the barbarian pried at the opening and found the door rotated into the chamber with minimal resistance. Hidden hinges ground softly as it swung wide, and the two men regarded a rectangle of solid black. A tarnished bronze handle was set into the inner surface of the door. The arguing voices of the prince and Shamtare died, and were immediately replaced by the sounds of the two men hastening across the room.

"What have you found, my friends?"

"Set eat me, if it isn't a secret door. The baron's cautions make my father's seem routine. The madman simply couldn't make himself safe enough." Prince Eoreck pushed past the men and stepped into the mouth of the lightless passage. He flourished his rapier self-consciously, wove a swift web of silver in the darkness. "I'll wager it leads to a secret vault of riches. Come on, men, follow your prince." Eoreck stepped over the threshold, and immediately hesitated. The prince's golden breastplate glimmered as he glanced behind to be certain that he was being followed and not heading off into the dark alone.

Shamtare shot Conan an exasperated glance, and the three mercenaries went after their prince. For once, the Cimmerian found himself bringing up the rear.

The passage was of bare stone, and so narrow that the barbarian's shoulders scraped either wall. The smell of dust was cloying in the enclosed space. The light from the balcony grew more and more diffuse as they advanced, until the men groped along in near total darkness. The cramped hall led straight back the way they had come, apparently running parallel to the barons' personal chambers. The floor remained smooth and level.

"What's this?" cried the prince. "A bit of glass in the wall?" There was much scuffling and cursing as the men maneuvered about in the narrow passage.

"Phaugh!" Shamtare's exclamation of disgust brought a thin smile to the Cimmerian's lips. "It's nothing but a peephole to spy upon those in the first room. Ishtar's arse, what manner of ruler watches his subjects frolic on his own couch?"

"Shall we keep going?" called Pezur.

"Yes," said Conan. "I think we're almost through with this fumbling in the dark."

"Watch out, all. There are three steps down here. What do you mean, captain?" said Eoreck, then, "By Pteor, a dead end! Arallu's fire, shall we never find any loot in this place?"

"Give the wall a good push," suggested Conan.

"What's that?"

"Put your hands on the dead end and shove, prince."

"What? Well, if you think it will... Derketo!" New light filtered into the passage, dim, but seeming bright to those in utter darkness. "It's another secret panel!"

One by one the party filed through the hidden door, and found themselves once again on the spiral staircase, only a few steps below the ebony door to the baron's private quarters.

The prince sat on the steps in dejection. His hangover had apparently faded to an unpleasant memory, and he had once again acquired his accustomed energy. He used all that energy to sulk.

"What shall become of me? Lord Eannus, my father, will disown me unless I can bring him the riches he expects. Damn that dolt Adrastus. I wish I'd seen him slain. I'd drink a toast to the plague-lich that gutted him. How about it, soldier? Any more wine?"

Shamtare was about to risk defying royalty by denying the prince the remainder of his wine, when Conan suddenly held up a hand.

"Be still." The Cimmerian looked up the wide spiral stairs, and his comrades' eyes followed. The steps swept up out of sight, empty but for dust. A faint sound came to their ears, a distant voice raised in a song or chant.

"What the hell?" whispered Shamtare.

Conan started up the stairs without a word, and the others scrambled to follow. He took the steps at a loping run, traversed the great circle of stairs again and again. The distant voice rose and fell like a barely tangible breeze. Those behind him began to pant and feel the dull ache of weary muscles, but the barbarian never slowed. Pezur wondered how far above the city they had climbed, then saw that the stairs came to an end ahead.

The steps opened into a high-ceilinged chamber in which the voice resounded clear and strong. And it was chanting: an eerie sing-song litany of growled and whistled syllables that formed alien words never meant for a human throat. But for the curious cadence and undeniable repetitions and refrains, Pezur would have sworn the voice spoke nothing but bestial gibberish. He hesitated at the top step. He knew that voice.

It was the voice of the wizard, Adrastus.

19

The high-arched chamber at the summit of the stairs opened into two halls that curved away to both east and west. Conan stood at the room's center, listened to the strange chant, and tried to determine its direction. The barbarian noted that the sounds seemed to emanate with equal clarity from either hallway, and reasoned that both east and west corridors must eventually meet, thus forming a great ring around the tower's periphery. So, it made little difference which hall he chose, as either would lead him back to this landing eventually.

Pezur, Eoreck, and Shamtare had time enough to clamber up the last of the seemingly endless stairs, spot Conan standing pensively in the chamber, and heave a few badly needed breaths before the Cimmerian started off down the left hallway.

"By Pteor," gasped the prince. "What gave the barbarian such tireless legs?"

"The Cimmerian hills," answered Shamtare, as he wiped his damp brow with a leather-clad forearm.

Eoreck slouched against the black banister, and might even have sat down if Pezur hadn't immediately taken off after Conan with

Shamtare at his heels. The prince sighed morosely, shoved off the railing, and followed.

The corridor described a great, gradual curve. The walls, floor, and ceiling were of pale and polished marble, its luster diminished by an even powdering of fine dust. The few lights, like those in the spiral stair, were smashed to white shards. Conan stole through the darkness like a wraith, and drew up short as an illuminated arch came into view on the right.

The arch was high and fretted, and it allowed a flat white glare, as cold as moonlight, to spill into the hall. The curved corridor swept on past the arch into more darkness. The sound of Adrastus's chanting voice was loud, and it didn't take a Cimmerian's keen senses to determine that it came from the room beyond the arch.

Conan slipped across the hall, skirted the chill pool of white light, and hewed to the shadows against the far wall. Skulking in the darkness like a prowling wolf, he dropped to all fours and peered into the illuminated room. His eyes dilated and shone with a feral fervor. He was scarcely aware of the quiet approach of his comrades.

The arch opened upon a huge circular chamber like none the Cimmerian had ever seen. The floor was an amazingly intricate mosaic done in tiny tiles of black and white. What little of the lofty ceiling he could make out appeared even more outlandish; it was a titanic dome of stained glass. Its countless panes were wildly variegated and chaotically colorful. The outer world was dimly visible through the dome's many-hued glass, but it was difficult to tell much of the sky as the chamber's walls were ringed with a brilliantly illuminated collection of the faceted light globes. An identical fretted arch was visible across the chamber on the opposite wall.

All this Conan noted in a heartbeat, before his gaze was captured by the tableau at the enormous room's center. In the swirling floor-mosaic's central whorl squatted a black dais of three steps, upon which sat a low ebony table. Kneeling on the dais, in front of the table, was Adrastus the Kothian. His back was to the barbarian, and he wore a long, flowing cowl that hung from his shoulders in rich folds of deep blue, emblazoned with small white symbols of arcane design. The sorcerer's left hand swept out, and in its palm was a small pyramid of lucent green crystal. The Kothian's chanting lowered to softer, more mellifluous tones.

Then Conan saw what stood before the kneeling mage, and it was as though a gauntlet of ice clenched in his belly.

The barbarian hunkered down and his lips peeled back from his teeth. He slowed his breathing unconsciously, as though he feared that which stood upon the dais might hear it and seek him out where he crouched hidden in the shadows.

But the thing on the dais saw only the tiny pyramid of crystal that Adrastus held in his outstretched hands. The dull black orbs of its eyes stared ceaselessly into the gem. The long, angular face bore no expression. No wrinkle creased the perfect, amber-skinned brow. It wore garments of black silk edged with cloth-of-gold, and they seemed to hang upon its lean frame with unnatural weight. The long-fingered hands lifted from its sides, and slowly reached for the proffered crystal.

Adrastus chanted on, though he grew hoarse, giving each oft-practiced syllable its perfect enunciation. Sweat streaked his face and gleamed in his beard. His fevered eyes shone as he gazed reverently upon the creature that stood before him. The small, glassy pyramid took on a deeper green color, and swift flickers of darkness danced in the air around it, like minute black sparks.

The thing that resembled a man extended its hands to take the crystal from the sorcerer, and Prince Eoreck stepped into the room.

"Adrastus! Damn your soul! What have you done with the baron's diamonds, you traitor?"

The thing's ebon eyes jerked up from the pyramidal gem. Adrastus started violently in surprise and the crystal jolted from his open palm. It dropped free, and the chant was choked off in the sorcerer's suddenly constricted throat. The mage dove forward clumsily, trying to catch the gem as it struck the second step of the dais and bounced. Adrastus floundered across the stairs. His hands reached in vain for the tiny pyramid as it struck the black and white mosaic tiles and shattered into crystal fragments.

The mage rolled off the dais and bounded to his feet with such alacrity that he might have been mistaken for a tumbling acrobat. But his face was not that of a jester. He looked to Eoreck with an expression in which murderous rage and stark horror fought for prominence.

"You thrice-damned fool! You've doomed us all!"

It was then that Conan stepped into the chamber with Shamtare and Pezur at his side. Swords were drawn. In the sudden silence the young archer's voice could be heard as he muttered a soft prayer to Ishtar. To the right of the entry was an elegant podium of dark wood, and beside the podium stood Balthano. The Argossean did not appear to notice Conan's arrival; his eyes were fixed upon Adrastus. The mage whirled to face the dais, then began to back haltingly away from it. "You fools," he whispered. "You thoughtless fools."

The creature on the dais cocked its head in a birdlike fashion and regarded the intruders. Conan's eyes met its empty black orbs, soulless as those of an adder, and the barbarian knew at once that he faced the same being which had looked upon him across the nighted city from the distant palace balcony. Its man-shape was a transparent deception; the thing gave off a tangible aura of unnatural menace. Pezur's prayers grew louder.

"What were you doing, wizard?" rasped the barbarian.

"Trying to stop it! Oh, you fools! What have you done?" Adrastus backed into Conan, who seized his shoulder. Balthano stepped away from the podium, as if to follow his master, and the thing on the dais abruptly moved forward. It seemed almost to float, scarcely touching the three black steps. No dancer ever moved with such weightless grace.

"Flee!" The mage's voice rose to a hysterical shriek. "Its touch is death! Flee or die!" Adrastus twisted away from the Cimmerian's grip and bolted out the doorway with Pezur close at his heels.

Shamtare stood his ground as the thing advanced, his eyes wild with terror controlled by raw discipline. His sword trembled in his white-knuckled fist.

"Shamtare, no!" Conan's voice rang out just as the man-thing darted toward the mercenary. A delicate amber hand reached out as if to caress the Shemite's brow, and Shamtare leapt back as if a torch had been thrust into his face. The demon moved to follow him, then hesitated and turned to Prince Eoreck, who still stood rooted in the spot from which he had so boldly interrupted the ceremony of Adrastus.

"I am the nephew of King Sumuabi of Akkharia!" blurted the prince. The black-clad thing tilted its long head as if weighing his words. And Shamtare, behind the demon, drove his shortsword into the small of its back. This action seemed to awaken Eoreck, who leapt into life, whirled, and ran for the entrance. Conan stepped around the fleeing prince and moved in, his heavy broadsword held ready to finish the strange being.

It took a mincing half-step forward under the impact of Shamtare's blow, then straightened. Conan froze in mid-stride, and felt his scalp prickle. The demon stared expressionlessly into the Cimmerian's face, then twitched slightly as the old mercenary tore his blade from its back. The great eyes held Conan in place, black and empty as the void that yawns between the stars, yet filled with an awful, shark-like hunger.

The prince's receding footfalls could be heard in the ringing silence.

"Ishtar's holies!" cried Shamtare in horror. "It doesn't bleed! It feels no pain! Flee, Conan!" The Shemite took two backward steps, then broke and ran for the arch on the room's opposite side. The demon looked over its shoulder and watched him go. The Cimmerian heard the scuffle of boots on marble behind him and knew that Balthano had fled as well. He was alone.

Conan lifted his blade to lunge forward with a decapitating strike, and in the fractured moment that his Herculean frame tensed for that action, the demon-thing turned back to face him.

And it smiled, drew thin golden lips back from rows of teeth like slivers of midnight onyx. It grinned at the Cimmerian like a black-fanged death's head, and lifted eager amber hands to clutch at him.

"Crom!" The curse was ripped from Conan's lips.

The barbarian's boots slid back a step, and his enemy floated forward like a hallucination born of mad nightmare, legs scarcely seeming to move, feet apparently skimming above the tiled floor.

Conan spun and sprinted through the arch.

And death pursued him.

20

The curtains moved listlessly in the cool breeze.

Shadows slowly lengthened in the lifeless city spread out below the lofty balcony. Pezur looked down upon the foaming crown of the Freshet far below, and tried to control the quaver in his breathing.

The tense voice of Adrastus came from the arch beside the ornate throne. "Most of that fountain is deep enough that we might well plunge into it from this height without injury. Do you think we could jump to it from here?" The mage peered down the hallway that led through the baron's personal chambers to the door that opened onto the great spiral stair.

He had closed and bolted it behind them just moments before. "No," said Pezur honestly. "Even with the benefit of a running leap over the railing, I doubt even Conan could do it. We'd fall short and be crushed on the flagstones."

"And you say the plague-liches have sealed the doors from without? Set's scales! Might we make a rope out of those curtains?" The wizard's voice snapped impatiently across the empty room. He remained stationed at the mouth of the hall, his wide eyes fixed on the door to the stairs.

"Yes," said the archer. "Conan suggested that." He drew the thick velvet fabric between his fingers. "We shouldn't have left them back there." He turned to Adrastus. "What was that thing?"

"Enough of that. I told your friends to flee, and if they were wise, they heeded me. The dolts disrupted the climactic moment of a year's desperate work, and whatever befalls them now is their own damned doing. Worry about saving your own life. If we can't get out of here shortly, we'll never get out. This is the lowest window I know, and I certainly don't relish the idea of searching through the other towers right now. Start cutting the curtains into strips."

Pezur felt as if he were imprisoned in an unlikely dream. He stared out over the city, saw inevitable evening coming on, as it always did. He laid a hand on the cool hilt of his dagger and shook his head. Conan would know what to do.

"Well, come on then!" Adrastus rapped. "Are you addled? Get on with it."

Pezur reached up and began to tug the blue velvet curtain from its golden rail when a sharp, splintering crash came from somewhere behind him. The sound of the mage's horrified gasp jolted the archer like a physical blow. He dropped the curtain, looked back, and saw Adrastus run across the chamber. The portly mage dodged between the empty chairs and divans, headed toward the black rectangle of the open secret panel.

A hollow thump, like the sound a hastily opened door might make as it rebounded from a wall, came from the hallway. Then there was silence.

Pezur's heart lurched in his breast. He moved to follow Adrastus, snagged his boot in the folds of the fallen curtain, and stumbled.

"Adrastus! Is it here? Has it followed us?"

In his frantic haste, the sorcerer hurled a chair from his path, but made no answer. Pezur kicked away the clinging curtain, then leapt toward Adrastus and the opening of the secret passage. The archer caught a flash of shadowy movement in his peripheral vision, and ran across the floor as quickly as he could move.

Adrastus ducked into the open passage, grabbed the tarnished bronze handle on the inner panel, and jerked the door closed. It shut with a muffled *click*, as loud in Pezur's ears as a clap of thunder.

"Adrastus!" The archer couldn't halt his headlong rush and came up against the shut door with enough force to rebound and stagger. He threw himself at the now featureless wall and clawed at it with frenzied fingers. There had to be a way to open the panel. He found nothing.

"Adrastus!" he screamed. "Adrastus!"

Something dark moved at the limits of his vision, and he redoubled his efforts, clawing at the wall and yelling the mage's name. He stopped abruptly, and stood silent with his hands flat on the cold marble wall. His breath burned in his throat. The shadow at the edge of his vision took shape.

There was a man standing behind him.

Pezur drew his sword and whirled to face his foe with a curse on his lips. His blade drove for the man's heart.

But it had no heart, for it wasn't a man.

21

Conan realized he was no longer pursued before he'd gone halfway down the spiral stair. Still, he fled at full speed, taking three steps at a time until he came to the huge square landing that formed the stairway's base. There, he paused to catch his breath and take stock. His naked broadsword gleamed like pale ice in the diffuse white light of the faceted wall globes.

Stifled gasps rose from the first floor. Conan moved soundlessly to the landing's rail, and looked down the sweeping stair that lowered into the oval room which was the palace's antechamber. He saw no one. The sounds continued: muted curses, gasps, and the occasional sob. The barbarian frowned darkly as he recognized both the voice and tone. He moved with easy speed down the wide stairway, approached the foyer, and paused in its doorway.

"Ho, prince, ease up there. There's no getting those doors open now."

Prince Eoreck had moved a chair against the palace's outer doors, stood upon it, and now tugged futilely at the massive, iron-bound bolt. He cast a glance back over a scarlet-caped shoulder, saw Conan, then returned to his fruitless efforts.

"Eoreck, cease. The doors have been sealed from outside. We must find another way out of this deathtrap."

The prince stopped pulling at the immobile bolt, turned, and dropped into the chair. He sat and stared at the Cimmerian, his face ashen and moist with sweat.

"We are already dead men. We might just as well lie down and start rotting."

"Do what you will," said Conan tersely. "I'm for finding a way out of here."

"Conan!"

The barbarian whirled about, automatically putting his blade between himself and the speaker, before he recognized the voice as Shamtare's. The old mercenary stood in the mouth of the left hallway, the hall he had taken when exploring the palace's first floor. He peered apprehensively up the stairs, then looked back at Conan.

"Got away from it, eh? It's good to see you alive. Come with me, brother. I've found a good place to hide out and plan."

"Hear that?" asked Conan of the prince. "Come along or lie down right here. It's all the same to me."

The Cimmerian moved to join Shamtare, and Eoreck heaved himself up from the chair to follow. The old mercenary was wringing Conan's hand and slapping his broad shoulders when a sudden hiss came out of the dimness of the right hallway.

"Hssst! Be silent, you fools." Balthano and Adrastus crouched furtively beneath the arch, and the wizard held a thick finger to his lips. "You'll bring it down upon us."

Conan's response was a deep laugh, open and honest.

Eoreck gaped at him as if the barbarian had lost his reason. "Ymir freeze me if we aren't a predictable lot," chuckled the Cimmerian. "We all run right to the door. Even though most of us know we can't even use it." He laughed again, and the sound was infectious enough that Shamtare smiled, and even the prince shook his head ruefully.

"It's just as well. Come along wizard, Shamtare says he's found a place to go to ground."

It turned out to be the palace kitchen. It was a good-sized square room with a door on every wall, each of which opened into a different ballroom. A massive wooden table sat at the room's center, still heaped with flour, the relic of a routine bit of breadmaking interrupted more than a year ago. A single, exceptionally bright light crystal glowed from the ceiling.

Shamtare pointed out that, should their foe appear in any door, they might easily scatter through any or all the other doors, giving the demon multiple targets of pursuit and thus increasing their chances of survival. He expounded on how the airy and open ballrooms would also allow them plenty of time to react to intrusion if they merely posted a guard at each door. He pointed out that the sound of an intruder's footfalls would surely be very audible, and Conan spoke up.

"Enough, Shamtare. Where is Pezur?"

The Shemite swallowed and looked about as if he might have missed the archer among his companions. "Damn me, I don't know."

"Have you seen him?" Conan's gaze raked over the prince, Balthano, and Adrastus.

"No," said the mage mildly. "Perhaps he chose a less predictable escape route."

Eoreck shook his head, and Balthano scowled arrogantly.

"The whelp's probably finished," said the Argossean. He rubbed his palms together. "The question is, what are we going to do now?"

"Hide," whispered the prince. "I can't face that horror again."

"The first thing we're going to do is get some answers," rumbled Conan. His blue eyes flashed dangerously. "What the hell was that thing, Adrastus?"

"Yes." The prince bristled, took a step closer to the Cimmerian, and stood taller with a strength born of righteous indignation. "What secrets have you been keeping from your royal master, sorcerer?"

"You'll watch your tongue!" snarled Balthano. His hands flashed to his belly and touched something at his belt. Immediately, his posture went rigid and a shudder ran visibly through his lean frame. "We're past the point of bowing to any of you, be you captain or prince! It would suit me to kill you all right here."

"Balthano, no," said Adrastus wearily. "Must I always be reining you in? Have you no sense of your own? If we don't work together to escape, we'll all die. And soon." The wizard's voice was low and forced. He passed a trembling hand over his haggard face, then touched briefly at his crystal pendant. "You want answers?" he asked, looking at the Cimmerian.

"To be sure," said Conan. "As long as we're safe here."

"Safe?" blurted Adrastus, and the others suddenly saw how he strained to keep his composure, how fear was a dark wind that billowed up from within him and plucked at his very sanity.

"It will find us. It's seen us all now, and knows us. It can sense us, feel our presence. Even if we manage to get out of the palace, it will hunt us down, smell us out as would a hound!"

The mage clutched his crystal pendant with both hands. Fear held him in a grip of ice, wrung cold beads of sweat from his furrowed brow, set his bearded jaw to quivering, his teeth almost to chattering.

"It? That man-thing you conjured with in the glass-domed chamber? What is it?" Conan faced Adrastus without threat, but also without pity.

"A man? It's not a man. It really isn't even a thing. It's the plague. Do you understand? The scourge itself. It is an incarnation, a living avatar of the plague. My old teacher, Tolbeth-Khar, and I sought to create a distillation of pestilence in the form of a serum. A simple liquid in a crystal flask." Adrastus drew a careful breath and looked around to be certain that each of the men heeded him.

"The baron commanded it. Hakure-Etah, a visiting Stygian sorcerer of the Black Ring, made the suggestion in passing and the baron wouldn't give Tolbeth-Khar and myself any rest until we'd accomplished it. The baron imagined he had hit upon the ideal defensive weapon to keep all potential threats to Dulcine's independence at a safe distance. If King Sumuabi became adamant about recovering his back taxes, the baron could threaten to loose a plague upon Akkharia. What city-state in all of Shem would dispute Dulcine's sovereignty if the baron was armed with such a weapon? A bit of serum in the water supply, or merely splashed about the city square, and a lethal sickness would sweep through the populace. It was a guarantee of safety." He paused. "In theory, anyway."

"What happened," asked Conan. "Did the serum get loose in Dulcine?"

"Oh no," said Adrastus. "Would that it had been so simple a problem. Something went wrong with the ceremony. I believe the baron's insistence that Tolbeth-Khar produce the plague-defense with all possible speed led the old fool to overestimate his own skills. Instead of a vial filled with plague-serum, he conjured a living being. Or, to be more accurate, a conscious entity that looked like a man and possessed a life of sorts. It was the sentient incarnation of the plague we had sought to distill as a serum. Tolbeth-Khar died at its hands. I escaped the city as it walked forth into Dulcine, and the deathly pestilence raged in its wake."

The mage stopped and drew a ragged breath. He licked dry lips. Shamtare drew a half-full bottle of wine from his backpack and handed it to him without comment. Adrastus pulled the cork, took a deep swallow, then lowered the bottle and continued.

"For a year I sought a solution to the horror my master had loosed upon the world. I journeyed through Stygia in search of sorcerous secrets. I was a lowly pilgrim in Kheshatta and a furtive scholar in Khemi. All the while I feared to hear that the plague demon had emerged from Dulcine and fallen upon the cities of Shem. Then, though scorned by my Stygian teachers, I did something that very few of them have ever dared to do: I led a band of thieves and rogues on an expedition to the haunted pyramids of eastern Stygia. Those cursed ruins are more shunned than those of dread Pteion. My researches led me to a forgotten crypt that held the remains of a thing that had walked and spoken before mankind climbed down from the trees. I stole treasure there. And secrets..." His voice trailed off.

"And now you have returned to battle the creature you inadvertently created," said Conan. "Why?"

Adrastus gaped guilelessly at the Cimmerian. "Why? What if it comes forth from Dulcine? It might stalk and ravage the whole of the world. Who is to stop it if not I?"

"It has stayed pent up in Dulcine for better than a year."

"Yes, but you must understand that, as an incarnation, it is not only new to this world, it is new to the flesh. In time it will learn to think, and to reason. And it will come to know hunger."

"Hunger?" mumbled Shamtare. His eyes had gone hollow, and when Conan glanced at him, he looked less a veteran soldier than an uncertain old man.

"Yes," continued Adrastus. "Remember that it is truly the plague. Thus it waxes stronger as the infection spreads. The more people it causes to sicken, the more powerful, the more alive, it becomes. The presence of those men who have been wracked by the plague and yet remain living doubtless offers it some small sustenance. But even the plague-liches cannot endure the pestilence indefinitely. Soon they must perish, and then the demon will be forced to leave Dulcine to seek its nourishment."

"The leader of the plague-liches called it Lord Death," Conan mused darkly. "They believe the thing is death itself."

"They're not far wrong," said Shamtare.

"But the ones still alive with the plague, the plague-liches—how have they survived?" asked the prince. "Does it allow them to live so that it might have worshippers?"

"I think not. I believe the plague is so unnaturally potent in the close vicinity of the demon that it afflicts even those who would ordinarily be immune. It simply takes longer to kill them. Those who are slain outright are the lucky ones."

"Can you stop this abomination?" The barbarian's eyes blazed as hard and bright as burnished steel.

"I would have. I might have, save that you interrupted my ceremony." The mage's mouth twisted bitterly.

"If you'd had the good sense to tell us what we were up against, and what you'd been planning to do in the first place, then you would have had able assistance."

"Sorcerers and their damned secrets," said Shamtare in disgust.

"You'll watch your mouth, old man," sneered Balthano. He still trembled with an unknown energy. Minuscule beads of sweat shone on his forehead and high, sharp cheekbones.

"Or what, stripling?" asked Shamtare coolly. "Will you pull your pig-stickers?"

Balthano's brows shot up in disbelieving rage. What manner of fool was this old man that he baited him so? The Argossean stared fiercely into Shamtare's face and suddenly realized that the gray-haired mercenary's features were much like his father's.

"For Ishtar's sake, be still!" cried Eoreck. "We don't have time to fight amongst ourselves!"

"The prince is right," Adrastus said. "We are trapped in here with the most lethal creature ever to walk the earth. It can sense us, and it will find us." The fearful quaver edged into his voice again, and his pupils rolled as they passed over each door in turn.

"There must be some chance. Can't steel harm it?" asked Conan.

"Of course not," burst out the Kothian with a hysterical chuckle. "Don't be absurd. It isn't even alive as we know life. Blades will slice its body without doing any harm. It may feel some form of pain, but it won't even bleed. It can't. Would you fight a disease with your sword?"

"There must be some chance," repeated the barbarian doggedly. It was not in him to admit the existence of a completely unassailable foe. The Cimmerian's untamed spirit rebelled at the sorcerer's fearful resignation. The untrammeled survival instinct of the primitive was his, and while Conan's barbaric fatalism told him that death was ultimately inevitable, he would never accept its grim embrace as long as he still had the strength to fight against it.

"Well, there is something." Adrastus stared at the wall and ran his fingers through his beard distractedly. His eyes were unfocused and shone with fear. "But I doubt I have the power to perform the rituals. It is too terrible…"

"What is it, man? Spit it out! We'll take any chance to survive. Are you so craven that you would lie down and die without a fight?" Conan's insult had the desired effect. The Kothian's eyes narrowed upon him. The mage licked his lips and smiled thinly.

"You are coarse, barbarian, but you are no fool. It won't be easy. In fact, it will almost certainly fail. Well, I am no stranger to failure. And as you suggest, anything is better than just giving up our lives to the plague demon."

"What can we do?"

"I must make my way into Tolbeth-Khar's library and find a certain book there. If you can keep the plague demon away from me while I make preparations for the ritual, and can ensure that it doesn't come into the Chamber of Conjuring while I am performing the spell, we may yet have a chance."

"This spell of yours can kill the thing?"

"Oh, no. Even if I can perform it correctly and achieve the

desired results, it won't be slain. At least, not right away. The spell won't affect the monster. It affects the palace."

Conan was silent while Shamtare shook his shaggy head woefully. "Have you gone mad, Adrastus? What is this you speak of? Conjuring spells upon the palace, indeed. We stand a better chance leaping from the windows of the fifth floor than listening to you."

"Hush, Shamtare," said Conan. "Hear him out."

Adrastus gave the barbarian a curt nod of thanks and continued. "You've all observed how well fortified this palace is. Well, the baron of Dulcine was even more obsessed with safeguarding his life and diamonds than you can readily see. Did any of you take note of the palace's foundation?"

"I did," said Conan. "There was an odd gap between the wall and the foundation itself. It served no purpose that I could see. It looked as though the whole palace was built in a bowl."

"Precisely," said the wizard in amazement. He looked upon the Cimmerian with a fresh, almost disbelieving appraisal. "The entire palace is designed to be sorcerously transported in case of an overwhelming attack. The whole of it can, with the appropriate spells, be magically moved to places already prepared to hold it. It is my understanding that there are at least two other hollow, empty foundations waiting patiently in isolated locations for the palace and its baron, should they have needed to flee Dulcine."

"All the good it did him," muttered Eoreck.

"Damnedest thing I've ever heard," said Shamtare.

"But of what import is this to us?" Conan demanded. "Wherever we may take the palace, we're still sealed inside with that walking pestilence."

"I don't want to take one of the baron's escape routes. What I want is to make use of the palace's built-in ability to leave its foundation. I want to take the palace to a place where the plague demon will have foes and can be slain by them."

"What madness is this?" asked Conan grimly.

"No madness," said Adrastus, his voice growing stronger and more confident as he went on. "It's our only real chance to survive. I don't know how much learning any of you have had, but perhaps some of you have heard of the theory of the Countless Worlds and how they overlay and impinge upon our own."

Silence answered him. Eoreck cleared his throat, but didn't speak.

"Well, it is a difficult concept to convey to those without schooling, but I'll do my best. It is said there are an infinite number of worlds that co-exist with our own, each occupying the same space, yet each invisible to the others, inaccessible to us without the use of the higher forms of sorcery."

"I have heard something of this," said Conan. "Some wizards are said to sunder the barriers of nature to draw upon these worlds for power."

"I trust I will cease to be surprised by your erudition shortly, barbarian. Whether there are countless worlds or not, I cannot say, but there is a specific dimension in which the many facets of life in our sphere are reflected in strange and terrible forms. Some mages call it the Plane of Absolutes. Others refer to it as the Dwelling Place of Magic. It is a realm of fearful power. Creatures can be found there, beings of such might that they could well be seen as gods. The plague demon will be vulnerable to them, and as a focused source of living magic, it will be a potent lure for their appetites."

"Appetites?" said Conan. His face resembled a mask carved from dark stone.

"It is a purely magical being. A very powerful thing. Some of these creatures will sense its power and be drawn to it. They will attempt to consume the plague demon. To draw its concentrated and contained power into themselves for sustenance."

"Devour it," said Conan.

"Exactly."

"This is lunacy," said Eoreck. "I forbid it."

"My apologies, prince," said Adrastus smoothly. "Forgive me, but if we act swiftly, perhaps we can avert our deaths. As soon as the palace completes its transition to the Plane of Absolutes, otherworldly predators will be drawn to the demon as flies to carrion. It will have more pressing concerns than preying upon us. If we don't attempt the transition, we simply forfeit our lives."

"And if we try this and it works," said the Cimmerian, "will you be able to return us to our own world?"

"Yes," said Adrastus. "It will be a relatively simple matter once the initial passage has been made. Our pathway between spheres will have already been laid down."

"A rope," put in Shamtare. "Couldn't we just make a simple rope and try to descend from the baron's balcony?"

"Even if we make an adequate rope and manage to escape the palace, I tell you the demon would seek us out. We'd never leave the city alive."

"We should try the wizard's plan," said Conan. He spoke quietly to Shamtare, but all the men heard him. "His is the only way we know to slay the monster. What good would our escape from the palace be if the plague came forth from Dulcine and swept across the world? Where would we flee to then? This may well be the only chance to kill the damned thing, and I say we take it."

Shamtare blew air from between pursed lips, then nodded curtly. Balthano stared at his boots and said nothing; his opinion was apparently secondary to that of Adrastus.

Only Eoreck couldn't accept the decision. He backed away from the little group, shaking his head.

"I can't do it. I can't face that thing again."

"By Bel," jeered Balthano, "this high-born toad's cowering turns my stomach. Let me cut his throat, Adrastus."

"Balthano," sighed the sorcerer. "Cease."

"No more threats," snapped Conan. "Speak against any one of us again and I'll split your skull. We stand or fall together now. Prince, you can stay down here and try to make a rope. Cut curtains and tablecloths into strips and tie them together. Even if this wild scheme works, we'll still need to climb out of that balcony window. And if the wizard's plan fails, I'd rather face that grinning demon in the open air than sealed in this palace death-trap. Are you game, Eoreck?"

The prince coughed into his fist, then nodded. "Thank you, captain."

"All right then," said the Cimmerian. "It seems that if we want to kill a devil, we've got to go to hell."

22

The spiral stair was a well of silence. Four men stole furtively up its coiled length, their footfalls all but soundless on the thick carpet. Often they stopped to listen, frozen momentarily in attitudes of alert trepidation, only to continue along their forbidding path.

The arched chamber at the top of the stairs was empty, and Adrastus led them into the east branch of the hall that wound in a great ring around the tower's circumference. In short order, they came to a closed door on the right wall.

Conan peered ahead, looking for the gleam of white light that would mark the open entrance to the Chamber of Conjuring. He thought he detected the faintest illumination from around the gentle curve of the left wall. Considering it was located parallel to the doorway on the chamber's opposite side, the barbarian knew it must be close at hand. He stared into the darkness, remembered the utter silence of the plague demon's attack, and felt an unpleasant chill along his spine.

"This is the door to Tolbeth-Khar's private chambers and library," whispered Adrastus. "I must disengage its protective wards, get inside, and find the book necessary for the spell that will move the palace. This will take a little time. I suggest that Balthano stays here and guards the door, whilst you two check the Chamber of Conjuring for the demon. If anyone sees it, set up a hue and cry so we all know where it is. Lead the thing away from me. I'll need all the time I can get to find the spell, prepare it, and then actually cast it in the chamber. Are you game?"

Conan looked at Balthano. The Argossean glared back at him in the gloom. It sounded as though Adrastus was playing favorites, but the Cimmerian would much rather have Shamtare at his back than Balthano. He nodded. "Work fast."

"Bravo, captain," said Adrastus and as the two mercenaries turned away, his lips drew into a small smile. Thin and cold, it vanished as the Kothian faced the door to his dead master's chambers.

It was of plain oak, thick and heavy and featureless save for a single plate of brass set into the uppermost panel. The door had no knob or ring to draw it open. Adrastus took a deep breath, then laid his palm flat on the brass plate.

Balthano heard a sudden hum, as if the sorcerer had cupped his hand over a wasp. Soft emerald light rippled across the brass plate, moved beneath the wizard's hand and silhouetted it briefly, black on green. Balthano blinked rapidly. For an instant he thought he'd seen the ebon outline of each bone in his master's hand, as if the green light passed unimpeded through human flesh.

The door swung open soundlessly and Adrastus stepped inside without a word. The door closed, and Balthano was left alone in the empty hall.

Conan and Shamtare followed the corridor's long curve until they saw the open doorway into the Chamber of Conjuring. Its fretted arch spilled white light that lay upon the hall's floor like a bright and frozen pond. The Cimmerian did as he had before, skirting the edges of the light to crouch in darkness and spy into the room. Shamtare shot a glance up and down the hallway, then crept alongside the barbarian.

The Chamber of Conjuring was empty. The light globes that lined its circular wall were bright, but outshone by the huge dome of stained glass, which was lit up to spectacular effect.

Each fitted shard blazed with tinted fire. Shamtare realized the sun must be directly overhead to create such brilliance, and was astonished to think that it was only noon. All this creeping about through nighted corridors had taken less time than he had imagined. Sealed inside the dark palace, it was easy to believe that night had fallen over all the world.

Conan stood. Shamtare followed his example, then tapped on the Cimmerian's mailed shoulder to get his attention.

"Do we go inside?"

"No," rasped the barbarian. "The demon's not within. We'd best stay out of the light. We'll follow the hall all the way around."

"Where in nine hells did it go? It pursued us, didn't it?"

"It chased me for a while, then it let up."

"Why?" The old mercenary's eyes shone faintly in the reflected light. The barbarian shrugged massive shoulders.

"I don't know. Perhaps something distracted it."

"If it fell behind you, why haven't we seen it yet?"

"Who can say what a demon like this might do? Come on."

The two men continued along the empty corridor, and with each step they thought to see the black figure of the plague demon emerge from the shadows ahead.

The door fell closed behind him and Adrastus found himself in utter darkness. For an instant the mage fought back a surge of panic, then he recalled Tolbeth-Khar's method of lighting his chambers.

"Ni ftagn Tothra Siir Cthugua," breathed the Kothian, and a warm red glow lit the chamber. In each corner of the square room stood a tripod of wrought iron topped with a flat dish of polished silver. In each dish danced a pent scarlet flame, burning brightly without fuel or smoke. The trapped flames whispered softly to Adrastus as he stepped around the circular table at the room's center and approached the dark wooden bookcase against the opposite wall. His brows knitted in an intent frown as he scanned the ranks of heavy tomes, some bound in faded leather, others in exotic woods, bronze, or gold. He ignored the plaintive whispers of the flames, knelt, and drew a thick volume from the bottom shelf. A curse broke from his lips when he saw that it was bound with heavy bronze fittings and sealed with a tiny black padlock. He didn't have the key.

Adrastus turned and set the ponderous book on the dusty table. The fetish mask of a Wadai shaman leered at him from the opposite wall. Its scarlet plumes appeared to twitch in the airless room, and its cruel grin seemed for him alone. The wizard pulled his gaze away from the upas-wood mask. A trembling hand sought his star-pendant and rubbed it absently. His mind raced.

He had no choice. He must break the seal regardless of the protective wards Tolbeth-Khar might have put upon it.

The sorcerer drew a dagger from within his doublet. He did not remove it from its sheath; the blade was of porous steel, steeped in the venom of the black Stygian scorpion. The slightest nick from its well-honed edge would bring a hideous, frothing doom. He set his jaw, readied his only magical defense, lifted the dagger over his head, then brought the pommel down on the little padlock.

"Dar Vramgoth!" shouted the mage, and the lock shattered like black glass. A jolt of electric pain shot along the nerves of his arm. Instantly, blue vapor sprayed from the broken lock, and sprang into three individual loops that uncoiled above the bronze-bound book.

The sorcerer made a hissed exclamation of pain and dropped the dagger. Its hilt had gone white-hot. He stumbled back from the table and beat at his right arm as if it were afire.

Floating in midair over the book was a three-headed serpent of blue smoke. It swayed gently from side to side and regarded Adrastus. Three pairs of eyes burned like flecks of golden hellfire. Its blue smoke-flesh roiled ceaselessly in upon itself, coursing wildly within the sharp confines of its snake form. Adrastus had but a moment to examine the guardian of the book before it struck at him.

Though his right arm was weakened by the terrible pain of breaking the sorcerous lock, and his mind was spurred to panic by the fearsome ward he had unleashed, the stout wizard still had the presence of mind to seize upon his only defense against a purely magical attack. Adrastus grabbed the crystal pendant with his left hand, snapped its cord from around his neck, and thrust the star convulsively at the guardian serpent.

Three blunt blue heads drove fiercely toward the Kothian's breast and encountered the interposed crystal star. There was a hollow clap and the demon-serpent dissolved into fading streaks of dusky vapor. Then came a sharp snap as the pendant broke in two. Its lower half fell to the floor and shattered.

Adrastus took a moment to recover himself, then laid the remnants of the pendant on the table and looked upon his broken handiwork with proud satisfaction. He had spent almost two months forging the crystal star. As a mage with limited skills who sought to consort with mighty sorcerers, Adrastus had made a device designed to absorb and deflect a magical attack. And it had worked. His arm throbbed and his body was damp with the sweat of fear, but the Kothian swelled with pride. Old Tolbeth-Khar's defenses had been overcome. Who was to say he was not a worthy wizard now?

Adrastus stepped to the table and flipped open the book. He was certain he would recognize the spell when he saw it.

Balthano stood in the dark hallway and tried to remain calm. He rubbed at the brand that disfigured his chest. It was to have been seared into the center of his forehead for all the world to see. But Balthano, wiry and fierce even at ten years of age, had writhed away from the two men who had tried to hold him down. The brand had slipped from the bailiff's hand and scraped along Balthano's breastbone. The horrific pain had given the youth the strength to flee.

That was twelve years ago, and he had never gone back. Often he had sworn that he would return to Argos and seek out the Messantian magistrate who had convicted him, and the lackeys who had marked his breast with the brand. Now, in the quiet dimness of the palace hallway, he swore again that if he survived this encounter with black sorcery, he would punish those who had made him an exile. With his magical belt to aid him, he would make his old enemies beg for the sweet release of death.

He touched the brand, and his thin face hardened with the hoarded bitterness of memory. The brand of a patricide. It mattered little that no one could see it; he was marked all the same. They had no proof. They had merely seized a youth of ten, convicted him in short order, and then tried to brand him preparatory to death by hanging. What kind of justice was that?

Balthano shuddered, and a fresh wave of acid rage seethed through him. They had no right. They had no proof. How could they convict him? They couldn't be certain he'd killed his father.

Even if he had.

Conan and Shamtare approached the pool of light cast by the second doorway into the Chamber of Conjuring. The strange room was still empty, and they had encountered no one in the hall. The continual silence was oppressive.

Shamtare was sweating, although he wasn't hot. The two mercenaries hesitated beside the doorway, looked longingly at the open sky visible through the chamber's glass ceiling.

"Eyes of Adonis," swore the Shemite. "I almost wish we would find the damned demon rather than continue this sneaking about in the dark." His stomach emitted a loud growl. "I'm also becoming somewhat hungry," he added needlessly. Conan flashed him a quick grin.

"Easy, my friend. Let us finish our sweep around the chamber, then we'll have a bit of bread before we start down those stairs again."

"Damn me, what I wouldn't give to be tipping a jug back in the Red Hand right now." Shamtare turned away and the Cimmerian seized his shoulder. The Shemite felt as if his complaining stomach chose that moment to plummet down through the floor. "What is it?" he gasped.

"Look."

Two figures had entered the Chamber of Conjuring through the opposite doorway, and now hurried to the room's center. It was Adrastus and Balthano, both moving quickly and fearfully. The wizard went directly to the dais and knelt on the second step. As Adrastus laid a shallow bronze bowl upon the ebony table, Conan saw his limbs tremble as if with fever. The Kothian wasted no time; his voice rose immediately in a peculiar, repetitious chant. He rolled up his left sleeve, pulled a small dagger from his doublet, and gashed his naked forearm without so much as a wince. He pinched the wound over the bronze bowl, squeezed out a thin stream of scarlet droplets. The chant did not falter, but echoed hollowly inside the expansive chamber.

Balthano made a quick circuit of the room. He slowed when he passed the doorway through which Conan and Shamtare stood hidden in deep shadow. Then he returned to his master's side.

"Should we tell them we're here?" asked Shamtare.

"Nay," grumbled the barbarian. "We might interrupt the wizard's magicks. All this sorcery sickens me, anyway. Let us keep on to the stairs."

"Gods!" The voice was Balthano's, shocked and frantic.

A black figure had followed the sorcerer and his manservant into the chamber and now stood silently just within the doorway across from Conan and Shamtare. The thing in black robes edged with cloth-of-gold cocked its narrow head at the kneeling form of Adrastus. Other than that, it was motionless.

The Kothian's chanted words acquired a shrill edge and his voice shook as he spoke, but the hypnotic cadence remained intact. Balthano took a single step toward the demon, then hesitated, unable to decide his course of action.

"What can we do?" whispered Shamtare urgently. "What?"

Conan drew his sword.

The golden-fleshed thing suddenly looked to the great ceiling and stroked at an ear with its left hand. It tilted its head, and an almost unnoticeable frown creased the smooth brow, as if it heard something inaudible to the men. Then the plague demon floated forward, toward Adrastus, ignoring Balthano.

The mage's voice grew shrill and tremulous, but the chant continued with unswervable, single-minded desperation. Balthano drew his black daggers, but stood still, unable to bring himself to attack the creature that threatened his master.

Conan leapt into the light and ran a dozen steps into the chamber. He halted and threw his arms above his head.

"Ho there, devil!" The Cimmerian's shout rang from the walls. The many-tinted rays of the sun burned upon his bright mail, limned his determined features with scarlet and gold. "Over here!"

The plague demon stopped beside the black dais, a mere step from the kneeling wizard's side. It might have reached out and laid a hand upon his shoulder, but instead it stared past the sorcerer at the gesticulating form of the barbarian.

Conan brandished his shining blade and roared in wordless defiance. Behind him, white-faced Shamtare came into the light and jeered at the demon.

Its lips parted, exposing the ebony needles of its fangs in a nightmarish approximation of a human smile. And it moved with fluid grace around the dais toward Conan. The demon seemed to fly across the mosaic floor, covering the distance between them in mere heartbeats.

The men turned and ran.

The corridor opened before Shamtare like a black funnel. His heart seemed determined to beat its way out of his ribcage and through his breastplate. Conan's long legs drew him effortlessly ahead of the Shemite, but terror led the old mercenary to discover a fresh and youthful vigor in his own limbs. The marble floor seemed to whisk away beneath his booted feet.

They hurtled into the arched chamber at the top of the spiral stairway. Conan did not hesitate an instant, but leapt down the waiting steps with a shout of encouragement to his friend. Shamtare reached the banister and was unable to restrain himself from snapping a swift glance behind.

Their pursuer came on, a dark form that moved along the shadowed corridor like a black vapor seething up from hell. Terror slammed adrenaline through Shamtare's body. With an incoherent curse, he stumbled onto the stairs, and lost his balance. His foot slipped on the heavy carpeting and dropped over the rim of a step. Pain sheared into his ankle like an ax-blade. With a cry that was as much rage as dismay, Shamtare's arms pinwheeled and he fell forward. The old mercenary had enough martial training to curl into a ball and roll as he hit the steps, a move that saved him probable broken wrists had he attempted to break the fall with his hands. The edges of the stairs bruised his body and drove the breath from his lungs. Then his arms and legs sprang out and halted his tumbling fall. He slid painfully along, then used his headlong impetus to shove himself to his feet and continue his flight. He reeled down the steps, half out of control, his ankle aflame with pain. The spiral stair seemed to unspool bottomlessly before him.

Ahead, on the curved wall of the great staircase, Conan stood in the open doorway to the baron's private chambers. Such was Shamtare's momentum that the barbarian had to reach out, grab the older man's arm, and drag him physically through the doorway. The mercenary hit the floor on his knees, wheezing great breaths that blew spittle into his beard. Conan slammed the door and saw that the bolt was shattered.

"Ymir! Get up, man. There's no time to rest. Maybe we can lose the demon if we flee through the secret passage."

Shamtare looked up to see Conan's broad back recede down the hall toward the room of the throne and balcony. He heaved himself to his feet with a grimace of effort and followed.

Cool air circulated through the open throne room. Shamtare spared a single glance at the clear blue sky that shone promisingly beyond the balcony's rail, then focused on the form of the Cimmerian. Conan stood at the wall where they had found the secret panel. His hands moved quickly and fruitlessly over the featureless marble.

"Hell's gates, someone's closed the damned door!"

Shamtare saw that a new body now lay beside the baron's blasted corpse. He was about to say something about it to Conan when he heard the door swing open behind him.

The Shemite looked back over his shoulder and saw the black figure of the plague demon glide over the threshold. He met its eyes helplessly. The thing's effortless movement seemed slow, yet it was halfway down the hall before he could tear his gaze away. Shamtare turned and hobbled painfully toward his friend.

"Conan! It comes!"

"Curse this door! We're trapped!" The barbarian smote the wall with a fist and caused the marble panel to boom like a bass drum. When he looked up, Conan saw his comrade stumble over a low bench and sprawl to the floor.

The shadow figure of the plague demon was suddenly there, looming over the fallen man like a storm cloud.

With a foul curse, the barbarian lunged away from the wall. Shamtare rolled onto his back and tried to drag himself away from his pursuer. The demon bent at the waist, and reached out a golden hand to touch the crawling mercenary's leg.

Conan howled a wild war cry and kicked a chair aside, sent it clattering across the room to crash against the balcony rail. The thing looked up from its prey and fixed dead, black eyes on him. The Cimmerian did not falter, but thrust forward with his sword extended in a flashing blur that cleft the demon through the center of its breast. Conan grunted with the brutal impact; pain shot up his wrist. It was as if he had driven his weapon into a ship's mast.

The demon shuffled back to keep its balance. Its black-clad foot slapped lightly on the marble floor and Shamtare had the incongruous revelation that it was the first time he had heard the demon make a sound of any kind.

Conan released his hilt, sidestepped lithely, and automatically drew his dagger. His blue eyes burned upon his transfixed foe with undimmed fury.

The gleaming length of the barbarian's broadsword had passed completely through the demon's torso. The leather-wrapped hilt was fixed to its black breast like some grotesque adornment. Silver steel stood out more than two feet between its shoulder blades, unsullied by blood. The thing regarded the hilt curiously. It plucked at the quillions with one idle hand, as if only vaguely interested in the nature of the weapon that pierced it.

"Bones of Crom! Is there no killing this thing?" As Conan swiftly bent to help Shamtare to his feet, the demon gripped the sharp-edged blade with both hands and drew the sword easily from its body. It examined the clean steel for a moment, then cast the weapon aside and advanced on the two men.

"Run, Conan!" shouted Shamtare. "I'll hinder it!"

Then came a sound like the tolling of some colossal gong. The men were struck by a ringing wave of noise so deep and pervasive that it thrummed upon their skin and reverberated in their marrow.

The demon stopped in its tracks and turned its angular head to the open balcony. Shamtare grabbed Conan's shoulder. His mouth worked frantically as he yelled questions inaudible in the eldritch din. The bell-like intonation was an unrelenting presence that saturated the senses, filled the ears, and blurred the vision.

Beyond the balcony, day became night.

The floor dropped away beneath their feet. It felt as if the tower had suddenly collapsed in upon itself and the throne room now plunged intact toward the earth. The men reeled for a suspended moment of nauseating vertigo as they felt the entire palace plummet into an unguessable void.

Shamtare fell, his mouth stretched wide in a soundless scream. Conan kept his balance in a fighting crouch, dagger held at the ready. His eyes rolled like those of a trapped animal.

The tolling ceased abruptly, and the horrific sensation of free-fall was simultaneously arrested with a jarring lurch. The plague demon was knocked to the floor. Only the barbarian kept his feet. Conan was reminded of a heavy object tied with a rope and hurled off a cliff to drop until the rope went taut and halted its fall with a savage jolt.

The sound of falling objects and breaking glass echoed for a long moment. Then there was a silence as complete and ominous as that of the deepest Stygian tomb.

Both Shamtare and the plague demon came to their feet at once. Though the Shemite and the Cimmerian immediately backed away from the invulnerable horror, it did not seem to notice them. Instead, it stared out over the balcony, then wheeled and fled from the chamber.

"What in Ishtar's name?" croaked Shamtare. "Look!"

The curtains that flanked the open balcony no longer billowed with the gentle afternoon breeze. They hung limp and lifeless. And they no longer framed a view of the city of Dulcine. The balcony opened on absolute darkness.

"It seems the wizard was successful," said Conan. The Cimmerian's voice was steady, but a chill fell over his neck and shoulders like a mantle of hoarfrost.

"Mitra help us." Shamtare's curse sounded much like a prayer. "Where did the demon go? Why didn't it finish us?"

"I wager it must have known what happened and where it was. Set alone knows where it went."

Shamtare combed back his thick hair with both hands and drew a deep, shuddering breath. "I, for one, am glad it's gone. Look there, who's that lying next to the baron?"

The two men walked across the throne room to where a new body lay silently beside the withered corpse of the ruler of Dulcine.

Conan retrieved his sword and peered warily over the balcony. His eyes met a blackness of such uniform solidity that it was almost tangible. His vision began to adjust, and it was as if he stared into a vast well of unthinkable depth. A cluster of tiny lights glimmered at the rim of his perception like a strewn handful of gems, half-lost in an ocean of darkness.

Conan blinked, shuddered, and looked away.

Shamtare knelt beside the new body. It was so ravaged by plague that the remaining flesh resembled tar that had melted and then solidified upon desiccated bone. Even though the corpse was curled in upon itself, enough of the armor was visible to send a sick pulse of recognition through the old mercenary.

"It's Pezur," said Conan. "Behold my armband."

"Oh Mitra," whispered Shamtare. "He was but a lad. He might have been my son."

The arm thrust through the cloth-wrapped ringlet had been reduced to a blackened remnant one-third its former size. The skeletal hand still gripped the hilt of his shortsword. When Shamtare gripped the armlet and lifted, the brittle limb broke in half with a sound like the snap of a dry twig. The Shemite cut away the cloth that wrapped the armband, then wiped it on a bit of velvet torn from a couch, and stashed it in his backpack.

Shamtare shook his head slowly. "Pezur."

"He died with a sword in his hand. A man can ask for no more than that," said Conan. "Now's no time to mourn."

"You're right." The old mercenary looked up. "What now?"

"Now we find that thrice-cursed wizard and stick by his side until he gets us out of this nether world."

Conan and Shamtare left the baron's private chambers and headed back up the stairs. In the silent throne room they left behind, the limitless ocean of primordial darkness beyond the balcony's rail gleamed with new lights. Tiny scarlet flecks, as frigidly bright as an earthly aurora, circled one another with restless purpose and, almost imperceptibly, drew nearer.

The curtains twitched, as if in the first subtle breeze of a coming storm.

23

The thing that resembled a man moved up the stairs as swiftly as it could. All it had learned and grown to take for granted about itself and the world around it had altered abruptly and without warning. The thunderous tolling and the dizzy plunge of the palace had been strange and terrible enough, but what followed was even worse.

The plague demon had felt the world disappear. As the balcony went dark, Dulcine's familiar skyline had vanished, and with it all the life that the demon had sensed around it.

The few survivors that wandered in the city, the ring of men outside the walls, even the distant glow of the clustered mass of lives beyond the southwest horizon—all were gone. The vast mass of the earth and the great heavenly light that shone down upon it were gone. The only thing that remained was the stone structure in which the demon had been born. All this it had sensed in an instant.

Although uncertainty was not new to it, the displacement of the palace created a deeper confusion than the demon had ever known, disrupted its position of centrality in the universe, assaulted its infant-like ego by thrusting it into a new and uncontrollable world. Its powerful senses reached out into the void that surrounded the palace and encountered forms of life it could scarcely identify as such. From the demon's initial confusion grew new emotions: anger, resentment, and fear.

There were creatures in this new world that were not at all like the men upon whom it preyed; unknown things that possessed life of a sort that the demon could not destroy. These things reacted to its presence, stirred, and took notice. The plague demon felt alien senses probe the palace and examine the demon in much the same fashion as it could sense humans. The creature felt horribly vulnerable, naked beneath the gaze of unknown and implacable predators.

So it fled. In all the city there was but one place into which its senses could not reach, one place impenetrable to its mystic sight.

It remembered the raven it had seen beside the Freshet and knew envy for the first time in its short life. The bird could fly away from its enemies. The demon reached the arched chamber at the top of the stairs and hesitated, looked back over a dark shoulder. It laid a hand upon its breast and felt the wound there slowly close beneath its fingers. The black-maned man had shown the audacity to attack it. He had driven his steel thorn through its body. He had stayed on his feet when the palace had fallen into this terrible new world.

Perhaps the black-haired one was responsible for all that had happened. Someone had to be responsible. The demon resolved to take the black-haired one as soon as possible. It would be a pleasure to kill such a bothersome creature. The plague demon moved into the circular hallway and its thoughts of revenge were replaced by a fearful emptiness. Before, it had been able to take whomever it pleased, whenever it pleased. Now it was thwarted, threatened, and seeking refuge.

"I am not the master of this world. I am not death. What am I?"

The demon's tormented questions went unanswered as it fled, seeking the protective haven of the Chamber of Conjuring.

24

Adrastus crowed in triumph, and lifted shaking hands to the lofty dome of stained glass. Its garish, multicolored panes were now uniformly black.

"I've done it!"

"What now?" asked Balthano, beside him. "How long before the demon is gone?"

"I've done it!" The sorcerer spun off the dais and danced across the black and white tiles of the chamber's floor. "Would that Tolbeth-Khar was here to see me now! The old dotard would choke on his envy!"

"Master, you have my congratulations, but we have to—"

"Silence!" bellowed Adrastus. His wild dance came to a stop and he walked quickly to stand face to face with Balthano. "What do we have to do now, pray tell? What do I need you for anyway? I need no one!"

The Argossean pressed his hands together over his breast and licked his lips nervously. "No, milord. You need no one."

The mage seemed to look through his servant, his eyes blank and distant. "So many days of bending to the will of others. Smiling and nodding and letting them have their way. Damn them all!"

"Yes, milord," mumbled Balthano. He didn't know what else to say.

"I've failed in my mission here, you know. Nothing can salvage my plan. Those idiots ruined it. But my time of failures is done. It's over. Now I have the power and the will to take what I deserve!"

"Yes, milord," said Balthano.

Adrastus looked over his manservant's shoulder and his brown eyes flew wide. His mouth dropped open and a choked and meaningless syllable came forth. For an instant, the Argossean thought his master was stricken with some fit; then he understood, and turned to see the plague demon enter the chamber.

It glided purposefully toward the room's center, stopped beside the black dais, and lifted its face to stare straight up through the domed ceiling. The presence of the mage and his companion seemed to make no impression upon it. The deep black eyes searched the equal blackness above, and though the golden face was as expressionless as ever, there was an air of tense anxiety about the creature, visible in its clenched fists and rigid posture.

The men had just enough time to recognize that the plague-demon was not going to attack them before Conan and Shamtare came into the chamber. Adrastus and Balthano met the mercenaries beside the doorway, and the four men regarded the demon from what seemed a safe distance.

"You were successful?" asked Shamtare.

"Yes," panted the sorcerer. "But the unholy thing is wiser than I imagined."

"What?" said Conan harshly. He shot a hard glance at the plague demon, saw that it remained motionless, then turned a scarcely less hostile gaze upon the Kothian. "What do you mean, wizard?"

"Attack it!" blurted Adrastus. "Wound it! We've got to get it out of this chamber!"

"Explain yourself, man." The barbarian gripped the mage's shoulder with a hand like a steel clamp. "I ran my broadsword right through the thing. I should have pierced the heart and shorn through the spine. It tugged the blade out as if it were a splinter. Attacking it is a fool's errand."

"Oh merciful gods! Don't you understand? It knows that the Chamber of Conjuring offers it a measure of protection. In here, I'm afraid that it's invisible to the predators outside!"

"What?" Conan's and Shamtare's voices merged in one note of incredulity. Balthano slumped back against the wall.

"The chamber," said Adrastus. "The dome is constructed to offer the sorcerer who uses it a measure of protection. As it intensifies the sorcery of the user, it masks him from outside scrutiny. The magical wards built into the chamber to protect human conjurers may well work to shield the demon from the attentions of the creatures we hoped would slay it."

"Ishtar," swore Shamtare. "Did you not think of this beforehand?"

"How could I know? How could it know?" burst out Adrastus. "Its senses must be far keener than I dreamed."

"Then we're safe from the things that dwell in this world as long as the demon stays in the chamber?" asked Balthano uncertainly.

Adrastus used a velvet sleeve to mop his pale brow. His eyes were haggard. "I don't know. It was outside the chamber's walls for our first few minutes on this plane. I... I don't know." His face hardened. "I do know that we must drive it out of here."

The sorcerer knelt suddenly and drew from his bosom the roll of velvet that held the ten slim blades of crystal. He unrolled the black fabric on the tiles and plucked each blade from its pocket.

"What's this?" asked the Cimmerian skeptically.

"His weapon of choice," said Balthano. Conan thought he detected a slight trace of scorn in the Argossean's voice. "Velvet and blades are all of a piece. He lays his hands upon the golden prints and then merely points at his foe, and the crystal knives fly true to their mark. It requires no skill. He said even I could use it. Cursed thing is probably worth a fortune."

"Crom," rumbled the barbarian, and stepped away from the kneeling magician. Under Conan's watchful gaze, Adrastus slapped both palms down on the glittering handprints at either end of the velvet strip. He held them there a moment while his face twisted in what might have been pain. Then his hands lifted and both forefingers pointed at the still form of the plague demon.

"Him."

Conan flinched as the transparent blades leapt up from the velvet and hurtled across the room like a flight of glass arrows. They struck the demon in the breast and throat, creating a volley of dull, heavy impacts that reminded the Cimmerian of tent pegs driven into hard clay. The demon staggered, and lowered its eyes from the nighted dome overhead.

"Hah!" yelled Adrastus wildly. He shoved the velvet strip back into his doublet and rose to his feet. "Wake up and see how I defy you! You are nothing but a mistake of sorcery! A foolish accident that I have come to correct! Hah!" The wizard waved his arms, attempting to antagonize the thing and hold its attention.

But it was more concerned with the crystal blades imbedded in its torso than the antics of the magician. Long amber fingers closed around the faceted tips of the crystals and drew them out. Each was examined in turn, then dropped.

The successive blades struck the floor without breaking and bounced with a sound like golden bells. When the last crystal lay on the tiles, the demon looked at Adrastus and cocked its head.

The sorcerer backed toward the doorway. "Over here, curse you!"

The demon started toward the men as abruptly and unpredictably as a shift in the wind. Curses broke from the little group as they headed as one for the doorway. They fled the chamber and their boots echoed in the dim marble hall.

The party sprinted along the curved passage and burst into the arched chamber at the top of the stairway.

"Hold!" bellowed Conan.

"The hell you say!" gasped Shamtare, poised on the top step with one hand on the rail. Balthano and Adrastus, already on the stairs, hesitated long enough to look back at the Cimmerian.

"Does it follow us?" asked Conan.

All eyes went to the dark mouth of the hallway. There was no movement there.

"Father Dagon and Mother Hydra!" swore the sorcerer. "It won't leave the chamber!"

"Then what are we to do?" said Shamtare.

"There's only one thing to do," said Conan grimly. "If the creatures that prey upon the demon can only find it outside of that chamber, then we must do whatever is required to drive it out of the chamber and into their sight."

"What do you mean?"

"Hallooo!" The voice resounded along the walls of the great stairwell from someplace beneath. "Ho, comrades!"

The men looked at one another. It was Prince Eoreck's voice. There was the thump of hasty feet on carpeting, and the prince came into view below. He gestured frantically. "I've found something! I think we can get out now!" Eoreck spun in a swirl of his scarlet cape, and trotted back down the steps out of sight.

"Do we follow him?" asked Balthano.

"What is he babbling about?" Shamtare wondered. "Has he lost his reason?"

"Such as he had. Let him go," growled the barbarian. "We've work to do."

"No." Adrastus started down the stairs again. "We've got to see what the idiot is doing. If that simpleton meddles in the wrong place, he could bring hell itself down upon us."

"As if we weren't there already," Conan grumbled.

JOHN C. HOCKING

They followed the wizard down the long stair until they came to the broad landing on the second floor. From this vantage point they caught a brief glimpse of the prince as he strode into the antechamber adjoining the palace's front doors. Adrastus began to run, taking the last flight of steps in a stumbling rush.

"Prince! Stop!" The sorcerer passed from sight into the foyer, and it was only moments later that Conan and the others joined him.

Prince Eoreck stood bent over before the great double doors. The glossy arch of the massive oak portal framed his brightly clad body. He pressed the side of his black-haired head to the smooth wood, his aspect tense with attention.

"Listen!" Eoreck lifted his ear from the door long enough to wave them closer and frown impatiently.

The men walked forward and slowed as they drew near.

The small room seemed claustrophobically narrow after the open stairwell, and Conan was keenly aware that it formed a cul-de-sac. The barbarian peered back through the doorway, half expecting to see the plague demon coming down the stair to corner them. Balthano hung back beside the Cimmerian, while Shamtare stepped forward and scowled at the prince. Adrastus stood close beside Eoreck and extended his hands imploringly.

"My lord, please do not—"

Eoreck interrupted. "Hush. Listen!"

For a pregnant moment, all was utterly still. Then came a slow, soft sliding sound, as of a great smooth surface slithering over stone. It came from outside, and seemed to pass ponderously over the door and the wall around it. The sound had a sinister pervasiveness; it seemed to blanket the face of the entire palace, as though some monstrous serpent had wrapped titanic coils around the keep and now drew them inexorably tighter.

"Do you hear that? They've come to let us out! *Hallooo!*"

Adrastus seized the prince by the shoulders and shook him violently. The wizard's face was transfigured with rage and fear.

"Be silent, you fool! You don't want to see what's on the other side of that door!"

Eoreck's eyes rolled drunkenly in his flushed face. He snarled wine fumes at the mage, twisted out of his grip and shoved him away. Adrastus stumbled back two paces and snatched the envenomed dagger from his doublet.

"Hallooo!" The prince thumped the door with a fist. "We're here! We're here!"

A tremendous blow slammed against the doors, shook the massive timbers in their sturdy frame with a power unmatched by any earthly battering ram. Eoreck reeled backward and sat down awkwardly on the floor. He gaped stupidly at Adrastus. The incredible blow echoed like a deep peal of thunder through the vaulted halls of the palace, then a second impact hammered the doors with force enough to crack the heavy timbers and smite the ears with deafening sound.

"Run!" Adrastus turned a face as pale as milk to the mercenaries. "Run—"

There was a mighty ear-rending crash as the doors burst inward in a blinding explosion of sundered bits of wood. A rain of lumber and splinters fell among the men, who staggered and shrank away. Eoreck was hurled back across the polished floor. What remained of the doors flapped in blasted ruins from the mangled hinges.

A wall of doughy white substance trembled in the shattered doorway. Its center puckered, extended, and then suddenly funneled into a fat tentacle that snaked into the palace.

"Don't move!" screamed Adrastus. "If you love your life and your soul, stand absolutely still!" Such was the frenzied urgency of his voice that the mercenaries froze in mid-flight. Some had got as far as the door, but most stood within a few paces of the invader.

The length of groping flesh was as big around as the battering ram it had emulated. It thrust blindly into the chamber, then swayed from side to side as if taking a scent.

Eoreck stood right beside it. His eyes sought the door helplessly while his white lips twisted without sound, though whether in silent curses or silent prayer none could say. It pushed past him.

Shamtare stood stock-still as the blunt tip of the thick tentacle drifted to and fro in the air before his face. It stopped moving. Its gelatinous gray-white surface began to roll and bubble like boiling suet. The tentacle lowered heavily to the floor, struck the marble with a mushy slap, then the first six feet of its length bent straight up at a right angle. The upraised tentacle-tip rippled and changed form fluidly. Lengths of flesh like knotted ropes broke free of its mass, whipped about, and then swiftly resorbed. The mercenary watched in ghastly fascination as it pinched narrow at its center, then shaped crude arms and shoulders topped by a head like a smashed blob of dough. A black-hole mouth appeared in the head and began to scream.

Overcome with horror, Shamtare collapsed, his hands pressed tightly over his face. The tentacle did not fall upon him, but hovered above his quivering body. The scream rose and fell without pause for breath, an inhuman, drawn-out wail that tore at the nerves.

At the door, Conan squeezed his hilt until his knuckles went white as bleached bone. His face was frozen in a rictus-snarl of atavistic horror and repulsion.

The tentacle's new-formed head stopped screaming. The lipless mouth sealed itself and disappeared. The thing's flesh continued to ripple and metamorphose.

"Stay still," said Adrastus. His voice trembled. "And be quiet. If it wanted to kill us, we would be dead already."

The only sound in the room was the liquid susurration of the thing's transforming flesh. A startlingly blue eye opened on the side of the lumpy head and rolled wildly. The orb seemed to plow through the head's pasty substance until it arrived in roughly the position of a normal human eye. A larger second eye, three-pupiled and scarlet, opened beside it. Beneath the eyes, another lipless mouth peeled open and gaped. The human-shape grew smoother and more symmetrical. It began to take on the embryonic aspect of a woman.

Against the wizard's advice, Eoreck moved slowly along the tentacle's length, approaching Shamtare, with an eye on the door. The fallen mercenary had recovered himself somewhat and now gingerly inched away from the thing that had thrust itself into the palace of Dulcine. Eoreck stepped carefully beside Shamtare, and was just contemplating a quick break for the door when the newly formed woman on the tentacle's tip abruptly leaned forward and thrust her waxen face into his. The mouth dropped open and a sound like the buzz and chirp of nocturnal insects came forth. The white throat worked and rippled.

Aghast, Prince Eoreck took a step backward and a flaccid hand whipped up and dropped on his shoulder.

Fingers separated in the meaty mass and gripped his upper arm firmly. The porridge-white visage smoothed and softened until it was the well-defined face of a handsome woman, normal in all but color. The eyes darkened to black and the mouth grew proper teeth. The hair was a tangle of pale, wormlike stalks.

"Ker-ith-rakar," said the woman-thing. "Lanz trinzini lob zan." The voice was recognizably human, though it was as thick and lifeless as if it had been forced from the throat of a drowned corpse. The words were of no language any of the party had ever heard.

Eoreck, held in place by the otherworldly nightmare, stared as if mesmerized into the woman-thing's face. His eyes had met hers and could not look away.

"Mang a zan lonztro," said the thing. "Where is it?"

Its voice modulated, became deep, firm, and imperiously commanding.

An icicle melted along Conan's spine. To see the shuddering wall of gray-white flesh in the doorway thrust out a pseudopod that grew ever more into the semblance of a woman toyed with

The Thing grows a beautiful woman's head
as the gang stares in horror

human sanity. The Cimmerian's skin crawled as he battled an almost overwhelming impulse to either flee or hurl himself upon the unnatural monstrosity with steel in hand.

"What?" croaked Eoreck. His mouth was dry, and the word crumbled against his palate like dead leaves.

"Where is it, little things? I hunger."

"It seeks the plague demon," said Adrastus. "It can't find the demon because it has concealed itself in the Chamber of Conjuring."

The prince leaned away from the heavy hand that held his shoulder. It would not release him. A pointed purple tongue poked out of its mouth and licked at the full lips. The eyes of the woman-thing remained locked with his own, and he stared into their fathomless, unknowable depths.

"Where is it, little thing?" it asked Eoreck.

"In the chamber, under the dome," he whispered.

"Dome?" The hand fell from the prince's shoulder and swung as bonelessly as a length of cable at the woman-thing's side.

"Yes." Eoreck took a tentative step away. He made a tent of his hands, touching his fingertips together to illustrate a dome. "Under the dome of colored glass."

The thing blinked and its jaw fell open, but instead of speaking, its entire body bobbed forward as swiftly as the strike of a viper. The limp arms whipped around Eoreck's body in an all-consuming embrace. The prince's terrified shriek was cut off as his face was pressed into the thing's malleable breast. His boots skidded over marble, then lifted free of the floor and kicked in midair. The woman-shape softened like a wax statue under a flame. Its body flowed around Eoreck's struggling form as its head lost all pretense of human features and drooped over its prey.

The huge tentacle abruptly withdrew, pulled back through the shattered doors with the prince still writhing as he disappeared into its mass.

Then it was gone, and the doorway was a portal opening upon a darkness like none of earth. It was a vertiginous void of preternatural blackness, a lost space between the worlds.

25

"Crom," said Conan softly. There was cold sweat on his body. "Is it gone?" Shamtare stood and made a show of dusting himself off.

"Yes," said Adrastus. "For the moment. I doubt it will be able to breach the dome, though."

Balthano was silent, afraid to speak lest he stammer and seem a coward. All four men stared out the blasted doorway into the black unknown. Shamtare crossed his arms over his barrel chest as he peered into the void.

"It looks much like the sky after nightfall. Almost as if we sailed a ship through the night. Are those white lights stars?"

"No," said Adrastus quietly. "They are universes."

"Truly?" said Shamtare, without comprehension. "And the red ones?"

"Red lights?" Adrastus came to the old mercenary's side in a rush. "Where?"

"There," said Conan. "Like scarlet candles. They're moving." As the Cimmerian pointed, the mage peered down his muscular arm and saw a collection of lurid pinpoints, like torches in the hands of a distant mob. The tiny flames swirled about in a vortex that ebbed in and out of visibility, half drowned in the darkness. The men saw them wax suddenly larger and brighter.

"Set's fangs! The Hounds! Get away from the doorway," sputtered Adrastus. "Get back!"

The group withdrew into the palace and closed the foyer's inner doors at the wizard's frantic urging. Eager hands shot the slender bolt.

"What now, sorcerer?" said Conan. "What horror will your plan yield next?"

Adrastus tore at his hair, as stricken with fear as he had been when the pallid tentacle groped into the palace. "The crimson lights. It's the Hounds. The Hounds of Thandalos! Oh gods!"

Shamtare scratched in his beard and grimaced. "Whatever these hounds are, they can't be any worse than the thing we just saw." The Shemite looked from Adrastus to Conan. "Can they?"

"The Hounds! That I should ever encounter them. Oh my gods!" The Kothian buried his face in his hands, only to have Conan pull the hands away and shake him forcibly.

"Keep a grip on yourself, wizard."

"You don't understand," sobbed Adrastus.

"Understand, hell," grated the barbarian. "I understand that you're our only way out of this pit, so you'd best keep your wits."

The Cimmerian's big hands pushed the mage against the wall and released him. Adrastus blinked and drew the back of a fist over his mouth. He nodded numbly.

"You're right. Of course, you're right." The sorcerer abruptly stiffened and turned to the foyer's bolted doors.

A hollow booming, as of mighty wings, swelled and resounded within the antechamber. It ceased, and sharp clacks echoed inside the shut room as though great talons lit upon the marble floor.

Adrastus cringed away from the bolted door. Audible through

the panels was an ugly snuffling. The sound was deep, liquid, and insistent. An acrid stench came to Conan, stung his nostrils like an acid mist. As he strained his ears to hear within the suddenly silent chamber, he became horribly convinced that whatever had come into that room was also listening intently for him.

With a quick beckoning gesture, the Cimmerian started up the stairs to the second-floor landing. Though he set a swift pace, the others kept close behind. Even Shamtare, who still favored his injured ankle, apparently had no difficulty in keeping up with the barbarian. They moved with little sound.

The group did not hesitate, but headed directly for the spiral stair. Conan fell back beside the laboring Adrastus.

"If I can get the plague demon out of the domed chamber, you're certain these things will hunt it instead of us?"

"Yes," gasped the mage. "Yes. Our souls are mere morsels beside its sorcerous might."

"Then I shall drive it out of the chamber if I have to hew the thing to bits."

The words were scarcely out of the barbarian's mouth when the stairs shuddered beneath their feet. The entire palace rolled slowly, like a ship on a rising tide. The men caught their balance, cursed, and kept on.

When they finally reached the arched chamber at the summit of the stair, Adrastus dropped to all fours, purple of face and wheezing for every breath. Shamtare sat on the uppermost step and massaged his injured ankle, while Balthano leaned over the rail to watch the stairs below. For a moment, all were content to rest and let their heartbeats slow.

The floor dropped, then give a giddy lurch from side to side, like a heavy branch swaying in a storm wind. From somewhere in the palace below came a deep cry like the howl of an outsized wolf. The ululation rose from a bass growl to a shrill and grating keen that rang with hideous hunger and unalloyed hate.

"Gods," panted Adrastus. He sat back on his heels and regarded the Cimmerian. "The palace is under siege. The dwellers in this dimension have come in force to investigate our intrusion."

"Shamtare, give me your gauntlets and bracers," said Conan. "And I'll take your cape too, Balthano. If I'm to tangle with this living plague, I'd best protect my flesh from its touch however I can."

Shamtare cast a glance at Balthano. He half expected the wiry Argossean to take exception to the Cimmerian's curt request. But the mercenary tugged the cape from his shoulders and offered it to Conan without protest. The floor heaved gently beneath their feet.

"Fruitless," muttered Adrastus. He shut his eyes and swayed to and fro on his velvet-clad knees. "My plans, my dreams, have failed me once again. What's the use, barbarian? Who among us truly believes you can succeed? You yourself said that your sword was powerless to harm the plague demon. It's mad to try."

"Is it mad to want to perish in battle instead of cowering in a corner until hunted down and devoured by demons out of hell?"

"The oil," said Balthano suddenly.

"What?" Conan and Adrastus looked to Balthano, but the Argossean didn't lift his head. He stayed in position, leaning against the banister and keeping watch on the stairs below. His narrow face was pinched with strain and glossed with a fine sheen of perspiration.

"The oil that repulses the demon. If you have any left, give it to the barbarian." Balthano's voice was little more than a whisper.

"What is this oil?" asked Conan.

"Doubtless another thing that our friend the wizard neglected to inform us about," snorted Shamtare. "Surely we should be accustomed to our sorcerer's little secrets by now."

"Shut up, old man. You'll get what's coming to you eventually," said Balthano, without looking away from the stairs. "Let the barbarian try to drive the demon into the open, Adrastus. What have we lost if he fails? We're no worse off with the Northman dead. Give him the oil if you have it."

Adrastus got his feet beneath him and, still breathing heavily, took a slender silver vial from a pocket in his doublet. He passed it to Conan, who regarded the object without enthusiasm.

"The vial contains an oil that the plague demon finds repugnant. I created it in one of my failed attempts to develop a cure for the scourge. It will not prevent the monster from attacking, but it may cause the demon to hesitate before it grapples with you."

"I'll take any advantage I can get," said Conan. He pulled the little cork and waved the vial beneath his nose. His face screwed up in a distasteful grimace. "By Erlik, it smells like a moldy dungeon." Despite his words, the barbarian was shortly smoothing the cool oil over his bronzed limbs. At the advice of Adrastus, he smeared the substance on his clothing, armor, and boots.

"I'll take what's left," said the mage. "For safekeeping."

Conan gave him a cold look, drew his broadsword, and poured the last of the oil along the blade's edge. He turned the sword over and allowed the thick liquid to coat the polished steel.

"If I can get it out of the chamber, you must help me drive it toward the stair," said the barbarian. The men nodded and Conan turned away without another word. He strode easily down the curved hall toward the Chamber of Conjuring as another demonic howl, bestial and athirst, rose up the stairwell and hung in the air like a pall.

26

Conan stood with his broad back to the wall beside the open portal for a brief moment, as if gathering his strength.

Then he swung around the corner and plunged headlong into the chamber.

"Ho, devil! I've come to send you back to hell!"

The plague demon stood at the center of the circular room, its head tilted back unnaturally as it stared straight up at the domed ceiling. It lowered its somber face to the barbarian and regarded him blankly. The black garments rippled, though there was no breeze to stir them.

In the white glare of the faceted light crystals, the stained-glass ceiling arched up in an interlocking web of reflective panels. On the other side of the glass, something waited. Suspended just above the wizard-wards of the dome was a titanic wall of crawling, amorphous flesh. It rippled and rolled like the surface of a lava flow. Strange limbs extended from its mass and were resorbed. Fanged mouths opened, raged in silence, and then were sealed forever. Countless dark eyes, polished disks of jet, peered in hungrily.

Conan drove forward without dissembling, without granting the blasphemy above the dome a second look, running straight for the silent demon in an attempt to close with it immediately. A Cimmerian battle cry burst from his lips. The barbarian held his sword ready for an unstoppable two-handed slash aimed at his foe's neck. He would see how the demon fared when bereft of its head.

The creature watched the man hurtle toward it, heard his boots hammer on the patterned floor, and idly lifted its right hand to stem the berserker attack. Conan halted his mad rush with a suddenness that set his boots sliding across the smooth tiles. He drew back and delivered his two-handed cut, not at his foe's neck, but at the proffered arm. The oiled blade tore through the plague demon's dense substance and sheared the extended arm away just below the elbow. The severed limb flew off, lost form in midair, and struck the floor as a rope of viscous slime. The demon's mouth dropped open and emitted a cry like that of a huge bird. It staggered back, its dull eyes focused on the black and bloodless stump of its right arm.

Conan felt an exhilarating, galvanic surge of battle-rage, for he had wounded the invulnerable. The mage's mystic oil lent his sword the power to cause the demon true pain.

Another fearsome war cry exploded from his lips as he swung his blade back to deal the demon a second blow. And the creature leapt forward, light as thistledown on the wind, hand and stump reaching for his face.

The Cimmerian recovered with pantherish speed, and his decapitating slash became a desperate thrust. The point drove into the black-clad midriff and stopped the demon's lunge. Again, the weird birdlike cry came from the expressionless face. When the creature grasped the sharp edges of the blade that impaled it, Conan saw that the stump was speedily growing a new hand. Both the complete, amber-toned hand and the new limb, a sickly white and fingerless tentacle, seized upon his sword and jerked it free.

Stunned with horror, the barbarian wrenched his weapon loose with a spasmodic heave that sent two fingers and a tentacle-tip sailing free to splatter on the tiles in liquid foulness.

The plague demon extended hands that mended themselves even as Conan looked on. He whipped his gleaming steel around his head, and the demon darted into action as lightly as a gymnast. The thing's good hand shot out, seized his uplifted left wrist, and squeezed. Shamtare's thick leather bracer protected Conan's arm from contact with the demon's envenomed flesh, but its grip was savagely strong.

Searing needles of pain drove up the Cimmerian's forearm. The stump of its right hand, with the new-formed tentacle twisting snakelike at its severed end, was raised and thrust into his face.

"Crom!" Conan's entire body twisted against the hand that held his left wrist. The thing's steely fingers seemed to rip his flesh through the bracer, but the full weight of his mighty form was enough to tear him free of its grip and send him reeling away from the hideously reaching tentacle. His heels struck the low dais of black onyx. He lost balance and fell heavily across the steps, beside the small ebony table.

Gasping, the Cimmerian rolled over in time to see the plague demon bear swiftly down upon him. The empty black eyes stared soullessly into his, as its intact left hand flew for his exposed throat. Conan's sword whistled through the air and lopped off the reaching hand. The limb fell on the stairs beside him, and spattered the sable stone with translucent slime.

Again came the birdlike cry, and this time the demon drew back from the barbarian.

It stared at its mangled hands and shuffled away. The new stump sprouted a questing tentacle, as thin and pale as the finger of a dead child. The thickening growth that sprang from its right stump divided into five boneless tentacles and each writhed with a life of its own.

Conan wasted no time contemplating its moment of weakness. He hurled himself off the dais and full upon his foe. His broadsword flashed and hewed into its left shoulder. The blade sank in thickly, as though he'd sunk it into solid tar. The terrible hands came up and the barbarian jerked his weapon free. He struck again, and this time his point cut a wide gash across the demon's dark-garbed torso. The slashed clothing did not gape and flutter. It writhed and shifted as the wound closed in upon itself.

The knowledge that the creature he faced was nigh invulnerable, regenerative, and that it had fashioned the plastic substance of its flesh into the imitation of human garments burned in Conan's brain like a black torch. He felt the full force of his instinctive fear of sorcery surge to the fore. Mad terror blazed through his blood, but Conan's survival instinct was such that he seized on his emotion and transformed it into a transcendent rage. With a howl of utmost loathing, the Cimmerian rained a blinding flurry of savage blows upon the demon-thing. Cuts and rents appeared upon its breast and belly, neck and thigh. It reeled away from the swordsman. It was unslain, but wounded; perhaps unkillable, but knowing, for the first time in its unnatural life, what it was to face an opponent who fought back.

Conan drove the demon back until it stood with its shoulders pressed against the wall, and he held it there with a relentless blizzard of blows. Sweat flew from the barbarian's brow, and his teeth gleamed white in a fixed snarl of battle-madness. His wild cuts and slashes never slackened, never slowed, and the demon's cries rose in a continuous ululation.

Suddenly, the thing thrust wide its ragged arms and lifted its battered head. Conan reared back for the slash that would finally decapitate his foe and test its immortality once and for all.

The blow never fell.

Titanic ebon wings burst from the demon's shoulders and stretched into twin arcs of darkness. The sleek feathers gleamed as iridescent as black satin. The wings snapped upward and then, violently, down. There was a sound like the cracking of an immense whip, and the plague demon jerked aloft with its new wings beating swiftly and smiting the air.

Concentrated gusts of wind buffeted the barbarian, drove tears from his squinted eyes. The dark wing tips slammed the air beside his head as the demon rose into the dome above. Conan dodged the crashing wings and leapt after his foe. His gauntleted hand locked onto the demon's right leg just below the knee.

The ascent faltered, then the black wings redoubled their efforts and Conan's feet swung free of the floor. The pair sailed awkwardly across the open dome, the Cimmerian's sword a silver blur as he hacked at his opponent. The demon's screeches reached an ear-piercing crescendo, and it groped down to strike at its nemesis.

The barbarian looked up to see a tentacled stump reach for his face and change form as it did so. The fat, wormlike fingers of its right hand swiftly hardened and darkened until they resembled the grossly exaggerated claws of a bird of prey. The black talon swiped at his eyes. He chopped at it, missed, and his blade sank into the thing's side.

The airborne pair swung wildly through the air and slammed bodily into the wall. Conan's head struck the hard marble and yellow light exploded behind his eyes. They dropped, slid down the wall, then the demon's wings caught at the air once again. They heaved up and spun in the room's center with Conan's feet dangling twelve feet above the floor.

Conan's vision was a bloodshot blur, but his hand stayed fastened upon his enemy's leg. He felt wetness course along his temple and spill hotly onto his neck. He snarled through the sweat and blood, saw the dusky talon grope for his face and turned his head. The black wings thundered as he tore his blade out of the monster's side. Needle-tipped claws touched his shoulder, rasped and clicked over the mail that protected it. The thing's right arm stretched, grew horribly longer. The barbarian recoiled, and the supernaturally sharp talons waved an inch before his eyes, touched his breast, and caught in the mesh of his chain mail. The talon clenched and links of stout Akbitanan steel popped as the mail was torn open over Conan's breast. Above the grasping talon, the plague demon's blank countenance stared down upon him.

Conan drew back his free arm and slammed his sword's point full into that expressionless face. A scream that dwarfed all before it split the air. The great wings hammered down and heaved the pair upward with swift, uncontrolled violence.

The thrashing wings hit the dome and blasted through the panes of stained glass. There was a crash like the splintering of a world and a brilliant rain of multicolored shards poured down over both the demon and his barbarian tormentor.

Conan ripped his blade free of the demon's face, and the black talon snatched his wrist and held it. Shamtare's bracer saved the Cimmerian's life a second time. The demon's face was split by a yawning, bloodless wound, as though the barbarian had thrust his point into a bust of soft clay. The Cimmerian twisted against the claw that sought to pull him upward as shattered glass and bits of metal frame showered past. An azure shard bounced off the back of his gauntleted fist and dug an ugly gash along his chin. Conan saw beyond the already healing head of the demon, saw the hole that gaped in the sorcerous ceiling. And he saw that which reached in from the darkness outside.

There was a rush of foul air, as frigid as the wind off a glacier. Doughy white ropes of flesh whipped around the demon's wings and stilled their beating.

Conan released his hold on the creature's leg and hung from the remorseless grip of the black talon. There was a ghastly moment in which he felt himself drawn upward with the plague demon, up into the mass of the amorphous nightmare that raged and bubbled with an alien and unknowable hunger. Then he passed the sword to his free hand, whipped the blade back, and severed the thing's right hand for the third time.

Conan tumbled free, and the black claw fell beside him.

He caught a single, unforgettable glimpse of the plague demon's impassive face sinking into greedy waves of pallid flesh. Then the Cimmerian twisted desperately in midair, trying to get his legs beneath him. He failed, and landed flat on his back on the ebony table atop the dais at the room's center.

Conan felt a terrific impact and heard the table's legs splinter. He knew no more.

27

Flickering sunlight played upon Conan's closed eyelids.

A voice penetrated his awareness. It rose and fell in the arcane rhythms of a sorcerous chant. The Cimmerian blinked, and consciousness returned to his body on a wave of pain.

Above, the huge hole in the stained-glass dome framed a clear blue sky. For a moment the heavens went black as death, then were a placid blue again, with the golden orb of the sun shining down like a benediction. Jagged shards thrust from the periphery of the dome like many-colored fangs, and the floor was strewn with a glittering carpet of broken glass.

Conan rolled painfully off the ebony tabletop and noted that his fall had crushed its legs. Landing on the table had likely saved him a broken back, though obviously nothing had spared him a few cracked ribs. Each breath lanced his sides with thin splinters of pain. His fine mail shirt was torn open across his brawny chest. The baron's diamond necklace was exposed and hung in the blood that seeped from his gashed chin. Conan sat up, cursed sulphurously, and plucked a thin spike of glass from the muscle of his thigh. He looked up at the sun, half expecting it to disappear again and leave the world in darkness.

The chant continued to rise in the open shell of the chamber, and Conan saw that Adrastus stood at the podium and moved his hands slowly over a shallow bronze bowl. The high sun blazed down and cast a brilliant illumination over a scene that would have been more appropriate in a gloom-shrouded dungeon. The mage drew his dagger and cut a small incision into his bared left forearm. He pinched the wound over the bowl, squeezed out a faltering stream of bright blood. Adrastus finished the chant, lifted the bronze bowl aloft, and then brought it to his lips. The ceremony was complete.

"By Mitra! It's noon again." Shamtare sidled into the chamber, his boots crunching on broken glass. He shaded his eyes with a callused hand, squinted up at the sun appreciatively.

"It is still noon. No time has elapsed. We were outside of this world, where there is no time." Adrastus licked lips encarmined with his own blood. Balthano stood silently beside the podium and watched the older man approach the prone barbarian.

"Ho, Conan, are you sound?" Shamtare tramped across the sparkling debris and scrutinized his battered comrade. The Cimmerian carefully got to his feet, shook himself, and, satisfied that he was more or less intact, stretched hugely.

"I'll live, though Crom knows I'd not like to do that again."

"Ah, the barbarian is up and around. And perhaps we owe him our thanks." The sorcerer smiled coldly at the mercenaries. His hands, hidden behind the rostrum, discretely removed the black roll of velvet from his robe and placed it upon the podium. Balthano noted his master's actions and a gloating smile creased his cruel face.

"Perhaps?" said Shamtare in amazement.

"The beasts that invaded the palace," said Conan tersely, "did we bring them back with us?"

"I think not," said Adrastus. He slowly unrolled the strip of velvet, and his fingers stroked the fabric as if to savor its softness.

"The demons that entered the palace had time to flee during the transition. Any foolish enough to remain were likely slain in the shift. Most of their breed are ill suited to this sphere."

He paused, frowned delicately. "You men, you understand that if you hadn't interrupted my ceremony when you did, the plague demon would even now be my slave?" The wizard's words were spoken with an idle gentleness that was a transparent mask for other, much darker, emotions.

"I could never believe your motives were as selfless as you described them," said the barbarian. His eyes lit with realization and grim curiosity. "You sought to control the demon? Did you think to use it as a weapon?"

"It should have been mine to command. I would have had it walk out the front gate into the army of Eruk," said Adrastus. His voice grew soft and dreamy. The crystal blades now lay upon the velvet strip and the sorcerer's hands hovered above the golden handprints. "It would have slain them all at my whim. I might have controlled the greatest power of the age but for your stupidity."

"Control that horror?" burst out Shamtare. "You're mad."

"Not at all," said Adrastus calmly. "You know, it took almost a year to forge the Viridescent Prism of Malgyris. It cost me time, blood, and something that I shall not name. The Prism should have bound the demon to my will. It was broken because of you."

"Then for all Eoreck's foolishness, he did a worthy deed when he blundered into your ceremony," said Conan.

"I would have wreaked much havoc with it at first," continued Adrastus, as if he spoke only to himself. "Not to please myself, you understand. It would have served to appraise the kings of the earth of the tremendous power I have at my disposal. Then I would have sold my services to the highest bidder. I might well have reshaped the age. I might have become the most powerful man in the world, but for you."

"I'm glad of your failure," said Conan flatly. "I think there is nothing any man could do to hold that demon in bondage for long. Be grateful that we escaped with our lives."

The sorcerer and the Cimmerian stared at one another for a timeless moment. Shamtare stirred uneasily.

"Come then," said the old mercenary. "Let us gather such treasure as we can and be rid of this accursed place."

"There is no treasure," said Adrastus. "The coffers are all but empty."

Conan snorted with rude laughter. "Dumped into the Freshet by the plague demon's worshippers."

Adrastus raised a thick eyebrow. "Yes, all save a few chests of coin. Oh, and that diamond about your neck."

Conan touched the gem, still wet with his blood.

The wizard's smile conveyed only a chill contempt. "I see that the legends have exaggerated its size considerably. I daresay I've seen a good many diamonds of greater worth. Still, it is more than adequate to keep a man living in reasonable comfort for years. I'll take it as a bit of compensation for my ill luck. Give it to me, barbarian, and perhaps I'll let you live."

"Go to hell, sorcerer."

A veil seemed to drop away from the Kothian's face, and revealed was a grotesque visage distorted by long suppressed rage and hatred. "Enough! Enough, by the gods! I have borne enough failure for a lifetime! Balthano, kill the old man!"

The mage's palms slapped down onto the golden prints emblazoned on black velvet. His face flushed scarlet, and his entire body trembled with bottled fury. He leveled both forefingers at the Cimmerian and his eyes gleamed black with murderous intent.

"Him!" he cried, and the crystal daggers flew.

The twin Karpashian knives appeared in Balthano's fists with equal speed. The wiry Argossean sprang from the podium's side with a shout of gleeful bloodlust. Shamtare drew his shortsword and took a defensive stance with a curse of defiance.

Conan saw the mage's hands slam down on the podium and knew what would follow. He made up his mind and acted on the decision in that instant; his sword arm snapped back and shot forward in one smooth motion, sent his weapon sailing through the air like a hurled spear. It met the crystal blades in midair with a jangle like temple bells. The sword, deflected from its intended course, winged past Adrastus's head, close enough to split his ear instead of his throat. The mage squalled and fell from the podium's stand. His blades came on relentlessly.

Conan whirled and fled, with the glittering crystal daggers pursuing him like a swarm of lethal hornets. He ran from the room at full sprint, dove into the hall, hit the opposite wall with his hands, and dropped to the floor. The Cimmerian rolled to the left as the foremost of the bright blades struck the stone wall at full speed. The first exploded into crystal dust, the second and third ricocheted with brittle impacts that chipped the stone. By then Conan had his legs under him again and was hurtling down the hall toward the spiral stair. The daggers hissed through the dim air in a close-packed cloud that quickly gained on him.

Conan ran as he had never run before in his life.

Balthano dodged around Shamtare's hard thrust with a contemptuous laugh. The Argossean's form seemed to blur before the Shemite's eyes; his speed was supernatural.

Shamtare tried to whirl, tried to get his sword between himself and his foe, but all he could do was stagger as a black dagger slammed into the juncture of his right arm and shoulder. The impact set the mercenary back on his heels, then the pain hit and he sat down hard.

Shamtare stared in disbelief at the hilt that stuck out of his shoulder and the crimson threads that already streamed from it. He tore his eyes from the hilt. There was a knife under his nose. Pain-glazed eyes followed the arm to the dagger-wielder's face. Balthano was grinning at him. His brow and cheekbones were beaded with sweat and the brilliant sunshine struck each tiny droplet with yellow fire. His eyes were inhuman.

"Get up, old man," taunted Balthano. "Where are your clever words now?"

Shamtare gasped for breath and clenched his eyes shut as if overcome with pain, then quickly passed his sword from his right to left hand, and lashed out with a rising slash that should have torn Balthano's throat open. But the Argossean stepped back with effortless speed and Shamtare's blow flew wide.

"Hah!" Balthano's laugh was a cruel bark of scorn. "Get up, old man. I want to kill you on your feet. I'll give you a chance. Look, I'll even turn my back." The Argossean, his face disfigured by a sadistic grin, slid his remaining dagger into its sheath and turned slowly away from the wounded man.

"Finish him, Balthano." Adrastus stood beside the podium and fidgeted. "Let us go and find my crystal blades. The Cimmerian cannot have gone far."

"Nine hells," said Balthano. "This grandfather has given me nothing but grief since we left Akkharia. Let me have some fun."

Adrastus was about to reply when Shamtare hurled himself from the floor and thrust his blade at Balthano's spine.

Boots thundered on dusty marble. Conan burst into the arched chamber at the apex of the great spiral stair. His sides heaved, drove wires of agony through his cracked ribs. In an instant he considered the stairs; perhaps the pursuing blades would weary in time, or lose their enchanted impetus at sufficient distance from the strip of black velvet and the caster of the spell. But he couldn't be certain of that, and both his friend and his enemies were here, on this floor. The barbarian ran past the stairwell and into the mouth of the east hall.

Adrastus's daggers whispered through the air, five feet from Conan's hard-driving back. Powered by a sorcery that would not let them rest until they buried themselves in flesh, the crystal blades closed on their prey.

Conan fled along the hall that encircled the highest tower in Dulcine. The barbarian anticipated the fatal bite of the daggers at any moment, as his steps led him relentlessly back to the Chamber of Conjuring.

Balthano turned and sidestepped in a blur of motion.

The black dagger that appeared in his left hand blocked Shamtare's desperate thrust with disdainful ease. Steel scraped and flashed. The heel of the Argossean's right hand hit the pommel of the blade still sunk in Shamtare's shoulder and punched it into the wound. The old mercenary cried out and fell to his knees.

Balthano stepped around the kneeling man and lifted his knife high. The sun shone on the black blade. "Didn't I say you'd get what was coming to you eventually? Didn't I? Where do you want it, old man? They say the back of the neck is quickest."

Footfalls slammed into the chamber behind him.

Balthano looked past Shamtare, saw the face of Adrastus go slack with shock, and whirled. Conan had sprinted through the chamber's opposite doorway and was upon him.

Balthano's dagger darted for the Cimmerian's throat, but his forearm slapped into Conan's interposed right hand, which snapped shut on his wrist. The Argossean strained back, found his weapon-hand trapped in a grip of iron, and repeatedly drove his free fist into the barbarian's face.

Conan's head jerked back and blood burst from his nose under the staccato volley of blows. He ignored them, seized Balthano's right leg, and quickly hoisted the man bodily from the floor. The barbarian spun, dropped to one knee, and held Balthano aloft for the hungry knives.

The crystal daggers hit Balthano in a fusillade of savage impacts that drove a choked scream from his lungs and knocked Conan sprawling beneath his flopping corpse. The stunned Cimmerian felt a surge of elation that his gambit had worked, sat up, and cast aside his blood-soaked human shield. Balthano rolled on the black and white tiles, his eyes wide and blank in the sun.

Shamtare knelt on the floor close by. His left hand plucked at the black dagger that transfixed his right shoulder. His right arm, streaked with scarlet, hung limp at his side.

Conan looked for his sword and saw that it lay beyond the podium, where he had cast it. He shook his dark head. To throw one's sword was an act of desperation.

Adrastus had stepped back onto the podium. His eyes were wild with disbelief.

"Impossible! No one can escape my blades!"

"Know any other spells, sorcerer?"

Adrastus looked into the barbarian's face and saw his own death. Conan strode forward purposefully, clenched fists swinging like war-hammers at his sides.

Adrastus slapped his palms down on the strip of black velvet, lifted them, and pointed at Conan yet again.

"Him! Him!" screamed the maddened mage.

There was a moist tearing sound. Conan's hackles rose, and he turned to witness the macabre sight of Balthano's lifeless body rising from the floor as if lifted by invisible hands.

The Argossean's arms and legs dangled limply, then shook as the crystal daggers ripped free. Balthano's corpse fell to the floor a second time, lay splayed and ruined beneath the nine surviving magical blades. They hovered in the air for a meager instant, their scarlet-stained crystal glimmering brilliantly in the sunlight. Then, as one, they darted for the Cimmerian.

"Crom!" Conan launched into a headlong dive. He flew past kneeling, white-faced Shamtare and landed, scrambling, on the steps of the dais at the chamber's center. He rolled over the top of the dais, grabbed the ebony tabletop from the splintered wreckage of its legs, and held it up to meet the airborne blades. A barrage of blows struck the smooth sheet of black wood. Glinting crystal dagger-tips burst from the side of the tabletop facing Conan. The impacts unbalanced him and sent the barbarian sliding down the dais steps. Fierce pain stabbed at his ribs and stole his breath. His skull struck unyielding marble and the Cimmerian saw blackness cloud the bright chamber.

"By all the gods, what manner of man is this?" The wizard's voice rang with incredulity and something much like horror. The Kothian jumped awkwardly from the rostrum and drew his poison dagger from his sash. He advanced upon the prone Cimmerian with stumbling speed. Conan lay beneath the sheet of sturdy ebony that had saved his life. The slender crystal blades stood out from the wood in an irregular pattern, imbedded in its fine grain.

"Now you will pay, you cursed savage! Your ungodly luck cannot protect you from the venom of the black scorpion."

The sorcerer's shadow fell over Conan, deadly blade held high. And the barbarian's elemental will to survive drove the numb haze from his brain and spurred his battered limbs to action.

With a bestial roar, Conan sat up and drove the dagger-studded tabletop into Adrastus's bulky body. It stuck, all nine of the trapped blades sheathing themselves in the sorcerer's flesh. Adrastus gave a shrill cry of pain and disbelief, stumbled backward two unsteady steps, and fell flat on his back. He lay still, hidden under the tabletop. A broad band of scarlet crept slowly from beneath the dark slab of wood.

Conan stood beneath the broken crown of the domed ceiling, in a circle of yellow-gold sunshine that struck a thousand multicolored glints from the shattered glass that covered the floor. He put a hand to the baron's diamond necklace where it hung about his bull neck. His blood had dried on the gem. He tucked it back into the torn neck of his mail shirt.

The Cimmerian spared a single brief glance at Adrastus, where the magician lay slain beneath a sheet of wood like the lid of a black coffin. Then he turned to Shamtare and walked across the ruined Chamber of Conjuring to help his wounded friend.

28

The two horsemen emerged from the dense forest and rode up the slow rise of a hill. A bright stream splashed and rolled merrily beside the little-used dirt road. At the hill's crest they came in view of a small mill of rudely hewn logs. The building sat in a grassy clearing beside a bow in the clear stream. As they drew parallel to the mill, the older of the two men pulled on his reins.

"Hold," said Shamtare. The grizzled Shemite's right arm hung in a sling of blue velvet embellished with white sigils. He looked at the silent mill, then at the reins in his hands.

"What is it?" asked his barbarian companion.

"I owe you my life a dozen times over, Conan. You bound my wound. You got us out of Dulcine." The old mercenary caught the blowing hem of his new cloak, and his callused fingers stroked at the richly embroidered colors of the city-state of Eruk.

Conan grunted in embarrassment. "It was no great feat. The surrounding army guarded against those who sought entrance into the city. They were ill prepared for those who wanted out."

"Well, the poor dolts that we met were, in any case. Do me one last favor, my friend."

"What is that, Shamtare?"

"Just wait here a moment."

"Little enough to ask," said the Cimmerian. He watched as Shamtare painfully swung a leg over his mount's back and slid from the saddle. A wince twisted the Shemite's features as his boots met the ground and the impact jostled his shoulder wound. His face went gray and he gnawed down on his lower lip. Then Shamtare set his jaw, walked to the mill's door, drew back a gauntleted hand, and knocked. He waited a long moment, while Conan looked on in silence. Shamtare had just lifted his hand to knock a second time when the door was pulled open.

A short, balding man with a fringe of gray hair and a leather apron looked out. The stout fellow ran a hand over his sweat-dampened pate and raised bushy eyebrows at his visitor.

"What can I do for you, soldier?" he rasped.

"Um, yes," fumbled the mercenary. "I wonder if I might be privileged to speak with your daughter?"

The graying eyebrows crept higher. "Certainly, provided she wishes to speak with you." The miller made as if to re-enter his mill, then turned to face Shamtare again. "Who shall I say is calling?" His eyes moved over the old mercenary's face.

"Two soldiers of Akkharia," said Shamtare, regaining some of his composure. "Tell her that one of them is the big barbarian who offered her some assistance last week."

The miller nodded, went inside, and shut the door behind him. Shamtare waited silently, occasionally casting a look at Conan. The Cimmerian sat his steed with impassive patience.

The door came open again and revealed the blonde woman whom the party had interrupted at her bath. She wore a simple dress of plain brown muslin, tied at the waist with a white cord. Powdery flour coated her arms to the elbow. The afternoon sun turned her hair into a cloud of spun gold. She blinked sea-green eyes at Shamtare, then looked past him to the mounted barbarian.

"Yes?" she said uncertainly.

"Good afternoon, milady," said Shamtare formally. His discomfort seemed to fall away and he stood taller despite his crippled arm. "I bring you a gift from the young man who lent you his cloak."

"Do you want the cloak back?" put in the woman hurriedly. "I can get it."

"No, milady. He has no need of it now."

The words took a moment to be understood. The woman nodded, her lips tight. "I'm sorry."

"He was much impressed with you. And I think he would want you to have this." With a slight grimace, Shamtare dug his good hand behind his sling and drew out the black Bamula armband. He held it out to her. "It has belonged to many brave men. Keep it and think well of its last owner."

The woman accepted the armlet. "Thank you." She watched Shamtare wonderingly as the mercenary executed a brief bow and turned away.

The old soldier remounted and rode off beside Conan without another glance at the mill or the woman framed in its doorway. The riders moved into the shade of the forest and passed over the wooden bridge with a clatter of hooves.

She watched them go, turning the armlet over and over in her hands.

29

The sun was smoldering in the west when Conan and Shamtare returned to Akkharia. At the Cimmerian's insistence they entered separately, by two of the lesser gates, and slouched low behind the turned-up collars of their cloaks. No one seemed to take any notice of either man, much less recognize them.

The barbarian dropped off the injured mercenary at the home of a doctor who was known to be adept with wounds of war. A fistful of golden coins from the looted treasury of Dulcine ensured his comrade the best possible care. Conan told Shamtare he would check in with Mamluke at the mercenary compound. Later that evening the two would rendezvous at the Red Hand, have a revel to celebrate their survival, and drink to the dead.

Evening slipped into night and the streets filled with shadows. Shopfronts went dark, while taverns and alehouses beat back the night with firelight and merriment. Conan strode around a corner into a deserted street. The low walls of Mamluke's compound were visible at the far end of the empty road. Conan quickened his pace, and felt a crossbow shoved against his side.

"Stop right there, big one," said a harsh voice in his ear. Conan drew up short. A second crossbowman stepped from the black maw of an alley and flanked him. The barbarian noted that the crossbows were of gleaming steel: formidable weapons designed to hurl a quarrel through armor.

Half a block away, Mamluke's sentries could be seen atop the wall, apparently engaged in a friendly argument.

Distant laughter rang mockingly in Conan's ears. If the cheerful guards saw their fellow legionnaire accosted, they didn't show it. It had grown dark enough that even had they bothered to glance toward the Cimmerian, it was likely they would have thought little of a trio of men loitering on the corner. Conan resolved to square things with the neglectful sentries. But now there was ample reason to wonder if he would ever have the opportunity.

"This is a stroke of luck," said the second man. "How long ago was he spotted at the gate? I'd have wagered one of the others would have picked him up by now."

"Their ill luck is our good fortune," said the first, philosophically. "Come along, barbarian. Out master wishes to speak with you. Take his sword, Duar."

The man addressed as Duar had a simple patch of black leather over his left eye. His right eye narrowed as he stepped gingerly alongside Conan and drew the Cimmerian's sword from its worn sheath. He almost dropped it to the street.

"Mitra," muttered Duar, "this is a heavy blade. Damned thing weighs as much as my wife."

"Which one?" sneered the first crossbowman.

Conan was shoved off the sidewalk, into the black alley. The pair were careful to keep him both between and ahead of them, ensuring two unimpeded shots should the Cimmerian decide to break and run. The barbarian moved cautiously ahead of his captors, conscious that at this range their crossbow bolts could rip completely through his body.

The alley came to a blind end, and there, amid the stinking refuse, waited an elegant closed coach drawn by two black stallions.

The barbarian relaxed somewhat as he realized the men truly meant to take him to their master, whoever he might be. Even a cursory examination of the carriage made it apparent that he must be a man of means.

The moon broke from the clustered clouds overhead. The paneled sides of the coach gleamed with thick black lacquer, and the bright fittings were of polished brass. This was the vehicle of a noble of high rank. Conan stole a glance back at his captors, discretely taking their measure.

Both wore severely plain breastplates and greaves of dull steel. Their helmets were conical and adorned with a dark flap of embroidered cloth that depended from the rear to dangle between their shoulder blades. Their tunics were dark as well, simply cut and bound at the waist by a wide military belt, from which hung both shortsword and dagger. Each held his heavy crossbow with the casual air of one who has used the weapon for so long it has become much like an additional limb. One-eyed Duar carried the Cimmerian's broadsword over his left shoulder, a bar of silver in the moonlight. His steady right arm shoved the crossbow into Conan's back. The armor-piercing bolt's pyramidal head gouged the barbarian's spine.

"He's looking at me, Rald," said Duar. "And he hasn't said a word to us yet."

"These brutish barbarians can but rarely speak the tongue of honest, civilized men," said Rald. "Can you speak, dog?" The trio reached the side of the carriage and Rald tugged open the door. It swung wide on smoothly greased hinges. The rich scent of leather wafted from the elegantly appointed interior. A soft, wavering light was cast by a single candle enclosed in a tiny glass lantern mounted on the satin-upholstered wall.

"I can speak," said Conan quietly.

"Good. Get into the carriage and cross your arms over your chest. I'll ride across from you. I promise to put a bolt through your belly if you so much as take a deep breath. Duar, you take the reins."

Conan did as he'd been bidden. As he settled into the comfortable seat, he reflected that he might have thrown himself against Rald, taken his sword back from Duar, and probably slain both of them under cover of the alley's protective darkness.

Rald slid carefully into the seat across from the Cimmerian and leveled the crossbow at his solar plexus. The barbarian considered how a swift kick might both lift and trigger the crossbow, sending Rald's quarrel tearing harmlessly through the coach's roof and leaving the crossbowman in his hands. But Conan had grown curious, and did nothing.

Rald pulled the door shut behind him. The carriage lurched forward and Duar's voice could be heard as he urged the horses around and out of the alley.

"Pull the curtains closed," said Rald.

"Why?" asked Conan mildly. "Do you think I don't know where we're going?"

Rald's mouth hardened into a cruel slash and Conan saw his hands tighten on the crossbow's lever. The thumb-thick bowstring seemed to quiver slightly, as if eager to release its load of steel-tipped death.

"Do as I say, dog."

The Cimmerian wordlessly tugged the heavy black curtains into place over the window, giving his guard time to do the same on his side. The solitary candle shed a wan, amber light over the two men.

"I saw you and your friend at the gates when I left the city with the prince's party," said Conan. "I didn't know then that you were lackeys of his father."

"Be silent." Rald's voice was heated.

"Why?" Conan growled. "You won't shoot me. Lord Eannus wants a full accounting of his expedition. He'll want to know what became of his son and the riches he was supposed to fetch from Dulcine."

"Silence, you impudent dog! I'll tell milord that you were trying to escape and I had to feather you."

"If you do, he'll never get the answers he wants, and you'll be the reason why. Would you risk his displeasure? I've been told he's a vengeful man."

"Open your stinking mouth just once more and I'll kill you right here. Lord Eannus would be unhappy with me, but it would be well worth it just to see you die with a bolt in your guts. You think you know what you're about, but you're just an ignorant savage who trifles with his betters." There was no mistaking the red rage that gripped Rald now. His half-closed eyes were glittering slits of hate and a vein throbbed insistently in his temple. He ceased speaking, but his lips continued to move; they twitched, drawn tight over his clenched teeth.

The coach rocked as its wheels ground over cobblestones. The candle's flame fluttered weakly, filling the carriage's interior with blackly shifting shadows. Conan, his suspicions confirmed as to the identity of his captor's master, stared ahead in stoic silence.

"Better," whispered Rald hoarsely. "Much better, dog."

They made the remainder of the journey without a word spoken. The coach ceased rolling over worn cobbles and began to bounce over a rutted road of loose earth. After several long minutes of jouncing, uncomfortable travel, the wheels bumped up onto smooth flagstones. Conan conjectured they had entered the grounds of a large estate by means of its garden gate. When the carriage drew to a halt and Duar jerked the door open, the barbarian saw that his surmise had been correct.

The moon cast silvery illumination over a sprawling expanse of well-tended gardens and shone in opalescent reflection from the windows of a three-story villa. Aside from a red glow through the curtains of a solitary second-floor window, the building was in darkness. Slim minarets rose from each corner of the mansion, their tapered silhouettes like titan daggers against the stars. The coach had stopped upon a wide, flagstoned court that lay beside the silent structure.

Across the court, half hidden in the shadow of a vine-grown trellis, Conan could discern a single door.

"Come on, heathen," said Duar. "No time to sightsee."

As Conan lowered himself from the coach, Rald slid quickly across his seat. The barbarian's feet touched the pavement at the same time that Rald, standing in the coach's open door, sent a sharp kick into the back of Conan's neck. The unanticipated blow sent the Cimmerian staggering into the road. He lifted a hand to the back of his head and turned to glare at his captors. Both crossbows were leveled at his broad breast. Conan's eyes burned like cold blue flames.

"Say something," snarled Rald. "Give me an excuse, you northern ape."

Conan rubbed the back of his neck with slow deliberation, and pinned the two men with an unblinking stare.

"Easy, Rald," said Duar wonderingly. "Bel and Erlik, what has he done to anger you so?"

"First he won't talk, and then he won't be silent. He thinks he's clever. He thinks he's the equal of his betters. Damned barbarians are all alike. They hire on as mercenary trash for a few coppers a day, and get to thinking they're as good as honest soldiers." The quaver in Rald's voice had grown worse and now he fairly trembled with suppressed violence. His face had gone pale with fury and mad hatred.

"Go easy, Rald. He belongs to Lord Eannus. Let the master deal with him."

"I've never killed a barbarian before. I've heard they have more blood than we city folk."

"Perhaps you'll have a chance to find out for yourself. But now we must do as milord commanded." Duar spoke slowly, in soft, even tones that seemed to penetrate his comrade's dark passion.

Rald spat, shrugged stiffly, then gestured with his crossbow.

"Move, dog. To the door. You can test your ill manners on the master."

Conan led the two men across the courtyard's swept and polished stones. He considered waiting until the door was open, diving through and slamming it shut between himself and his captors, then disregarded the idea. They would raise an alarm, he would be sealed in the fortress of his enemy, and his curiosity would still be less than satisfied.

A braided cord hung from a slot in the wall beside the door. Duar tugged at it and produced the distant sound of chimes. They waited a long moment, stood silently as the cool night breeze plucked at their garments and chilled their flesh. Then the chimes rang again in response. This was apparently the awaited signal, for Duar pulled the door open and the trio entered a luxurious corridor lit by hanging clusters of golden oil lamps. The aromatic oil burned with brightly guttering flames that shed warm illumination while producing a cloying, flowery perfume. The walls were paneled with exotic woods and hung with lush Vendhyan tapestries. The scented air was warm, torporific, and seemed to absorb sound.

No one was in sight, but neither Rald nor Duar appeared to find this remarkable. They urged the Cimmerian down the corridor's length until they came to an imposing double door, studded with copper and set with a huge bronze knocker. Duar reached for it.

"No," snapped Rald. "Let him do it. Go on, savage, knock for admittance to your master's chamber."

Conan reached out lazily, drew back the heavy knocker, and released it. The clapper struck its panel with a hollow boom that seemed to resonate throughout the building. The three men waited in silence once again. Rald shifted his weight from one foot to the other.

"What if he's not in? What if he doesn't expect us?"

"Enough. We are following his instructions exactly. He'd gladly waken for this."

"Enter!" The voice had the timbre of a shout, yet came weakly through the massive door. The barbarian and his captors obeyed, and came into a high-arched hall that stretched away fifty paces to end in a wall set with a small balcony that hung twelve feet above the tiled floor. A bearded man stood on the balcony. He was clad in wrinkled sleeping garb and was in the act of wrapping a robe of deep crimson around his corpulent body.

Everywhere Conan looked his eyes met the same sullen scarlet tones. The burgundy of the floor's tile was echoed by the bloody hue of the tapestries, and both seemed to smolder in the lurid glow of the ruby-encrusted lanthorns mounted along the walls.

"Lord Eannus, it is your servants Duar and Rald," cried Duar. "We bring a member of your son's expedition. We found him about to return to Captain Mamluke's compound."

The fat man bound his scarlet robe about his broad belly with a cord of fine woven silk. He laid hands winking with jeweled rings upon the balcony's carven rail and regarded his visitors.

"I recognize my servants when I see them. Come forward so I might have a better look at your captive." The party had advanced no farther than the hall's midpoint when his voice rang out again. "Far enough! No closer! No closer." The room's near-perfect acoustics filled their ears with the swelling sound of his voice.

Lord Eannus, brother to King Sumuabi, was of average height, but he outweighed most men of his size by a third. His dark beard was fashioned into a dense column of ringlets that fell upon his breast, yet it could not conceal the multitude of chins that wobbled below his jaw. His mouth worked nervously. Beneath black and arched brows, his tiny eyes moved fitfully over the men before him.

"I was told of you, mercenary. You're the barbarian that Mamluke had wield the wooden sword. I've forgotten your name."

"I am Conan. Mamluke himself sought my assistance on your son's expedition to Dulcine."

"Answer only the questions I put to you. Where is the rest of your party?" Eannus's voice was a treble whine, but it was full of the overweening confidence of one who has grown accustomed to others obeying his commands promptly and without question.

"Dead," said Conan bluntly.

"All of them? Even the wizard?"

"All of them. Even your son."

"The devil can eat my wastrel son. Hmm. I feared the wizard might have overestimated his own abilities. It seems I was correct. How regrettable. What about the treasure?"

"Lost."

The figure on the balcony stiffened visibly and gripped the rail a little tighter. For a moment, Eannus seemed to have difficulty finding his voice.

"Lost, you say? Not merely left behind?"

"Hurled by the people of Dulcine into the Freshet in an attempt to appease the gods and end the plague."

Duar and Rald shifted uneasily where they flanked the barbarian, but their crossbows hovered steadily at his ribs.

"Ishtar's Holies." Eannus tugged at the curls of his beard with ring-glittering fingers. "Did nothing survive?"

"Nothing."

"Guards, knock him to the floor!"

Booted feet slammed into the backs of Conan's knees and the barbarian let himself drop. He pushed up on all fours, crimson tiles cold under his fingers, and felt Duar and Rald press in above him, their crossbows at the ready.

"All for naught, eh? And it seems that you alone survive as evidence of my folly. Well, truthfully, the end will be much the same for you, barbarian, as I would have had all of you mercenaries executed even if the mission had been a success. Little point in sharing, whether it be the treasure of Dulcine or the knowledge of my ill judgment and failure." The king's brother paused, then waved a regal hand. "Duar, put a bolt through him."

"Hold!" Conan snarled. Even on all fours at the guardsmen's feet, the Cimmerian seemed to loom larger than his captors. The elemental power of a creature of the wild coiled in his body and shone untamed in the volcanic flash of his eyes.

"Yes?" Eannus was all eagerness now. "Did you lie? Do your comrades live? Have they hidden the treasure?" The questions blurred together in their speaker's panting haste.

Conan drew his legs up beneath him and sat on his heels. He shook an unruly strand of black hair out of his face and grinned coldly. His left hand dug beneath his broad belt.

"My comrades are dead and the treasure is lost, but I would buy my life with the one thing I saved from the plagued city of Dulcine."

"Diamonds, perhaps? Or some other trinkets? Guards, give him room." The disdain in Eannus's voice was belied by his attentive interest. His gaze was rapt upon the kneeling barbarian. Conan could hear Rald's breath hiss slowly between his clenched teeth. It was a sound of distilled frustration.

"Better still." The Cimmerian's hand drew a roll of black velvet from behind his belt and placed it on the floor before him.

"What is it? What?" Eannus's pale brow creased as he strained his eyes to see what Conan held. "What do you have there? Is it the baron's fabled necklace?"

"Better than that, even," rumbled the barbarian. He unrolled the velvet, spread it out on the tile in front of his knees. Twisted runes of gold leaf glimmered on the lush fabric. At each end of the strip of thick velvet was a full-size golden handprint.

Duar and Rald inched forward in curiosity, looked down over Conan's broad shoulders, and saw that the length of cloth held a series of narrow pockets. From nine of the ten pockets, Conan drew a hand-sized length of transparent crystal and laid it on the gilded velvet.

"Diamonds? Diamonds of that size?" Choked with greed, Eannus bent over the balcony with his bloated belly pressed into the rail.

"No," said Conan. "Mere quartz crystals."

The Cimmerian pressed his palms flat on the golden handprints, and it was as if he had plunged his hands into a frigid mountain spring. His knuckles paled to white, and his flesh went numb. Time seemed to slow in its course and the air around his body to thicken like gelatin. There was a tiny voice whispering quickly in his ear. It spoke with unnatural speed, spewed a vile litany of strange words in a language at once utterly unknown and instinctively repellent to the barbarian.

Nausea bloomed in his belly.

"You would buy your life with worthless crystals?" Eannus's voice almost cracked with incredulity and his face darkened with anger. Conan saw the face as if from a vast distance.

"No," said Conan again, sick with the foul voice in his skull. "I would buy your death." He lifted nerveless hands from the velvet strip and pointed at Eannus with both forefingers. "Him."

The transparent daggers sprang from their velvet cushion and hurtled down the hallway like glittering birds of prey. They whistled over the balcony and hammered into the body of Lord Eannus with a series of meaty impacts that lifted him from his feet and hurled him back a dozen paces to spill on his back and lie motionless.

Still on his knees, Conan seized upon his guards' inevitable moment of astonishment. He slammed a numb fist up beneath each crossbow, driving them high while he ducked below.

The sharp thrum of the released bowstrings blended into a single note. The bolt from Rald's crossbow tore through Duar's eye patch and brain, bursting from the back of his skull to splinter against the wall behind him. Duar toppled as rigidly as might a marble statue, dead on his feet with his bow still gripped in stiffening hands.

The quarrel thrown from the dead man's bow passed harmlessly between Rald's left arm and side. It was to the warrior's credit that he recovered swiftly; Rald wasted a mere instant in contemplation of the sudden havoc before he swung the heavy crossbow at Conan's head.

The haft of the bow slapped into the Cimmerian's ready hands. Iron fingers closed on the weapon and the flesh of Rald's arm. Conan rose up and twisted his body, wrenched his standing foe from his feet, and flipped him over his shoulder. Rald hit the floor with a clash of metal and a cry of fury, the bow ripped from his grasp. He rolled nimbly, came to his feet almost as swiftly as the barbarian, and drew both shortsword and dagger.

"So come on then," panted Rald.

As Conan gripped the crossbow's metal haft, feeling began to seep back into his frozen hands. The horrid voice in his skull had fallen silent the instant he lifted his palms from the golden handprints, but now his head throbbed and his ears rang. The Cimmerian let the crossbow swing idly at his side, and watched his foe.

"Are you a barbarian sorcerer, then? Wielding enchanted knives?"

"Hardly," said the barbarian. The two men circled one another slowly, alert for any opening. "The plunder was so meager that I hoped to sell the cursed thing. It bought more than I hoped."

"Have you run out of tricks to play? Surely you don't think an unloaded crossbow is match for a sword and dagger? Come on! If you charge me, I'll make your death quick and clean. If you make me come to you, then I'll take my time about it and see if you barbarians truly have more blood than we civilized men."

Rald heard Conan's low chuckle; then the Cimmerian was both lunging forward and throwing the crossbow. The heavy haft flew into Rald's face with such speed that he couldn't lift his sword to block it. The blunt end cracked into his forehead with force enough to stagger him and fill his vision with dizzying lights.

Then Conan's hands fell upon his neck.

In the garden, shadows grew slowly longer as the moon lowered to the waiting horizon. A breeze rattled along the sculpted hedges, carrying a chill that promised autumn. In the distance, a lone dog howled mournfully once and was still.

The door that opened from Lord Eannus's mansion into his garden courtyard was flung wide. It poured forth warm light and silhouetted the form of a tall man. The man loped to the side of an elegant carriage that stood in deep moon-shadow. He climbed into the driver's seat and found there a massive broadsword. With a grin, he leapt from the coach and cut the two black stallions free of their reins. He mounted the larger of the two and rode it bareback from the garden grounds.

Behind him, flames flickered redly in the windows, broke free of the walls and roof, then lifted ragged, raging pinions over the mansion of Lord Eannus, brother of King Sumuabi.

30

The Red Hand was a rambling, ramshackle establishment of two stories that sat on a busy street corner in one of Akkharia's marginal districts. The area was close enough to the thieves' quarter to have a less than savory reputation, yet it was near enough to mercenary compounds and the housing of the palace guard that it was considered safe by slumming nobility. The presence of so many armed soldiers made for a menacing yet secure environment, as any fracas that broke out was swiftly extinguished by ready hands. A drunken brawl between mercenary factions was occasionally known to escalate into a full-fledged battle, but the punishments for this were so severe that it was a rarity. Whores and swindlers were always on their best and most subtle behavior, and a thief who had the daring to ply his trade in this district was either highly skilled or a fool.

The Red Hand was a tavern that catered almost exclusively to Akkharia's mercenaries, and was favored by those of Mamluke's Legion in particular. When Conan strode into the main room he was confronted with a full score of men in the armor of his troop, many of whom shouted his name, slapped tabletops, and demanded that he sit and drink with them. The barbarian smiled, traded a few bawdy insults with those closest to him, and made his way toward a table near the wide fireplace. A small fire burned in the center of the expansive hearth, packed coals warming a stained iron kettle.

Shamtare sat at the table beside the fireplace with a leathern jack in his left fist. His right arm hung limply across his armored breast, suspended from a clean white sling. He turned a dull expression to Conan as the Cimmerian dragged up a chair and sat down heavily.

"How goes it then?" asked the barbarian.

Shamtare blinked at his friend with red-rimmed and weary eyes. He ran his free hand over his mouth and beard, then grabbed the handle of the jack once again.

"Ill news, by Ishtar. Ill news, indeed. The sawbones told me this arm will never be as it was. If I'm lucky, I may someday be able to lift it from my side. That Argossean dog took my sword arm from me, may his soul writhe eternally in the fangs of Erlik." Shamtare spat bitterly into the fire. "I must give up soldiering, and it is all I have ever known." The old Shemite concluded his gloomy speech by lifting his jack of wine and gulping from it deeply.

The barbarian leaned back in his chair and rubbed his jaw. A big hand plucked at the torn neck of his mail shirt, pulled forth a thin chain of finely wrought golden links and a transparent gem that shone in the firelight like an errant star.

"What the devil," growled Conan. He tossed the necklace to Shamtare, who managed to loosen his grip on the leather jack in time to snatch the treasure from the air. He bobbled it, almost dropped it into his wine, and gaped at Conan, whose hard face was transformed by a wide, white grin.

"Buy yourself a tavern," said the Cimmerian. "That's the baron of Dulcine's fabled necklace. Not a bad pension, eh?"

While Shamtare tried to make up his mind whether to stare at Conan or the gem, the barbarian stood and faced the fireplace.

He moved between the old mercenary and a torch mounted on the far wall, and for an instant Shamtare saw Conan's black-maned head surrounded by a fiery nimbus, as though the Cimmerian wore a crown of ruddy gold.

Conan pulled a lax length of crumpled black velvet from behind his belt. With a careless motion, he tossed the empty fabric into the glowing heart of the coals. It lay a moment beneath his stolid gaze, then burst into hissing green flames.

"Gods," exploded Shamtare, finding his voice. "What burns with such a foul stench?"

"My career as a sorcerer," said Conan.

The barbarian turned his back on the rapidly fading embers and faced the teeming tavern. "Ho, barkeep!" he bellowed lustily. "Wine for the house!"

ACKNOWLEDGMENTS

Thanks to Steve Saffel, patient editor and guide. To all those at Titan Books who've taken up the Cimmerian's bold banner: Nick Landau, Vivian Cheung, and Dan Coxon. And to those at Heroic Signatures: Fredrik Malmberg, Jay Zetterberg, Matt Murray, Chris Butera, and the noble Steve Booth.

To those who supported my Hyborian efforts through advice, direction, or simply being there when needed: Howard Andrew Jones, Deuce Richardson, Vincent Darlage, John O'Neill, Jen Hocking, Cinda Hocking, John Evan Hocking, Charlie Erickson, Pat Rowland, Andrew Rowland, Michael Kope, Chris Pelon, Tom Bowden, Tim Martin, Fritz Freiheit, and Tim Anderson.

To Robert E. Howard, and to all those who have worked to keep the Cimmerian flame alive down the many years.

ABOUT THE AUTHOR

Winner of the Harper's Pen Award for sword and sorcery fiction, John C. Hocking is the author of two novels starring Conan the Cimmerian. His short fiction has appeared in the *Flashing Swords* ezine, *Black Gate*, *Skelos*, *Weirdbook*, and *Tales from the Magician's Skull*. Recently retired, he is currently working on a new novel. He lives in Michigan with his superhumanly tolerant wife and can be found online at facebook.com/people/John-C-Hocking/100063350343450/.

For more fantastic fiction, author events,
exclusive excerpts, competitions, limited editions and more

VISIT OUR WEBSITE
titanbooks.com

LIKE US ON FACEBOOK
facebook.com/titanbooks

FOLLOW US ON TWITTER AND INSTAGRAM
@TitanBooks

EMAIL US
readerfeedback@titanemail.com